THE COELHO MEDALLION

A DAN KOTLER ARCHAEOLOGICAL THRILLER

KEVIN TUMLINSON

THE COELHO
MEDALLION

WHAT TO DO WHEN YOU
SPOT A TYPO

They happen. That's why I built the Typo Reporter.
If you find a typo or other problem with this book, you can
report it here:

https://www.kevintumlinson.com/typos

As a special thank-you, you can opt to be included in the
Change Log for this book! If I use your suggestion, and you
agree to be included, your name will go into a special
section in the book, so future readers can appreciate you as
much as I do!

Happy reading,
Kevin Tumlinson
Very Grateful Author

PROLOGUE

Prime Alert Fire Safety Products, Inc. — New Mexico

Alarms were already blaring, echoing through the canyons of corrugated aluminum among the outbuildings and warehouses of Prime Alert Fire Safety Products.

Alarms were a bit unusual here. The facility was located in an expanse of desert nestled in among a collection of foothills in New Mexico, near the Colorado border. The closest town only had a few hundred people, officially. Unofficially, maybe a few hundred and fifty. None of them had any interest in breaking into a bunch of warehouses a hundred miles south of anywhere, where nothing better than smoke detectors were manufactured and stored.

Except for tonight.

Henry "Hank" Lott was pretty sure this would turn out to be a case of some bored teenagers getting a little too drunk and a little too rowdy. He figured he would find them next to one of the metal out buildings with a can of spray paint and more than a few bottles of beer, tagging the giant metal canvases of the warehouses to show their virility before slinking off to diddle each other in the brush.

Guys and girls, Hank figured. *Kids.*

Hank was the night shift here, and he had no issues with that. It was hours and hours of being alone, with nobody but Hank Williams Jr. and Johnny Cash and a few other bad seeds for company. And that was a bit of alright for Hank. He'd had enough of most folks. They could keep their Facebooks and Tweeters. Hank would stick to a good book and a country music soundtrack.

It helped quite a bit that the job was pretty routine. Nothing much ever changed, and Hank liked it that way. He made his rounds in the same beat up Chevy pickup that the company had issued him almost three decades ago. He stared out at the same New Mexico desert, night after night, and woke up around noon every day to go fishing in the same creek, with the same rod and reel he'd used for thirty years. And every so often he ran off the same sort of teenagers who were probably causing all the ruckus tonight.

The monitoring service had called just 20 minutes ago, and Hank rolled out from his little spot overlooking the mountains and the flat-pan of the surrounding desert. He was a little grumpy about putting down the book he was reading—a Nick Thacker thriller that was really killing the hours. But he so rarely saw any activity here, it was tough to be mad for too long. There was always the chance he might catch some burglars trying to steal computers from the offices or something. He'd be a hero, in the morning. Maybe he'd get a bonus, or a raise. He hadn't seen either of those for a few years now.

He pulled up to Building Three, one of the staging warehouses where boxes of smoke detectors were stored before shipping. From here, Prime Alert reached out to the Walmarts and Targets and Home Depots of most of the United States, selling a reliable and inexpensive product to the masses. Hank felt a certain amount of pride, working for a company that actually did save lives—even if it was indirectly.

The roll-top door of Building Three's front entrance was open when Hank arrived, and a large moving truck—one of those that could be rented from a home storage center—was backed up to the bay. From his vantage point, Hank saw two men moving within the barely-lit interior of the warehouse. They were using hand trucks to load stacks of boxes into the moving van as rapidly as they were able.

Hank shut off his radio and then stepped out of the Chevy as he drew his weapon—an aged .45 that he'd had since he left the service. It was his personal weapon, and much more comforting to him than the little .9mm pea-shooter the company had tried to issue him. It would make a big bang and a big hole, if the need arose. Thankfully the need never had.

Hank also took out his mobile phone and dialed 911. In a whispered rush he told the operator the situation and his location and said that there was a robbery in progress. He advised them that he was armed, and about to engage the suspects. Before the operator could tell him to stand down and stay put he hung up. The police wouldn't be here for quite a while—the facility was at least half an hour from the closest police station. But by then Hank hoped to have these guys rounded up and held at gunpoint. He might have to lock them in one of the offices in the back of the warehouse, he figured. That was, as long as they didn't try anything.

He stepped away from the Chevy without closing the door and crept quietly toward the gap between the moving truck and the door frame of the loading bay. When he was close enough, he saw that there were actually four men moving around inside, not just two. They were quickly loading the hand trucks and then rolling boxes of smoke detectors into the van, before speeding back to reload.

"That's enough," he said loudly, aiming his weapon at the men, who were clustered around the next batch of boxes.

They froze, and then turned on him.

They were dressed all in black except for olive drab coats, which looked to be military surplus. Their faces were covered in black ski masks, so that only their eyes were visible, and their hands were sheathed in black gloves.

Definitely not kids, Hank thought. For the. First time, he was feeling as if this might have been a mistake. Four masked men, and only one Hank. At least he had the gun.

"Just step away from the boxes with your hands in the air. Get down on your knees, out here in the open floor."

Hank had stepped through the gap and into the loading area of the warehouse, and he kept the gun trained on the men, as he moved. His mind was racing with the possibilities of what he should do with them. He glanced to the back of the warehouse to Eugene Spencer's office and realized that all of the keys were hanging from the ignition of the Chevy at the moment.

Dammit you old fool, Hank thought. He'd have to keep them on the floor, and wait for the police to arrive.

The men made no move to do as he had ordered.

In fact, it almost seemed like they had no idea what he was even saying.

There was a sound then, from behind him. It was a series of clicks that Hank immediately recognize, and it sent goosebumps up his back and made him break out in a sweat. Hank had heard that sound before, back in the war. He knew what it meant.

It meant he was a damned fool for not checking the truck.

"Lower your weapon," a voice said from behind him. It was strongly British, and the man sounded a bit young. But it was firm and left no room for doubt as to what the owner of that voice would do if Hank didn't do as he was told.

Hank raised his left hand even as he knelt down and placed his weapon on the ground. When he stood up again he raised his right hand and turned slowly to look into the back of the moving van.

A man stood among the stacks of boxes that the burglars had already loaded. It was quite a number of boxes, actually. In the short time it had taken for Hank to put down his book and get to Building Three, these men had systematically emptied a very large portion of the warehouse. There were thousands of smoke detectors already loaded into the van.

"You called the authorities, I assume?" the man asked. He, too, was wearing a mask and gloves, as well as the olive drabs. And he had a weapon aimed directly at Hank's head.

"Yeah," Hank said. "They'll be here any minute. So I'd ..."

"You couldn't have called them more than ten minutes ago. It will take half an hour at best for anyone to get here." The man stepped carefully down from the back of the truck, the weapon, trained on Hank, never wavering. "We have ample time."

"They'll be here any—"

Before Hank could finish the man raised the weapon and fired a single shot, striking Hank in the chest. He flinched back, and then fell, slamming to the ground. He clutched at the wound, coughing and sputtering from the pain. He rolled and tried to crawl away, but the man stepped forward until he was practically hovering over him.

Hank looked up at him, rolling onto his back. The man stood above him, held the weapon in one hand, and put a bullet in Hank's head.

With the deed done, the man said something in Arabic to two of his men, and they rushed to move Hank's body out of the way, then scrambled back to the boxes. In moments they had emptied the warehouse and sped away into the night even before the sound of sirens rose in a warble somewhere distant in the New Mexico night.

MEMORIAL PARK — HOUSTON, TEXAS

Dr. Evelyn Horelica tried to ignore the pain in her wrists as the thin zip ties cut into them.

She ignored the gag in her mouth as well—as best she could—and concentrated only on breathing as steadily and calmly as she could around the gag pulled tight over her mouth. Her nostrils flairs. Her eyes were wide with fear. Her heart was thumping hard enough that she could hear it pulsing in her ears.

She had no idea why she had been kidnapped. She feared rape, but the kidnappers had given no sign that they were even remotely interested in that. They had simply grabbed her, with no warning, before she'd even fully realized they were there.

She had been nearly finished with her run—the full three-mile circuit around Houston's Memorial Park Golf course—when two men had rushed out of the tree line, gagged and tied her, and dragged her into the woods before she could even react. They'd been so fast, and so efficient, Evelyn hadn't even put up a fight. It was over before she'd even realized she was in danger.

Once they had her trussed up, they swiftly lifted her onto their shoulders and rushed her into the woods, emerging into a secluded clearing where the van waited.

The graphic on the side of the van read "Menton Landscaping and Irrigation." Evelyn had seen vans like this a thousand times around Houston. She used Menton for her own landscaping, in the rental house she was using during her time here. The guys who showed up were always nice and polite, even if most of them didn't speak English. She'd never felt unsafe around them.

She was thrown into the darkened interior of the van, and the door was slammed shut, leaving her bound, gagged, and now blind. The sounds from outside were also muffled, and she realized the walls, the floor, even the ceiling of the van were all covered in some sort of spray foam, deadening all sound from the outside—and from the inside.

Dr. Horelica kicked at the side of the van, and tried to scream, but the sounds were muted, falling back on her in dull tones.

These men had been too good—too methodic—to be mere rapists or kidnappers. Grabbing her wasn't part of a whim, it was part of a plan. She was being kidnapped by professionals.

But why? What could someone want from her? She was a linguist. She specialized in dead languages and ancient symbolism. She wasn't part of any government contracts, and she had no connection with national security or anything that could influence tides of money or politics. She was, as most of her friends thought of her, the most boring type of researcher there was—one who reads for a living.

She felt more than heard the slight thud of the van's doors closing, and the rumble of its engine starting. In seconds they were moving, and Evelyn started screaming through the gag, kicking frantically at the sides of the van, the floor, the back doors. Some part of her knew it was pointless, but these were the options she had left to her. This was the only fight she could give.

It wouldn't be enough.

AMERICAN MUSEUM OF NATURAL HISTORY — NEW YORK, New York

The medallion was part of an exhibit of ancient American artifacts.

The very phrase seemed like an oxymoron to most museum patrons. The words "ancient" and "American" just didn't belong in the same sentence, and that was precisely what made it intriguing. America was, and always been, the new world. The civilization that currently stretched between her shores had a lifespan that could be measured only in centuries, not millennia. There wasn't anything ancient here.

At least, that was the way most people thought of it.

The truth was, European descendants were relatively new to the ecosystem of the Americas. They'd been preceded in North and South America by cultures extending thousands of years into history: Aztec, Mayan, Inca, hundreds of indigenous tribes—the so-called "Indians"—all had cultures that stretched back almost infinitely beyond the arrival of the Niña, Pinta, and Santa Maria.

In fact, as it was turning out, Europeans weren't even the first non-natives to set foot in the Americas. Now making headlines, in archeological and historic circles at least, was mounting evidence that Vikings had once landed on the eastern shores of what would become Canada and the

United States. And as it turned out, Eric the Red was just the tip of a Scandinavian iceberg.

It was all so astounding.

Vikings—making a home for themselves in a world that was so far from their native soil it wasn't even supposed to exist. This was the edge of everything, to the ancient seafarers. But nothing as trivial as the edge of the world, or a harsh and freezing expanse of empty ocean, could possibly keep Vikings at bay.

The possibility of something ancient in the new world might be bizarre to most of modern society, but it was no less a reality. The medallion hinted at that new reality, providing tantalizing proof of something ... well, something impossible by the standards of current archeological research and the known historic record.

Named for its discoverer, Dr. Eloi Coelho, the *Coelho Medallion* had been found in perhaps the most startling location anyone could think of—a dig site near Pueblo, Colorado.

This was the spark that ignited a raging fire of public astonishment and excitement. Pueblo, deep in the center of the North America and surrounded by an expanse of mountains and foothills, was the very last place anyone expected to find any sign of the seafaring Vikings.

It seemed impossible.

It was captivating.

It hinted at an alternate history of the United States, filled with mystery and adventure and a strange new perspective that no one in either the public or the scientific community had ever considered.

No one knew for certain what the history of the medallion might actually be, and that was its most attractive feature.

Deepening the mystery further, there were markings on the surface of the medallion, both front and back, that could count their origins among any number of Native American cultures. But it was the symbols that looked for all the world as if they were Norse that were fueling a flood of speculation from both inside and outside the scientific community.

This led a few brave researchers to wonder—aloud and in print no less—whether there had been some kind of intimate contact between several of these pre-European North American cultures and the Norse.

Why not? In light of recent discoveries, it seemed plausible enough. Sure, it went against hundreds of years of established facts and known history, but discovering something like the medallion—a sort of Rosetta Stone of ancient American culture—put every former idea under a microscope for reexamination. These were new and exciting days.

These well-meaning researchers, of course, were quickly snubbed, and their careers briefly called into question, highlighting the dangers and foibles of daring to question the status quo in academic and scientific circles. New ideas and new perspectives were not always welcome—hardly ever welcome, if one were being honest.

All of that aside, however, the controversy surrounding the medallion, and its lack of an origin story, made it just the sort of mystery that the American Museum of Natural History needed. It had given the Museum a much-needed boost, amounting to the biggest attraction in decades.

Dr. Albert Shane, the museum's Curator of Human Origins, was tickled by the press coverage of the event. He particularly liked a quote from the New York Times:

"At the heart of the exhibit, a mystery: What is the origin of the Coelho Medallion, which headlines the event? A circular object, two inches in diameter, covered with ancient symbols and

images—the medallion inspires the imagination toward fantasies of khaki-clad archeologists on a quest to solve the mystical riddles of a lost culture."

That had just the right flavor, Dr. Shane thought. It set the tone for the entire exhibit. It attached a bit of mystery and intrigue to the medallion that overrode any academic or scientific controversy. And the controversy itself, he had to admit, only propelled more people to want to see the medallion for themselves.

So far thousands of people had come through the museum's doors, wandered among the glass cases and reading the placards, looking to be even a small part of that figurative "khaki-clad archeologist's" quest. Those same patrons bought trinkets and souvenirs in the gift shop, concessions from the cafe, and more than a few season passes.

These were good days for the bottom line. Dr. Shane felt they had a winner on their hands—and it was about time.

For most of his tenure here, the museum had seen only modest and fairly dull returns on exhibits and showings. Frankly, they made more money on the novelty events—cocktail parties and high school lock-ins among the exhibits, all of which required having unhappy employees on hand to keep people from messing with the displays.

The most popular exhibits tended to be novelties as well—cringe-worthy collections such as "royal sex toys" and "ancient cursed treasure." The public just didn't have an appetite for mummies or dinosaur bones or broken shards of pottery anymore. They could see all of that on YouTube while seated on the toilet, and it cost them nothing. Why should they shell out money to see these things in a stuffy building that didn't even have a Starbucks?

But the Coelho Medallion was different.

Nothing stirs the public like an ancient mystery. The

mere fact that this object and the other artifacts from the dig site pointed to Vikings in the mainland was stirring all sorts of interest from the public, who had a constant craving for something new and interesting and exotic, especially if it was right in their own back yard.

Of course, that mini-series on the History Channel had helped a bit. Some of the museum patrons even recognized Dr. Shane as he moved about, his bow tie and suspenders making him easy to recognize. He was even being asked for his autograph—definitely not an everyday occurrence!

It was definitely a banner event for the museum, and for Shane's career.

Dr. Shane felt so good about the exhibit, in fact, and about the positive impact it was having on the museum, that very day he'd given the green light for an extension. The artifacts would be on display for an additional two weeks before they were taken on national tour. By his calculations, that would mean another hundred thousand dollars in ticket sales alone. The concessions, the souvenirs, and season pass sales would be through the roof.

It was enough to make him feel ok with his life choices again.

Back at the start of his career, Shane had wanted very badly to be like one of those khaki-clad adventurers mentioned by the times. But life didn't always take the turns one expected, and his experience, not to mention his need for a steady income, had eventually made working in a museum the best alternative to a career spent crawling around in ancient ruins, and digging up artifacts from lost cultures.

He might still have preferred being out in the field, actually being part of the discovery, to sitting behind a desk in an office tucked into the back corner of a museum. Being in the field had always been the dream of his youth. He had never wanted to be the Curator. He'd wanted to be that khaki-clad adventurer. But this was good too. He had learned to be satisfied with his career and his life. It was comfortable, and it gave him some notoriety and respect. That was reward enough, he had long ago decided.

It was later on a Thursday night, after Dr. Shane had retired for the evening and was just pulling into his garage, when his mobile phone rang. The caller ID showed the number for museum security.

His stomach twisted instantly, and all of his life choices once again seemed to press in upon him.

"This is Dr. Shane," he answered.

"Sir, you'd better get back here right away," said Neil Gossner, head of museum security.

"Neil, I've just arrived home," Shane replied. "Unless this is something of vital importance ..."

"The exhibit has been robbed."

It was so abrupt. So matter of fact. Not a hint that Gossner was aware of the crushing, existential meaning that came with the words.

"Robbed?" Dr. Shane said quietly. He felt like throwing up, and before he even asked the question he knew what Gossner's answer would be. Still, he had to ask. It was his job. "What was taken?"

"We're not sure how they did it, sir. Not yet. But it looks like the only item stolen was the medallion."

The only item stolen?

The medallion?

The center piece of the entire exhibit?

"I'm on my way," Dr. Shane said, his voice hoarse from the feeling of dread that was gripping him.

He sat for a moment, feeling his heart pounding, feeling

the blood rushing in pulsing waves through his body, his face and neck flushed and warm and wet with perspiration.

Then, as if he'd been shocked awake, put the car in gear and stepped on the accelerator.

He slammed the brakes at the last second as he almost lurched through the back wall of his garage, having put the car in the drive without thinking. He shifted into reverse then, calmly and deliberately, then sped backwards out of his driveway and onto the street with a thud, squealing away in the direction of the museum.

PART I

Chapter 1

"As far back as the 10th century AD, there is evidence of ... well, let's call it Norse dabbling in North America."

There was a minor chuckle at this, mostly from the heavy academics in the room, and Dr. Dan Kotler was grateful for it. When he had agreed to speak on this topic the research was already making its rounds through the scientific community, but it hadn't yet caught on. Most of his fellows thought of it as absurd, despite all the best evidence.

Kotler was able to lecture openly about Norse influence on North America only because he wasn't bound by the usual limitations of academia and science. He was an independent—as credentialed as any of his contemporaries, holding multiple PhDs in Anthropology and Quantum Physics. But he had the good fortune of being his own benefactor, thanks to his personal wealth. This, coupled with his lack of direct affiliation with any given university or institute, ensured he was free to posit any absurd theories he wished with very few repercussions.

Well, other than occasionally being blackballed from certain peer review journals and thought of as a fringe lunatic by his peers. Consequences he could live with, for the most part.

He worked hard, however, to present impeccable research and evidence for any claims he made or conclusions he drew, which kept him more or less in the good graces of the scientific community.

More or less.

His musings on the Norse influence on North America had ridden the fine line of academic absurdity and legitimate archeological research for years now, and he was fully aware of that. The theories were starting to gain acceptance in the larger scientific community, an inch at a time, but only grudgingly. Kotler felt sure he'd been invited to do this talk only because of recent findings in Pueblo, including the medallion unearthed by Dr. Eloi Coelho and his team. If not for the popularity of that medallion and the exhibit associated with it, Kotler might still be lecturing, just on a very different topic. The symbolism of ancient pottery, perhaps.

Then there was that History Channel miniseries.

Vikings in America had been rushed through production, spurred at least in part by the exhibit that included the Coelho Medallion itself, but that hadn't stopped it from catching fire with the public. For an audience weaned on *Ancient Aliens,* and other programs that routinely presented wildly speculative theories and viewpoints of history and archeology, *Vikings in America* was almost tame by comparison. The show had just the right mix of dramatized reenactments, as well as testimonials from some of the rock-star level researchers and scientists in History Channel's roster, to create a frenzy with the public. Everyone wanted to know: How had Viking artifacts come to be found nearly 2,500 miles from where they'd initially landed in the New World?

It was the sort of baffling mystery that set public curiosity on fire.

Kotler had been asked to be a part of the program, as an expert on both Norse history and mythology and as a general anthropologist and cultural expert. During his interview, he'd spoken at length about symbology, specifically pertaining to the symbols discovered at the site, and he had outlined much of the history he was discussing today, in this very lecture hall. A lot of what he'd said ended up on the cutting room floor, but some of the more sensational revelations had come directly out of his mouth. And that had given him a nice boost as a minor celebrity, he had to admit.

The miniseries event had aired over the course of four nights, and it had brought in high ratings for the channel. It had fueled a passion for finding out more about this strange idea—Vikings discovering America before Europeans had ever set foot here. Suddenly the whole discovery became wildly popular, drawing a crowd to the exhibit and, somehow, to this lecture that had never been intended as anything serious. This was supposed to be a cheeky nod to the quirks of history, with the Viking discovery presented as a one-off anomaly. Now, suddenly, it was a standing-room only presentation.

They were forced to upgrade the venue at the last minute to accommodate all the ticket-buying patrons who wanted to learn more. Now, instead of the few dozen academics and graduate students Kotler had expected, the auditorium was jam-packed with highly interested ...

What was he to call these people? What was the half-joking nickname that Evelyn Horelica had used? History groupies?

"We've long known that Vikings had at least two settlements in Greenland. But what has come to light more recently is evidence of a small settlement in *L'Anse aux Meadows*, in Newfoundland." Kotler touched the screen of his iPad, and the large display above him changed to show a collage of shots from *L'Anse aux Meadows*. "What looks like a fenced-in grassy knoll at first glance is actually the remnants of what we have confirmed to be former Viking houses." He paused for effect. "This is a Viking village, on the shore of Médée Bay, right here in North America."

He advanced the presentation again, and now the audience was treated to a computer model of what the village might have looked like circa 1,000 AD. Kotler was again pleased to hear some satisfied *ahs* and *oohs* from the audience.

He advanced the presentation to show some artifacts. This was one of the things the history groupies came to see. The weird and mysterious stuff. The unusual that hinted at some tantalizing and hidden history.

They hung on his every word as he described the function of various pieces, their role in Viking culture, and the conditions under which they were unearthed. He cycled through various carved stones and markers, to the pleasure of the audience.

"This is one of my favorites," Kotler said, pausing on an image of man in a top hat standing beside a large stone with white runes carved into it. "This is Dighton Rock, which was discovered half-buried in the mud of the Taunton River, in Massachusetts. It was discovered as early as the 17th Century, when it was at first mistakenly determined that these markings were made by Native Americans. Later, in the 19th Century, they were thought to be Phoenician and later still they were even thought to be Portuguese. But I prefer a 20th Century interpretation," he paused, looking around at the rapt faces in the audience, "which identifies them, correctly, as Norse runes."

He let that soak in. Norse runes in Massachusetts of all places? Even the academics in the room were whispering to each other at this point, though Kotler decided they were probably discussing how best to crucify him.

Kotler had personally concluded that these were unquestionably Norse runes, despite the current academic position that they were unverified. He had brought more than his own expertise to the table with this. Doctor Horelica—Evelyn—happened to be a top-notch linguist, as well as someone dear to him. She had verified that the runes were more than just random carvings.

There was a message there. There was meaning.

That was enough to convince Kotler, but he'd gone ahead and had their speculation and insights verified by a few more independent experts anyway. Every one of the them came back with the same conclusions, and after the third or fourth confirmation Kotler no longer had any doubts.

Again, he advanced the presentation. "This is Viking Tower, in Newport, Rhode Island." And again, "This is Thorvaldsen Rock, in Hampton New Hampshire." And again, this time a shot of several easily identifiable swords, axe heads and other ancient objects, "All of these artifacts—nearly two hundred of them—were discovered near Cheboygan, Michigan, on the coast of Lake Huron. A lot of good things come out of Cheboygan, but it's surprising to learn that an ancient armory was one of them." He got the laugh on that, and went on. "And lest you think that Vikings only spent time in the Northeast ..."

On the large screen, several images were gathered in a collage. "The Beardmore relics, of Beardmore, Ontario. The

Heavener Runestone, in Le Flore, Oklahoma. And, most infamous and most controversial, the Kensington Runestone, found in Alexandria, Minnesota."

The crowd really appreciated those little tidbits, and thrilled to the idea of Vikings coming inland, hitting the interior of the United States. Kotler imagined everyone asking the same questions he had asked: How had they gotten there? Some of these places weren't accessible by lake or river, so did they portage their ships across dry land? How far did they get?

Those were the questions that quickened Kotler's own pulse, but they had surprisingly raised the eyebrows of the public as well. Kotler had become accustomed to a somewhat apathetic reaction from the public, so this booming interest in his field of expertise was both welcome and invigorating.

Kotler glanced at some of his colleagues in the front row of the auditorium. He took note of several looks of disapproval and expressions of out-and-out denial. He was schooled in reading body language—was quite good at it, in fact—and could see from their postures and expressions and impatient ticks that they weren't enjoying this talk nearly as much as he and the rest of the audience. He was already on the academic naughty list after his participating in *Vikings in America*, and now he was sure to see some blowback, as the maven of this event.

And he hadn't even gotten to the good part, yet.

He sighed, steeled himself, and then said, "These finds are remarkable, and point to a hidden history of the Americas that we're only just starting to uncover. Our history is more ancient than we realize. But even more intriguing is that we are finally discovering evidence of something entirely unexpected. There are artifacts coming to light that provide tantalizing proof of a connection between Norse culture and that of several pre-Columbian native cultures— including the Aztecs, the Mayans, and most recently the Pueblo Indians. Effectively, we now have evidence that Vikings may have had more influence on ancient Americans than we ever realized. And it's a discovery that changes everything we know about American prehistory."

As the audience reacted to this, and his colleagues grumbled to each other in the front row, Kotler brought up a side-by-side image of the front and back of a disk-shaped gold medallion, inscribed with hundreds of marks and symbols. "This is the Coelho Medallion, discovered by Portuguese archeologist Dr. Eloi Coelho, while on a cooperative dig in Pueblo, Colorado. The area is rich in Pueblo ruins, and during an exploration of these Dr. Coelho found a structure that had been buried in an avalanche for more than five hundred years. He and his team were able to determine the general timeframe by carbon dating the remains of animals that were killed in the collapse. It's safe to say that no one has seen this structure for at least that 500-year range, and possibly a great deal longer. It went undiscovered during the whole of United States history."

Murmurs of appreciation and speculation from this, and Kotler let that simmer just a bit before continuing.

"The medallion contains markings from numerous pre-Colombian cultures. But it is these markings—"

Kotler tapped the iPad and the image onscreen expanded and dimmed, with a bright circle illuminating a short series of symbols near the center of the medallion.

"—that has caused such a big stir in the research community. That, ladies and gentlemen, is a confirmed set of Norse runes."

He turned to the crowd, all of whom were silent, rapt by

the presentation. "Evidence, it would seem, of ancient contact between the Norse and pre-European Americans, deep in the interior of what would become the United States of America."

"DR. KOTLER?"

Kotler had just signed dozens of autographs, including copies of some of his books, and at this point he was really just interested in getting to the men's room. His colleagues —all of whom had glared at him even as they marched out of the auditorium in a stodgy line—would be in touch later for a bit of rebuttal, he was sure.

The man who had addressed him stepped in front of him, dressed in a dark suit and white shirt. He had a plain, dark tie, and his shoes were shined and very practical looking. They looked as though they were designed to fit a more formal look, but it could give plenty of traction in a sprint if needed.

"I'm sorry," Kotler smiled, "I really have to use the restroom. Can I sign whatever you have once I'm back?"

"We're going to need you to come with us," the man said. And for the first time, Kotler noticed there was another man, dressed exactly like the first, standing just on the other side of the door. Both wore very sober expressions, though the other man was watching the crowds rather than Kotler himself.

Kotler had let himself be distracted by the urging of his bladder, and only now looked at the man before him with a more critical eye. His body language told Kotler that the man was disciplined, probably ex-military. He was fit and had the bearing of someone who could spring into action any moment. There was a slight bulge to his coat that practically screamed "weapon." The man stood directly in Kotler's path, hands held in front of him, one over the other, ready to do whatever needed to be done, if Kotler didn't comply.

"FBI?" Kotler asked.

There was the tiniest register of surprise in the man's eyes before he reached into his coat and produced an ID and badge. "Agent Roland Denzel," he said. Then, as with a slight, amused quirk on his lips, "FBI."

He nodded to his partner, "This is Agent Richard Scully."

As Kotler smirked and raised his eyebrows, Agent Denzel quickly added, "No relation to the X-Files. And he would appreciate it if you didn't mention it."

"Fair enough," Kotler nodded. "But I was serious about the restroom. If I could ..."

"I'm afraid you'll have to hold it, sir," Denzel said. "I'm sorry."

"No more than I am," Kotler said, and grimaced as Denzel put a hand on his arm and led him down a side corridor, away from the crowds, and into a conference room, where he was instructed to wait.

Denzel and Scully took positions outside the door. Kotler sat in one of the leather chairs. And crossed his legs.

A few minutes later, the door opened, and an older man entered wearing a suit only slightly different from those of the agents—a bit more tailored, and a bit more expensive. He was balding, but well-groomed, and he had the sort of wry-looking expression that Kotler had always interpreted as intelligent but skeptical. it was the sort of expression one wore when they thought they had more information than you knew. They were usually right, and it usually meant trouble.

"Dr. Kotler," the man said, shaking Kotler's hand and

motioning that he should stay seated. "I apologize for shuf-
fling you away like this, but it was unavoidable."

"Who are you?" Kotler asked, his ability to play games of
politeness or politics with these people was severely
compromised by the pressure on his bladder.

The man sat across the table from Kotler and opened an
iPad that was in a clamshell case, with a keyboard that made
it look like a tiny laptop. The older man peered down his
nose at the screen, tapping and swiping until he came to
whatever it was he was after.

"You are an acquaintance of Dr. Evelyn Horelica? The
linguist?"

At the mention of Evelyn's name, Kotler felt a wave of
mixed emotions. He had just been thinking of her, during
the talk. But if he was being honest with himself, he'd
thought of her often over the past couple of years. They still
talked frequently, still had contact when they could, despite
...

"Actually, yes. I've spoken to her recently. A couple of
days ago, I believe. Is she ok?"

"You've spoken to her numerous times over the past
several months, according to phone records."

Kotler blinked. "Yes. Though I don't see why that's any of
your business. Unless something has happened. Has something ... is she hurt?" Kotler felt dread at the thought of what
this man was about to tell him.

The man looked up from his iPad, and then leaned
forward slightly, twining his fingers together as he propped
himself on his elbows. "Dr. Kotler, I'm Director Matthew
Crispen, with the Manhattan offices of the FBI. I'm afraid
Dr. Horelica was recently abducted. It happened on a Friday
evening, unfortunately, and so it was nearly 72 hours before
anyone realized she was missing. The FBI is investigating

the abduction, in the course of that investigation your name surfaced. Numerous times, actually."

"Abducted?" Kotler felt his stomach clench. "Wait, 72 hours? My God! That's ... That means the trail ..."

"Cold," Crispen nodded. "But we have a few leads. We believe the abduction had something to do with the work she was engaged in. And there, again, we found a connection to you. She was in Houston working with a new employer, but she was also continuing to collaborate and consult with you on some of your work. This ... Viking thing," Crispen said, waving vaguely in the direction of the lecture hall. "But in looking through emails on her laptop, not every communication she had with you was professional in nature."

Kotler felt his face flush, and nodded. "Well, I won't make any secret of our relationship, Director Crispen. Evelyn and I were dating. For a while, anyway. These days, we're mostly pen pals." Kotler smiled lightly, hoping it would break some of the tension, but the Director remained tensed.

There was something about the man's body language that was setting off alarm bells for Kotler. Something about the way Crispen was conducting himself, as if he held all the cards, and was about to deal Kotler a blow. Kotler had no idea why, but he was suddenly feeling as if he'd been caught doing something wrong. He couldn't imagine what it could be, but there was always that sense, when dealing with people in authority, that there may have been some mistake you'd overlooked. It was similar to seeing police lights come on behind you—even when you knew you weren't speeding, you became paranoid that you were being pulled over and given a ticket.

"I haven't seen her in person for a few months. She's

been in Houston working on a project funded by an oil company there. Something about determining whether some of their land overseas should be classified as an historic site, which would prevent them from drilling without a lot of special precautions. She was helping with translations and some of the research."

"But that's not why you were in contact with her," Crispen said.

"No," Kotler said. "Most of our calls and emails were personal."

"Most, but not all," Crispen replied.

Kotler considered this. "I did send her scans of the Coelho Medallion, which were passed to me by Dr. Eloi Coelho himself. She was helping me to identify and translate some of the symbols and languages. I have a background in languages and symbology, but she's a specialist, and I wanted her insight. She and Dr. Coelho have also been in touch about this."

"The Coelho Medallion," Crispen said, peering once again at his iPad. "That's the artifact that you believe links Vikings and Aztecs?"

"As well as Mayans, Pueblos, and several other indigenous American cultures we are still cataloging."

"Very interesting," Crispen said, and for once he looked up from his iPad and smiled. "I have something of an interest in archeology myself. But ... you're not an archeologist, are you Dr. Kotler?"

Kotler raised his eyebrows. "I am, actually. However, if you mean that I'm not officially affiliated with a university or museum, you're right. I'm a private researcher. I have a background and PhDs in archeology, anthropology, etymology, and symbology. I also have PhDs in quantum physics and quantum mechanics."

"Quite a resume!" Crispen said, tapping the table between them with the fingers of his right hand, before leaning back a bit and folding his hands together. "And diverse. From quantum physics to symbology? How does one make that transition?"

Kotler shrugged. "It's not really a transition, if you're still doing it. When it comes down to it, I'm on the same quest everyone else is on."

Crispen waited, then prodded Kotler, "Which is?"

"Meaning," Kotler said. "I'm looking for meaning. In history. In the Universe. Even in cultural relationships."

"It seems to pay very well," Crispen said. "You have no employer, and yet your lifestyle seems to be fairly comfortable."

"I'm not short of money. I have an inheritance. And investments."

"Quite a few," Crispen said, nodding. He was looking at the iPad again, scrolling through whatever was hidden from Kotler's view.

Kotler immediately caught on to the fact that Crispen had been deliberately misleading him. Was he testing Kotler? Trying to see if he'd be honest about his finances? Or was he simply trying to keep Kotler off balance for some reason?

"I'm sorry, are you investigating me for Evelyn's disappearance?"

Crispen looked up at him, as if surprised. "Should we be?"

Kotler peered at him, trying to figure out the game. "You've seen something. Something in the research I shared with Evelyn. What is it?"

"It's your research, Dr. Kotler. Why don't you tell me?"

Kotler shook his head. "Nothing from the translations

I've gotten, so far. Mundane greetings, that sort of thing. But there were the new runes. A series that looked like 'city' and 'gold.' They're in an associative relationship with the rune for 'river.' Evelyn thought that together they might be taken as a place name. The name of an ancient North American city, perhaps. Possibly a translation of something the pre-Europeans introduced to the Vikings. Or vice versa."

"You seem to know quite a bit, Dr. Kotler. Why don't you tell me ... what do you know about this city itself?"

"Exactly what I've told you," Kotler said. "Why, what do you know about the city?"

Crispen laughed, then shrugged. "I know that Dr. Horelica sent you an email about that translation, then went for a jog. And an hour or so later, she was gone. Which, you have to admit, is somewhat suspicious."

Kotler thought about this and realized there was a lot about it that just wasn't adding up. "Director Crispen, why exactly is an FBI Director handling an interrogation like this personally? And why cast suspicion on me? She was in Houston—I couldn't have abducted her, even if I'd had reason to. If you've seen our emails, you know that Evelyn and I were intimate at one time, and that we still have a good relationship. I care for her very much. I would certainly never do anything to harm her, and especially not over anything to do with the medallion. So, what's really going on here?"

Crispen shook his head, as if disappointed in Kotler. "Dr. Kotler, you were the last person to be in contact with Dr. Horelica. Can you account for your whereabouts on Friday?"

"I was here, in Manhattan," Kotler said.

"Can anyone corroborate that?"

"I'm sure someone can. Do they need to? Do you have something that might indicate I'm lying?"

"Give me the names of people who can place you in New York on Friday. Also," Crispen reached into his coat and pulled out a thin sheaf of papers. "This is a warrant for full access to your apartment, your phone, and your computers."

Kotler took the warrant and read through it. "I'm being investigated for the kidnapping of Evelyn Horelica?"

"In part," Crispen said. "You're also being investigated for your role in a potential terrorist collusion."

Chapter 2

THIS HAD ALL the earmarks of the FBI covering its own butt, and Kotler was apparently just the pair of tighty-whiteys for the job. That was enough to make him want to take a swing at somebody, but at the moment he was more concerned about Evelyn.

As breakups went, theirs wasn't necessarily that bad. It was almost mutual. She had gotten the offer from Houston, and it was too good to pass up.

Kotler, on the other hand, liked his life essentially the way it was. He traveled and visited excavations and archeological sites, he spoke and lectured at museums and universities, he did his research and he wrote his books—and then he returned to his apartment in Manhattan, living in the sort of building one would normally be unable to afford on an anthropologist's income. Perks of being wealthy.

Kotler loved traveling, and loved spending time in remote sites, learning new and interesting things about ancient and modern cultures alike. But he always returned to Manhattan. The city was home. It was where he recharged. And he liked it that way. There had been nothing to draw him to Houston.

Which was the problem.

His needs were more than simply taken care of by his inheritance—he'd be considered wealthy regardless of where he lived in the world. The only thing he ever felt was missing in his life was companionship. And ... well, that was usually just a temporary deficiency. For an academic, Kotler kept in good physical shape. He was considered handsome, though not particularly on the cutting edge of fashion. And despite being somewhat of a pariah in certain scientific and academic circles, he often found himself associating with the city's elite—another perk of wealth. His books, the television appearances, and his speaking engagements gave him that air of minor celebrity as well. All of these combined had given him plenty of opportunities with the opposite sex. He couldn't complain.

For all the trysts, though, Kotler often still felt a bit lonely and isolated in his daily life. He had always needed someone who was an intellectual equal—someone who shared his passions if not his viewpoint. So it was good that he'd found someone who was both a loving companion and a good friend, with an intellect that he found as attractive as her physical beauty.

Things had been good with Evelyn. The two of them had been running in the same circles for years, catching glimpses of each other at symposiums and academic events. They had spoken to each other often, on topics ranging from lofty personal insights and speculations over the purpose of the Great Pyramids to mundane conversations about restaurants they liked and their favorite flavors of ice cream.

Kotler had suspected for some time that eventually they might take a turn together—slipping away from friendship and delving deeper into the waters of a more intimate relationship.

Evelyn was a knockout, with a model's figure and a mind that could put most of her male counterparts to tearful shame. Kotler was attracted to her immediately, but he had never acted on it until he felt for certain that she reciprocated. Which did happen. Eventually.

That first night, after a museum banquet, it had been almost inevitable that the two of them would sneak off for some private moments in the ancient hominid exhibit. In fact, it was almost cliché that they'd snuck away in the middle of a black-tie event. Which might have been what appealed most to Kotler. His life was often so unpredictable, sometimes even dangerously so. A bit of inevitability was good every now and then. A spot of predictability was soothing for the soul.

But predictability soon wears out its welcome, and Kotler found that he didn't particularly want to be in a committed relationship at this point in his life. He was too mobile. His life was too fluid. And, if he was being honest, he liked women a little too much to settle on just one at the moment.

He knew what that would look like to anyone on the outside. He was sure to be billed as a philanderer. A womanizer. And in today's over-politicized, militantly correct climate, such a thing made him almost an anachronism, and certainly someone to be sniffed at derisively, if the topic ever came up.

That didn't really bother him.

It didn't seem to bother Evelyn, either. In fact, she didn't seem to mind the breakup at all. When she gave Kotler the news that she was taking the job, and moving to Houston indefinitely, her entire demeanor was that of a woman who was tying up a loose thread. She was still sweet, and kind, and loving. They still had passion between them. But now it had the tone of something laced with farewell, rather than monogamous commitment.

Maybe she sensed that Kotler was getting restless. Or maybe she had just had enough of him and wanted to move on and explore other avenues herself. Or it could be that she never thought Kotler was "serious relationship material," which would have been a fair point.

He knew that he could be distracted to the point of it being ludicrous, when he was working. It might be days before he even looked up from what he was reading or examining, whatever ancient puzzle he was trying to solve, and uttering more than a grunt or monosyllabic exclamation upon discovering something new. He tended to travel frequently, and with just an instant's notice, which often shredded plans and cancelled dates. And his conversations inevitably drifted away from the mundane world and into whatever it was that had caught his interest. His life was his career. It always had been.

Even Evelyn, a peer in his field, didn't want to talk shop all the time. She loved her work as much as he did, but it was hardly the only thing in her life. She had friends. She had hobbies. She had family—something Kotler himself only had in limited supply. It stood to reason that she might want a life that consisted of more than solving the next ancient riddle or deciphering the next mystery of the universe. So maybe she was as ready to move on as he was.

Despite that possibility, however, and despite the 1,600 miles between them, the two of them still talked often.

Their initial attraction was still there. They still wanted to know what the other thought, whenever they made a discovery or needed to make an intuitive leap.

Evelyn was often traveling as part of her new role, and sometimes their destinations overlapped. They would spend quick evenings together, usually something small and intimate. They made the most of the time they had, and for now that seemed to be enough.

At the moment, however, all Kotler wanted was to see Evelyn alive again.

He was less worried about being investigated for her abduction than he was bothered by the fact that the FBI was wasting time. The real kidnappers were still out there, and every day the trail would grow colder as Director Crispen kept efforts focused on the wrong man. And Kotler was definitely the wrong man. Far from being a viable suspect, Kotler would actually better serve the investigation as a consultant, if they'd let him. If Evelyn's abduction was, in fact, tied to the translations on the Coelho Medallion, Kotler was one of the most versed people on the planet, when it came to that. Only Dr. Coelho himself might possibly know more.

The fact that Kotler was under suspicion was, ironically, the most suspicious thing of all.

Kotler had all of these thoughts while finally relieving himself in the restroom just down the hall from where he'd met with Director Crispen. The Director had left several minutes ago, with the dire warning that Kotler should "not leave town," until they could complete their investigation.

Agents Denzel and Scully were still guarding him—one inside the restroom and one outside. As Kotler washed his hands, he looked at Denzel in the mirror.

"Why does a fairly run of the mill missing person's case require the Director of the FBI to make a personal visit?"

Agent Denzel paused before saying, "That isn't for me to know, sir."

"And why are you two agents still with me? Do you intend to follow me home?"

"We do have orders to escort you home," Denzel said. "After that, Agent Scully and I are relieved."

"Meaning that someone else takes over and watches me?" Kotler asked.

Denzel said nothing.

Kotler dried his hands and threw the paper towel in the bin. He was thinking about everything he'd managed to learn from Crispen. Which wasn't much.

Whoever had Evelyn took her because of her work—that much seemed clear. Crispen had brought up the emails that had gone between Kotler and Evelyn, and of late most of those had to do with translating the symbols on the Coelho Medallion. So it seemed reasonable to assume that the medallion was at the heart of this.

But how did all of this tie into collusion with terrorists?

That was the scariest bit, to Kotler's thinking. Crispen had refused to give him any but the sketchiest details about what that collusion might look like, and how it might involve Kotler. Crispen would only allude to vague discoveries and evidence, making no attempt to elaborate. Kotler could tell that the Director was baiting him, pausing after his accusations in the hope that Kotler would start talking and filling in the gaps. He was giving Kotler plenty of rope to hang himself.

Kotler, realizing what was happening, didn't take the bait. As uncomfortable as the stretches of silence might be, he volunteered nothing. It was safer to stay silent, even if it made him look as if he were hiding something.

In today's rampant terror-*noid* climate, security agencies were more likely to simply bury you in a cell somewhere rather than deal with determining if you actually represented a threat to national security. Much like the Red Scare trials of the 50s, the mere suspicion that you might have ties to a terrorist organization made you a threat. It was a dangerous climate.

The fact was, it wouldn't take much to tie any given person to a terrorist group, especially someone who travelled frequently and often visited conflicted regions of the world. To that point, Crispen's veiled threat was weighty enough to put some pressure on Kotler, regardless of his innocence.

Which made Kotler wonder—what if Crispen was only using that charge specifically to put some heat on Kotler?

What if it was meant to make Kotler act, so they could see what he did next? If they needed Kotler to reveal something through his actions, then they would want to put as much pressure on him as possible.

So how should he respond?

As far as he could tell, without knowing the real motives of Crispen or whomever might be pulling the strings in the background, there was nothing for it but for Kotler to play along and do exactly what they wanted. For now.

Evelyn was missing, and despite the apparent frame-up the FBI was trying to push, Kotler really would do anything he could to keep her safe. He would start by looking at his own research materials, to determine what he might have said that resulted in Evelyn being abducted, and to see whether he had any culpability in this.

Going back to the research seemed obvious, which meant it was the most likely outcome that Crispen was hoping for.

So that was exactly what Kotler did.

He took out his iPhone and opened Evernote. He kept all of his research in Evernote these days, rather than on paper documents, so he could access it from anywhere. Many of his colleagues still relied on bulky file cabinets filled with reams of paper—unindexed, and sometimes impossible to cull through. Kotler preferred to be far more fluid and mobile, and to have access to information instantly and on demand. He paid a service to scan every document, photo, and map that came across his desk, and then send the digital files to him in Evernote before archiving all of the physical materials off site. It was an efficient system, and it gave Kotler the ability to index and search by keywords, which made things much faster.

More often than relying on the service, however, Kotler would simply photograph something from his phone, while in the field, and tag and categorize it himself. It made things quicker. Kotler liked quick results.

In a folder labeled "Coelho Medallion," the service had created a note with an overview of everything he'd uncovered to date. And there was quite a bit.

Hundreds of notes contained photos and quick scribbles about symbols and translations—some of which he'd done himself, but many of which he had received from Evelyn or other experts. He sorted these by clicking on *Evelyn Horelica* in his list of tags, bringing up everything tagged with her name. So far, nothing jumped out at him.

Kotler had a habit of copying and pasting relevant emails into notes, keeping the paper trail alive and linked to the right topic. He spent a few minutes sorting through

Evelyn's messages regarding the Coelho Medallion. After a moment he had a comprehensive list, which contained mostly suggestions about possible translations for some of the more obscure symbols on the medallion.

Near the top, among the most recent messages, was the translation that mentioned the key words *river, city,* and *gold.* He had mentioned these in his lecture, earlier that evening, and had given them only a causal reference, because they were fairly casual terms, after all.

At least, they had seemed that way, at the time.

The unique combination of *city* and *gold* in the Norse symbology was a curiosity he had intended to explore later, perhaps the next time he spoke to Evelyn on the phone or in person. It wasn't typical. Though Vikings were fond enough of gold, to the point of ransacking villages, towns, even churches to get their hands on it, there were no Norse legends of a city of gold.

It was more likely, Kotler and others had felt, that this might be a reference to a much better-known *city of gold,* and one that had captured the imaginations of adventurers and the public for centuries—the fabled *El Dorado.*

The medallion raised the tantalizing prospect that the Vikings might have had knowledge of *El Dorado,* centuries before the Spanish would learn of it.

Speculation about this—and it was simply speculation, at this point—was the newest bit of information to wind its way between Kotler and Evelyn. The email was from just over a week ago. All of their communication between then and now was more mundane, more personal, sometimes even intimate. Kotler tried not to let himself feel outraged over the fact that the FBI had access to those emails. He stayed focused, trying to puzzle out what the FBI saw in his communications with Evelyn that might somehow connect him to her abduction or bizarrely, to some terrorist action.

Maybe it was the city of gold.

Kotler wasn't prone to unchecked speculation or hyperbole, but even he couldn't pass on the opportunity to bring up *El Dorado*—the fabled Aztec City of Gold. Or, rather, the Muisca city of gold, if one were being historically nit-picky.

El Dorado was largely suspected to be a pipe dream, by modern scholars at least. Some suspected it was a complete fabrication, concocted by European explorers as a means of fueling the fires of well-funded exploration for kingdoms and empires looking to expand their power and wealth by exploiting the resources of the Americas. Spanish sailors could find backing for expeditions to the New World much easier if kings and queens and lords of all standing thought there could be an entire city of gold in it for them. And, to compensate for never having found such a city, the spice trade at least kept many coffers filled. Tobacco alone was worth the journey.

In one of his emails to Evelyn, Kotler had quipped, "Maybe the reason Europeans never found *El Dorado* was because the Vikings already sacked it before the Spanish got there!"

A joke. Only slightly funny. And Evelyn had responded with the intellectual equivalent of rolling her eyes and indulging his moment of boyish speculation. It was clear, from the email at least, that there was nothing serious in the idea. It was meant as a joke, and it was taken as a joke.

As Kotler considered it now, however, in light of Evelyn's abduction and the FBI's peculiar interest, he wondered if maybe this was the trigger after all. Which brought him to an alarming conclusion ...

Someone, other than the FBI, had access to their emails.

Kotler had never made any public statements about the *El Dorado* idea, and Evelyn certainly hadn't. The only mention of it was in these personal communications, which the FBI had accessed after Evelyn's abduction. If this was the reason she was taken, it could only mean that someone else had access to her email and files from a week ago. Possibly earlier.

Who? And why?

The most obvious answer as to why would be the money, of course. A city of gold would be a tremendous financial windfall in any century. History was replete with the horrific deeds of those who had searched for *El Dorado*, willing to obtain it at any cost. It was possible that someone had seen the announcement of the Coelho Medallion, and all of the discoveries coming out of the Pueblo dig site, as a piece to a larger puzzle. If they had the resources, they may have made a connection between the medallion and *El Dorado* all on their own, and had begun tracking anyone associated with it.

That, of course, would mean they weren't so much watching Evelyn as they were watching Kotler himself.

It was a chilling prospect, but it carried with it implications that made Kotler uncomfortable beyond his personal safety. It was true, then onus for Evelyn's abduction might actually be on his shoulders. By consulting her, he had inadvertently put her in jeopardy.

He shook this thought from his mind. He couldn't afford to think like that, at the moment. He needed to keep his thoughts on how to find Evelyn and ensure she was alright. His culpability, as well as his innocence in her abduction and this accusation of terrorism, had to come second to that.

For now, however, he felt he could safely assume he had the *why* settled, at least enough to use as a starting point.

The *who* question was a bit more problematic. Whoever was monitoring their emails had also arranged for Evelyn's abduction, and was so far eluding the FBI. Hacking emails, kidnapping researchers in broad daylight without anyone so much as hearing a whimper—these things took planning and resources. It earmarked her captor as both powerful and wealthy.

And what about the FBI, and this alleged terrorist action?

It was odd enough that an FBI Director had made a point of personally approaching Kotler as a suspect. Kotler didn't know FBI protocol, beyond what he'd learned through books and movies, but he was certain that Director Crispen wouldn't normally be so involved in an abduction case, even if terrorism were a factor. He should, by rights, be far too busy to take a personal hand.

The implications were ... well, actually, Kotler wasn't entirely sure what any of this implied. It certainly hinted at Crispen having some agenda of his own. It also indicated that whatever the terrorist activity was, it would be centered on the discoveries at Pueblo.

What did Vikings have to do with modern day terrorists?

There were questions here that Kotler couldn't answer, given the limited information he had, and that limited his options. At the moment all he could do was behave as if the FBI was on the side of the angels, and continue to help them with the investigation in any way he could. It was what was best for Evelyn, and for Kotler as well. He could hardly be of any help if he found himself in a cell somewhere.

Agents Denzel and Scully escorted him to the elevator, and then down to the lobby. Kotler had been scanning Evernote during all of this, and they hadn't so much as tried to peek over his shoulder, much less restrict what he was doing. Which meant they were either monitoring his activities in some other way or they knew that with the subpoena the FBI would eventually have access to everything he was doing anyway. It was possible they were already monitoring him somehow, though Kotler didn't want to give over to quite that much paranoia. Yet.

The one thing Kotler had going for him was the fact that even though his notes and emails might be accessible to anyone who might be monitoring, his private thoughts and his conclusions were entirely off the record, air gapped from his digital notes and files. The spies could know the details of everything he'd committed to the page, but they couldn't know the connections he would make between the various points of data, in light of events.

A small victory, and a small comfort, but Kotler clung to it. For now, his best tactic would be to shift his perspective. He needed stop focusing on the who and why, for the moment, and start asking new questions: What connections could he make, using the data he had? Which details mattered, and which were useless?

Kotler using his phone to schedule an Uber when Agent Scully said, "This way sir. We've arranged for you to have a ride home."

"Guys, I appreciate that I'm under suspicion, but unless you're going to arrest me, I see no reason to be treated like a prisoner."

"It's for your protection," Denzel said soberly, almost apologetically. "There's a possibility that you may be a target."

"If I'm not the mastermind behind Evelyn's abduction, you mean?"

Denzel and Scully said nothing, but they insisted on guiding him to the car.

Kotler sat in the back seat while the two agents sat in front. As they drove, Kotler considered again the information he had, rolling it over and over in his mind, letting connections form, glow into embers, fade back into darkness when nothing sparked to life.

Was it really possible that this was all about his silly joke? Could this really be about his notion that Vikings might have found the city of *El Dorado,* or its equivalent?

It had been such a passing remark, and so recent, that he hadn't spent any time seriously considering it. He hadn't so much as thought of it since, if he was being honest. The idea was kind of silly, and he'd had no reason to keep it top of mind.

But now he wondered if he should start reaching out, making contact with people who might have some answers, and digging up a few answers of his own.

Who should he reach out to? And would contacting them put them in the same danger as Evelyn?

Several minutes passed in silence as Kotler rode in the back seat of the FBI vehicle. They arrived at his apartment building without so much as asking him directions, and Kotler noted at least three vehicles parked nearby that might have been more agents. Or, potentially, even kidnappers or assassins. This game was already dangerous.

Kotler nodded to the agents without a word and stepped out onto the sidewalk in front of his building. He walked past Ernest, the building's door man, and gave him a friendly smile and wave, as he always did. If the FBI had already searched his place, Ernest gave no sign of knowing about it. Kotler cringed a bit at the idea that he'd be the talk of the building, once the FBI barged in, but controversy wasn't all that new to him. He'd be fine.

As Kotler waited in the lobby for the elevator to arrive,

he realized that his best bet for settling some of his questions, and for making any headway in helping Evelyn and himself, was to start from the beginning. He needed to go to the source, as it were.

He needed to speak to Dr. Eloi Coelho.

Chapter 3

THE RESTRICTION on travel kept Kotler within range of his home, for the foreseeable future. Crispen had told him he had the run of Manhattan, but that was as far as the leash stretched. It was a good sign that he wasn't under house arrest, Kotler thought. Or it could be that Crispen wanted him to be free to do things that might incriminate him. If Kotler was under suspicion and being monitored closely, they might be giving him plenty of rope to hang himself. They were likely looking for whomever he'd reach out to, searching for anyone he might be working with.

Kotler had considered this, long and hard, before deciding to reach out to Dr. Coelho. He didn't want to put his friend in undue jeopardy, nor put him under undue scrutiny from the FBI. At the moment, though, Kotler was a bit short on leads. Particularly since he was tethered to the island, unable to fly to either Houston or Pueblo. He would have to restrict his search for answers to Manhattan, for now.

Luckily, Coelho was currently working here in Manhattan, and not unreasonably far from Kotler's apartment, at the American Museum of Natural History. The fact that this was one of Kotler's more frequently visited destinations was an advantage.

The day had turned a bit dreary outside, so Kotler opted to take the subway, noting that at least two men in suits boarded the same car, and when he exited a few blocks from the museum he saw that two more dark-suited men were stationed and waiting to follow him to street level.

How many resources was the FBI expending on him? It added to Kotler's impression that something else was going on here, below the surface of what Director Crispen had shared with him. It was a foregone conclusion that Crispen wouldn't share all of the details of the investigation, and he would most certainly lie if he did give Kotler any information. It was obvious that Kotler had somehow found himself in the middle of something big, without even trying. And what irked him most was that he had no idea what it was or how he'd gotten here. He was used to trouble finding him, eventually, but he preferred the kind that he could see coming.

The walk from the subway to the museum was long enough to both clear Kotler's head and make him rethink walking in this weather. There was a drizzle of rain making everything sloppy and miserable, and there was just enough chill in the air to make it uncomfortable without a coat, but too warm while wearing one.

He was grateful to reach the museum when he did, and he vowed to take a car going back.

When most people think of research into antiquities and ancient artifacts, they picture stodgy old men in outdated fashions, hunched over large oak tables strewn with dusty bits of jetsam and debris recovered from the soil of some ancient dig site. That vision was not far from the truth, Kotler had to admit.

Rather than some dingy basement dungeon, however, most modern research was conducted in fairly clean rooms, with modern equipment and lighting. Most researchers, these days, were youthful, casually but nicely dressed, and generally intelligent and inquisitive in a more practical way, rather than obsessed with the minutia of antiquity the way the public perceived them.

Dr. Eloi Coelho was of an older generation, likely more in line with what the public imagined an archeologist to look like. He had platinum hair that contrasted nicely with the bronze of his skin, though his hair was starting to thin slightly on top. He sported the sort of wire-rimmed spectacles that might be considered cliché for his breed, and was wearing a light blue button-down dress shirt, the sleeves rolled to his elbows. He wore khaki chinos, pressed and neat, but which had clearly seen the field on more than a few occasions—noted by the tiny bit of fraying at the cuffs, and the small bit of fresh needlework near the belt line. Folded and hanging over the back of a high-backed stool was the Doctor's tweed coat, with requisite leather patches on the elbows.

Coelho was an archeologist and academic who certainly met the expectations of the public.

"Dr. Kotler," Coelho said, smiling and extending a hand as Kotler entered.

Kotler took the hand, and the two made a warm greeting. "Dr. Coelho," Kotler said, returning the smile. "It's good to see you again."

"You've had a visit from the FBI?" Coelho asked, cutting to the chase. His Portuguese accent made him sound jovial, but Kotler picked up on a slight irritation all the same.

"You too?" Kotler asked.

Coelho nodded. "Evelyn," he said, sadly. "They asked me many questions. Most of which I could not answer." He peered around, as if ensuring the FBI agents were not in the room with them. "They asked me many questions about you as well."

Kotler nodded. "I'm a suspect, thanks to my relationship with Evelyn, and some emails they pulled from her computer. Though I believe there may be something else going on."

"And is this why you are here? Are you trying to find something that clears your name?"

Kotler thought about this before responding. "In part. I'm here to see if there's something about the research into your medallion that might have gotten Evelyn abducted. And I'm hoping it will save her."

Coelho examined him for a moment, then nodded and said, "Evelyn was not the only abduction."

Kotler was surprised. "Who?" He asked.

Coelho frowned and shook his head. "Not who. The medallion. It was taken from the museum a few days ago."

"A few days!" Kotler exclaimed. "I haven't heard a thing in the news!"

Coelho waved a hand, dismissively. "The museum closed the exhibit immediately, claiming there were some issues with public safety, or some nonsense. I only heard when Dr. Shane called me personally. I believe he was ordered to tell no one, but he felt I should know."

"Do they have any leads on the theft?" Kotler asked, though he suspected he knew the answer.

Coelho shook his head. "Dr. Shane tells me they're not even certain how it was stolen. There is no evidence of an actual break in. It was there one moment, and the next it was simply gone. Quite mysterious."

This was odd and interesting news, and it intrigued Kotler. At the moment, however, he wasn't sure how the theft of the medallion tied in to Evelyn's abduction, if at all. For now, he filed this information away, with the thought that perhaps he could follow up on it later.

He looked at the table where Coelho had been working, and he noted the less sensational artifacts recovered from Pueblo. Though these were not as glamorous or sensational as the medallion, they were no less important. They provided vital clues about the discovery, and some insight into how and why Vikings came to live, for a time, in the interior of North America.

"I was emailing Evelyn just before she was abducted," Kotler said, his voice quiet and intense. He looked up at Coelho and saw that the old man's face was registering some of the pain that Kotler was feeling. Coelho and Evelyn were colleagues, on occasion—it was hard not to be in this work. Small world, and all that. And though they might not have been close, Coelho was clearly a man who felt deep emotion over anyone's misfortune, particularly that of a friend and colleague.

"Did Evelyn ever mention to you an idea about a city of gold?" Kotler asked.

Coelho nodded. "Once. A day or so ago, on the phone. She mentioned the translation, and that you had brought up *El Dorado*." Coelho chuckled. "It would be very amusing, no? To discover that the Vikings had sacked *El Dorado* before the Spanish ever set foot on these shores!"

Kotler smiled and nodded. "It would. But even the presence of the Vikings is in question at this point. Just because those symbols happen to resemble Norse doesn't mean they truly are. We need more corroborating evidence to move this from a question to a fact."

Coelho grinned then and motioned for Kotler to follow him.

He led Kotler to one of the clean rooms at the back of the lab, where two technicians were working on something that Kotler could not quite make out from the other side of the glass. In Portuguese, Coelho asked through the intercom if the two would stand aside and move the rolling table closer to the glass, so Kotler could see what they were examining.

Kotler leaned in, and gasped as he saw what was on the table.

It was a wooden figurehead, from the prow of a ship, carved in the shape of a dragon.

The wooden surface was carved in an intricate pattern of scales, as well as an unmistakable knotwork motif that was instantly recognizable as Norse in origin.

It was old, and the wood had rotted over the centuries, degrading the carvings. It had gaping, jagged holes, and the pattern occasionally disintegrated into splinters. It was, however, very obviously the figurehead of a Viking ship.

Kotler had personally seen hundreds just like it, but it was still a shock to find it here, in the context of Coelho's dig.

"When did you find this!" Kotler exclaimed.

"We brought it back from Pueblo two days ago. We located it in a newly unearthed underground cavern that we believe links to an aquifer system. An underground river."

Kotler looked at him, unbelieving. "Underground?"

"We gained access to the caverns through a surface cave near where the medallion was found," Coelho said. "I have found markings matching those from the medallion, carved into the mouth of the cave. We've determined that before its collapse, several hundred years ago, the cave mouth was an archway. It appears to be a natural formation that was further carved and adorned with symbols from numerous languages. All of which appear on the medallion."

Kotler was still staring at the carved figurehead, not quite sure if he should believe what he was seeing. Before him sat actual proof of a Viking presence in deep, interior North America. In Colorado—far from the Great Lakes, and even further from the Atlantic Ocean. There weren't even any major rivers connecting this central part of the United States to the East Coast. Kotler could only imagine the journey that would have to take place for the Vikings to find themselves here, closer to the Pacific Ocean than to the Atlantic they were familiar with.

He had always imagined it as an overland trek, a long and grueling portage with Vikings either abandoning their boats on the shores left behind, or manhandling them over the terrain, in search of the next body of water. Now, however, a new and thrilling possibility emerged, and it was difficult for Kotler to accept.

He looked back to the table, and the wooden remains splayed there like a cadaver being autopsied.

The figurehead not only verified a lot of Coelho's research—research that Kotler was participating in—it opened up possibilities that turned American history on its ear. Nearly everything known about pre-European America would have to be reexamined and reconsidered. It was perhaps the biggest pre-historic discovery in the US since unearthing dinosaur fossils in the 19th century. It hinted at volumes of lost history and cultural influence yet to be discovered.

"Eloi, this is ... this is simply amazing."

Dr. Coelho smiled and nodded, and led Kotler back to a small office, where each of them poured a cup of strong, black coffee. Coelho peered through the crack in the door, then reached into his desk and removed a small flask, splashing some of the amber liquid into his cup. He offered it to Kotler, who appreciatively offered his cup to be 'enhanced.'

"You must come to the site," Coelho said, leaning back in the creaking office chair. "The markings are incredible. And we believe the figurehead is just the beginning. There are many fragments of oak scattered within the cavern. My team leader, Richard Barmoth, is dating those finds now and preparing them for shipment to here. He's verified that they are from the same source as the figurehead. We are carbon dating all of the samples as they come. It's quite exhilarating."

Kotler sipped his coffee, winced a bit at the first taste of whiskey, and nodded. "I would love to visit the site. I think that's going to be tough to arrange at the moment, however. The FBI have me under guard and surveillance. They've made some pretense of saying it's for my protection, as much as out of suspicion. I'm pretty sure they're not going to make any allowances for me to leave Manhattan, though. They're actually here in this building, right now, looking as indiscreet as possible."

"Why would they possibly believe you'd harm Evelyn?" Coelho asked, shaking his head. "Anyone who knows the two of you would see that as ludicrous."

"I think it's more complicated than it looks," Kotler replied. "They've tied in this 'collusion with terrorists' claim, which I believe is meant to put added pressure on me. They figure I know something, and they want to give me proper motivation to reveal it."

"And what do you know?" Coelho asked, peering at Kotler over the top of his coffee mug.

Kotler thought for a moment, considering, then shook his head. "The only thing I've been able to come up with is *El Dorado.*"

Coelho scoffed. "Do you honestly believe the FBI has any interest in a mythical city of gold? It seems very unlikely."

Kotler considered this, sipped his coffee, and shook his head. "No. But I believe someone does. And I think that somehow has pull. Enough so that they can have me come under special attention from some powerful people. That isn't the kind of scrutiny I'm comfortable with."

"No," Coelho said, shaking his head. "I imagine not. So you are unable to leave Manhattan?"

"For the moment," Kotler answered.

"Pity," Coelho said. "I believe you would be useful at the site. My benefactor has provided us with quite a few resources. This is perhaps the most well-funded expedition I have ever been party to. We have made tremendous progress. I believe our continued findings there would be of particular interest to you."

Kotler thought about this, and agreed. He wasn't quite sure why or how, but he had the sense that Coelho's work was intimately tied to Evelyn's abduction, and this new discovery in Pueblo was bound to be part of it. He wasn't yet sure how *El Dorado* might factor in, if it did at all. But his gut was telling him that Evelyn's abduction was linked to the mysteries spiraling out of the Coelho Medallion. He needed to see where it was recovered, with his own eyes.

"You said the medallion has been stolen?" Kotler asked. "Do you know if there are any leads?"

Coelho shook his head. "No, my apologies. I know only

what little I have shared. I have not even been approached by the police."

Kotler was surprised. "You haven't?" he asked. "No one has reached out to you? The entire exhibit is the result of your work. The medallion was named for you!"

Coelho laughed. "I do not think that holds quite as much interest for anyone beyond the two of us," he said.

Kotler was about to comment on that, to assure Coelho that his work and contributions were history-making in their importance. Just as he was about to speak, however, there was a storm of noise from outside the research lab.

Gunshots, Kotler realized, alarmed.

"Eloi, come with me!" he shouted. He stood, opening the door and gesturing rapidly for Coelho to follow. The older man seemed confused for a moment, perhaps startled by the abrupt chaos, but he did as Kotler said, hurrying through the door as Kotler led the two of them toward the back of the facility.

Kotler had been in this part of the museum on many occasions. He knew the layout well, including all of the ways in and out. He had no idea what was going on in the corridors outside, but he did know that there was a freight elevator in the back of the research suite. That could take them up a flight to the street-level loading docks. This was where exhibits were brought in by truck, and items tagged for study were diverted into the research facility in the basement level.

On instinct, Kotler kept low, and gestured for Coelho to do the same. The cacophony from the corridors was getting louder, which meant it was getting closer. There were screams of pain from outside the room, and the sounds of authoritative shouting that Kotler assumed—or hoped—were coming from the FBI. The two agents who had followed him into the museum might be the only people standing between Kotler and Coelho and whoever was blasting their way inside.

Kotler intended to get away from here as quickly as possible, and to take Coelho with him, and figure out who was shooting later. He'd seen enough live fire in his time, and had dodged enough bullets to last two lifetimes. He wasn't feeling nostalgic about either experience.

Unfortunately, whatever the final barriers were to the gunmen entering the facility, they must have fallen. As Kotler and Coelho reached the service elevator and waited impatiently for the car to settle in place from above, the doors to the facility burst open and several heavily armed men ran in shouting.

The chaos was too loud for Kotler to make out everything they were saying, but the gist was clear. Kotler and Coelho were being ordered to stop, and that was an order Kotler had no intention of obeying.

The elevator finally settled in place, and Kotler yanked the metal-grate doors open, shoving Coelho inside and to the floor before following closely behind and slamming the doors closed. He hit the button to send the car up, and then dropped to the floor of the car just as bullets began ricocheting from the metal grating. Sparks danced all around them as the bullets struck, reminding Kotler of something akin to crazed fireflies. He covered his head with his arms and concentrated on not panicking.

Kotler heard more yelling, and this time he was able to make out a few words in Arabic—and not anything that sounded all that pleasant. One man was yelling to the others to stop firing, to take the two of them alive. Comforting, in its way, but Kotler knew they couldn't depend on gentle treatment, if they surrendered. Their lives might be spared, but they'd find themselves in a worse predicament.

It was better to run.

Finally the elevator rose beyond the threshold of the ceiling, and in a moment it stopped at the loading bay floor. Kotler slammed the elevator gate open and practically dragged Coelho out behind him.

It was then that he noticed that the older man was a bit sluggish.

Kotler eased Coelho to the floor behind some large wooden crates, near the elevator. He peered over the top of the crates to make sure no one was rushing in on them. This was a bad place to pause, but one look at Coelho and Kotler knew they had no choice.

The older man had taken a bullet to his right shoulder.

Blood was soaking the man's shirt, and Coelho was already looking pale from the loss of it. He was sweating and panting from the pain.

"Eloi," Kotler said quietly, "I'm sorry. We have to keep moving. Can you manage?"

Coelho nodded, even as he winced. "I will need ... some help."

"You have it," Kotler said. He gently put Coelho's left arm over his shoulder, assisting the older man in standing, and then guided him toward the large bay doors of the loading area. Mercifully, these stood open, giving them access to the street.

Despite this, however, it wasn't an ideal exit. There was no way to know what waited for them on the other side of those large, rolled doors. But the street was public, and Kotler could see people wandering by, completely oblivious to the gunshots and chaos happening just below their feet.

A young man in a green hoodie, pulled down low over

his face, glanced up at them as he rushed by, hands buried deep in his pockets. After he'd passed, the sidewalk beyond the bay doors looked more or less empty, with a crowd of people moving along on the cross street, which Kotler could just make out from this angle. The kid in the green hoodie disappeared into this crowd, and Kotler found himself thinking that was probably the best move for them as well. If he could get Coelho out of here safely they could disappear in that crowd and find a place to regroup, to call for help and get Coelho the medical attention he needed.

It was a plan, at least. At the moment, Kotler felt they were woefully short on those.

It was time to move.

They scrambled as quickly as they were able toward the opening, and Kotler kept glancing back over his shoulder, hoping he would not see armed men burst into the loading bay. With the gates of the freight elevator still propped open, the elevator's safety systems wouldn't let it respond to any calls from below. That was good. But there were stairs close by, and it wouldn't take long for their pursuers to find them.

As they neared the exit, with the street in sight, a man stepped around the corner, weapon drawn and leveled on the two of them. "Down! Down! Hands on your heads!"

Kotler stopped in his tracks, shifting slightly to stand between Coelho and the armed gunman, in an effort to shield the older man in case of gunfire. In an instant, however—and to his great surprise—Kotler found himself laughing. The man taking aim at them was Agent Denzel.

Upon recognizing Kotler, Denzel lowered his weapon and rushed forward in a crouch, looking past them to make sure no one was in pursuit. "Dr. Kotler," he said. "We got the call from our agents inside. Weapons fire. Are you ... Have you been hit?"

Kotler looked down to see that quite a bit of Coelho's blood was on his shirt. He looked a gory mess, but the older man was the one slumping from his injuries. "Dr. Coelho has," Kotler said. "I'm fine."

"Come this way," Denzel said, and led them out of the loading area with his gun raised.

Police sirens had started blaring, and people were being herded away from the building as a SWAT van squealed to a stop nearby. In moments, several armored men swarmed out of the van. Police were placing barricades and blocking street access, waving gawkers away from the scene.

Denzel helped Kotler get Dr. Coelho to a safe place behind the barricade, and in moments paramedics were on the scene, tending to Coelho's wounds. Kotler assured them he had not even injured, refusing to comply when asked to lie down. Instead, he stood and found Agent Denzel, who was speaking with the SWAT team leader.

"Who are they?" Kotler asked as he marched up to them, nodding toward the museum.

Denzel eyed him for a moment, as if debating whether to tell Kotler where to go, and whether the options should be friendly. He apparently made some internal decision and shook his head. "We have no idea. Not yet. We had four men in the building. Two are dead. The other two have barricaded themselves in one of the rooms. Did you see the attackers?"

Kotler nodded, catching his breath, though he hadn't been aware he was breathing heavy. "I saw three men enter the research lab. They were firing at us, but once we got into the elevator I was able to take a quick head count. They were speaking Arabic."

"Arabic? Are you sure?" Denzel asked.

Kotler nodded again. "Absolutely. I'm fluent. "

Denzel took out a notepad from his coat pocket and jotted these details down. He asked a few follow up questions to see what other details Kotler could provide.

Which wasn't much. Kotler had been as surprised by the attack as anyone, and the adrenaline of the moment was still coursing through him.

"Why do you think they're after you?" Denzel asked.

Kotler considered for a moment, unsure how he should answer. The honest answer was that he didn't know why they were after him or Dr. Coelho. But he had a suspicion. He just wasn't certain he wanted to share it with the FBI, just yet. He wasn't certain where they were in all of this, and any information he had that they didn't might make a difference in the outcome. Kotler wanted to make sure he controlled that outcome as much as possible.

Then again, Denzel had just saved his life. Kotler was highly skilled at reading people, and he couldn't sense any duplicity in Denzel. The agent seemed as genuinely concerned as he was professional.

Could Kotler trust him?

He needed allies, he decided.

"I think they're trying to gain access to any information about the dig in Pueblo," Kotler said. "I think they want to find the city of gold."

Chapter 4

FBI OFFICES—NEW YORK,

THE FBI OFFICES were a bit different than Kotler had expected, based on what he'd seen on television and in movies. He had expected a high-tech war room of a space, with agents seated at curved tables, engrossed in their sleek and cutting edge personal displays while a large screen dominated the room, providing most of the light for the space as it rotated through criminal dossiers, surveillance footage, and satellite imagery.

The reality was more like a cubicle farm.

There were plenty of windows in the outer offices, where hundreds of agents sat before computer terminals that were edging on toward being outdated. The room was filled with office sounds, from the whirring of copy machines to the constant chatter of phone conversations. All told, it was far less exciting than an episode of 24.

There were offices lining the outer rim of the cubicle farm, with large glass walls that, more often than not, were sheathed in slatted blinds, pulled closed to provide privacy for the occupants. Since those offices used the outer windows of the building as a fourth wall, those with closed blinds effectively cut the interior off from any natural light, casting the entire galley into the greenish haze of overhead fluorescents.

Kotler had been able to observe some of those offices from both sides, thankfully. Otherwise, he wasn't sure how he would have handled the hours of questioning and thinly veiled interrogation. He'd started to become annoyed with the subtle assertions that he was somehow responsible for Coelho's injuries, and possibly even the front man for the attack on the museum.

There was little he could do about it, at the moment, beyond keep as sunny a disposition as possible, cooperate fully, and wish fervently that the FBI had the budget for better coffee.

After hours of being handed off from one set of agents to another, he eventually found himself seated in Director Crispen's office. It was a cut above the rest, of course. Crispen had an expansive window view, for starters. His desk, though supporting its own stacks of folders and files, was neat and organized, and adorned with a few photos and personal items. Kotler noted that these were angled so that both Crispen and is guests could glance at them, without having to turn them for a better view. It was a subtle psychological indicator, that Crispen cared about his family and kept them on the same level of priority as anything else on his desk, and thus his career. That, at least, was a comforting touch of humanity, and Kotler clung to it, hoping he could perhaps appeal to it, if the need arose.

Opposite the desk and the window, in one corner of the office, was a round meeting table. The chairs were oriented toward a wall-mounted whiteboard, which was filled with unintelligible notes about ongoing investigations. Or so

Kotler assumed. It could be something else entirely. He wasn't quite sure, and knew he'd get no answer if he asked.

They were seated around the meeting table now, as Kotler sipped from a coffee mug emblazoned with the FBI seal. It was his third, or possibly fourth cup, and it had not gotten better with practice.

What tasted more bitter and acidic to Kotler, however, was the fact that he was still sitting here, recounting the events in the museum. He had already told his story to numerous agents, while seated in numerous cubicles and offices and conference rooms. He had told it to Crispen himself, just now, as they sat sipping coffee and going over details again and again and again.

It was tedious.

Of course it was. It was meant to be. Every syllable of Kotler's telling and retelling would be recorded and scrutinized to find details he might have meant to keep secret, or to uncover clues he had not meant to give. It didn't matter how often he said he had nothing to hide, and that he was willing to cooperate fully. The assumption was always that he would try to keep something from them.

After enduring another hour of this, finally Kotler said, "Don't you think it's time you gave me a little more information from your side of this story? Can you at least tell me if Dr. Coelho is alright?"

"He should be fine," Crispen said, leaning back in his chair and propping an elbow on the table. He sat with his legs crossed, as relaxed looking as anyone could be, while discussing a terrorist attack. Of course, Crispen, like all the other agents, had the freedom to leave the room at any time, and had not been forced to endure hours of questioning.

Kotler, by contrast, was feeling an ache at the base of his

spine, and in his neck and shoulders. All he wanted was to walk out of these offices.

Crispen continued. "He was in surgery within an hour of leaving the scene, and the bullet was removed without major complications. He's still in the ICU, but recovering for now, and under heavy guard."

"Where was he taken?" Kotler asked.

"We'll just keep that information quiet for now," Crispen said, giving Kotler a condescending smirk. "He's safe."

Kotler nodded. He was happy enough to know that Coelho was alive and being treated. It was the best he could hope for, and it was all he really needed to know. For now.

"Before the attack, you say that Coelho showed you the figurehead?"

Kotler nodded.

"We've recovered that, along with the research tied to it. We ..." Crispen hesitated, then said, "We could use your help in determining how it ties in with all of this."

Kotler scoffed and shook his head. "Now you want my help? Yesterday you all but accused me of kidnapping and terrorism." Kotler rubbed his eyes with one hand, then looked back up. He considered, weighed what he was about to say, and decided he'd had his fill of playing nice. "Tell me, Director Crispen, what is your agenda in all of this?"

Without hesitating, Crispen replied, "We want to find Dr. Horelica."

"And what about this terrorist connection?"

"We're investigating that as well."

"And do you still believe I'm cooperating with them?"

Crispen smiled. "I haven't ruled it out. Yet."

Kotler nodded. "And who is pulling your strings, Director? Because this has all the signs of being some sort of snow job. What has the FBI muffed up? And how is it you expect me to help fix it without giving me any information? And while you've tied my hands with veiled threats?"

Crispen's expression remained more or less the same, but Kotler picked up on some of his micro expressions. It was clear that Crispen was not used to being challenged or having his motives questioned. It was also clear that Kotler had hit on something—a raw nerve that maybe Kotler could exploit, though he couldn't be sure what it was.

Crispen stood then and went to the small wet bar, where his personal coffee maker stood. He poured a fresh cup of coffee and gestured with an offer to freshen Kotler's cup as well. Kotler shook his head.

"Consider your hands untied," Crispen said as he sipped from his mug. "We're suspending the investigation into you as a suspect in Dr. Horelica's abduction, effective immediately. Upon certain conditions."

Kotler felt his gut clench. "And what would those conditions be?"

"You work with us. You help us decipher the research from Coelho and his team. And you help us in our investigation into the terrorist actions tied to this case, in any way we see fit."

"That sounds a bit broad for my tastes," Kotler said. "I prefer terms and conditions that don't leave me to the whims of someone I don't trust."

"Trust is a strange thing, Dr. Kotler. It's not earned, the way many people think. It's a decision. I'm making that decision now. You should do the same."

"To a point," Kotler said.

"To a point," Crispen agreed.

"Anwar Adham," Crispen said, sliding the image into view on the iPad.

Kotler laughed lightly, and when Crispen stared at him he explained, "His name is ironic." Crispen continued to stare, and Kotler shook his head. "It's wordplay. 'Anwar' means 'radiant and full of light.' But 'Adham' means 'Black or dark.' Kind of a built-in pun. It's amusing."

"Not so amusing to his victims," Crispen said, advancing the images again to show several badly mutilated corpses.

Kotler had seen his share of mutilations, from severed limbs to beheadings, and far worse. The images on screen did not terrify him, particularly. But they were in no way pleasant, and Kotler wasn't exactly happy to be ambushed by them. He said nothing but noted that Director Crispen was watching him for a reaction. He'd done this intentionally, sending Kotler a message, not just about the stakes but about potential consequences. A subtle threat.

"These are the latest murders to be connected to Adham directly. He either performed these mutilations himself or he was overseeing them while in the room, we're not entirely clear on which. The photographs have been scanned by systems within the NSA and run through deep analysis. These aren't the only photos, of course, but you get the idea."

"Clearly," Kotler said.

Crispen advanced the screen again and this time photos of two different men appeared. Kotler recognized one of them. "That's Dr. Lewis Alman, from the Colorado School of Mines," Kotler said. "I don't recognize the other man."

"Dr. Alan Ridgway. He was here from Britain. Both were working with Dr. Coelho at the Pueblo dig, and both went missing almost three weeks back. Missing until two days ago, that is, when they were found in the condition you saw a moment ago."

Kotler felt his face flush with shock and anger. Dr. Alman wasn't a close friend, but Kotler had worked with him several times. He was a good man, quick witted if a bit nerdy. It was unnerving and frankly offensive that anyone would do that to another human being, and the shock was all the more poignant because it was someone Kotler actually knew.

Kotler felt an even deeper fear at the thought that Evelyn could just as easily be murdered in this way. It lent even more urgency to an already heavily-laden situation. Kotler felt an even greater pressure to take action, to do something to save Evelyn and stop these atrocities.

"As far as we can determine," Crispen continued, "these men were abducted directly from the Pueblo site and taken into New Mexico, and then across the US border into Mexico, near El Berrendo. They were found by Mexican authorities, who at first suspected they were victims of a drug cartel. They called us when they found the video tapes and photos, and the IDs of both men. The current Mexican administration considers terrorism to be an 'American problem.'"

"And these murders are connected to Evelyn's abduction?" Kotler asked, dreading the answer.

"Based on some of the evidence we uncovered, we believe they are. Along with at least three other murders— all people who had some connection to the Coelho Medallion. We believe that you and Dr. Coelho himself were marked for elimination or possibly abduction by Adham's group, and the prospect of you both being in the same location at the same time was too good to pass up."

"Elimination? Why would they want to kill us rather

than abduct us? Not that I'm advocating either course of action."

"We're not entirely certain, but we suspect that if they couldn't capture you they would want to remove you as assets to our investigation. They may have everything they need, with Dr. Horelica."

Kotler nodded. "So, you've known about these two murders and the other abductions for at least two days."

"That's right," Crispen said.

"But you only came to me yesterday."

Crispen said nothing.

"I don't appreciate being bait, Director. Especially when I have no idea I'm even in danger."

"We've had men on you 24/7 since we determined the link between these men and Dr. Horelica. You were in no more danger than you would have been otherwise. And we needed some way to draw out Adham and his people."

"You apologize for nothing, then. Got it," Kotler said, dismissing Crispen with a wave. He leaned in to the images on Crispen's iPad, trying to ignore his worry over Evelyn and to think as he would when approaching any enigma. Just as with investing a crime, when anthropologists want to puzzle out the actions of an ancient culture, they go back to first principles. All human actions came back to one thing: Motive. "You're after Adham," Kotler said. "What is Adham after?"

"We believe Adham is after funding. We think he's gotten wind of a potentially massive windfall in Pueblo, and he believes he can use it to do a lot more damage in the US, and worldwide."

"You're talking about *El Dorado*," Kotler said. "You think he's after a mythical lost city of gold?" Kotler shook his head, and then laughed. "It doesn't fit. We only just discussed this as a possibility a few days ago, and that was entirely a joke. My joke, I might add. There's absolutely no serious evidence that Vikings actually found *El Dorado*, or anything resembling it. We've only just uncovered reliable evidence that Vikings even had a presence in the area, a couple of days ago."

"We have a source that believes you're on the trail of something very big," Crispen said. "Coelho's discoveries have fueled a fire. And your joke was taken as more of a hunch—which we believe served as just enough confirmation to put Adham to work."

"Terrorists in Colorado, looking for an ancient Aztec treasure, presumed stolen and hidden by Vikings." Kotler laughed and rubbed his eyes with the forefinger and thumb of his left hand. "When do the Nazis and UFOs get here?"

"Now that you mention it," Crispen said, and he slid the iPad across the table. On the screen were scans of some old documents—shipping records, it appeared—that were in extremely poor condition. "These are pages from a ship's manifest from 1945. They were taken from one of Hitler's U-boats. And while the ship they were taken from contained no Aztec treasure, it did contain a collection of maps and documents from archeologists who had been searching and studying Pueblo at that time. Hitler was on the hunt for gold and had a particular fascination with Norse mythology and with Vikings. We think he had spies in that original Pueblo camp, and we think they were reporting back to the *Fuhrer* about what they uncovered. Nothing solid. Only hints. But the hints were enough to intrigue a few people in the Nazi party, as well as the archeologists and researchers who kept all of this secret for decades. Until recently, that is. When Coelho uncovered that medallion and the other artifacts, it triggered a black-market bidding war on these old shipping manifests."

"But you have them, don't you?" Kotler said, pointing to the iPad.

Crispen shook his head. "These are just a few of the documents. They were in the private collection of our source. The rest, we assume, were sold off to anyone who bid high enough. We have bits and pieces only, mostly from the shipping manifest, but none of the maps or the logs. We believe Adham may have those. He's certainly obtained some information about the site."

"And he's using that information to hunt for a buried treasure," Kotler said, skeptically. "Which he'll then use to fund attacks on the United States."

"Something along those lines, yes," Crispen said.

Kotler studied the manifest for a few minutes. His German was pretty good, but he was having trouble deciphering the content of what he was reading. Some of it was pure gibberish.

He realized, then, that the manifest contained bits of code—ciphers meant mostly for masking some of the descriptions of the content of various shipping containers. "You have a key for this cipher?" Kotler asked.

Crispen nodded and smiled lightly. "Impressive. It took the NSA a full day to realize there was a cipher." He took back the iPad, swiped through a few files and images onscreen, and produced a new image—a complete document that had English translations for the scraps of the manifest, along with the decoded contents. Kotler read through these and stopped when he saw a phrase that sent chills through him.

"*Barnstokkr,*" he said aloud.

"Yes," Crispen said. "I'm not sure why that wasn't translated from German to English."

"It's because it isn't German. This is Norse. Barnstokkr means 'child-trunk.' It was a tree that stood in the center of King Völsung's hall. Sigmund, father of Sigurð, the mythical dragon slayer. He was a hero to the Norse."

Kotler shifted position, sipped from his coffee cup, and continued. "One day a one-eyed stranger appears and pierces Barnstokkr with a sword. The stranger turns out to be Odin, in disguise. Which really shouldn't have surprised anyone, it was almost always Odin in disguise. Whenever you hear about a one-eyed stranger in a Norse tale, it generally indicates the special significance of the story. And in this case, Odin announces for all present that the man who can remove the sword from Barnstokkr will have it as a gift. And though many strong and powerful men tried to remove the sword, it was only Sigmund who could pull it free." Kotler chuckled and shook his head. "There are a lot of historians who believe this may be the root of the legend of King Arthur, drawing Excalibur from the stone."

"Fascinating," Crispen said, though he clearly was not impressed by Norse mythology, or by its potential link to the fables of the round table. "What does this have to do with anything?"

"Barnstokkr was sometimes used as a symbol of oath. Usually an oath of marriage, but sometimes as an oath between the Vikings and some of the other cultures they encountered. A symbol of Barnstokkr would sometimes be used as a sort of seal of agreement—a way to tell other Vikings that the locals were under protection, or that there was an alliance. And according to this manifest, one of the missing documents was a translation of markings found at Pueblo, one of which was the symbol of Barnstokkr adorning a stone. It's ... well, it's further proof of a Viking presence in ancient America, frankly. And it's a strong hint that the Vikings struck some sort of accord with the indigenous people of the area."

"Dr. Kotler, I appreciate how exciting this is for you, but unless it has some direct bearing on this case ..."

"It's motive, Director."

"Motive? How?"

"If the Vikings were willing to pledge an oath to the Pueblos and Aztecs and other ancient American cultures they encountered, there must have been something they wanted but were uncertain they could just take. Vikings were very good at taking what they wanted, but they weren't idiots. If they found themselves in an indefensible position, such as encountering a force that could match them in ferocity as well as overwhelm them with numbers, they would not be above diplomacy and negotiation."

"You're saying they signed a deal with the Aztecs? They made a trade in return for gold?"

"I'm not certain it was gold, but yes. They made a deal with the Aztecs and a number of other cultures. As far as I can determine, this site in Pueblo was some sort of indigenous United Nations. Several cultures coming together, marking the occasion by carving symbols into that archway cave entrance, and forging the Coelho Medallion out of gold. The Vikings must have sparked some sort of major cultural alliance that brought a lot of disparate native tribes together." Kotler shook his head and grinned. "It may be one of the first times in history that the Vikings were responsible for bringing peace to warring nations."

Crispen considered this. "So someone gets wind of Coelho's discovery, sees the connection with documents he already had in his possession, and contacts Adham, giving him the resources he needs to go find an immense lost treasure. A patron to terrorism."

Kotler shook his head. "That's where things start falling apart for me. There's something weird about the connection there. Whoever has possession of those maps and other documents clearly has an agenda, but what would be the benefit of bringing a terrorist cell onto US soil? How does Adham factor into this person's plans? What good could come from helping a terrorist, if they're just after the city of gold?"

Crispen shrugged. "Since 9/11 we've uncovered evidence of terrorist movement on US soil that would make you hide in a bunker forever. The motives of the people who support them range from absurd to delusional to purely treasonous. Their motives are irrelevant."

"I disagree," Kotler said. "In my experience, motives are everything. People make decisions with clear reasons. Whoever the patron is, if they actually are a patron, they have their reasons for doing this. They would support Adham for a definable reason. Their motives matter."

"And what motives might you have, Dr. Kotler?"

"None," Kotler said, shaking his head. "Or, rather, my only motive is to rescue Evelyn, if she's still alive. And I think you know that by now. In fact, I think you've known it all along. You've been using the terrorist angle of this to push me and get me onboard with helping you investigate this. And I don't believe your motives are to find Dr. Horelica. It's possible all you want is Adham, and you could care less who gets hurt, or worse, while you hunt for him."

Crispen regarded him for a moment, then nodded. "Alright, I'll give you this much. I will admit that Dr. Horelica is not the top priority in this investigation. That does not mean we have stopped looking into her abduction. But our resources are being funneled into finding Adham, as a priority."

"I'm just going to assume, then, that you're using Evelyn's abduction as an excuse to get me involved in the hunt for Adham."

Crispen nodded.

"Why?" Kotler asked.

"You're a special talent," Crispen shrugged. "We've looked into you, Dr. Kotler. You're an independent with few solid ties. A wild card. You're beholden to no one because you have money, and you have freedom to pursue any area of study you please. Someone like you might be a perfect asset, but you're very difficult to enlist."

"I would have helped to find Evelyn," Kotler said, feeling tension rise and his jaw muscles tighten.

Crispen nodded. "I believe that. But this goes beyond the kidnapping, Dr. Kotler. And if we had come to you and asked for your assistance with the investigation into Adham, would you have agreed to come onboard?"

Kotler said nothing. Crispen would believe whatever he chose, that much was clear. Kotler know, though, that he would certainly have come onboard to help, if asked. He knew the stakes, of letting a man like Adham run free. He said nothing to Crispen, because he was too busy considering what this conversation meant.

Crispen had said they had looked into him as a resource.

When had they done that?

Crispen picked up his phone and made a call, speaking partially in English and partially in some sort of FBI code that Kotler didn't even try to decipher. Instead, he focused on the rest of the translation of the manifest, trying to find any more hints or clues. Anything that might help him to help the FBI, whom he hoped would be equally as focused on finding Evelyn as they were on taking down Anwar Adham.

Crispen hung up and went to a coat hook near his office door. He pulled on his suit jacket, buttoning the top button and smoothing the lines. "Your flight leaves in an hour, Dr. Kotler."

"My ... my flight? To where?"

"To Pueblo, Colorado. I've made arrangements for you to personally inspect the base camp and the ruins. With an escort, of course."

Kotler nodded and stood. "Good. That's good. I think I can best help from there. But can I make one request?"

"You can make it. I won't promise to give it you," Crispen said.

"I'd like Agent Roland Denzel to be my escort."

Crispen considered this. "Denzel is a good man. And he's already familiar with you and the case. Consider it done." And with that, Crispen gestured for Kotler to exit the office.

As they passed the desk outside of Crispen's office, the Director gave instructions to his secretary, who then stood and led Kotler past the cubicle farm and to another room, where he was instructed to wait for Agent Denzel.

Kotler was given back his phone and other personal items. He checked and answered emails and text messages as he waited, and he did a quick search for information about Dr. Coelho's medical condition, with no results. Even the attack on the museum was still being referred to as "an incident," with only a few, sketchy details.

He then searched Evernote for any information he already had that might be useful, in light of everything he'd just learned. There wasn't much.

Before long, Agent Denzel knocked and opened the door, and asked Kotler to follow him. In moments the two of them were stepping out of the elevator and into Denzel's car, *en* route to the airport.

Kotler hadn't even had time to pack a bag. Which, as it turned out, wasn't necessary. Some items had been prepared for him, obviously taken from Kotler's apartment by whomever was there searching through his belongings. And in amongst his clothes was an iPad containing all of the information Crispen had shared earlier. At least Crispen had shown him that courtesy.

The flight would be nearly four hours long, and there would be plenty of time to catch up on research. But what Kotler wanted most, at the moment, was to catch up on sleep. He used one of the flight pillows provided by the attendant, and propped himself against the window of the plane, settling in to catch a quick nap before landing in Colorado.

As he drifted off to sleep, however, he had the nagging sense that he had overlooked something.

It wouldn't occur to him until later that Crispen had never actually answered Kotler's question—about who was the FBI's source in all of this, and what their motives might be.

Chapter 5

PUEBLO WAS BITTERLY COLD.

They were arriving late in the evening, and as the chill from earlier in the day dropped from the low 40s to an icy 24°F, Kotler found himself once again wishing he'd been allowed to pack his own damned bag. If he had, he certainly would have brought more than a sports coat and a few long-sleeved button ups. Thanks to whoever the FBI had sent to his apartment, Kotler found himself shivering against the cold in clothes better suited for a board meeting than an archeological dig.

Thankfully, one of the camp's live-in researchers was kind enough to loan him a coat, but it was a bit small, and couldn't be buttoned in the front. As a result, Kotler was forced to pull on practically every scrap of clothing in his bag and make do with the coat as best he could. It wasn't quite enough, but he could suffer through.

They were standing around a folding table in a medium-sized portable building, set up on the spot to serve as a sort of home base for the dig. Everything they did here had to be extremely low impact—anthropogenic ecology had already shifted the local flora and fauna away from what was native to this region during the time this site was active. The last thing anyone in the scientific and archeological communities wanted was to incur more damage, and potentially wipe out the faint footprints of a lost civilization.

The very fact that this location was proving to have so much Aztec and Mayan influence, not to mention Vikings, was somewhat shocking to the historic purists in the region. Some locals resented men like Coelho, who had come and turned local history on its ear a bit. In their view, the archeologists and researchers working at sites like this weren't so much uncovering long-forgotten history as they were spitting in the face of the cultural identity of everyone who lived here.

Kotler was always fascinated by the idea that people might rather remain ignorant and hold on to their lingering beliefs about history or culture, rather than explore any new information or consider any new perspectives. It ran counter to his nature, and to the nature of all explorers and knowledge seekers. It was an argument against the advancement of knowledge, Kotler felt, and usually perpetrated by those who proclaimed they were preserving history.

Some of the locals had taken to openly debunking any finds that the researches took from this region, going so far as to accuse Coelho and his research team of fabricating and planting artifacts, in an effort to justify the team's continued presence here, as well as the funds they were receiving. Of course, nothing could be further from the truth, Kotler knew. Coelho as impeccable, and he was meticulous in the details of his research. He was openly accountable as well, never shying away from answering the accusations of his detractors head-on.

Still, when faced with new facts, the sort that challenged

what everyone "knew to be true," it was normal for there to be ... well, doubt, to put it mildly.

Kotler had to admit, from the outside a lot of what was being discovered in these canyons was so incredible, he might have doubted it himself. If not, that was, for the fact that he had personally examined artifacts from this region, as had his good friends Eloi and Evelyn.

Both of some have paid a price for this, Kotler thought, then immediately pushed it aside. There was work to do, and if he was going to find Evelyn he had to keep sharp.

"This is the area where Dr. Coelho uncovered the medallion," said Richard Barmoth, pointing a finger at an area of the map outlined in a gerrymandering pattern with red ink. "This line indicates what we're finding to be a series of structures, most of which are Long destroyed. We've uncovered most or the most prominent artifacts in this area."

Barmoth was the lead for the primary dig team. He was the first to put hands on the figurehead, and he had been present when Dr. Coelho found the medallion. Short of Coelho himself, Barmoth was the most knowledgeable person on the planet when it came to this dig.

Which could make him a target, Kotler mused. He glanced around to assure himself that Agent Denzel was nearby.

Of course, security here at the dig site was incredible. Just getting into this building had meant passing through three different checkpoints, and the personnel were not shy about brandishing rifles. They had been a rough sort of onsite security, Kotler felt, but showed signs of the sort of discipline that came with being ex-military. Most dig sites, in Kotler's experience, employed security guards that were more of the would-be-police variety—the type who might have failed police training, or failed to even enter the academy, and were now working in the closest field they could manage. The security personnel guarding the Pueblo site, however, were no would-bes or wanna-bes. Kotler could tell by their postures and even their micro expressions that they were trained and had seen combat.

Kotler looked back to the folding table, where Barmoth slid his finger across the map to a different spot, marked this time in simple circle of green ink. "The archway is here, about fifty meters from the medallion site."

"How is it that the archway wasn't found sooner?" Kotler asked. "There are hikers all over this region at any given time of the year, aren't there?"

Barmoth nodded. "Hundreds of hikers come through here every year, but the archway was collapsed and buried by a rock slide, centuries ago. It's pretty difficult to spot without a technological assist. We used ground penetrating radar to pick up the gap, and it was almost blind luck that we happened to be in that particular spot. Most of our searching has been focused on the area immediately surrounding where the medallion was found."

"What were you hoping to find there?" Kotler asked.

Barmoth shrugged. "Buildings. Dug outs. The medallion was buried under a lot of rubble, alongside several other artifacts. We thought the archway might be the entrance to some sort of temple, but now we're not so sure. It may have been more like a vault or a tomb."

"Any human remains found inside?" Kotler asked, suddenly very curious.

Barmoth shook his head. "No. All we found were animal carcasses, which we were able to use for carbon dating. The chamber that held the medallion was sealed off when tectonic activity collapsed the hillside, covering the archway and the opening."

Kotler considered this and examined the maps and photos in silence for a moment.

Barmoth was approached by a couple of the site's researchers, who asked mostly about mundane operations for the camp. These included making accommodations for Kotler and Denzel.

Kotler looked up to see the FBI agent studying his own collection of data—testimony from the researchers regarding the two murder victims. Since arriving here, Denzel has been actively engaged with a number of Coelho's team, including Barmoth. Kotler had watched some of this, studying the dynamics in body language between Denzel and the archeologists and graduate students who manned the camp. He was impressed by the agent's ability to glean a larger picture of the facts by noting even tiny, obscure details. It was similar to how Kotler himself worked, when trying to figure out some ancient riddle. In that respect, Kotler knew, the agent's job was not so different from that of an anthropologist or a theoretical physicist—each of these fields required building a bigger picture from whatever details might be at hand, filling in the gaps with intuition and insight.

Kotler could see that Denzel was good at what he did. In his way, the agent was as much a scientist as Kotler or Barmoth or even Coelho himself.

With the increased security in the camp, there was an ongoing debate about whether the dig should be shut down altogether, and the people moved to safety elsewhere. Someone along the ladder was preventing that, Kotler figured. Maybe the same someone who had the pull to get high-level Federal agents to put pressure on Kotler, to force him to play along.

Kotler was becoming increasingly convinced that the

onsite security ex-military—their bearing and demeanor had military written all over it, at any rate, making them seem more like trained mercenaries than the typical security detail. They were well-armed, with high-powered automatic weapons.

They had also turned a fairly unremarkable dig site into something resembling a military base. There were multiple checkpoints, with armed guards at every entrance and exit, plus an armed patrol around the perimeter, and God knew what else. Kotler was impressed with their efficiency. Denzel was just annoyed.

Kotler looked again to the photos, spreading them out in a haphazard grid on the table. Each was marked with map coordinates, and Kotler could cross reference these against the map itself. Looking closely, he was able to see that everything found and catalogued at the site so far had come from the same general area—a circumference of about 150 meters starting with the medallion's location as a center point.

That's odd.

Whoever had crafted the medallion had held it in high regard. It was adorned with the languages of multiple cultures—symbology, largely, rather than language. But everything about it suggested reverence. This was a holy artifact.

The archway, as well, signified something sacred. Barmoth could be right about it being a tomb or vault. But ornate artificial archways weren't a typical feature among Native American cultures. So this one had to be something special. Maybe it was influenced by the Vikings, who surely would have encountered similar designs in Europe. The fact that it existed at all, however, told Kotler that it was a sacred site.

So why had the medallion been found fifty meters—over a hundred and sixty feet—from the archway?

And what about the city of gold? So far, the medallion was the only bit of gold anyone had uncovered. If there really was a city of gold here—*El Dorado* or otherwise—where the hell was it?

Kotler heard some loud conversation start up just outside of the temporary building and saw Agent Denzel dismiss the grad student he'd been speaking to, put away his notebook, and go out to investigate. Kotler wasn't getting anywhere with what he had in front of him anyway, so he decided to do the same.

Outside, Barmoth and a few others were in an argument with three of the private security team.

"We need access to that site! You can't just barricade it!" Barmoth shouted.

"We have orders, sir," replied one of the security team. He was a tough-looking man in his early 40s, and Kotler could see the volumes of muscle bulging under his uniform. Just like the rest of the security force, this man was holding an automatic rifle, and wearing full desert camo, complete with a helmet and what appeared to be night vision goggles resting on top. He looked the part of a solider in every way, with the exception that he was wearing Metallica T-shirt under his fatigues. Definitely not military issue.

"Your orders include keeping us from doing our work?" Barmoth replied, with open skepticism.

The guard patiently explained, once again, that orders were orders, to the clear frustration of Barmoth or again demanded access to the site. Kotler watched this exchange for a moment and had to admit he wasn't sure why a security detail should have to barricade part of an archeological dig from the actual archeologists. In fact, it was just about the most curious thing going at the moment.

Kotler sidled up to Denzel. "Can we get into that site? Do you have authority to get past security?"

Denzel snorted. "I'm an FBI agent. They're a private security firm." He paused, during which time Kotler looked at him, expectantly. Denzel rolled his eyes. "Yes, I have the authority to get us into the site."

"Let's go," Kotler said, starting in that direction.

"I have the authority," Denzel said, not budging from where he stood. "But I didn't say I would do it."

Kotler turned and looked at Denzel. The agent was wearing a thick, warm-looking, well-fitted coat with FBI stitched across the front and back in large yellow letters. "You're my escort? You're guarding me wherever I go?"

"Those are my orders," Denzel replied.

"Good. Keep me from being shot by this private security firm," Kotler said, and turned again to walk away.

He heard Denzel curse under his breath, and then heard the sound of the agent's boots crunching gravel under his feet as he followed Kotler deeper into the dig site.

They came to the barricade in just minutes—the base camp was central to everything, and nothing here was more than a few minutes' walk from the command center. As Kotler approached the checkpoint, two heavily armed guards raised their weapons.

"This is a restricted area," one of them said. "Turn and go back to the main camp."

"Restricted by whom, exactly?" Kotler asked.

"You will not get another warning," the guard said.

Denzel stepped into the light just behind Kotler, his badge already raised and glinting in the large security lights, mounted on poles to either side of the entrance. "I'm Agent Roland Denzel, with the FBI. Dr. Kotler and I have full authority to survey any part of this site. Lower your weapons."

The two guards hesitated, glanced at each other, and then pointed their weapons at the ground. "We have very strict orders, sir."

"Keep at them," Denzel said. "Now, let me and Dr. Kotler pass."

They exchanged glances again, and reluctantly stepped aside as Kotler and Denzel walked through.

Before continuing on, Denzel paused and asked the guards, "Who's your superior? How can I reach him if I have questions pertaining to our investigation?"

"We report to Will Canfield, sir. Everyone calls him Sarge."

"And who does Sarge report to?" Denzel asked.

"We get our orders directly from Mr. Cantor, sir."

Kotler was startled to hear the name. "Cantor? Mark Cantor? The founder of Zelot?"

"Yes sir," the guard said.

Denzel gave Kotler a strange glance, then said to the guards, "Thanks for your cooperation, gentlemen." He then moved away with Kotler beside him.

"Who is Mark Cantor?" Denzel whispered to Kotler. "And what is Zelot?"

"Zelot is a social media site for academics and researchers. Sort of a Facebook for scientists. Actually, it's more of a tool for crowdsourcing research. People who are really passionate about a topic, and who do loads of independent research, can publish their findings for the community to access, without worrying about pesky trivialities like peer review, or credentials."

"Sounds like you're not a fan," Denzel said, smiling smugly.

"It had promise, when it was first created. I contributed articles myself, and I was pleased to get very good feedback and quite a few leads on new lines of study. But it quickly became a haven for conspiracy theorists, over time."

"Doesn't everything on the Internet become a haven for conspiracy theorists?" Denzel asked.

Kotler chuckled. "I can't deny that."

"So what is Cantor's interest in this dig site? And why would he have his men block access to it?"

Kotler shook his head. "That's what I intend to find out."

KOTLER DIDN'T HAVE THE MAPS WITH HIM, BUT HE HAD TAKEN photos on his phone, and he was zooming in on these now, determining their current location in the dig site. "This is the archway," Kotler said, pointing first to his phone and then waving a hand at their surroundings. "They're blocking access to the most important area of the site."

"On the grounds that it presents a present danger to the researchers," Denzel said.

Kotler shook his head. "Without access to the archway, this camp may as well pack up. What's the point of keeping everyone around if they won't be allowed to do the job they came to do?"

"Just in case," Denzel shrugged.

Kotler looked at him.

"We've assumed that the research team is the only group studying this, but if Mark Cantor has a private security team built entirely of ex-military and special ops, you can bet he has at least one person inside the site, doing private research."

That made sense, and Kotler was surprised he hadn't thought of it. He had a growing appreciation for Agent Denzel, beyond the feeling that he owed Denzel for saving his life. The man was smart, calm under pressure, and willing to play something out—even if he didn't understand it entirely—just to see where it was going. Rare qualities for anyone. But perhaps they were necessary qualities, considering Denzel's line of work.

They continued down the stony path, their way lit by the occasional solar lamp, until they came to another temporary building, this time nestled against the side of a rock face. Kotler and Denzel exchanged glances, and then entered the building.

Inside were two men, one of whom was dressed in the sort of casual khakis and button-downs the rest of the researchers wore under their coats. The other man was dressed in well-tailored business wear, though his suit jacket was hanging from a hook by the door. He was young— maybe in his late thirties at the most—and had a close-cropped beard that was clearly meant to age him a bit. He was fit and had the bearing of someone who was used to being in charge, but he had to keep to a tightly contrived personal image to maintain the air of respect he felt he deserved.

Kotler immediately recognized the man as Mark Cantor.

Cantor and the researcher looked up from whatever they'd been studying as Kotler and Denzel entered, and there was the briefest flash of annoyance on Cantor's face. Kotler was good at reading micro expressions—he'd trained with some of the best in the field, as part of what he had thought of as "expanded anthropology"—and for the briefest instant what he saw in Cantor's features was not the annoyance one feels when their authority has been bucked, but the sort of deep anger that comes when expectations have been suddenly derailed. Cantor did not want them here.

"Mr. Cantor," Kotler said, making no move to step forward, but instead placing his hands in the pockets of his own khakis—a passive aggressive signal that would send the message that Kotler wasn't under Cantor's authority.

"Dr. Kotler," Cantor replied, nodding.

"You two know each other?" Denzel asked.

"By reputation only," Cantor said. He looked again at Kotler. "I'm a fan of your work. I saw your lecture on the Coelho Medallion."

"From yesterday? You do get around," Kotler smiled.

Cantor returned the smile, though it lacked some of the warmth one would expect. "I had someone in the crowd streaming it to one of our servers. I watched it on the flight in."

"I wasn't aware anyone was taping," Kotler said.

"Taping?" Cantor said, laughing. And this time it actually was genuine. "No one uses tape anymore, Dr. Kotler."

"Right," Kotler said wryly. "My anachronism is showing."

"What brings you here?" Cantor asked, nodding to the interior of the temporary building. It was a large, open space, with a few square tables pulled together to form a rectangle in the middle. High-backed stools surrounded this. And spread out on the table were maps, photos, digital tablets, and a few artifacts that had obviously been recently liberated from the dig.

What was more impressive to Kotler, however, was the large, gaping maw in the back of the room. Through a blind of several clear plastic panels draped over it, Kotler could just see the jagged outline of an excavated cave entrance. And on one side, just barely visible through the dangling plastic, he could see a hint of carvings. The most visible carving was a Viking rune, which gave Kotler a small thrill to see in person.

"I was going to ask you the same question, Mr. Cantor," Kotler replied, smiling and looking Cantor in the eye.

"Call me Mark," Cantor said.

"Dan," Kotler replied. He indicated Denzel with a nod. "And this is Agent Denzel, with the FBI."

Denzel nodded and said, "You can call me Agent Denzel."

Kotler fought to keep from laughing, though he couldn't keep the smile from his lips. Cantor seemed to ignore Denzel's bravado, and instead turned his attention back to Kotler.

It was calculated, Kotler knew, to indicate to Denzel that Cantor was the one in charge. It was also a bluff, because Kotler could read plainly on Cantor's body language that he was trying to distance himself as much as possible, preferably by convincing the two of them to leave.

"We're here for essentially the same reason you are," Cantor said. "I'm funding this project, so I'm very interested in what we find here. But I'm also concerned about the researchers, and the actions of Anwar Adham. I want to prevent any more of my researchers from being abducted or murdered. And I want to do anything I can to help bring back Dr. Horelica, safe and unharmed."

Noble purposes, Kotler had to admit. But something about Cantor's body language wasn't quite matching up. It was true, he did have a vested interest in the dig, and in keeping the researchers safe. But when he mentioned Evelyn, he didn't seem quite as concerned as he claimed.

That might be because he wasn't personally affiliated with Evelyn Horelica and had no real personal stake in her well-being. It might also be that he was only concerned with the researchers because of the impact their deaths had on the work he was funding. Cantor could be a sociopath, for all anyone knew. Kotler couldn't be certain about any of his motives at the moment.

Kotler stepped closer to the two men and peered at what they'd been studying. "Is that a heat map of the area?" Kotler asked.

For the first time, Cantor smiled, and it was a smile of genuine pleasure. "Yes, it is. Do you know how to read one?"

"For area surveys? Not particularly. We've used similar technology to look for hot and cold spots in tombs and other sites, to find cavities in the walls—that sort of thing."

"That's basically what we're doing here," Cantor said. He pointed to the map, "These images are taken from three of my satellites. These red and yellow areas are the surrounding stone, lit up by stored heat from the sun. But this ..." He indicated a blue ribbon that crooked and curved its way through the map until it disappeared in a black mass, several miles away from this location. "This is underground. The computers use a combination of heat scanning and ground penetrating radar, plus a few patent-pending technologies I'm not at liberty to discuss. What you're seeing is a composite of layers and layers of scans piled on top of each other to give a more complete picture."

"When was this taken?" Kotler asked.

Cantor hesitated, though it was very brief. Only an instant. "I believe this image is from several months ago. Maybe July."

Kotler nodded, letting it pass, though he stored that information, unsure why, but certain that Cantor was lying.

"You said this is underground," Denzel said, pointing at the blue ribbon. "What is it, exactly? It looks like a river."

"That's exactly what it is," Cantor's companion said.

It was the first time the other man had spoken, and as everyone turned his way, his face flushed. "Sorry. I'm David Reese." He gave an awkward wave.

"And what is your role here, Mr. Reese?" Denzel asked.

Reese made a brief glimpse at Cantor, as if looking for permission.

It was Cantor who replied. "Mr. Reese is my lead researcher. I found him on Zelot. He's very knowledgeable about the technology we use in our satellites. He was a contributor on several of the new patents, though he has a confidentiality contract that prevents him from discussing them." Cantor gave Reese a pointed glance, as if ensuring that the man remembered his non-disclosure agreement. "I felt he would be invaluable here."

"I don't remember seeing your name on the researcher log," Kotler said.

"Neither do I," Denzel interjected, glancing at Kotler as if saying, *I was just about to say that.*

Again, Reese looked to Cantor, then said, "I came in with Mr. Cantor, when he called me. I've been studying the findings from this site in my home office. I was very excited to get a chance to see it in person."

"And you're saying this is an underground river?" Denzel motioned to the heat map.

Reese nodded. "The technology we use can penetrate several hundred meters, and we estimate this is about 800 meters down in this region. Almost half a mile. And these lines," he breathlessly indicated a few wispy streaks of white, "are the roof of a cavern. Metrics put that gap at about at around 18 meters."

Kotler looked up, startled. "18 meters? You're saying there's a river down there that has 60 feet of clearance?"

Reese quickly looked again to Cantor, and Kotler followed his glance.

Cantor was peering hard at Kotler, watching. He nodded. His expression told Kotler everything he needed to know.

Denzel, on the other hand, was lost. "When the two of you finish talking telepathically, can you let us mere mortals in on what you're saying?"

Kotler looked to Denzel, shaking his head in disbelief. "There's enough clearance down there for a vessel that was 50 foot tall. Essentially, a sailing vessel could have navigated that river."

"And what does that mean?" Denzel asked.

"It means, Agent Denzel," Cantor replied, "That we have found an underground river that could well have allowed the Vikings to reach Pueblo, Colorado," he said. "By boat."

Chapter 6

THE WALLS of the cave were dry and dusty, indicating that despite the alleged presence of a river, somewhere below, the dry air of Pueblo kept any moisture at bay. This wasn't unexpected, but it did raise several questions for Kotler.

The notes he'd read from Coelho's team had indicated that the figurehead had been found about 30 meters down, embedded among boulders and debris from a collapse, at some point in the cave's history. There were signs of the collapse further down into the cave, but the figurehead had been found in an area away from worst of it.

That was odd.

It hinted at a demise for the Viking boat that might have had nothing to do with a cave in. The vessel that had been buried here was seemingly crushed by unknown forces, before the collapse itself.

The pressing question, Kotler though wryly, aware of his own pun, *is how did it get up this far?*

According to Cantor's data, and Coelho's notes, the figurehead had been found well away from where the entrance to the underground river would have been. Essentially, it had been found in the highest point of the cave, where no water would have been present. It seemed unlikely that the Vikings or anyone else would drag an entire ship up from underground, just to place it in this cave to rot and deteriorate for centuries. So how had it come to be here?

Mark Cantor and David Reese were accompanying Kotler and Denzel into the freshly opened cavern. Each of them had flashlights, but they were hardly needed at the moment. Work lights had been brought in and mounted on stands throughout the space, with tight bundles of power lines running along the walls and out through the mouth of the archway to a nearby generator. In some corners of the cavern it was nearly daylight in intensity.

On one wall, several meters in from the entrance, there were more inscriptions, from a variety of sources. There were very few Norse runes in this part of the cave. Most of the markings were the equivalent of cave drawings—primitive looking pictographs of animals and humans.

These are older drawings, Kotler realized. *They must have been here long before even the interactions of the Vikings with the indigenous cultures.*

Though there was some evidence of Aztec and Mayan writing, alongside some symbols Kotler didn't recognize, there seemed to be less intrusion here. It was as if this place had been held in some reverence even thousands of years ago, long before the Vikings had made an appearance.

Evelyn would love this, Kotler thought.

Immediately he felt the worry and fear return. Where was she? And was she safe? He hardly believed she could be, given the circumstances surrounding her abduction, and the horrific torture Anwar Adham had used on the abducted researchers. It seemed as though any hope of Evelyn being alive might be pure fantasy. These were terrorists, after all.

But that was the strange thing, wasn't it? According to what Director Crispen had shared, all available evidence indicated that Evelyn had been abducted in broad daylight, in a very public place. Whoever did it had to be able to blend in seamlessly.

Kotler had seen photos of Anwar Adham and his men. They were distinctly Middle Eastern in appearance and features—olive-toned skin, coarse black hair, and the characteristic beards that were essentially demanded and required by their culture. Even in western clothing, they would stand out as Middle Eastern. And today's *terror-noid* populace would home in on them as a potential threat just from cultural prejudice and bias alone, making them more memorable for their passing.

It wasn't out of the question that they could have pulled off the abduction. There was just something about it that seemed a bit off to Kotler.

"Up ahead is the spot where the figurehead was found," Reese said, leading them down a sloped and rock-strewn cave floor. "It's the furthest point the research team has reached so far. The cave collapsed at that point, and it's taking a while to clear. Structural integrity has been a huge priority for Coelho's team."

"We appreciate that," Denzel said tightly.

Kotler looked at him, noticing that he was pale and sweating. "Claustrophobic?" Kotler asked.

"I'm fine," Denzel said, clenching his jaw.

Cantor stepped up ahead of Reese, turned on his flashlight, and shown it down into a shallow recess. "That's where it was resting," he said.

Kotler stepped forward and knelt, peering into the circle of light from Cantor's flashlight, then taking his own flashlight out and sweeping a beam across the floor, up the concave sides of the cave, and to the ceiling above. He spotted something strange.

"Have they started excavating yet?" Kotler asked.

"Not yet," Cantor replied. "We're using scans of the cavern to determine the safest course of action. We're scheduled to start excavating tomorrow."

Kotler looked back at him, and then turned and aimed his flashlight squarely at one section of wall. "Those marks. That's scoring from metal tools. Someone widened this opening. And from the looks of it, I'd say it was likely done around the time our Vikings paid their visit."

Cantor and Reese both stepped forward, excitedly examining the marks on the walls. "Why didn't anyone else notice this?" Cantor asked, his voice quiet but laced with irritation.

"Zebras," Kotler replied.

Everyone turned to stare at him.

"An old doctor's adage. When you hear the sound of hooves, you think horses, not zebras. When the researchers began exploring these caverns they assumed every gap here was a natural formation, because almost everything after the opening in the cliff face is a natural formation. No one thought to look for evidence that a tunnel was carved into the rock. The very idea of metal tools wouldn't have occurred to them, because the indigenous cultures here used stone tools."

Cantor was watching him, thinking. "Zebras," he said.

Kotler nodded.

Cantor turned back to examine the wall, a cross expression on his face. "I wonder what other zebras my men have overlooked?" he said.

"Don't be too hard on them," Kotler said. "There have been a lot of amazing discoveries here. Attention goes to the most intriguing finds. Eventually, with more time, the team would have found this. Although it seems that of late no one has been allowed access to the cavern."

Cantor's eyes flashed at Kotler's gentle jab, but he said nothing. And in just a moment his composure returned, as if nothing had ever bothered him. Kotler had to give him credit—Cantor was adaptive.

They backed away from the gap, leaving it in shadows as they regrouped in an area that was brightly lit by work lights.

"So what's the plan?" Denzel asked Kotler. "Are you going to stay down here?"

"I think I've got all the information there is to have, at the moment," Kotler said. "I know there were more artifacts found here." He turned to Cantor and Reese. "What about writing? Any symbols or drawings we haven't seen?"

Cantor shook his head. "Nothing I've been made aware of. But you have full access to all of our research. Dig in. All I ask is that you share with me and Mr. Reese anything you discover."

"I'll do that," Kotler said. "And what about the other researchers? Why are you keeping them out of this site?"

"Safety," Cantor said.

Kotler scoffed. "Mark, please. Safety? These men and women crawl around in caves like this for a living. What's your real motive?"

"I can tell you that I have my reasons, and that's as much as I'm willing to share."

"Even with the FBI?" Kotler asked, tilting his head toward Denzel, and playing his one trump card.

"I'll cooperate fully with the FBI in finding Dr. Horelica, and in finding the men who killed my researchers. I want to see them brought down. But unless you produce a warrant, I have no intention of handing over the keys to my little kingdom here, and I would prefer to keep a tight chain of custody on this research. There is already a great deal of speculation in the scientific and academic communities, and I want to keep from fueling the fires. Now, you've seen the site. You have the research. I have been very accommodating to this investigation so far, in my opinion. My men and I have work to do, so it's time for you to leave."

Kotler exchanged a look with Denzel, who only gave a brief nod. They then followed Cantor and Reese out of the cavern, into the temporary building at the cave's mouth, and from there out into the cold night of Pueblo.

———

WHEN THEY WERE PAST THE SECURITY CHECKPOINT AND making their way back to the main camp, Denzel asked, "Did you pick up on anything while we were in there? Besides the scoring? Anything that might provide some leads or maybe give me grounds for getting a warrant?"

Kotler shook his head. "No, nothing like that." He was feeling frustrated, and even a bit angry at the moment. There was something nagging him about all of this. Details were jumbling together, and all the new discoveries were clouding his view. He needed time to reflect on this, to work out how the pieces came together.

Somehow Evelyn's abduction was tied to the discoveries here. She had been taken because of her expertise. The "city of gold" was the most logical motive, for the moment, but that didn't make it fact. The complete lack of any trace of gold here was reason enough to suspect that maybe they didn't have the translation quite right. Or that it was a reference to something else entirely.

What could the carvers of the Coelho Medallion have meant by "city of gold?"

These cultures were all steeped in symbolism and metaphor, and they often lacked a cohesive written language. Often, they fell back on symbols that represented abstracts, legends, and fables, rather than literal words or terminology.

Which made it fiendishly difficult to do a direct translation. Once you factored in the notion that these writings may have been some form of accord between several very different cultures, with different languages and historical traditions, the waters became even murkier.

When Kotler and Denzel arrived back at the main camp, they split up to find their mutual quarters. They were given directions by one of the security guards and pointed to where they'd be sleeping that night.

They would settle in—it had been a long day, and it was getting quite late by now, even after gaining two hours with the time difference between Pueblo and New York. Kotler had to admit, he was feeling the hours and the tension, and would welcome some rack time.

In the morning, after a night's rest, they would reconvene. Kotler would examine everything the research team had uncovered, and Denzel would question everyone present for leads in Evelyn's case, as well as in the hunt for Adham and his people.

Kotler had just stepped into the small trailer he'd be using for the next few nights and had liberated himself from the under-sized coat and the layers of clothing, when he heard yelling from outside. A moment later there was the sound of a gunshot, followed by more yelling.

Kotler pulled on the small coat and ran outside, ducking behind a vehicle to stay under cover. Prudence might have suggested that he stay inside and barricade the door for safety. But Kotler's instincts were always pushing him to identify the threat and choose an informed course of action. He wasn't opposed to hiding, nor to running away if the threat was overwhelming. But he had to know what he was up against, before deciding a course of action.

Besides, he'd been shot at before. And worse. It wasn't his favorite experience, but he could handle himself.

He was looking across the campground, lit by a couple of large, portable security lights. The ring of temporary buildings, really a series of small trailers, formed a sort of courtyard. It was a large, open space, and well lit. There was no sign of anything there. But to his right, near the research headquarters, he heard a new series of gunshots, and he made his way in that direction, keeping to the shadows.

He had no weapon, and that was a problem. Looking around he spotted an open toolbox near a vehicle with its hood up. He pilfered a pry bar from this and hefted it a couple of times to get a feel for its weight. He slipped back into the shadows and edged his way toward the sound of gunfire.

At the edge of the narrow alleyway in which he stood, he stopped and peered around the corner. Across the way he could see Agent Denzel, standing and firing before ducking back for cover behind a parked security jeep.

As Kotler watched, four of Cantor's security team rushed forward to join Denzel at his position. One of them was an older, burly man with a red handlebar mustache. He was barking orders at his men and into a handheld radio.

That would be Will "Sarge" Canfield, Kotler assumed.

What Kotler could not see from his vantage point was the enemy. Someone was among the buildings opposite Denzel and the security team, and they were taking quick shots that sounded as if they were coming from several different positions. Kotler couldn't get a solid head count on how many of them might be out there. But he did pick up on the fact that he was closer to them than Denzel and the security team, who were pinned in their position by the barrage of enemy gunfire.

Kotler gripped the pry bar, and quickly made his way back down the alley. He peeked around the corner, looking across the courtyard. He saw no one. The researchers must be huddling inside, staying low. That was good. It was probably where he should be, he figured. Though as he eyed the thin aluminum walls of the trailers, he couldn't imagine being any safer inside than he was outside. At least out here he could see what was happening, and maybe do something.

Kotler darted along the front of one of the buildings until he came to the next darkened alleyway. He did a quick peek around the corner and saw nothing.

He sprinted to the next, and this time as he looked around he saw four men with weapons—mostly small arms —firing at Denzel and the others. As Kotler waited and watched, he noticed that more gun shots were coming from elsewhere.

When he was certain no one was looking, Kotler sprinted past the alley and made his way to the next.

Here he saw two more men, also staying low and firing periodically. They had with them a large crate, about six-foot-long and three-foot-high. It was difficult to see from his position, but as Kotler craned his neck for a better look, he noticed a logo emblazoned on the side of the crate.

He recognized it immediately. The same logo had been stamped into every crate used to store the objects being recovered from this site. It meant that these men had stolen an artifact, and now they were struggling to escape with it.

Kotler shook his head. What could they possibly have stolen that would be worth fighting back a very well-armed security team? Kotler had seen the manifests, detailing the finds form this site. He couldn't think of anything that a bunch of armed thieves would find so valuable.

Maybe there're are more than just thieves, he thought.

One of the men stood suddenly and stared at the end of the alleyway where Kotler was trying keep hidden.

Not well enough.

The man shouted something in Arabic that was washed out from the sounds of gunfire, and both men were now on their feet and rushing in Kotler's direction, weapons raised.

Kotler cursed and sprinted across the courtyard to the most convenient cover he could find. He rolled under one of the Jeeps that was parked at the edge of the open space, hoping that he'd made it there before the two men saw him.

He scrambled and turned around, facing the direction of the alley he'd just fled from, and gripping the pry par so hard his hand ached.

The two men emerged from the alley, each with a handgun raised and stretched in front of them. They were crouch-walking into the courtyard, scanning every direction for possible attack, and for a clue as to where Kotler had gotten to.

Kotler, for his part, managed to calm his breathing and remain still, watching. So far, they didn't seem to know where he was, but it might occur to them any minute that he couldn't have gotten any further than the Jeep.

He wasn't sure what to do at this point. His pry bar would be no use against their weapons. They'd cut him down if he tried to make a break for it, and there was nowhere for him to run at any rate. He was stuck here. It would take a miracle to get out of this.

The two men were edging closer to the Jeep, at which point it must have occurred to them that this had to be where their prey was hiding. They whispered to each other, and then split up to circle the Jeep.

Kotler held his breath.

As gunfire continued nearby, Kotler hoped it would be enough to mask any sounds he might make as he shuffled on the ground beneath the Jeep's undercarriage. He waited for the first man to walk up to the Jeep's passenger side door and peer in, making sure no one was inside. The other man was continuing on, past the Jeep, walking in the direction of one of the temporary trailers. There were crates and other vehicles in that area, making it a good hiding place for someone trying to remain out of sight.

This Jeep, on the other hand, was not such a great hiding spot. It wouldn't be long before the man thought to look under it, and at that point Kotler would be soup.

Kotler waited for the man to edge his way to the back of the Jeep, and then he carefully crawled out on the passenger's side, rose into a crouch, and made his way as quietly as possible to where the man was standing.

Kotler peered under the jeep, and could see the man's boots, nearly on tip-toe. He must have been stretching to look into the back of the vehicle, and as Kotler watched, the man's heels lifted from the ground. Kotler could hear noisy rummaging as the man searched under a tarp and through a load of tools and other items.

Kotler stood quickly, stepped around the corner of the Jeep, and slammed the pry bar into the man's head, right at the base of his skull. Stunned, the man fell forward, but was struggling to get his hands under him and stand again. He was off balance now, leaning over the back of the jeep with his feet kicking.

Kotler hit him again, and this time took advantage of the man's stunned state to reach in and grab his handgun.

Kotler was about to order the man to keep his hands in sight and to roll over when the man slumped, apparently unconscious from the second blow.

Kotler quickly checked the weapon, pulling the magazine to see how many rounds were left. He found six rounds in the magazine and one in the chamber. He patted the man down and found another fully loaded magazine as well as one empty magazine, and a pack of cigarettes, a lighter, and some car keys.

Kotler shoved all of this into his jacket, and then paused.

The man was approximately his size.

Kotler rolled him and quickly pulled off the man's coat. He shrugged off the small and inadequate jacket he'd gotten on loan from one of the researchers, and then pulled on the terrorist's much warmer coat, zipping it in the front.

This had the advantage of keeping him warm, but it might also serve as a bit of camouflage if he encountered any more of these men. It could keep them from shooting him long enough for him to make an escape.

Of course, it could just as easily get him shot by his own side, if they mistook him for one of the enemy.

He'd have to chance it for now.

Kotler looked up to see if the other man was anywhere

around, but there was no sign. He then took off the belt of the first man and used it to lash him to the roll bar of the Jeep, where he slumped and hung like wet laundry on a line. He fished in the bed of the Jeep and found an oil-soaked shop towel. He felt slightly bad about shoving it into the man's mouth, but under the circumstances it seemed justified. Kotler found a bungee cord and used it to tie the gag in place.

With the first man out of the way, Kotler raised the gun and scrambled in the direction of the other, reasoning that it would be better to take the man by surprise and subdue him, rather than make a run for it and leaving him in play. If he encountered one of the researchers, there could be a hostage situation to deal with. Or he might end up taking out one of Cantor's security team. Or possibly even Agent Denzel.

It was too dangerous to let him go.

Kotler came to the corner of the building and peered around into the darkness—just in time to come face to face with a very surprised enemy.

Quickly Kotler trained his weapon on the man, "Don't move!" he shouted. But it was in vain.

The man raised his own weapon and fired without hesitation. Kotler ducked around the corner just in time to hear the whine of a ricochet, and without looking he flung his hand around the corner and fired blindly. He got off three shots before he heard a gurgled yelp, and when he again peered into the alleyway he saw the man lying on the ground, face first and one foot over the other. The "dead man's fall," as it was called it in forensics. It was a sign that someone had died on their feet.

To be sure, Kotler rushed forward with the handgun trained on the man and put a knee on the man's back while he checked his pulse, confirming that he was dead. There was blood on Kotler's fingers as he pulled them away. The man had taken a shot to the throat.

A lucky shot, for sure, but Kotler would take luck. He could prove his marksmanship some other day, when he wasn't also trying to keep from being shot.

All around him there was a sudden and abrupt silence, as if confirming this man's death had ended the bigger battle. The gunfire had been so constant that this new silence felt eerie. Kotler's ears were ringing in the new silence.

He stood and walked to the other end of the alley, looking around to see if he could work out what had happened, and why the gunfight had stopped. He had a hope, that Denzel and the others had won. But it could just as easily have gone the other way, and Kotler was prepared to deal with that, if it was the case.

He saw several armed men moving at a slow and deliberate pace, sweeping the area, looking for any potential threats. Among them were Denzel and Sarge. Kotler tucked the handgun into his waistband and raised his hands above his head before stepping out in to the light.

"Agent Denzel!" he shouted. "It's Dan Kotler! I'm in the alley back here, and I'm wearing a coat I pulled from one of the enemy."

"Come on out slowly, Doctor," Denzel said, training his weapon on the alley.

Kotler could have done without having yet another gun pointed at him, but he did exactly as he'd been told. He stepped out with his hands clearly visible, high above his head, and waving them slowly to show he did not have a weapon.

Denzel chuckled. "Were you really so cold you had to become a terrorist to get a coat?"

Kotler smiled, lowering his hands. "I also stole his cigarettes." He reached into his pocket and offered the pack. "Want one?"

Denzel shook his head. "No thanks. I quit. Those things will kill ya."

Chapter 7

"LET's see what they were after," Sarge grumbled.

He was a stout man, a little over six-foot-tall—though Kotler suspected some of his height came from his thick-soled boots. Sarge struck him as the type of man who saw strategic advantage in having an imposing appearance. Which explained the severe military haircut, cropping his red hair into a square block at the top of his head, and the well-kept but socially sad handlebar mustache that drooped down either side of his chin, giving him a permanent frown.

Sarge had arms like ship cannons, bulging to the point of threatening to burst out of his desert camouflage sleeves. This definitely added to his imposing persona.

Sarge pulled a large knife out of a sheath on his belt and used it to pry open the lid of the crate they had just recovered from the gunmen. Once the crate was open, Sarge swept a hand through the nest of straw being used as packing material.

Kotler peered inside along with Denzel and the others.

"It's a totem," Kotler said, intrigued.

"A what?" Sarge asked.

"A marker," Kotler explained. "Symbolic, usually. It's carved from a tree trunk. Some indigenous tribes would carve these as a symbol of their tribe or family. They typically have carvings of animals and other figures that represent spirit beings."

"They worshipped these things?" Sarge asked.

Kotler shrugged. "Maybe. Maybe not. Some speculate they represent a tribe's animal guide, or an animal they felt a special connection with. It could be form of worship, I suppose. But it was also a common symbol that united their community. The same way a cross unites Christians in a church, or the American flag unites Americans."

"Got it," Sarge said, taking a cigar out of the beast pocket of his vest and shoving it unlit into the corner of his mouth. "So what did these terrorist bastards want with it?"

Kotler looked closer at the totem and shook his head. "That isn't the first question I'd like answered," he said.

"Seems like an important one," Denzel replied.

"It's important, but what interests me is the fact that this isn't an animal totem. That carving looks a lot like a human male. And one that should not be there."

"I see it," Denzel said. "Eyes, nose, mouth, beard. What's so unusual about it?"

"First, Native Americans didn't have beards," Kotler said. "So this is a depiction of someone they met. It's more proof of a Viking presence."

"Great," Denzel said. "We needed more of that."

Kotler shook his head. "There's more to this, though. This has significance. Something big happened here. The Vikings ... They didn't conquer or pillage while they were here. They were ... it's as if they were revered. There are hints of some kind of union or agreement between the Vikings and the indigenous tribes here in Pueblo, such as the carvings in the archway, and the symbols on the Coelho Medallion. But this is a step beyond. A totem meant something very significant to the indigenous tribes here—a spiritual reverence. And then there's this," Kotler said, pointing to a series of twisting patterns in the center of what would be the Viking's chest.

"What does it mean?" Denzel asked.

"It's a series of runes, and I recognize them. These," Kotler said, running his fingers over part of the pattern, "are the same runes we found on the medallion. It's talking about a river, and a city of gold. Whatever happened here, I think it has something to do with that underground river that Cantor and Reese found. And I think the men we encountered tonight want access to it for some reason." Kotler looked up at Denzel and Sarge, who were watching him closely, expectantly.

Before anyone could respond or ask further questions, however, a voice spoke from behind them.

"That will be enough," said Mark Cantor. Everyone turned to see him and David Reese hurrying forward. "Sarge, I want that crate sealed and moved to a secure location. It will be transported out of this site by morning."

"Yes sir," Sarge said, and waved to two of his men, who hurried forward and replaced the top of the crate, hammering nails into place.

"Mr. Cantor," Denzel said, standing to his full height and turning to face the billionaire full-on. To his credit, Cantor didn't cringe or back down in any way, despite Denzel's imposing form. "That crate isn't going anywhere. The men who attacked this place were willing to kill and even die for that totem, and that leaves me with some very big questions. That crate is part of my investigation now."

"That may be," Cantor said. "But it's clearly not safe here.

It won't do you or anyone else much good if any more of these men arrive and manage to get their hands on it. And aside from being a part of your investigation, it happens to be my property. So unless you can provide some sort of assurance that there aren't more terrorists coming to take it?"

"I can't say that for certain, no," Denzel said. "But I think it will be safest with the FBI."

"I disagree. And since it's my property, I'll have it taken to where I see fit. The FBI can have full access to it. Under my discretion."

"Mr. Cantor, you may not fully grasp what I mean by 'part of my investigation,'" Denzel said coldly. "This crate goes where I say it goes. Or I can place you under arrest for obstruction, and let your lawyers try to talk you out of it."

Cantor stared hard at Denzel for a moment, then shook his head, letting a smile play on his lips. "We'll see, Agent." He turned to Sarge. "Put the crate in a secure location, here in the camp. I want guards on this at all times. We'll wait. For now."

"Yessir," Sarge said gruffly, and gave orders to his men.

Cantor looked at Kotler now. "I don't have you in a confidentiality agreement, Dr. Kotler. And that bothers me. I trust I can depend on you to be discreet about this?"

"That depends very much on what else you're hiding from me," Kotler said. "That totem was not included in the manifest of artifacts recovered from this site. We have full access to all research and discoveries here, as part of Agent Denzel's investigation. When were you going to reveal this to us?"

Cantor shook his head. "I didn't deem it as relevant."

"Ah, see, there's the problem right there," Kotler said,

smiling. "You're not the one who gets to deem anything relevant."

Cantor smirked, then turned and left, with Reese in tow. Sarge and his men followed quickly, with the crate hefted between four well-armed men.

Kotler let out a huff and looked at Denzel, who was watching the progression.

"Well, that tells a story, doesn't it?" Kotler asked.

Denzel eyed him. "And what story is that? Cantor is hiding something?"

"For starters," Kotler said. "But it also indicates that these terrorists were not responsible for stealing the Coelho Medallion."

Denzel's eyebrows went up in surprise. "How so?"

"Because the totem essentially gives them the same information they would already have. There may be more to it, obviously, but why take this relic? If they have the medallion, they have the same information we have."

Denzel considered this. "They wouldn't risk a play like this for no good reason. Maybe they're trying to keep this information away from anyone else?"

"Doesn't track," Kotler said. "We had the Coelho Medallion for the better part of a year. We've photographed it extensively. We could replicate it with no trouble. Basically, we have all the measurable and quantifiable information we can possibly glean from the medallion itself. So the only thing these men could have been after was information these two relics have in common."

"The city of gold?" Denzel asked.

Kotler shook his head. "Maybe. But something about that doesn't feel quite right. We keep thinking it's a reference to *El Dorado*, but that was just a joke I made, not an actual translation. The truth is, there's something hinted at in all of this that none of us has put together yet. I think our new terrorist friends were after something else."

"What would that be?" Denzel asked.

Kotler glanced in the direction that he and Denzel had come from earlier in the evening, where they'd first met Cantor and Reese. "I think they're after the river," he said.

———

THEY WERE IN ONE OF THE BUILDINGS THAT WAS BEING USED as an equipment storage shed. It was one of the few places that had any resemblance to a cell, with a mesh cage that could be locked from the outside, to prevent anyone from making off with tools or other items. The site was populated primarily with researchers and graduate students, however —none of whom were likely to want to steal bolt cutters or a shovel. Kotler and Denzel had asked a couple of Sarge's men to clear most of the tools out of the cage, and they had then appropriated it as a makeshift prison.

Two men had been taken alive from the firefight. The first as the man that Kotler had bludgeoned and tied up in the Jeep. He was bruised, and likely had a slight concussion, but was otherwise fine.

The other man had been shot in the scuffle with Cantor's security team. He was a bit worse off, though his wounds had been tended. He was on minimal pain medication, however, and it was likely he wasn't feeling his best.

At the moment, both men were chained to heavy pieces of drilling equipment on opposite sides of the room from each other. Two guards were standing by just outside the tool shed, to keep watch overnight.

Kotler had been grateful that Denzel thought they should wait until morning to interrogate the two men. He was going on very little sleep, at this point, and the events of the past several days had been taxing. Having a night to crash, followed by a hot shower and a good breakfast, had refreshed him and given him a boost. He had approached the tool shed right on time, with a Styrofoam cup to of coffee warming his hands. He felt pretty good.

Their prisoners, on the other hand, hadn't had such a great night.

Just outside the cage, there were two chairs where Kotler and Denzel could sit, if they chose. That was Denzel's suggestion. He wanted those two chairs to sit there, unused, during the whole talk, as he and Kotler stood and looked down on the men. It gave them a psychological edge over the prisoners, to see that these two fully refreshed and rested men didn't even need to sit during the interrogation.

Both men were dirty, and their clothes were soiled. Their wounds had been dressed in clean bandages, but otherwise they looked as if they hadn't been clean in a decade. They were also chained in uncomfortable positions that didn't allow them to stand without bending full at the waist. While seated, their hands couldn't be brought down any lower than shoulder height. The result was that they were never quite comfortable, and probably had a number of physical aches and pains in addition to their injuries.

"Gentlemen," Denzel said, standing with his hands in his pockets and looking down at the men. They stared away from Denzel, looking at the darkened corners of the tool shed, refusing to respond.

Kotler mimicked Denzel's stance, hands in his pockets, chin tilted to his chest. It was like an expression of pity. All part of the psychological game, Kotler decided.

He glanced at Denzel, who gave him a nod, and in

Arabic Kotler asked, *"Why were you trying to steal the totem? What is it for?"*

The men didn't answer, but Kotler saw from their body language that they were surprised to hear their own language. Despite this, they showed very little sign of wanting to cooperate.

That was ok. This was the warmup. The real questions would start as soon as Kotler had a read on how they responded to the soft stuff.

"Are you affiliated with Anwar Adham? Do you follow his orders?"

Again, they made no reply, but Kotler could see plainly that they recognized the name. They made very little movement, remaining stiff while he talked, as if their bodies were trying to keep their secrets through muscular tension.

"We recovered the totem you were trying to steal, and I was able to read the symbols on it," Kotler said in Arabic. *"Do you know what the symbols mean?"*

More silence, but Kotler saw a slight shake of the head from the man who had been shot. It was brief, only an instant, but it told Kotler that these men were only following orders to obtain the totem. They weren't privy to why they were taking it.

"What do you know about a city of gold?" Kotler asked. Nothing about them indicated they knew anything at all.

"And what about a river?" he asked, watching closely.

This time he saw both men stiffen, and quickly glance at each other. It was slight, but readable. And it told Kotler exactly what he needed.

They knew.

It wouldn't hold up in court, but it told Kotler everything he needed to know. The river really was what they were searching for. Now they had the real motive driving Adham and his men. It told them what Adham was after, though it gave no hint as to why they were after it. The odds would be that these men would have no idea what Adham's plans for the river might be. They were soldiers in this, following orders. Nothing more.

Kotler had one more question to resolve, however.

"Why did you abduct Dr. Evelyn Horelica?" he asked in Arabic.

And he was surprised to see a brief and confused exchange between the men. It was less than an instant, and subtle to the point that even Kotler questioned whether he'd actually seen it. He pressed again. "Where is Dr. Horelica being held?" he asked, watching closely.

Again, the men showed signs that they had no idea what Kotler was talking about.

He stepped back, hands still in his pockets, and gave Denzel a perplexed look. He then turned and walked out of the tool shed, with Denzel shadowing him closely.

The guards let them out and then locked the doors behind them, resuming their posts. When Kotler and Denzel were clear and able to talk privately, Kotler leaned close. "They have no idea what I'm talking about. They don't have Evelyn."

"How can you tell?" Denzel asked. "They never said a word."

"I was reading them," Kotler said. "Body language. They definitely work for Adham, but they have no knowledge of or any interest in a city of gold. They didn't seem to even know anything about it. When I mentioned the river, though, they lit up. That's what they're after, although I have no idea why."

"And when you asked them if they knew what the symbols meant they were clueless," Denzel said, nodding.

Kotler was surprised. "You speak Arabic?"

"I'm not proficient, but I can understand it," Denzel said. "Surprised?"

"A little," Kotler smiled.

"Yeah, the FBI doesn't hire idiots. Go figure. Now, what about Dr. Horelica?"

"They had no idea who she was. They were surprised by the question."

"So ... what? They don't have her? Then who took her?"

Kotler shook his head. "I have no idea. And it changes the game, doesn't it? We know what these men are after now. But that's it. We no longer have any suspects who might have abducted Evelyn. And the trail is so cold now ..." He let the statement hang.

Denzel glanced back at the shed. "I'm going to want to ask them a few questions myself."

"Of course," Kotler said. "I'll help any way I can. Just ..."

"I know," Denzel said. "We'll take another look at the details on Dr. Horelica's abduction once we have everything we can get on Adham. Something about all of this really stinks."

Kotler said nothing, but silently agreed.

The two of them went back to the shed and spent the next few hours asking questions and receiving very little in way of answers. Kotler helped, as promised, but the entire time he was preoccupied with thoughts of how all of this fit together.

And he had to finally admit to himself that none of it did.

Chapter 8

CANTOR AND REESE left the camp the next morning.

Despite the conflict and head butting over the totem, Cantor ordered for it to be handed over to the FBI, without restrictions. Denzel and Kotler learned of this from Richard Barmoth, who seemed to be agitated enough for all of them.

"I didn't even know the totem existed until yesterday," Barmoth complained. "None of my team has had a chance to examine it. I'm the bloody lead here!"

"It's fine," Kotler said. "The FBI doesn't need the totem."

Denzel arched an eyebrow. "Shouldn't that be the FBI's call?"

Kotler grinned. "I think Cantor's security force has proven it can handle itself against incursions, don't you agree? And we have detailed photographs and measurements of the totem. I'm more interested in the symbols carved into it, and what they might mean. The terrorists didn't win this one. They were making a play, and it didn't pan out."

They hadn't learned much from the two men they had in captivity, but Denzel had managed to get the injured one to start talking. He was in worse shape than they had thought, and badly needed medical attention. Denzel arranged for him to be transported to a medical facility nearby, where he had arranged for agents to take over for local police by late afternoon, keeping the man under guard.

His partner, meanwhile, was taken to God knew where. He wasn't cooperating, and he had no real medical needs to attend to, so Denzel had opted to put him in a hole somewhere. Kotler didn't know the specifics, and decided he didn't really want to know. He had learned everything he could from both of these men, frankly, and it hadn't put him any closer to finding Evelyn.

Before the injured terrorist had been sent to a hospital, however, he had given them at least some useful information.

When Denzel had pressed him about why they needed the totem, the injured man had slipped, and used the word "confirmation."

This was an odd choice of wording, and it told Denzel and Kotler three things.

First, that they had been right about Adham wanting the totem to provide information about the river. Whatever his reasons, Adham wanted access to that underground waterway. And regardless of those reasons, his desire alone was enough for the FBI to want to prevent it.

Second, it was clear that the security presence here had been unexpected. Adham wouldn't have bothered with this throwaway mission, had he been aware that Cantor had beefed up security to near-military grade.

But the third and most important fact was the one Denzel seemed most interested in.

Adham was close by.

The men who had attacked the facility had driven two

small SUVs, which Sarge's security team had recovered from a ridge about half a mile from the camp. The two SUVs provided enough room for the men, their weapons, and the totem, and precious little else. They had made an incursion into the camp before, to kidnap the researchers, and had likely anticipated they'd meet some small security team. They hadn't counted on Cantor's proclivity for extremes. Never underestimate a determined billionaire.

It was Cantor's overkill that had not only prevented Adham's men from taking the totem but had ultimately saved the lives of everyone in the camp. Denzel had said as much to Sarge, when they'd talked about additional security measures.

They had practically fawned over each other in their mutual respect. The two of them had developed a weird sort of bromance, from Kotler's point of view, but he wasn't there to judge.

Kotler briefed Barmoth on everything he'd deciphered from the totem—which wasn't much more than they already knew. He asked Barmoth to keep him apprised of any new finds. And then he and Denzel got into one of the camp's Jeeps and left the site, ranging out into the foothills and expansive landscape surrounding Pueblo. They eventually connected to 96, heading northeast toward Cañon City.

Cañon City was a municipality with a population of a little over sixteen thousand people. It was the sort of sleepy town that the Cohen Brothers would have loved—perfect as a backdrop for small-town life disrupted by the absurd. Kotler couldn't help but feel that he and Denzel were bringing some of that absurdity with them.

They were driving into Cañon City ostensibly to resupply, get a hotel room for a few nights, and spend some time reviewing what they'd learned. In reality, Denzel had a contact in town who might be able to provide information about Adham's whereabouts.

"Why didn't we talk to this person earlier?" Kotler asked.

"Because until yesterday I didn't know for certain whether Adham was in the area," Denzel replied. "And if he was, I didn't want to tip him off that we were looking for him. My contact is a local that knows all the best places to hide here."

"He sounds like he might be a bit unscrupulous," Kotler said, smiling.

"She," Denzel said.

"She? Your contact who knows the lay of the land is a woman?"

"Something wrong with that?" Denzel asked.

Kotler smiled and shook his head. "No, actually, there's everything right with that."

They pulled into a small gravel parking lot that was surrounded by a chain link fence. Denzel had been using GPS to guide them, and he was checking their location against an address he had on his phone. He peered out through the windshield, scanning the fronts of the buildings along the street.

"Are we lost?" Kotler asked.

"I don't think so. The GPS says this is the place. I just don't see the ... Oh. There it is."

Denzel gestured with his phone toward a building that had a large oak tree growing in front of it, and a green and white striped awning obscuring part of its entry. It was across the street from the parking lot, and there were cars parked all along its front. Kotler peered and strained to read the sign on the door, just as a man opened it and entered the building from the street. As it closed, Kotler could make out the white vinyl letters stuck to the glass.

"Montezuma Cantina," Kotler read. "This is the place?"

In answer Denzel stepped out of the Jeep, reached into the backseat to grab his suit coat, and pulled it on, smoothing it as he worked the buttons.

Kotler nodded and stepped out, grabbing his own coat—the one he'd "liberated" from the terrorists. It was drab and a little soiled looking, but it was the best he had at the moment. He weighed the current temperature, decided it was warm enough this morning, and left the coat in the Jeep.

The two of them crossed to the Montezuma Cantina, and when they stepped inside a little bell hanging from the door announced their presence.

It was afternoon, around 1 PM, and there was a light crowd lingering from lunch. The Cantina had a smattering of tables covered in red checkered cloths, and a few old timers sat at a couple of these—reading papers and talking about sports or politics or whatever else they had on their mind. Old country standards played from a set of speakers mounted in the corners or the cantina, near the ceiling. Kotler recognized a cover of "Whiskey River," though he didn't recognize the singer's voice.

The bar itself was empty except for the man Kotler had seen enter moments earlier. He sat at the end of the bar with a mug of beer in front of him, and didn't seem interested in them or anything else.

Kotler had been in places like this thousands of times in his travels, and oddly he felt right at home. He wasn't much for dive bars or cantinas as a patron, but from an anthropology standpoint they were a goldmine. There was no better way to discover the quirks and nuances of a culture than to sit down to a meal and a stiff drink with some of the locals. All it took was paying the tab, most of the time, and people would open up about all sorts of things.

Kotler had spent hours sitting in places like this with people he was interviewing, or with people he was sharing information with, poring over maps and old journals, looking at small bits of artifacts or photos from digs. It was some of his favorite work. It was a universal rule of human nature, that the most interesting thing to any individual was their own life, so any anthropologist worth his salt was a good conversationalist, by way of being a good listener.

He bellied up to the bar, and Denzel joined him.

A large woman came in from a swinging door at the back of the bar, carrying a crate filled with freshly washed glasses. She lowered the crate to a stand just under the bar's edge and was taking the glasses out and placing them on the bar back. She gave Denzel a slight nod, and eventually came over to ask what they were having.

"Ginger ale," Denzel said.

"Lightweight?" The woman asked.

Denzel smiled. "On duty."

She looked at Kotler. "Jameson," he said. "Neat."

She smirked, as if impressed, and poured him a double without his having to ask. His kind of woman.

She left for a moment, then came back with Denzel's ginger ale—a can that she cracked and poured over ice.

"You're early," she said as she slid the drink across to him.

"Well, it's been a while, Sharon. I couldn't wait to see you again."

Sharon made a noise in the back of her throat. "I'd be fine not having to see you or any of them others again," she said.

"Is that any way to talk to the guy who got you out of prison?" Denzel asked.

"I only had two years left, Denzel. I could have done that while knitting." She scowled, but then softened. "But you boys did take care of Rodriguez for me. And because of that I got the Cantina back. So I owe you."

"Well, there's that," Denzel said. "And the fact that helping us is part of your parole."

She shook her head, disgusted. "Can't just let a lady have a minute, can you?"

Kotler watched all of this in fascination. "I had no idea you had such close contacts here," he said to Denzel.

"I spent some time here a few years ago, working with the DEA to track a local drug cartel that was moving through here from New Mexico. We took them down thanks to Sharon here. In part, anyway. It's been, what, five years?"

"About that," Sharon nodded.

It became clear to Kotler that despite their talk, Sharon had a fondness for Denzel, and it seemed at least partially reciprocated. It clearly wasn't romantic, but they were close nonetheless. Friends, of a sort. Denzel's demeanor around Sharon was authoritative, but also relaxed. It hinted at familiarity and respect.

Kotler marveled at the complexity of his new FBI friend. He would never have guessed, from the agent's occasionally stiff and gruff persona, that the man had a softer side. Kotler liked it. The idea of Denzel as an all-American good guy was appealing.

"We're looking for the most likely place for some heavily armed folks to hole up," Denzel said, glancing around to make sure no one was close enough to hear their low-key conversation. The music playing helped to drown them out, and the only person who might be close enough to hear was the man at the end of the bar. He was seemingly too engrossed in his own thoughts to care about any of their talk.

"Anyone I know?" Sharon asked.

"It'd be best for you if it wasn't," Denzel said.

Sharon nodded. "Lots of places could be likely. I'll need more information."

Denzel pulled out his phone and brought up a map of the area where the research camp was located, to their southwest. "We figure it would have to be within twenty or thirty miles of this location," he said. "Close enough for a couple of SUVs to get ten or so guys in and out under cover of darkness, with guns and a crate in tow."

Sharon studied the map and shook her head. "Not enough," she said. "There's a thousand places a camp full of smugglers and gun runners could be hiding out there. Don't you boys have some kind of fancy spy satellites that can show you a mouse farting from outer space?"

"Maybe," Denzel said. "But there are a lot of gassy mice out here, and it would help if we could narrow things down a bit."

Sharon again looked at the maps and then pointed a stubby finger at the map on Denzel's phone. "This place has some promise. There are caves there that we used to use for storing ..." She glanced up at Denzel quickly, apparently deciding she might not want to incriminate herself. "Well, let's just say 'goods.' Some of those caves connect to a network of natural and man-made tunnels. You can get from one side of this rise to the other entirely underground, if you work at it. Made for a good escape route." She said this last with the wispy air of nostalgia, which made Kotler smile.

Denzel nodded, and then touched the screen to drop a pin on the location. He made a note in the little notepad he carried in his coat pocket, as well. Kotler again smiled. The more time he spent with Denzel, the more nuanced the man became. He was comfortable enough with technology, to a degree, but had the demeanor of someone who was anachronistic, and clinging to old standbys such as notepads with real paper, scribbled in with real ink. It was the sort of dueling nature that made men like him fascinating to study.

Not that they would approve of being studied.

Kotler sipped his Jameson and savored it. The past few days had been rough, but he was starting to slip into the loose and relaxed feel he always got when he was on a quest. True, most of his ventures were a bit more tame, and involved a bit less gun play—most of the time. But he'd seen and dodged his share of live fire over the years. And he'd dealt with armed Middle-Easterners on more occasions than he'd like to count. Some of those encounters still haunted him.

Despite all of the danger, however, he always ended up slipping into a state of calm enjoyment. Zen of the adventure, he guessed.

Or—and maybe it was time he admitted this to himself —it could have been because of the danger and action that he would find himself starting to loosen up and have fun. His academic work could be a bit stiff and stodgy, and he would often get antsy, wanting to get back out to the field. And though he liked putting his hands in the dirt and crawling around in spider-infested spaces buried deep under the earth as much as the next anthropologist, it was the interaction with people and cultures that really drew him. And interactions with people could sometimes get messy and dangerous.

His tendency to get bored with academics and to race to the closest dig site was part of the reason he and Evelyn had started drifting apart. He was willing to admit that. It was rough, he was sure, dealing with someone who couldn't sit still for long, and who, even when he was home, talked of faraway places with a certain yearning. Kotler and Evelyn had done their heart-to-hearts on a number of occasions, and he'd been fully aware of how distant he could be with her. It wasn't intentional. It just was.

The whiskey warmed him, knocking off the last of the chill he still felt from the morning. He listened to Denzel and Sharon as they discussed details about the approach to the smuggler caves and tunnels, where Adham might be hiding.

Kotler's attention wandered a bit. He started looking around the cantina, observing the environment through the reflection in the ancient-looking mirror behind the bar. The mirror was spotted with years of nicks and dings, the silver fading in small leopard spots here and there, especially around the edges.

He saw the old timers, a couple of which had broken out a deck of cards for an impromptu hand of Spades. He then noticed the man at the end of the bar, who had stood slowly, and moved so that he was on the other side of his stool. He reached his right hand into his thick coat, and as it drew back ...

"Down!" Kotler shouted, turning and grabbing Denzel, throwing him from the bar stool and down to the floor just as shots were fired.

Denzel scrambled and turned one of the tables on its side, hunkering to his knees as he drew his own fire arm. He peered over the table's edge and then brought his own weapon up to fire.

Kotler had no weapon, and he found himself using Denzel's return fire as cover while he belly-crawled as quickly as he could to the opposite side of the bar. He circled around its edge and had to raise himself over a small step and onto the platform of the bar's floor. He registered briefly that pipes must run under the floor here, an upgrade from when this cantina was built, during a time when indoor plumbing hadn't been invented, perhaps.

Staying low, Kotler moved along the raised floor, which was covered by a rubber grate mat that would allow spills to pass to a metal drain sloping toward the middle. When Kotler glanced through the mesh of the rubber mat he saw a faint trickle of red mingling with water or some other clear liquid. He looked ahead to see Sharon, splayed on the floor behind the bar.

Dead. She'd taken a shot to the chest during the initial shooting and had fallen among several shattered bottles.

Kotler felt a brief sting of regret that he hadn't been able to save her, but this was quickly replaced by anger and rage. Whoever this guy was, he had to be tied to Adham.

Once again Kotler found himself dodging bullets from weapons wielded by Adham's men. Once again, innocent people were being hurt and killed by this monster, all by remote control, as the coward himself hid out somewhere in the mountains.

"Federal Agent!" Denzel shouted from out of Kotler's sight. "Put down your weapon and lay face down on the floor, now!"

The man responded by firing two more rounds, and Kotler was able to determine that he'd ducked behind the end of the bar for cover. In fact, as Kotler looked he could see the man's back as he crouched down. Kotler had a clean line of sight on the guy, but nothing to use to take him down.

He crawled forward.

More shots fired, and Kotler hoped someone had the presence of mind to call the police. But he realized they'd get here far too late—no matter the outcome. It was up to him and Denzel to take this guy down.

Kotler came to Sharon's body and didn't hesitate as he crawled over her. He could allow himself to feel anger and grief and revulsion later. Right now, he had to ...

What exactly? He was crawling toward the bad guy, with no plan. What was he thinking?

The man disappeared from Kotler's sight briefly, and there were gunshots again. Kotler heard a muffled grunt and was suddenly filled with dread that Denzel had taken a bullet.

That was all he needed. Whatever else happened, Kotler was determined to take this man down. He sped up his crawl, moving forward as fast as he was able, and as he got close enough to touch the guy he rose to his feet and leapt outward, tackling the man against the swinging door at the back of the bar.

The two of them slid across the slightly wet tile of the back room, and Kotler managed to pin the guy's gun arm. He slipped on the damp floor, losing his balance and ultimately throwing an ineffective punch against the man's jaw.

The gunman wasn't fazed. Instead, he managed to land a punch of his own, connecting with Kotler's nose and making him see stars.

Kotler lost his balance and fell, rolling onto his back. He was dazed and raised a hand to his nose as if he'd somehow woken up with the realization that he'd been punched.

The gunman wasted no time getting to his feet, and he stood over Kotler, leveling the gun, taking aim at Kotler's head.

His senses returning, Kotler braced himself for the shot.

He felt a sudden stab of regret that he had let Evelyn down, that he had failed Denzel, and that everything had gone south so quickly.

The sense of calm and ease he'd felt earlier had returned, however. Somehow, facing his death, he realized it didn't bother him that much. He'd given it everything he had. If he had to go ...

But instead of shooting him, the man knelt, raised the pistol, and brought it down hard on Kotler, knocking him into black before Kotler could have another thought.

PART II

Chapter 9

AGENT DENZEL WOKE to the sound of rapid, tensely serious talking.

He couldn't quite make out the words, but they seemed somehow familiar, and were certainly urgent.

He felt something on his face, covering his nose and mouth, and he tried to reach up and remove it, but his arm was restrained. Both arms, now that he tried them. There was some sort of band across his chest, keeping him in place.

He managed to open his eyes and saw flashes of fluorescent light blur by, rhythmically breaking a pattern of drab and stained panels from a suspended ceiling.

"Agent Denzel," a woman's voice said. "Just remain calm. You're in the hospital. You've sustained a gunshot wound to your chest. Just stay calm and we will take care of you."

"*Ktlrr*," Denzel muttered, but no one seemed to hear him much less understand him. He barely understood himself.

What happened to Kotler?

He must have blacked out at that point, because from his perspective he blinked and in his next moment of consciousness he heard a steady series of beeps, and realized it was a heart monitor. His groggy brain reminded him of the nurse or doctor or whoever she was—the woman who had told him to remain calm. Told him he was in a hospital. Told him he'd been shot.

He pried his eyes open, almost painfully, and felt groggy and nauseated. Everything was slow at the moment. His brain wasn't fully engaged yet. He felt like someone had replaced his blood with over-used motor oil.

The room was typical, with his bed at the center and the walls lined with equipment, cabinets filled with medical supplies, and a couple of uncomfortable looking chairs near his bedside. There was a coat hung from a hook on the back of the door to his room, and it was one that looked familiar but otherwise indistinct. It wasn't his.

There was the sound of flushing from behind the other door in the room, and it opened to reveal Director Crispen, drying his hands on a paper towel before tossing it into the little metal waste can.

"You're awake! Good to see you pulled through, Agent."

Denzel tried to speak, to say "Thank you, sir," but his throat was raw, and his mouth was very dry. He started to cough, and Director Crispen hurried to a small rolling table beside the bed. He took a cup and poured water from a small pitcher, then helped Denzel to sit up a bit as he brought the cup to the Agent's lips.

Denzel sipped, and felt the cool water soothe his throat. He nodded, grateful, and Crispen set the cup on the side table.

"You gave us a scare, Agent," Crispen said.

Denzel tried to smile. "Sorry, sir," he said, his voice a bit raspy. He cleared his throat painfully a few times. "I was caught off guard."

Crispen nodded. "Two people died. Your CI was one."

Denzel took a second to take this in, and then nodded, feeling a stab of grief. Sharon had been more than just a confidential informant. She'd been a friend, of sorts. She was a rough sort of person, and she had her hands into all sorts of shady deals. But she'd been a good woman. She didn't deserve to be shot down in her own bar.

"What about Kotler?" Denzel asked. "Was he the second?"

Crispen shook his head. "The second was one of the patrons. He apparently took a bullet in the back as he tried to run for the exit."

Denzel nodded, feeling guilty. He knew there was nothing he could have done to protect the bystanders. The gunman had the advantage, and Denzel was lucky to have escaped alive himself. Still, his job was to protect people, and having two people die on his watch wasn't easy to take.

"And Kotler?" he asked.

Crispen studied him for a moment, as if considering before he spoke. "Kotler was taken. Witnesses say that after you were shot he took on the shooter, tackled him to the ground. It sounds like he gave it a good go, but the other guy got the upper hand. The witnesses claim he dragged Kotler out of there, through the back."

"Any leads on where they took him?" Denzel asked.

Crispen shook his head. "Not at the moment. I was hoping you might have some ideas."

Denzel thought about this and said, "Did they recover my phone?"

Crispen nodded, reached into the pocket of his coat, and produced the phone. He handed it to Denzel, who unlocked it and opened the map he and Sharon had been pouring over earlier. Denzel brought up the pinned area that Sharon had given him, the possible location of Adham's base of operations.

He gave Crispen all the details he had, starting with a full debrief on the events at the dig, the interrogations, and some of Kotler's observations.

Crispen had taken out a small notebook and was jotting down details. "And you think they're hiding out in caves and tunnels nearby?"

"Makes sense," Denzel said. "If they really are after access to this underground river, for whatever reason, they'll want to stick close."

"And do you have any speculation about why they want access to an underground river?"

Denzel shook his head. "No. Neither did Kotler. That was something we were going to work on once we'd located their base camp."

Crispen nodded, jotted something else down in his note-book, then closed it and put it away. "Good," Crispen said. "I'll have people start looking into these details, and canvassing the area you've given us. Good work, Agent. Now, focus on getting better. We can have you transferred to New York in a couple of days, once your doctors clear you."

"Thank you, sir," Denzel said. "But what about Kotler? I'd like to speak to whoever is in charge of the investigation into his abduction."

Crispen nodded. "I understand your concern, and I know you want to help. I have agents looking into Kotler's ... *abduction*. We'll see what that turns up."

Denzel caught the inflection and doubt in Crispen's voice and was confused. "You don't think he was abducted?"

Crispen shook his head slightly. "I'm not ruling anything out. It's a bit suspicious that his abductor tried to kill you, but took Kotler with him, wouldn't you agree?"

Denzel considered this for a moment.

No, he decided. He definitely did not agree. In fact, nothing about Kotler being abducted was suspicious in any way, as far as Denzel could determine.

What was Crispen plaything at? It was suddenly clear that the Director had some agenda and was purposefully skewing the narrative to cast doubt and suspicion on Kotler. Denzel hadn't known Kotler long, but he was absolutely certain the man was in no way working with Adham. The last thing Denzel wanted was for Kotler to be railroaded into charges of collusion or conspiracy.

He kept all of this to himself, however. He wasn't sure what was happening, or what game Crispen was playing, but for now he needed to be a good soldier. He needed Crispen to believe that he'd swallowed his BS without question.

"Director, I appreciate you coming to see me personally," Denzel said, as sincerely as he could manage. He felt tired and weak from the drugs and the surgery, and he hoped it would help mask any hint of suspicion in his voice or demeanor. "I wouldn't have expected you to come here personally." Denzel's unspoken question—*Why are you here?* —would have to go unasked and unanswered, for now.

Crispen waved this off, oblivious. "I was in the neighborhood. And when I heard you were injured I made sure to get here right away. The FBI takes care of its own."

Denzel nodded. "I'm honored you took the time sir."

Crispen nodded, smiling and looking a bit too smug for Denzel's tastes.

"It's no trouble. But I do need to get going. I have Agent Scully coming in to get the details of what happened. I'll forward him my notes, but I'd like you to speak directly to him, especially if you remember anything more."

"Yes sir," Denzel said.

Crispen nodded and left the room.

Denzel was still holding his mobile phone, and now he tapped out a text message to a friend back in the New York offices, asking for a favor. He was certain that destroying Kotler's phone would have been one of the first things that the gunman did, but there was always the possibility he forgot in all the chaos. Or maybe he didn't get to it right away, which could give Denzel some clue as to where the man was taking Kotler.

While he waited for a response he also sent messages to some of his old contacts in the DEA, some of his combat buddies, and anyone else he could think of who might be able to help.

He hated to admit it, but he didn't trust Crispen to follow through. He felt a pang of guilt about that, and for contacting an outside agency to work around Crispen and the FBI itself. This was his career, after all, and he'd taken certain oaths. But in truth, there was something really off about all of this, and Denzel was going to have to turn to people he knew he could trust.

The gunshot wound ached now, and he was starting to get drowsy, probably from the IV drip in his arm. He knew they'd want him to rest, and to sleep as much as possible. And he'd be glad to do that. He was worried for Kotler, but knew he was in no shape to help anyone at the moment.

Before setting the phone aside and drifting off, Denzel heard the chime for an incoming text message. He looked at the phone, his eyes starting to get bleary, and read the message from his home office contact.

We have Kotler's last known location as about twenty miles south of where you were shot. I'm including coordinates.

Denzel nodded, as if the text were a disembodied voice

he needed to acknowledge. He was too drowsy to do much else. He quickly forwarded the message to his friends at the DEA, and then placed the phone on the table next to him. He was asleep before he'd even managed to bring his hand back to rest on the bed.

Chapter 10

UNDISCLOSED LOCATION

VICTOR RAMIREZ DIDN'T MIND TAKING freelance work—that was really what his entire career was about. What he didn't like, however, was playing jailer. It was too much like being a babysitter. And in this case, it was just too hands off for his taste.

The woman, Evelyn Horelica, was no real trouble, at least.

He watched her as he always watched her. There were numerous cameras in the room where she was being held, and his equipment let him switch to any view he liked, instantly and fluidly. Through the cameras he could also listen to anything that was happening in the room, which wasn't usually necessary. Evelyn tended to work in near silence.

Victor could zoom in any camera at any angle to see what Evelyn was up to, and what she was working on. He could look at every keystroke she made on the terminal, on the tablets, on any piece of equipment in the room. And all of this was continuously being recorded so that if he needed he could hop back a few seconds to see something from a different angle.

His employer had everything well covered. It must have cost a small fortune.

Victor himself wasn't exactly inexpensive. In fact, he hired himself out at ridiculously high rates so as to discourage those who were not truly committed. It was good to weed out the low rents, and to discourage those who lacked the heart for the type of work Victor was known for.

Per the usual process, Victor had been contacted by a third party for this gig. But what was unusual was how quickly the client had chosen to bring Victor directly to his own property, to set him up with everything Victor needed to do the job. That showed real trust, and Victor appreciated that. Trust was something difficult to cultivate in his line of work. He had, in fact, taken an additional week to agree to the client's terms, spending the time doing a very deep dive into the client's past. He was effectively building his own trust, and it paid off. The client was above reproach, at least by Victor's standards. Of course, Victor had stored away much of what he'd uncovered. Just in case.

Because of all of this vetting and planning, Victor had an escape route all mapped out, for when this whole series of events finally met its ultimate conclusion. This sort of thing always ended in certain ways, and Victor had stayed in business this long, and had been this successful, by being aware of all those inevitabilities and possibilities. Victor had always done his best to act with precision and, as much as possible, certainty.

What Victor wasn't entirely certain about, however, was why this woman mattered so much to the client. As far as Victor had determined, there was no personal connection between them at all. No professional connection either, when it came to that. Not officially. As far as Victor could tell, Dr. Evelyn Horelica was just a source of information, and not even a particularly useful one by Victor's estimate. There wasn't much she could tell his client that couldn't be found by other, more efficient means.

This seeming incongruity had led Victor to do some digging and research of his own, as part of his preparations and planning. He learned about the Coelho Medallion, and about those who were studying it. He learned about Eloi Coelho, and about Dan Kotler. And, though his employer might not have wanted Victor to have this information, he learned about the FBI, and the contacts—and more importantly, the influence—his client had within the agency.

And through all those things, Victor learned what the client was after, and why it was so important.

In the end, there were the usual components of greed and power, which did not surprise Victor. What did surprise him, however, was that his client was so clearly acting in the service of honor.

It was admirable, in its way. It was surprising, as well. Victor was never much of a fan of surprises, but this was different. This was inspiring, in part. And thrilling. He admired his client for his brilliance, actually. A plan of this complexity, being carried out using his personal resources, and playing so many groups, factions, and elements against each other—there were pawns at play in this scheme who might never realize they were doomed to failure from the start. It was a complex game that showed all the organization and planning and meticulous detail that Victor himself relied upon. And, if Victor was being honest, it showed a level of brilliance that Victor himself lacked. It was admirable in every facet.

Despite the client's brilliance, however, and despite the

trust he had chosen to place in Victor, the real reason Victor had finally decided to accept this job was because of his own personal hobbies.

As a professional, Victor demanded a high price, and thus felt obligated to perform at a high level. Often, in his work, he would deny himself some of his most basic urges, in the name of performing with excellence. This delayed gratification added to the anticipation Victor felt, awakened his senses, and kept him always alert. Rather than work against him as a distraction, his eagerness kept him focused. He kept his attention on the job, performing at the peak of his abilities, and then, upon receiving payment and moving on, he would allow himself the reward of satisfying those other urges.

This job, however, came with a bonus.

The money he was being paid was more than adequate to meet his needs. It would keep him comfortable and allow him to go to ground for quite some time. That was important, in his work. It wouldn't do to allow himself to become fatigued, or careless, but it also helped him to remain off of the radar of certain agencies and factions, when he could spend time away from the work. Much like a magician, when someone in Victor's line of work demonstrated his tricks too frequently, the audience began to catch on. By spacing things out, taking a careful approach to which clients who worked with as well as when, where, and even how he accomplished his work, he could avoid creating suspicion. He could confound any organized attempt to track him down. He could survive and thrive, free to take the next job at his leisure.

He charged quite a bit for those jobs, because his leisure was so vital. He was not hurting for money, to be certain.

Money, however, was not the only thing driving Victor,

and never had been. Aside from his need to lay low, to rest, to recuperate and to enjoy the spoils of his work, Victor had other needs. Unique needs that could only be met under the right conditions. His employer, having been made aware of these needs, was more than happy to grant Victor's request for a bonus.

Once this had played itself out, Victor could claim Evelyn as his own.

It really was a win-win scenario for everyone. Victor's appetites could be met, and the client could rid himself of any connection with Evelyn's abduction. This facility, built on his employer's property, could be razed to the ground, with all evidence destroyed, and life would go on pretty much as it always had for the client.

To Victor would go the spoils.

He smiled at that. It was an old joke, and one he really enjoyed. He was fond of puns, actually, though he rarely made them himself. He liked to hear them. He liked to think of them and congratulate himself on his cleverness. Puns were a play on words, turning a phrase that seemed to be taking the listener in one direction, but suddenly twisting to reveal a hidden and unexpected outcome—seemingly random, but actually very cleverly constructed, with intention, and meant to divert the attention of the listener so they never saw the end coming.

Victor liked that. He thought of it as a metaphor for his work. He spent a great deal of time preparing and planning so that the job could be executed with an exact result, while anyone who might be paying attention would be fooled or misled, their expectations frustrated by an outcome they never saw coming. While Victor, the punster, would slip quietly away to enjoy other pursuits.

In time, Victor thought, considering those pursuits in light of Evelyn Horelica.

Victor checked the monitors again. He scrubbed the streaming recording back a few minutes, looking over Evelyn's most recent activity. Nothing seemed unusual. She was doing the work, which was all that was required of her for now.

She seemed to understand, intuitively, that the work was the only thing keeping her alive.

Well ... perhaps not the only thing. Victor's employer was using her as leverage against Dan Kotler, and that might well be more important than her actual research. It was clear that the client was looking for something, but that, too was just one more facet of his plan.

Just like a pun, Victor's employer was weaving a story just to twist it at the end.

Evelyn Horelica was simply one interesting piece of this whole story, and in the end, her role played, her fate was already determined.

In the end, she belonged to Victor.

Evelyn Horelica had stopped being afraid a week ago.

She wasn't entirely sure of the exact moment, of course, and as she thought about it there was the possibility that she'd really stopped much sooner. After all, you can only feel abject terror for so long before the effects start to wear off. The adrenaline fades when the dreadful thing you're anticipating doesn't happen, and continues to not happen for hours, days, weeks. Eventually, Evelyn reasoned, you begin to forget that you're in danger, when the threat is no longer immediate. Over time, as it became obvious that she was trapped but that no one was making a move to harm her, she began to accept the inevitability of her situation, to a degree. She relaxed, the panic subsided, and she started to fall into a rhythm.

It helped that there was the work.

Evelyn had to admit that even though these were less than ideal circumstances, she was very glad to have a project to keep her busy and sane. The work was the only thing keeping her from going absolutely bonkers. As it was, her first week here had been a cycle of breaking down into tears out of fear and frustration. It wasn't until she'd relented and started to immerse herself into the work that she'd found any sort of peace or resolve. She wasn't entirely sure what was expected of her, but she figured she stood more of a chance if she could keep things moving, keep being productive and useful. Besides, with the work to distract her, she could also start thinking about ways to escape.

If escape was possible.

She still had no idea who her captor was. But he—or she, mustn't rule out that possibility—seemed to want her alive, which was a relief. For now, at least. Circumstances might change later, but for the moment she felt she was safe as long as she kept at the translations.

She had been a little surprised when she'd woken to find herself in this room, surrounded by reference books, old ship manifests, and several artifacts that were clearly from the Pueblo dig site. She had immediately recognized some of the reports and documents produced by Dr. Coelho, as well as duplicates of work from Dan Kotler. Dan had shared most of this material with her, in fact, over the past several months. It hinted at some connection, and at the notion that her captor had been watching her for some time. She tried not to dwell on that.

But seeing work from Dan, she did wonder—was he ok? Had he been kidnapped as well? Was he still alive?

Whenever her thoughts returned to this topic, she would dive even deeper into the work. She couldn't afford to worry over Dan now. For the moment, she had to concentrate on keeping herself alive, and on being alert for any opportunities that arose.

The makeshift lab that served as her cell was festooned with an array of resources. There was a computer, and of course she had immediately tried to get a connection out, to make contact with someone and ask for help. But the computer had no internet connection. It was on a local area network only, and the only communication she had was with someone who seemed to be elsewhere in the building. They issued orders to her via a chat application, and they delivered information she needed whenever she asked.

Basically, they were a buffer between her and Google.

It was a little cumbersome, to operate this way. It was a bit like trying to play piano with oven mitts on. But she hadn't yet requested information that was denied to her. Whoever it was, on the other side of the screen, wanted to make sure she had everything she needed to do the work.

They also sent her new information she wouldn't have thought it request. She was looking at a report now, in fact. It was an inventory of a few new artifacts, scanned and cataloged from the Pueblo site, along with some notes and speculation.

She had opened the laptop with the intention of making some notes of her own and updating the log she was forced to keep. She checked her inbox, as she always did when logging on, and found a ZIP file containing a large packet of photos, documents, and digital scans.

Normally, content like this would be physically delivered

via the chute—the fancy dumbwaiter with a small elevator that delivered her food as well as artifacts and documents she would need to study. For the past few weeks she'd procured quite a collection of objects that had clearly been retrieved from the Pueblo site. There would occasionally be photos or scans of documents in her inbox, but most of what she examined came in through the chute.

So why was she getting all of this digitally?

It wasn't a problem. There was plenty of information here. True, it would have been better to study everything first hand. Primary sources were always more revealing than secondary sources. Whoever had documented these findings, however, was at least very well organized, and obviously intelligent. There were notations about where the objects were found, corresponding to coordinates and indicia on satellite imagery. These came alongside some remarkably insightful observations about the patterns of symbols and the iconography found at the site. There was even a note about the discovery of scoring and tool marks found in the cave, indicating the use of metal tools at a time when indigenous American tribes were still using sharpened flakes of flint.

That was exciting. If you were a nerd. Which, Evelyn would freely admit, she was. In fact, it was just these sorts of details that she loved discussing with people who knew they were important. That was the one thing that made it impossible for her to be so absorbed in this work that she could forget that she was a captive—there was no one to share her enthusiasm, or the excitement of discovery. She had no one she could excitedly bounce ideas off of, to see what crazy connections could be made that might abruptly shift the direction of the research. She had no one to talk to.

Evelyn wished she could talk to Dan.

Dan Kotler had been something of a pet project of hers, over the past few years. He was the consummate man child, in some ways. He was incredibly intelligent—maybe even as smart as he thought he was. She had to admit, grudgingly, that you didn't get multiple PhDs in multiple and disparate fields if you were anything less than brilliant.

He was also handsome. And funny. And kind.

But when it came to their relationship, he was a total child.

When the offer had come from Houston, Evelyn had decided it was perfect timing. It was clear that anything she might be building with Dan was going to take some time to mature. And Evelyn had started to grow tired of the wait. She loved Dan—she could admit that to herself. She wasn't so sure she was *in love* with him, though. Not anymore. Maybe she never really was.

She thought that maybe if they separated for a while and lived far enough away from each other that it was less than convenient to spend time together, they might find themselves just parting ways. But it hadn't happened that way. Her move just seemed to lighten Dan's spirits, if anything. They ended up communicating more often than they had before and opening up to each other in new ways she never would have expected. And when they did get together, out in the real world, it was fun again. It felt new and exciting, as it did when they'd first met. They enjoyed each other's company, after all, and had so much in common to talk about and explore.

It had taken time for Evelyn to realize, however, that this was about as far as it was ever going to go.

She knew Dan's history. She knew about his parents, about his strained relationship with his brother and the quirky but cute relationship with his nephew, and about the drive Dan had to empower himself, to ensure he was always free, always mobile. She knew why he kept an apartment in Manhattan that he barely spent time in. And she knew why he spent more time ingratiating himself to those who could give him access to dig sites around the world than he did trying to keep his relationships on track. Dan was as complicated as he seemed to be, and for a time Evelyn had found the challenge of their relationship to be charming and endearing.

It was only after it became clear that she was always going to be in competition with the dead, with lost cultures, even with the underpinnings of the cosmos and the nature of reality, that she had finally decided that "charming and endearing" weren't enough. She needed more, and so she had moved on.

Still, in a moment like this, all other considerations aside, she longed to talk to him. He would have just the right insight, she knew. He would be able to help her figure out exactly how all of this fit together.

He might help her escape, too. Mustn't forget that.

She peered at the data she'd just received, and immediately started putting puzzle pieces together. She'd been at this for a while now, and the strangeness of her situation had finally worn off. This was her work, at the moment. This was what she had to do. She wasn't sure if refusing would mean her death or not, but there was no reason to chance it.

Just keeping herself busy was enough justification to do the work. Being trapped here would drive her insane if she couldn't keep busy.

She read one of the new reports and stopped.

By this point, it had become pretty clear to her what her mysterious captor was after. Practically everything she'd been given had been focused almost exclusively on the "city of gold." Dan's little joke had set all of this into motion, it seemed. Evelyn couldn't even be angry with him for it. He was so brilliant, he hadn't even realized the intuitive leap he was making, or where it would lead. He had, somehow, been right, without even trying.

At least, that's what she'd thought at first.

As she studied the artifacts and pictographs and other materials more closely, she came to realize that Dan had been wrong after all. Or, at the very least, he'd been slightly off.

It wasn't his fault, of course. He hadn't been making an informed observation about facts so much as he'd just been making a joke. But his translation—indeed, even Evelyn's initial translation—had been just a bit wrong. In this line of work, of course, slightly wrong was as good as being completely wrong. History books were filled with bad assumptions that had gone on to fuel everything from McCarthyism to the Neo-Nazi movement. Being slightly wrong or slightly misinformed could lead to trouble.

And the trouble with 'translating' symbolic languages, such as those used by pre-Columbian Native American tribes, was that there really was no direct translation. There were hints. Notions. Impressions. However, there was nothing that she could use as a one-for-one substitution to get these ancient signs and symbols into readable English. The best hope she had for deciphering what all of this meant was the Rosetta stone of the Coelho Medallion, and the scant collection of Viking runes it contained. Those, of course, were mostly vague.

The reality was, even with all of the new data and information pouring in from the Pueblo dig, an exact translation might be impossible. In fact, based on what she'd been receiving from the dig site, they'd gotten it all wrong from the very start.

She had come to this realization only a few days ago but had kept it to herself. She couldn't be entirely sure what her captor was after, but she knew that withholding information could be useful. It might even be all that kept her alive.

She had started to suspect, based on everything she'd studied and translated over the past few weeks, that she could definitely put down any rumors of a city of gold, at least as they had understood it. With this new data and the photos and scans, she was absolutely sure.

El Dorado did not exist. At least, not in the way they had assumed.

She was also absolutely certain that her 'benefactor' was convinced that it did exist, however, and that was the most likely reason she'd been kidnapped. Whoever her captor was, he or she expected Evelyn to make them richer than they already appeared to be.

They were going to be sorely disappointed.

Evelyn kept this information completely to herself, never revealing what she'd discovered in the log she was keeping. Whenever the "city of gold" came up in any artifact, she glossed over it, leaving her initial translation intact. She wasn't sure if it would help anything, but it was the one advantage, the one thin piece of leverage that she had over her captor.

Still, despite the fact that they were chasing something that didn't exist, Evelyn was still getting closer to revealing where it could be found. As of now, she also knew what it was—a quirky bit of irony that made her smile, despite everything.

The river—now that was turning out to be real, and it was an exciting find. A passage from somewhere in the

Northeast region of North America, which led all the way to the interior of the continent? That was something that could change everything they knew about the history of this region. It could open discussions about ancient history that seemed mostly to be fantasy before. There were numerous Native American customs that mentioned underground cultures, passages to the world below, and caverns and caves where god-like beings lived. Finding a river that could provide passage through long and treacherous swaths of land, all underground, could explain a lot of the more intriguing quirks of Native American lore. It was thrilling.

It could change everything, and yet she couldn't share the discovery with anyone except the man or woman on the other side of that computer.

Dan Kotler might be a man-child when it came to their relationship, but right now she would give anything to talk to him.

She wondered, briefly, where he was and what he was doing. She wondered if he was going crazy with worry. She wondered if he was safe.

And then she put her own worry away in some back closet of her mind and got back to the work of translating and speculating on rivers and Vikings and cities of gold.

Chapter 11

SMUGGLER'S CAVES—NEAR PUEBLO,
COLORADO

KOTLER AWOKE TO UTTER DARKNESS, and the smell of damp
soil. The air felt chilled and a bit humid. He was laying on a
stone surface, next to a wall that felt as if it curved up and
away from him. His hands and feet were tied, with his hands
in front of him, and it was something of a struggle to wriggle
into a sitting position and lean against the wall.

His head was killing him.

He couldn't reach up to the sore spot on the back of his
head, to see if there was blood or a welt, but he could feel a
faint throbbing where the gunman had struck him with the
butt of his pistol. He worried briefly that the reason he
couldn't see might be that he'd been blinded by the concussion, but he calmed himself quickly, and relied more on the
facts than the panicky assumption. He took in the details,
studying the environment with what senses were available
to him, and making conclusions based on the facts he
uncovered.

He could hear the slight echo of sounds from his movements and small coughs, hinting at a stone ceiling that
curved into the darkness overhead. The smell, the moisture,

the feel of stone beneath him and behind him, and the complete darkness that swallowed him—he was in a cave.

He must be in the network of smuggler's caves controlled by Anwar Adham.

This was bad.

The man in the cantina must have been one of Adham's operatives, tracking Kotler and Denzel, waiting for his moment. The two of them had allowed themselves to relax a bit, in the comfortable setting of the bar, and people had died because of it. Sharon, the bartender, had been killed for certain, and Kotler's last memory of Denzel …

He shook his head. If the agent was dead, there was nothing Kotler could do about it at the moment. He had to keep his mind focused on the here and now, if he had any hope of escaping this pitch-black prison.

The darkness was impenetrable. Except …

In the distance, barely noticeable unless he was looking at just the right angle, there was a tiny, narrow sliver of light. It was about as substantial as a glowing strand of hair in the distant darkness, but it gave him some relief that he wasn't blind after all. It could also hint at a way out.

He listened hard, but heard no one in that direction, or any other for that matter. Only the echoes of his own movements came back to him. It made Kotler feel isolated, and this gave him a slight twinge of panic.

Could they have decided to leave him here, where no one would ever find him?

But then, why would they do that? His captors had gone to the trouble of keeping him alive long enough to bring him here, more or less uninsured, so leaving him to die in the darkness simply wasn't logical.

No, if they had wanted him dead he would most certainly be dead. He was reminded of the attack at the museum, in which Dr. Coelho was critically wounded. Director Crispen had said that the FBI believed either Coelho or Kotler was the target, and that their capture was the likely objective.

The fact that Kotler was here, alive, appeared to prove that out. It meant that Adham had some purpose in mind for him. Which, in itself, might be neither good nor pleasant, but for the moment it did mean he was alive. As long as he was alive there was some hope that he could escape.

Theoretically.

His hands and feet were bound with zip ties. He might be able to rub the ties binding his hands against the cave wall and use the rough texture of the stone surface to wear through the plastic. This might also relieve Kotler of a fair amount of skin, but if it helped him to escape it'd be worth it. The trouble was it would take time, and Kotler wasn't entirely certain how much time he actually had.

What if he wriggled his way toward the light? He might be able to better assess his situation.

That seemed dangerous for multiple reasons. He had no idea if there was perhaps a gap between him and the light, for a start. He might end up crawling right into a sheer drop. With his hands and feet tied he might not be able to stop himself from falling, or might be unable to climb out, if he somehow didn't die while being dashed against dark and invisible stones.

Another consideration—he didn't know how long he'd been here, or where his captors were. If he encountered them while making his way forward, he'd prefer to do it with his hands free.

So his best bet was to stay put, for now.

With that settled, Kotler managed to get himself to his feet by pressing against the cave wall and worming his way upward. He had plenty of head room, as it turned out. He had half worried he'd knock himself out again by smashing his head into the cave ceiling, but this cavern seemed to reach interminably upward into the darkness.

As he got fully to his feet, Kotler turned and placed his tied hands against the wall. He began working up and down, trying to scrape more plastic away from the band than he did skin away from his hands. It wasn't going well.

Suddenly he heard a noise, like boots clomping on a stone floor, and a flashlight beam swept over him. Kotler had turned at the sound of the noise, and was now leaning back against the cave wall, his bound hands in front of him and raised slightly, attempting to shield his eyes.

A bright cone of light blinded him, and he found himself pressing back against the stone wall, as if he might phase right through it. There was no hope of hiding in this place, however. As his eyes adjusted to the light he saw that he was in a cavern that sloped to a narrow gap at one end. The only exit was the path toward the light, and there was nothing in the space behind which he could hide. His only hope of escape would be the narrow tunnel through which his captors had arrived. This space was perfect as a cell.

Two men approached him rapidly, grabbed his arms, and roughly dragged him through the cavern, toward the exit. With his feet bound he couldn't walk, and so he ended up being mostly dragged as the men gripped his arms painfully.

The cavern opened up until a larger tunnel, after a couple of sharp bends, and the light in this larger space was bright and total. Kotler blinked into the overpowering glow of a network of electric work lights strung throughout the space, making it as bright as day here.

Tables were set up throughout the space, and these were

covered with everything from maps to small hand guns. On one small table was a tray of instruments that made Kotler cringe to think of their use.

He'd seen this sort of thing before.

Afghanistan. The high heat of the desert pressing down on him and his team of fellow researchers and archeologists. The sneer of the man who had captured them. No amount of explaining or bargaining could convince the man that they were just an expedition of historians and scientists, working with the full permission of the Afghan government. No amount of pleading could keep two of Kotler's colleagues from being ...

Kotler shook the thought from his mind. This wasn't the time, and those were the dangers and horrors of the past. There were new dangers to deal with here.

The two men who had been propping him up now dropped him hard into a wooden chair surrounded by bright lights. Kotler felt his stomach clench. He knew what this was. What it could be.

He said nothing. He knew that, too. He was a thing now. An object. He had no rights, no humanity, no hope, except the hope that came with answering all of their questions and doing exactly as they asked.

There were other men in the room, and one of them stood from behind a far table and moved toward him. As bright as the room was, there was a swath of shadow just before the bright circle where Kotler sat, and the man stepped into this darkness and stood, watching.

It was dramatic. It was effective. The bright lights kept Kotler from seeing the man's face, which meant he was also unable to read his micro expressions. Despite this, the man's body language was clear, even in silhouette, and it sent a message.

This was the man in charge. This was the one person in these caves who had any real freedom, any real choice, and any real power.

This was Anwar Adham.

"You are Dr. Daniel Kotler," Adham said.

His accent was surprising. It was British, not Arabic. It felt immediately incongruous to Kotler, giving the man the air of someone who was sophisticated and well educated. It made him seem oddly civilized. Somehow Kotler found that more off-putting than anything.

"Yes," Kotler said, attempting to make his voice sound weak, pathetic, broken. He knew from experience and research alike that men like Adham were often motivated by the fear they could inspire in others. Any sign of strength from Kotler might trigger unpleasant results. Kotler would play this close, to the best of his ability. If he had any chance of escaping this, it was going to come with a cost. The best Kotler could hope for was to minimize that cost as much as possible.

Adham turned to a nearby table and picked up a sheath of photos. He held them out, expectantly, and Kotler took them in his bound hands.

Kotler stared at the top photo. It was the totem. He managed to fold it down a bit to see the next photo, which was an image of the medallion.

These were familiar images. They were the exact photos he'd studied earlier. In fact, the photos of the totem were images that Kotler had taken himself, after the interrogation of Adham's men. He'd emailed them to only three people, so finding them here was not just a surprise, it was a revelation.

"The symbols on these artifacts," Adham said, his accented voice quiet, almost kind. "What do they mean?"

Kotler saw through this immediately. It was a test. Would Kotler try to lie? Would he tell the truth?

There was nothing to hide, really. Nothing about these symbols should be all that dangerous. In fact, by now Kotler was certain that Adham already knew what they meant and had likely gotten that information from the work of Coelho, Evelyn, even Kotler himself.

With little hesitation, Kotler flipped between the top two photographs and said, "There are numerous symbols from a variety of cultures. The runes you see common to both of these photographs are Norse. They roughly translate to 'city of gold' as well as 'river' and 'union.' The others are from dialects I haven't spent much time studying, so I'm not entirely sure what they mean."

"Guess," Adham said, smiling.

Kotler looked at him for a moment, then back down to the images. "There are a couple of Aztec symbols here that also mean 'gold' and 'river.' There's at least one symbol that refers to *cipactli*, or the crocodile. Judging by the presence of the Norse language and the obvious homage to a Viking in the totem's motif, I'm going to guess that *cipactli* was the word closest to 'dragon' for the Aztecs. Likely a description of the Viking ship's figurehead."

Adham laughed and clapped his hands once. "Very good! I did not know that, about ... what was the word? For crocodile?"

"*Cipactli*," Kotler said, volunteering no more than he was asked, but not hesitating in answering.

It was a tricky game he was playing here. Adham was definitely testing him, attempting to make him feel at ease despite his captivity. Any wrong moves on Kotler's part, though, and the results would be bad. This was the sort of tactic that men like Adham used often—build a bit of hope, then tear it down, then start again. Keeping your victims hopeful could be useful in getting them to share what they knew. Tearing that hope away could be useful in showing them that you are the one in charge of their fate.

It was clear that Adham wanted Kotler for something. Likely, Adham wanted him for his knowledge of the symbology on the artifacts, as well as any information Kotler might have regarding this mysterious underground river. But that was all in Kotler's head. He certainly wouldn't need his hands or feet or ears in order to do translations, or to share what he knew. Kotler preferred to keep all of those body parts attached, of course. So for the moment he would cooperate fully with everything Adham asked or demanded.

Adham nodded to one of his men, who pulled another wooden chair forward. Adham sat in this, still in the band of shadow, still obscured from full view by the bright light. He was facing Kotler as if they were dining across a table from each other, in a restaurant with an oddly *terrorist spider hole* motif.

"I have followed your work, Dr. Kotler. You're not like the other researchers or archeologists I have known. You are not motivated by the things that motivate them. You certainly do not require money. You also appear to have all the notoriety that someone in your position might expect. I recall you have been a guest at many prestigious parties and galas, alongside a number of celebrities!"

Kotler nodded. Acknowledgment, but not response.

"Money and notoriety seem to be the biggest motivators for one in your position," Adham continued. "Power, perhaps, would be another possibility. But you do not have the bearing of a man who seeks power. Which does beg the question: What does motivate you, Dr. Kotler?"

Now he was given permission to speak, though that did

not mean he could simply speak freely. He would have to measure every word, calculate the possible responses.

He tilted his head slightly, glancing up and to the left—signifying that he was thinking about Adham's question before answering. He wasn't sure if Adham might have studied body language, but someone as suspicious and as intelligent as him would likely have learned a few things by instinct alone. Kotler had to avoid any sign that he might be lying.

"I suppose that I'm motivated by discovery. I want to know the meaning behind everything."

Adham smiled, nodding. "And what have you discovered, Dr. Kotler? What underlies the small part that humanity plays on the Earth?"

"I haven't found those answers yet," Kotler responded. "That's why I keep looking."

Adham laughed again, nodding. "Good answer. Any other answer and I might have had to kill you!" He laughed once more, and to Kotler it sounded near maniacal, though he knew that might be his imagination. The stress of this situation was going to play with his perceptions. He had to stay calm if he wanted to think of a way to get out of this.

"So, still looking," Adham said, shaking his head as if this was just too bad. "And the Vikings ... How do you see those ancient warriors fitting into the meaning you seek?"

Kotler considered this, and measured his response, though he attempted to sound almost conversational as he spoke. He hoped that by subtly asserting himself as a teacher, a lecturer, in this scenario, he might trigger something within Adham. The man was clearly educated and cultured, and Kotler hoped to associate himself with any perception Adham had regarding perhaps a respected professor or beloved teacher. It was a long shot of a hope.

"I'm not certain, actually," Kotler said. "Not yet. But I do see everything as connected. Whatever meaning may underlie the existence of the universe, it binds everything we know."

"How very philosophical," Adham said soberly. "And this bond, do you share it with me? With my men?"

"I'd say so," Kotler said without pause. "Given our present circumstances, I'd say we're very much bonded, at the moment. What do you think?"

Adham stiffened, and Kotler knew he'd broken the protocol. He hadn't been able to help himself. He was falling into the rhythms of the sorts of conversations he had with colleagues. Ask, answer, ask. But this wasn't a conversation between colleagues. There was no equality here. Kotler had to keep that in mind. He could never, for an instant, make it seem as if he thought himself to be Adham's superior, or even his equal. Kotler was the lowest form of life, here in these caves. A rat or an earthworm would have more of Adham's respect.

"Dr. Kotler, we have ... talked ... to some of the researchers from the camp in Pueblo. We have learned a great deal."

Kotler nodded, not bothering to point out that *talk* was a bit understated, considering the mutilated corpses of the men Adham had abducted.

"What we have not learned, however, is the one thing I seek. I want to know more about this river."

There was a brief pause, and suddenly Adham slapped his knees, and stood. He stepped forward into the light now, and Kotler could finally see the man's face and features. "So, Doctor ... tell me. What do you know?"

Kotler didn't hesitate. He kept his words even, as if they were occurring to him as he spoke, and as if he was as safe as he could possibly be. "I know that the river runs through a series of connecting caverns that were at least tall enough for a Viking vessel. Which means it also had to be wide enough for oarsmen to do their work, or shallow enough for someone to be able to pole them through. I know that the river connects to the dig site in Pueblo, likely somewhere on the other side of the collapsed rubble of the cave where the figurehead was found. And I know that it is impossibly long. It would have to be, to somehow reach all the way to the North East region. Or to at least get close enough to a surface river or lake, so that the Vikings would have stumbled across it."

"In other words," Adham said, "You don't really know much."

Kotler smiled now, because it couldn't make his situation any worse. "No," he said. "I don't know much. I mostly have educated guesses. Which I'm willing to share, for what they're worth, if you would consider releasing me."

Adham chuckled. "Dr. Kotler, I think we both know that releasing you isn't something I'm willing to consider."

"No," Kotler said. "I didn't think so."

A thought occurred to him then, and he asked, because there was no reason not to. "Did you have anything to do with the abduction of Dr. Evelyn Horelica?"

There was a brief flash from Adham. Kotler saw it as recognition, but it was followed quickly by confusion, and then Adham hid both emotions.

"Perhaps we did," Adham said, smiling. "But, of course, I have no need to answer to you." He nodded to his men, and the two who had dragged Kotler into this chamber now took hold of him and roughly dragged him out again. They took him back to the dark cavern and dropped him in a heap on the ground.

Kotler gasped, and briefly had the wind knocked out of him, but managed to squirm his way into a seated position, leaning against the wall. He heard the men move away, and briefly saw a break in the slim bit of light from the entrance to this cave. Then all was quiet, except for Kotler's own labored breathing and the rasp of his movements in the cold darkness.

Chapter 12

AGENT DENZEL HAD ONLY BEEN in the hospital for a couple of days, but he was already planning his escape.

He'd gotten visits from several agents, mostly quick follow-ups on bits and pieces of information they had obtained during their investigation. Agent Scully had flown in from New York on the first day, and Denzel had updated him on literally everything he knew about Adham and the most likely location where he and his men were hiding.

Denzel had also offered up everything he knew about Kotler's abduction—including the last known location of Kotler's phone, which was confirmation of at least the general location of Adham's camp. Scully seemed completely uninterested in any information about Kotler, however. He nodded along, and jotted a few things down, but asked no follow up questions.

That settled things for Denzel. Director Crispen definitely had an agenda, and he had just as clearly directed his agents—including Denzel's own partner—to all but ignore Kotler's abduction.

That left it to Denzel himself. Which meant he had to get out of this hospital.

The nurse had been in that morning, right on time. She changed his bandage and assisted him in getting to the bathroom. At least he was ambulatory. When she was helping him back to his bed he asked, "Whatever happened to my clothes? I know the things I was wearing were probably ruined, but what about the carry-on bag I had in the Jeep?"

She considered for a moment. "I think they brought it in, so you'd have something when you checked out. It's probably in the dresser."

She nodded to the cabinet that was tucked into one corner of the room, and then walked over an opened it up. There, at the bottom of the space meant for hanging clothes, was Dan Kotler's bag.

He groaned inwardly.

Denzel had packed that bag himself. At the time, he hadn't been so thrilled with Kotler. The guy had seemed like kind of a prick, to be honest.

So Denzel had packed only light clothes, despite knowing it was going to be bitter cold in Pueblo. It was sort of a passive aggressive little swipe, he would admit, but it had been immensely gratifying—especially as Kotler had shivered through that first night.

It had only been after the firefight that Denzel started to feel a twinge of guilt over his actions. A slight twinge.

The clothes in that bag would be plenty warm enough for Denzel as he slipped out of the hospital. He could always buy new clothes somewhere local. The problem, however, was size.

Denzel had a few inches on Kotler, and he was at least a

couple of inches broader. These clothes were barely going to fit, if they fit at all.

Karma, Denzel thought. *Dammit.*

He smiled at the nurse, who closed the cabinet and then helped him into bed. When she left, he waited until he heard the click of the door closing, and then scrambled out of bed, limped to the cabinet, and grabbed the bag. He managed to wriggle on the pants and shirt, which were indeed a bit snug. He looked like a large sausage stuffed into a small casing, but he could pass. He'd just look slightly ridiculous doing it.

Leaving the bag and everything else behind, with the exception of his phone, Denzel made his way out of the hospital room.

He was moving a bit slowly. The pain was pretty bad, and he could feel it radiating from under the bandages. His muscles were loosening a bit as he walked at least. He went from a slow limp to a slow walk, and as he passed the nurse's station he swiped his right hand up and alongside his face and scalp, as if smoothing his hair and then rubbing his neck at the shoulder, hiding his features with the bend of his elbow. No one looked up, and soon he was standing in front of the elevators.

"Hey," a stern male voice said from behind him.

The elevator had arrived but hadn't yet settled into place and opened its doors. Denzel waited, keeping his eyes front and wondering if he should try to make it to the stairs. He was still a little unsteady on his feet, and not thrilled about the idea of pounding his way down a few flights with his shoulder flaring like it was on fire. But if it came to it, he figured he could make the stairwell in just a few steps, and gravity could assist him in making speed to the bottom.

If he didn't end up falling and breaking his neck first.

"Hey," the voice said again. "Could you hold the elevator when it opens?"

Denzel glanced around now and saw that the voice was coming from an orderly guiding a gurney toward the elevator.

Denzel smiled and nodded, and when the elevator dinged he stepped aside and let the orderly roll in first.

Denzel stepped inside and hit the button the orderly asked for, as well as the button for the ground-floor lobby. He rode in silence, let the orderly out at his floor, and when he came to the ground floor he made his way quickly to the glass doors that led to the parking lot beyond.

A couple of blocks from the hospital Denzel called a cab.

His wallet, and his badge, were still in the hospital somewhere. There'd been no time and no chance to find them. But Denzel had some friends here—military buddies who would be happy to lend him some cash, and a little help. Of course, what he really wanted right now was a new set of clothes. Kotler's pants were a little tight in the crotch, and that fact was becoming more noticeable the longer Denzel found himself wearing them. There would be chaffing.

Denzel called up one of his old military buddies as the cab rolled out, and then repeated his friend's address to the cab driver.

"So, who is this Kotler guy?" Denzel's buddy asked over the line. "Old friend?"

"New friend," Denzel said. "And he has a knack for attracting trouble."

"My kind of guy," his buddy said.

Denzel shook his head, then grinned. "Yeah," he said. "Mine too."

Chapter 13

TIME STOPPED HAVING ANY MEANING, and for all Kotler knew he'd been in these caves and tunnels for months. He never saw sunlight—only the artificial light that Adham's men used in the caves. He spent much of his time huddled in the dark cavern, mostly recovering.

They had started beating him soon after his talk with Adham. He'd taken beatings before, and he knew how to roll with it. They still hurt, of course, and they still took their toll on him both physically and mentally. He knew that things could get much worse than a few bruised ribs and a black eyes and busted lips.

In fact, Adham had threatened to make things worse several times, and Kotler had to work fast to keep the man from getting a little too loose with the pliers and power drills. Kotler knew that his only leverage was information, and so he worked hard to keep small bits in reserve. He would dole out enough to keep Adham from thinking he was holding back, but he was definitely stalling for time. Through hard work and focus, he managed to drag out revelations sometimes by days, giving Adham scraps of the information he uncovered. It was grueling, but with diligence he was able to narrow the stream of information without alerting Adham that he was holding anything back.

The rest of the time he lied.

Actually, Kotler had to admit that a lot of what he was telling Adham's men was less about lying and more about educated guesses that were pure conjecture on Kotler's part, and which he would never have never uttered to anyone in the academic or research community. Where he would vet his speculation to preserve professional integrity, however, he now relied on these wild and expansive conclusions as part of a survival strategy.

The underground river was only one of the mysteries that Kotler was struggling to solve, however.

Adham and his men had stolen quite a few artifacts and documents from the research site, before Cantor's security forces put a stop to it. Yet somehow, they were still getting information, in the form of documents and scans and photos that could easily be sent in digital format. Information was leaking from the site.

It was clear Adham had someone on the inside.

Kotler wasn't sure who the mole might be. He'd only met a few of the researchers, during his brief time at the site. He was absolutely certain that someone there was leaking information to Adham, though.

The data was not something of a trickle, compared to what it must have been before Sarge and his men had taken over security. Still, what Adham had here—the documents and artifacts and photos Kotler was forced to examine and translate and speculate over—told an interesting story.

The totem photos didn't provide much more than confirmation of a Viking presence in the area, hundreds of years before the continent was discovered by the Europeans.

The totem also provided the same strange hint about the underground river, and a city of gold, that Kotler and Evelyn had already uncovered from studying the Coelho Medallion. As Kotler pored over the photos, he began to see more hints of an underlying mythos, and a deepening mystery.

He was also noticing, for the first time, that despite the similarities between the iconography on the totem and those on the Coelho Medallion, there were some symbols missing. Notably, some of the actual Norse symbols were gone, or slightly altered, and so were some of the Aztec symbols. The totem was a good hint at whatever message was encoded in the medallion, but the medallion itself was the Rosetta stone.

A fact that Kotler kept to himself.

Actually, what fascinated Kotler most about the totem was that it was clearly a marker for expressing reverence toward the Vikings. In fact, after studying a few of the present symbols from native cultures, Kotler realized that whoever had carved this totem had merely been copying the Norse runes, which explained why they were a bit off, and a bit vague. Whoever had carved the totem may have been working from memory, with no understanding of what the runes represented or symbolized. Essentially, the totem bore several transcription errors.

The rest of the language of the totem—if it could be called language—referred to the Vikings as if they might be gods themselves. It hinted at a tale in which the Vikings emerged from a sacred cave, and established a bond with the indigenous people, showing them many wonders before re-entering the underworld laden with gifts and treasures provided by the Aztecs and Pueblos and other cultures.

Vikings weren't exactly known for diplomacy, but it was clear they had made an exception here.

Kotler thought about this as he was once again hunched, stiff and bruised, over photos from the dig, as well as associated notes and papers that the mole from the research camp had brought to Adham. No one was onto this theory yet—that the Vikings had somehow made themselves akin to great spirits in the eyes of the locals. It changed quite a bit about how Kotler interpreted the information he was getting.

It didn't help him much, though.

Adham's men wanted access to that river, and the consensus at the moment was that the only way to get to it was through the cave entrance in the camp. The cave itself had its own symbol, which Kotler had eventually managed to translate across three of the numerous languages used in carvings. As far as he could tell, that cave was the only entrance, and that information wasn't making Adham or his men very happy.

If it turned out that there was no other way in, that Kotler was at a dead end ... an almost certainly literal description.

"There might be another tunnel or cave connecting to it," Kotler suggested, his voice a little raspy. One of the men had punched him in the throat earlier, and Kotler had coughed and sputtered for a long while after. Now everything was sore and hurting, and everything he did took more effort—not just talking but simply breathing could be a chore.

"For your sake," Adham had said, bending at the waist and holding the back of Kotler's neck in a painful grip. "There had better be."

Kotler would have to find another way into that river, if he hoped to survive much longer. While he looked for it, his strategy was to find and feed little bits of information to Adham for as long as possible. He didn't have a plan of escape and wasn't making much headway on coming up with one, but maybe if he could drag his feet enough the FBI would eventually find him.

It was a slim hope, but it was all he had.

At least Evelyn isn't here.

It was cold comfort, considering he didn't know where she was. He'd rather her be almost anywhere but here. These men had taken it easy on him so far, but things were going to get much worse. He was glad Evelyn was spared that at least.

There was also the problem of Evelyn being leverage. Adham had never fully admitted that he didn't have her stashed somewhere, precisely because he could use that ambiguity to keep Kotler working. Kotler, however, knew that Adham was bluffing. He could read it in the man's body language, if the subject ever came up.

Another mystery to solve. Kotler was feeling them rise around him like water filling a well. He just hoped he didn't end up drowning.

Kotler was studying one of the stolen artifacts—a chunk of iron shaped vaguely like an axe blade, and which should definitely not be in a Native American dig site. There was nothing about the artifact that would give him any clue about an alternate entrance to the river, but he had managed to persuade Adham and his men that everything was a potential lead.

He had to admit, he had some vague notion that he might be able to use this axe head as a weapon and make his escape. As plans went, it was ridiculous. From an ironic standpoint, Kotler rather liked it. Too bad he'd be stone dead before he could ever tell anyone how brilliantly his plan had failed. Still, merely having his hands on something that could, under the right circumstances, be used as a

weapon made him feel at least a slight tingle of empower-
ment. He clung to that, needing it desperately at the
moment.

There was a sudden cacophony of shouting from somewhere deeper in the caverns, away from where Kotler was
working, and his guards loomed. The guards stiffened, then
crept forward, weapons raised, taking positions near the
entrance to where they were hole up.

Gunfire erupted from somewhere in the caverns,
echoing loudly and bouncing from the walls, making it
impossible to know its true direction or origin.

The two men were so distracted by the noise that Kotler
had a sudden inspiration—he should make a move. He
should do something and make his escape!

But what could he possibly do? He was bruised and
beaten to the point where he could barely move. He was
pretty sure he had at least one broken rib, and a couple of
broken fingers on his left hand. His left eye was swollen
nearly shut, and his throat felt bruised to the point of
making it painful the breath.

He also had no weapons, other than an ancient and
pitted axe head. Though he thoroughly enjoyed the ironic
fantasy of using that axe head to bludgeon one of the
guards, the follow-up would be a barrage of bullets tearing
him in two as the other guard noticed the attack.

For the moment, Kotler was still trapped.

He looked around the cavern and decided it might be
best if he simply hunkered down. He turned the table in
front of him on its side and hobbled with bound hands and
feet to crouch behind it. He dropped to his knees, then
rolled, laying on his back. He used the axe head to start
gnawing away at the zip ties around his feet—at least he
could run if he had to.

It took time, because the axe wasn't exactly a sharp instrument after centuries buried in the desert. It served, however, and soon the bonds were cut. He began awkwardly working at the straps around his wrists, making slow progress.

The guards were shouting in Arabic now, which Kotler understood.

"Who is there! Reveal yourself!"

More gunfire, and now some of it was definitely coming from within the caverns. The guards had been fired upon, and they were shooting back.

Kotler stayed put. This was the safest place he could be, at the moment. Which wasn't saying much. He kept working at the bands around his wrist, which were tougher because of the angle he had to work with.

There was the sound of a man screaming, and a wild series of shots, and in a moment things went very quiet. Kotler risked peeking around the edge of the table and saw that the room was filled with acrid gun smoke, wafting in the gentle currents of the vent fans that were set up in a line along the walls of the cave, guiding clean air into the room from the outside. Tendrils of smoke curled around the work lights, and the overall light in the room had dimmed considerably.

Kotler couldn't decide what to do. He was still bound, still injured, and still pretty screwed. But things seemed to have died down—quite literally. He wasn't hearing any more shots, but no one was talking, either. Adham's men would have been babbling to each other by now, Kotler knew. So whoever had come in here had won the day.

The question was, who? Was it the FBI? Or was it local drug runners, clearing people out of the network of caverns they considered their home turf?

Kotler went back to hacking away at the binding on his wrists. The rough and pitted edges of the axe blade were taking small chunks from the plastic zip ties, and eventually he'd damaged them enough that he could snap them with a quick, hard pull of the wrists.

He then sat up, still hiding behind the overturned table. He looked once again around the table's edge.

It felt good to have his hands and feet free. He rubbed his wrists, letting circulation return painfully and slowly, as he watched the clouded entrance to the cavern where he was hiding.

The two guards were splayed on the ground, blood splattered on the walls around them and pooling in puddles beneath them before running to the low spots of the room. Their rifles were both pinned under them. Kotler was thinking about trying for one of them, to see if he could quickly pry it free, but spotted a handgun in a holster at one guard's side.

Moving as quickly as he was able—which wasn't very quick—Kotler scrambled to the guard's side and pulled the handgun free. He quietly pulled the weapon's slide partially open to check for a chambered round. He didn't bother checking the magazine. It would be fully loaded.

He held the weapon out in front of him as he did a quick peek around the mouth of the tunnel. The gun smoke and dust filled the air all along the tunnel's length, blocking some of the work lights further down. It made it impossible to see anything, or to determine whether anyone was alive out there. Kotler looked around the cavern and decided that regardless of the unknowns his chances were better out there than in here. He'd rather be shot while trying to escape than executed and left to rot here in these caves, if

Adham and his men happened to survive and circle back here.

Slowly Kotler edged out into the tunnel, moving to the far wall, away from the string of work lights. He slid along, staying low, with his weapon leading him.

Up ahead he saw movement and stopped in his tracks.

Shadowy figures were moving in the smoke, gliding their weapons from side to side, as if trying to cover every possible direction. There were at least three of them, and they were edging their way toward Kotler.

What should he do?

These men had taken out Adham's group. Or ... had Adham's group won? Could the figures just ahead be Adham's men sweeping for more enemies?

Kotler felt his heart pounding, but took deep breaths, centering himself, calming himself. He was in a bad situation, and in any bad situation, filled with unknowns, you look to what you know.

He was trapped here, regardless of whomever was up ahead. He had one handgun with ten rounds at best, while the men ahead were clearly armed with semi-automatic weapons. If these men were with the FBI, great. Kotler should put down his own weapon and call out to them. If they were Adham's men, not so great. Kotler should still put down his weapon and call out. It would be better to be taken alive, surrendering willingly, than to be shot trying to escape.

Except now Kotler was feeling something else entirely. He was angry. He'd been pinned here for God knew how long, tortured and beaten, and now he was finally free and armed.

No, putting down his weapon and surrendering wasn't something he was prepared to do, regardless of who might be ahead. Maybe it was the smarter and more strategic play, to surrender. Being smart hadn't gotten Kotler very far here, however. No, it was time to make a stand, and take whatever consequences came of it.

"Put your weapons down and surrender!" Kotler shouted, raising his weapon and taking aim at the closest figure. "I am armed, and I will shoot if you do not identify yourselves."

There was a surprised murmur, and Kotler heard what sounded like someone talking into a mobile phone or radio. He couldn't quite make out the words, but it had that tone of someone speaking directly into a microphone.

"Dr. Dan Kotler?" A voice asked from the smoke.

Kotler felt his heart pound. "Identify yourself!"

"Dr. Kotler, my name is Agent Carl Rickson. I'm with the DEA. We're here with Agent Denzel of the FBI."

Kotler couldn't believe what he was hearing. Literally. He calmed himself again, and said loudly, "Agent Denzel is dead."

"Actually, he's alive," Rickson said. "He was hospitalized, but he got over it."

There was a light chuckle from some of the men with Rickson.

"Prove it," Kotler said, refusing to lower his weapon.

"It's true, Kotler," Denzel's voice said over a radio speaker. "It's me. We're here to rescue you."

Kotler finally lowered his weapon and slumped against the wall. He laughed, though it hurt his throat, and wasn't very loud. "Agent Denzel," he said. "What took you?"

He heard Denzel laugh. "I had to buy new pants."

Chapter 14

KOTLER SAT on the tailgate of a pickup truck as one of the DEA agents tended to his wounds. Kotler wasn't making the guy's job any easier, wincing at every dab of the alcohol-soaked swabs and out-and-out pulling away as the agent applied sutures to some of the worst wounds.

Once the gruesome and painful work was done, and Kotler was finally left to smolder from the burning of dozens of wounds and bruises, he was handed a thermos of cold water. He drank greedily, gulping the cool liquid down.

Denzel stood nearby, ready to take the thermos away as Kotler sputtered from water going down the wrong way.

"How long have I been in there?" Kotler asked the agent, rasping from his injured throat.

"A little over two weeks," Denzel said. "I would have gotten here sooner but I was in the hospital."

"Food poisoning?" Kotler asked, managing a smile.

Denzel smiled in return. "Gunshot wound. Our shooter in Cañon."

Kotler nodded. "I'm sorry, Roland. I was worried you'd been killed."

"I damn near was. But I was also worried we'd find you in worse shape. You don't look so bad, though."

Kotler laughed, and winced from the pain in his side. "Tell it to my ribs."

Denzel nodded. "I convinced my contacts at the DEA to help on this. If anyone asks, those guys in the caves were running cocaine from across the border."

Kotler nodded. "They might have been, for all I know. I spent most of my time in a hole in the back of the tunnel where you found me. They had me translating and interpreting artifacts and papers."

"What are they after?" Denzel asked.

"The river," Kotler said. "We were right. They seem to have no interest in the 'city of gold,' or anything else. But they're scrambling to find another way into that underground river. So far as I can tell, the only known entrance is the cave. I think I know why it's covered with symbols, though. I think the Vikings emerged from it, and the locals thought they were great spirits."

"Awesome," Denzel said. "That's about as helpful as a *Star Trek* reference, as far as I can tell."

"There's a lot going on here, actually," Kotler said. "Adham knows absolutely nothing about Evelyn's abduction. In fact, I got the impression that there's another player on the board. Maybe one with a slight connection to Adham. It was hard to tell. I think Adham has a benefactor, but I couldn't determine whether it was the same person who abducted Evelyn."

"Well, my buddies in the DEA will debrief you and get all the details, and they've already promised to share, if they find anything in those tunnels. Meanwhile, I have to fly back to New York and take my lumps."

"What happened?" Kotler asked.

"Crispen," Denzel scowled. "He's reassigning me."

Kotler nodded. "I'm sorry."

"I think it's probably for the best. I'm still recovering from my injury, technically. But I'll be honest, I think it's mostly about getting me away from you. He has some weird hang up when it comes to you."

"I noticed," Kotler said. "I'm sure he'll find a way to make it look like I was colluding with Adham while I was here."

"I'll make sure that doesn't happen," Denzel said grimly.

Kotler was touched by the show of loyalty and support, but he knew that Denzel was practically powerless when it came to Director Crispen. Whatever Crispen's agenda, he saw Kotler as an impediment. And judging by the details Denzel was sharing, Crispen would just as soon have left Kotler in that cave than mount a rescue. So things were pretty serious.

Kotler was going to have to watch his back.

"So what's your plan from here?" Denzel asked. "Maybe you should call it quits and go back to New York."

Kotler shook his head. "Something tells me that isn't really an option," he said. "And even if it was, I wouldn't take it. Evelyn is still out there, somewhere. Adham was a dead end for finding her, so I'll have to start over."

"It wasn't a total loss," Denzel said. "Thanks to you we shut down a terrorist base camp"

"But Adham escaped," Kotler said. "And you can be sure this wasn't his only foothold in the states. He's still out there somewhere. And he still wants access to that river."

"Which means we have an advantage," Denzel said. "We control the only entrance."

Kotler nodded, though he wasn't sure how much of an advantage that really was.

"We should spend some time figuring out exactly why

the river is so important to him," Kotler said. "Do you think you can help with that? Is it going to be too difficult with Crispen watching you?"

Denzel shrugged. "Yes and no. I'll call some of my contacts—the same people who helped me track you down. Crispen doesn't know about their involvement in your rescue. I'll see what we can determine based on the data we have."

"You might want to get in touch with Cantor. His satellite data might give some clues we can use."

"If he is forthcoming with it," Denzel said, shaking his head. "He's being very guarded. And without just cause, I can't force him to hand anything over. I'll ask, as firmly as I can, but Cantor isn't the type to roll over just because I have a badge."

"Reese might be, though," Kotler said. "He's just one of Cantor's crowd-sourced researchers. But he's had access to all of that data."

Denzel nodded. "I'll see what I can do. And I'll share what I can, if it doesn't impede the investigation into Adham or into Dr. Horelica's abduction."

That was all Kotler could ask for. He desperately needed to be kept in the loop in all of this, if he was to remain useful. But with Crispen watching both Kotler and Denzel closely, Kotler would have to live with whatever scraps of information he could get.

A short time later Denzel shook Kotler's hand then climbed into the passenger seat of a friend's truck, which then sped off, presumably to the closest airport. Kotler watched it go, feeling oddly sad. He'd just spent two weeks being beaten and kept against his will, with no human contact other than his captors, and yet seeing Denzel leave was still like the closing of a chapter. He would have to circle up with him later, see how things turned out with Crispen.

The DEA agents offered to take Kotler to the hospital and debrief him after he'd been checked out, but Kotler wanted to get out as many details out as he could while everything was still fresh. He told the agents about the stolen artifacts, his suspicion of a mole at the campsite, Adham's goals to find the underground river, even what he'd learned from studying the artifacts and paperwork while in captivity. There were lots of follow up questions, and Kotler did his best to answer everything.

Soon, however, he felt exhaustion starting to overtake him. The DEA agents finished up and promised to contact Kotler if they had any further questions. Then the ambulance took him to the hospital.

After being cleaned up, bandaged, given a series of shots, and having more X-rays and CAT scans than seemed safe, Kotler was given a bed in a vacant room, and a mild sedative to help him sleep. A guard was placed outside of his door, in case any of Adham's agents came along to tie up loose ends.

Kotler could not have cared less about that threat, at the moment. He was so exhausted—physically, mentally, and emotionally—that he was asleep in his hospital bed in moments.

The next morning, Kotler awoke to discover two FBI agents standing over him, and he ended up giving them all the same information he'd just shared with the DEA. So much for inter-agency sharing.

The FBI agents took plenty of notes but said very little. When they were done, they told Kotler he was free to return to New York.

"I'll be staying here for now," Kotler said. "Evelyn is still missing, and I believe I can do the most good here."

"We have the investigation under control, Dr. Kotler," one of the agents said. "You'll be safer back in New York. Director Crispen asked us to arrange a flight."

"Good of him," Kotler said. "You can cancel it."

The agents glanced at each other. "Doctor ..."

"Unless you're about to tell me that I'm under arrest, I have no intention of going anywhere. I'm not impeding your investigation. I was invited here. I'll be staying until I'm satisfied that there's nothing more I can do to help find Dr. Horelica. I suspect she's just about the lowest priority on Crispen's list, so I'm not inclined to leave it to you to find her."

"Sir ..."

Kotler hit the call button beside the bed. "I believe I need a bit more rest, Agents. Thanks for dropping by."

A nurse came in, "Mr. Kotler?" He asked.

"Doctor. Kotler," Kotler said. He rarely insisted that anyone use his title, but at times like these he wanted to leverage what little social authority he could. "I'm feeling a bit tired, so I think visiting hours are up."

The nurse looked at the two agents, and both nodded lightly before leaving the room.

His stubbornness wasn't going to make things easier, Kotler knew. The FBI—Director Crispen in particular— could make a case that he was interfering in their investigation. They might be able to force him to leave. But before they did that, Kotler intended to make one more visit to the Pueblo site.

In all his debriefings, there was only one detail he'd held back. He told both the DEA and the FBI that Adham had no interest in the 'city of gold,' and that was true. What he hadn't told any of them, not even Denzel, was that in studying the photos of the totem and other artifacts closely for the past several days, he had figured out what the city of gold was. Maybe not where it was, exactly. Though he had a good guess on that, too.

Adham's men had no interest in the city of gold. But Kotler was beginning to suspect that someone else did.

It was the only clue Kotler had when it came to finding Evelyn Horelica. And he was going to follow where it led.

Chapter 15

THERE HAD BEEN some slight changes in the camp since Kotler and Denzel had driven off to Cañon a couple of weeks earlier.

Most of the research personnel had been relocated or reassigned. Coelho's people had been removed to some other project, by Coelho himself, it seemed. Or by one of Coelho's people.

The old man had been released from the hospital while Kotler was in captivity, though he was still bed-ridden back in New York. He wasn't doing well, judging by what Coelho's assistant had told Kotler on the phone. And now, as Kotler stared at Coelho's thin and pale face via Skype, Kotler feared his old friend might not be around much longer.

"Daniel," Coelho said, his voice just above a whisper.

That seemed like bad news to Kotler—not just Coelho's voice but the fact that a he'd referred to Kotler by his first name. For the entirety of their relationship, Coelho had always referred to him as Dr. Kotler. There may have been an occasion where Coelho called him "Dan," maybe over drinks or during some celebration. But he'd never called him Daniel, and that told Kotler a lot about the man's condition.

"How are you feeling?" Kotler asked.

Coelho attempted a weak smile. "I've had many better days. But what about you? My assistant told me you were abducted. You look like hell."

Kotler smiled. Only Eloi Coelho could suffer through a gunshot wound and still think someone else looked like hell.

"It wasn't the most pleasant experience, but I'm fine now," Kotler said, trying to brush past the entire incident. The past few weeks were still too fresh, and Kotler preferred not to think about them for the moment. He would have plenty of time to process and consider it all after he managed to find Evelyn. "You pulled your team from the research site," Kotler said.

Coelho nodded. "I thought it was best. Mark Cantor has installed his own people there now. I've relinquished the contract I had with him."

"Just like that?" Kotler asked.

Coelho gave him a pitying look. "Come now. Things have become far too dangerous there. Had I known sooner I would have pulled my people weeks ago. The FBI never told me. It has become a contested site, to say the least. I'm told the FBI and DEA are actually blocking anyone from coming in and out."

That wasn't entirely true. The two agencies were working on a joint mission to find Adham and his people, and part of that involved a stricter control of the site and the area surrounding it. Locals and even tourists could still come and go through the region, they were just submitted to more scrutiny than usual.

"Dr. Coelho, while I was ... in captivity ... Adham had me

digging into files and research that could only have come from the camp. Some of the documents he had actually came from my own notes, which I shared with only a handful of people." He paused before saying the next part, wary of how it might affect the older man's health. "I hate to say this, Eloi, but it seems like there is a mole here, sharing information. Would you have any idea who that might be?"

Coelho first looked surprised, then a bit deflated as he shook his head. "No. I've known most of the people on that team for decades. I trust them. None of them would have thrown in their lot with a terrorist."

"Unfortunately, someone did," Kotler said quietly.

Coelho nodded. "And do you believe this person was involved in Evelyn's kidnapping?"

Kotler shook his head. "No. It became clear early on that Adham had nothing to do with Evelyn's abduction. He was clueless about her."

Coelho considered this. "Very strange."

"Yes," Kotler nodded. "It looks like we have two different problems on our hands here. In fact, I believe we're dealing with two different parties, with their own separate agendas. But I believe both want essentially the same thing."

"The city of gold?" Coelho asked.

Kotler shook his head again. "No. At least, not entirely. I have no doubt that may be a factor, but Adham didn't seem interested in it in the least. It's my opinion that he's after the river, though I'm not sure why."

"The underground river," Coelho nodded. "Very impressive."

"You've caught up," Kotler said, smiling.

"I got the short version from my assistant. It seems incredible. If the Vikings really did sail in on an underground river it must stretch from Colorado to the Great

Lakes!" In his excitement Coelho started coughing, sputtering into a handkerchief that someone handed him from off-screen.

Kotler waited for his coughing to subside, then said, "That would be incredible, but I'm not sure that's possible. There are quite a few shifts in geology between those two regions. I'm thinking they must have found something on the other side of the St. Lawrence divide, which would put them further inland. It's possible they were using inland rivers and portaging from one body of water to another in an effort to move west. I imagine they found the entrance to the underground river far from the Great Lakes."

Coelho nodded, though his expression was one of speculative wonder.

"Once we can get into that river, we may find all sorts of new and interesting things," Kotler said, trying to stoke the ember of Coelho's enthusiasm. It might be good for the man, to have that spark of excitement and fascination.

"I regret that I will not be a part of the discovery of it," Coelho said morosely.

Kotler knew Coelho was referring to his health. In an effort to distract him, he replied, "I'm sure that Mark Cantor would allow you to visit here. It was your dig, after all. He could probably be persuaded to continue sharing information with you, at least."

Coelho waved this off. "Oh, I still get reports. Richard was asked to stay on at the site, and he sends me emails frequently, sharing what he's learned. I appreciate them, though I know he must be risking his position to send them."

Kotler blinked. "Richard Barmoth?" He asked.

Coelho nodded.

Kotler hesitated, then changed his expression, smiling.

"I'll have to look him up while I'm here," he said. "I haven't spotted him so far."

"He seems very busy," Coelho said.

"I'm sure that's it," Kotler nodded. "I'll track him down. But I don't want to keep you any longer. You need your rest!"

Coelho waved another weary hand. "All I do is rest. Please, let me know if your theories on the city of gold and the underground river lead to anything interesting. And please, Daniel—let me know when they find Evelyn. I worry for her."

"So do I. And yes, absolutely."

They disconnected, and Kotler closed the laptop before shoving it into the leather messenger bag he had picked up from town. He'd been forced to do some shopping, after a couple of weeks in a cave, and had bought a new laptop along with some new clothes. He was used to traveling light, but since becoming embroiled in this he'd come to appreciate the luxury of being able to choose his own clothes and resources. Denzel had confessed to being the one who packed the sparse bag—a passive aggressive swipe that now they could both laugh about. But Kotler was happy to shed all of the borrowed clothing and hospital gowns for some new threads of his own.

He left the small trailer that was serving as his home for the moment and wandered toward the tent standing at the entrance to the cave, where Cantor's people had now set up, using the space as home base. Kotler didn't recognize anyone on his way into the restricted area, but that wasn't all that surprising. He'd only met a handful of the people who had been here previously, and all of them were now gone. All, that was, except Richard Barmoth.

The guards checked his identification and let him

through. He entered the tent and was immediately impressed by the bustle of the place.

All of the artifacts that had been recovered and remained on site were now spread out among several work stations. They were being catalogued and packed into shipping crates, for transport to another location. Everything was photographed and scanned with 3D scanner wands, as well as with devices Kotler didn't recognize.

Kotler had to admit, one advantage of having Mark Cantor funding the project was a wealth of advanced technology. There were devices here that Kotler had only read about. It was truly impressive.

So why is Mark Cantor funding this project? he thought.

The question so abrupt, it startled him. In all the chaos, and with his mind focused on finding clues that might lead to Evelyn's rescue, as well as dealing with his abduction and torture at the hands of Adham, Kotler had failed to ask the most basic question. The first principle question.

That bothered him—because it was exactly the sort of thing he lectured about. He was continuously challenging the "zebra" problem, when it came to scientific research and analysis. He wanted people to question the sound of hooves, even if they thought the answer was obviously horses. Ask all the basic questions, to eliminate them if for no other reason.

And yet, this time at least, he hadn't done that himself.

Cantor was a larger-than-life figure, with an impressive background. He had been a child prodigy and had earned his first million before leaving high school. He had written software that the government eventually purchased and instituted in training military personnel and federal agents, accelerating the learning curve for what had always been thought of as "pure brain skills." Thanks to Cantor's software, agents and soldiers could learn to distinguish patterns faster, to remember faces easier, and to calculate odds for tactics quicker—among other useful capabilities. Language learning alone had been a big draw for federal agencies, but the implications of Cantor's software went so much deeper.

Cantor had a knack for creating products that had a narrow but lucrative appeal. Zelot was a good example of this—Kotler had been impressed by the idea that someone could build a purely academic social media tool that was actually profitable. At least ... he had assumed it was profitable. Zelot had such a strong marketing presence, and had gained such popularity among his colleagues, Kotler had once again made the mistake of thinking those hooves had belonged to horses instead of zebras. Maybe he should reexamine that assumption, and perhaps do a little digging into the financial standing of Zelot, once he had an opportunity.

As he wandered among the researchers, he did finally spot a couple of familiar faces. David Reese, who had been by Cantor's side during Kotler's first visit to this site, was talking with Richard Barmoth, Coelho's former lead researcher here. They were sharing an iPad and discussing the recent finds from the dig.

Kotler made his way to the two men, and stood patiently, waiting to be noticed.

"Dr. Kotler!" Reese said. "I heard you were back. Mr. Cantor said to assist you with anything you need."

"I appreciate that," Kotler said, shaking Reese's hand.

He turned to Barmoth and shook his hand as well. "I was surprised when Dr. Coelho told me you had stayed on," Kotler said.

Barmoth smiled. "I've been with this project since the beginning," he replied. "I would like to see it through. My role here may have changed somewhat, but Mr. Cantor was kind enough to give me the same level of access I had before. I have to admit, I'm enjoying connecting with the new team. Many of them have no real academic background, but they're very passionate about the work. I haven't felt this excited about a dig since I was an undergrad."

"I'm sure it helps that this discovery is going to change the way we all view history on this continent," Kotler smiled.

Barmoth nodded enthusiastically. "There is that," he beamed.

Kotler looked now at some of the tables in the room, and the artifacts and equipment strewn over them. Somewhere in all of this was a clue, he hoped, that would lead to finding and rescuing Evelyn. Assuming she was still alive. But how could he get from ancient Vikings in the interior of North America to the abduction of a researcher several hundred years later? That seemed like a lot of layers to cut through. And he was going to be working at odds with whatever game Crispen was running.

It made him feel weary to think of it all. He turned to Barmoth. "When I was being held by Adham's men, they had me studying data from this dig. It was clear they had an inside man."

Barmoth shook his head. "I can hardly believe that. I've known most of the people who were working here for the better part of a decade. It just seems impossible that any of them could have been working with terrorists."

"Can you think of any motive someone might have?" Kotler asked. "Money? Ties to their home country, perhaps?"

"None of the team was from that region," Barmoth said. "So I don't think that's it. Money? Maybe. This work doesn't exactly pay well, and if someone has student loans and medical debt to pay, I can see the temptation. I have those worries myself." Barmoth chuckled. "But I can't think of a single team member who would have done it. Besides, not only did the FBI vet everyone, Cantor's security team grilled all of us as well. Once all the problems started, we were all scrutinized pretty closely. Even our communications in and out are monitored."

"Oh?" Kotler asked.

"Yeah," Barmoth said. "I have to get permission from Sarge Canfield just to call home, and I'm pretty sure all those calls get recorded and listened to. All this scrutiny for an archeological dig—I feel like I'm part of the Manhattan project."

Kotler smiled at that. It was one of the things that had struck him as odd throughout his experience with this dig as well. The level of interest in this project was higher than any Kotler had ever previously participated in. Though he personally felt it was of tremendous importance, he never would have assumed it would be a matter of national security.

Denzel had told him that the FBI had requested the site be shut down until further notice, but Cantor had pulled strings and used his influence to keep it going. Whatever it was that Cantor wanted out of this dig, it had to be bigger than pure historical interest. He showed no serious inclination toward finding the river, as Adham did, yet somehow his interests and those of Adham had crossed, with Evelyn, Coelho, and Kotler himself in the middle.

Something Barmoth said caught Kotler's attention. "Where is Sarge, anyway? He saved my life, the last time I was here. I don't think I ever properly thanked him."

Reese checked something on his iPad. "He's at the main security building," he said. "He has a small office there."

"Right," Kotler replied, nodding. "I'll check in with him. And I'll let you two get back to work. I apologize for interrupting."

"Are you kidding?" Reese smiled. "Dr. Kotler, it's a privilege to be able to talk to you! If you have any questions about the progress of the dig, or anything we find here, please ask!"

Kotler nodded. "I will, thank you."

He left the two men to their discussions and wound his way out of the secured area to the small, portable building that was being used as security headquarters.

There were essentially two rooms in this tiny, temporary office—one large space with chairs facing a podium, presumably where Sarge held briefings; and one smaller space with a door that Sarge could close for privacy. At the moment that door was open, and Sarge was sitting at a desk reviewing something on a laptop. He looked almost comical, as a very large man hunched over the sleek, modern machine, stabbing at the keys with large fingers. His expression, Kotler noticed, was one of engrossed wonder, as if the screen in front of him were some sort of magic portal that granted knowledge to the user.

In a way, it is, Kotler mused. Though he wasn't sure Sarge would find the whole analogy all that flattering or amusing.

Kotler knocked lightly on the frame of the door, and Sarge looked up, gruff and grizzled, clearly not appreciating the interruption of his work. "Kotler," he grunted.

"Sarge," Kotler said, nodding. "I wonder if I could have a chat with you. If it's a bad time ..."

"It's always a bad time," Sarge grumbled. "But come in. And shut the door."

Kotler closed the door behind him, and then took a seat

in the folding chair in front of Sarge's desk—which, as it turned out, was a folding table that had seen better days. It seemed everything here was made for immediate evacuation. Nothing felt permanent.

"What can I do for you, Dr. Kotler?" Sarge asked. He leaned back in the creaking office chair and patted at a pocket on the front of his coat, apparently not finding what he was looking for.

Something about that seemed familiar, and it clicked with some other half-remembered information in the back of Kotler's mind. He blinked, inhaled, and left it to think about later.

"I was wondering if you'd had any success in tracking down the mole that Adham has planted in the camp."

Sarge barked—or at least, it sounded like a bark. Kotler realized it was a quick laugh, filtered through Sarge's gravel voice and handlebar mustache. He watched as Sarge leaned back, turned slightly, and produced a small, ornate wooden box. He presented this to Kotler, opening it to reveal a row of cigars.

Kotler waved, "No thank you," he said.

Sarge grunted, took a cigar and nipped its ends, then lit it with a wooden match he seemingly produced from nowhere. He puffed on this a few times, and when he spoke Kotler watched a swirling cloud dance from his lips. With Sarge's fire-red mustache, the whole thing gave the impression of a grizzled dragon, preparing to launch into an attack if his victim didn't properly answer *these riddles three.*

"I've had some of my best guys looking into how it's happening," Sarge said.

"How what's happening?" Kotler asked.

"The communications," Sarge replied. "Somehow this

bastard is in contact with the terrorists, and he's doing a pretty good job of hiding his tracks."

"Doing? You mean he's still at it?" Kotler asked.

"We think so," Sarge said. "The DEA found all kinds of equipment in those caves where you were getting the crap kicked out of ya. And before anyone mentioned anything to the bunch here, they were still getting data from this site. They're monitoring."

"Interesting," Kotler said. "Do you have a suspect?"

"No," Sarge groused, disgusted. "Nearly everyone who was here with Dr. C's original team has been replaced, and those who are left have all passed some pretty thorough background checks. We're watching everyone all the time anyway. No one makes a phone call or sends a letter or even farts in Morse Code from this place without us knowing it. All internet activity is monitored. And there are no landlines coming in, so there ain't any phones. We're using signal blocking tech to keep a bubble around this place. I can't figure any way for someone to get a message in or out."

"Except someone is," Kotler said.

"Well, yeah. Somehow," Sarge said, puffing on his cigar and scowling.

"No," Kotler said. "I mean that I know that someone is. I have proof, though I have no idea how he's doing it."

Sarge was leaning forward. He had the cigar in a corner of his mouth and had just taken a puff when he reached up and pulled it free. Smoke billowed from his nostrils as he asked, "Who is it, and what do you know?"

"Richard Barmoth," Kotler said. "He's been in touch with Dr. Coelho, filling him in on what they're finding here. Old habits, perhaps. Or a sense of loyalty. But he's doing it under the radar. Which means he has a way to connect to the internet without being noticed."

Sarge spat a particularly cringe-worthy combination of words, then rose from his chair. "Where is he?" Sarge growled.

"Before you drag him out in chains ..." Kotler eyed Sarge, who had a couple of troubling veins bulging in his neck and temple. "... or worse, it might be best if we monitor him for a bit. If we can catch him in the act, we might gain an advantage."

Sarge once again chomped on his cigar, pausing to consider what Kotler was saying. Finally, after a long moment, he said, "What advantage ya go in mind?"

"Disinformation," Kotler replied. "If it turns out that Barmoth really is leaking information to Adham, then we might be able to use his methods to lure Adham into a trap."

Sarge nodded. "I like it. How do we do it?"

"The best way is to leave Barmoth in play," Kotler said. "Feed him false information about the underground river."

Sarge grinned. "You're a sneaky bastard, Kotler. I wouldn't have pegged you as the type."

Kotler smiled lightly and shook his head. "If Barmoth really is the mole, I'm glad to help. But this doesn't really move me any closer to my own goals. Dr. Horelica is still out there, somewhere. Adham didn't have anything to do with her abduction, and I still have no idea who did."

"Too many players on the field," Sarge nodded. "We'll narrow the bastards down. Help me nail Adham, and I'll help you track down Dr. Horelica."

Kotler stood, shook Sarge's hand, and said, "Deal. Now, I'm going to go outside for some fresh air before I suffocate from cigar smoke."

Sarge laughed and puffed another cloud in Kotler's direction.

Chapter 16

FEEDING false information to Barmoth was tricky.

For starters, Kotler would have to work against an entire team of researchers with varying skills of observation and varying levels of natural inquisitiveness. He couldn't simply plant a fake artifact and wait to see if it was discovered. He'd have to manipulate the data being gathered in a way that wouldn't derail the research but would catch the eye of Barmoth. It would be a delicate balancing act, but fortunately Kotler knew exactly what Barmoth would be on the lookout for.

He started with the camp's digital records.

Sarge gave him access to the intranet that the researchers were using, and Kotler became the only person on site who could access the system from outside of the secured area. He was able to monitor everything that was entered into the database, including guesses and observations about recent translations.

Sarge's security team had a couple of IT people, and they had installed keystroke trackers on every computer in the camp. Using these, Kotler was able to monitor individual usage, and eventually was able to home in on Barmoth's personal folder. This was where Barmoth stored his notes and observations.

There was nothing incriminating in this folder, of course. Combing through Barmoth's notes, however, helped Kotler to get a bead on the man's areas of special interest. Barmoth was being subtle about his pursuit of information regarding the river, but it was definitely there, right alongside notes about the alleged "city of gold" and his speculations on where the Vikings might first have entered the underground river.

Kotler was surprised to see some of his own theories written out in detail, among Barmoth's notes. He hadn't shared any of this with Barmoth. He hadn't even shared it with Coelho. In fact, the only way Barmoth could have gotten this information was if he'd somehow followed the research Kotler had done while in captivity. This was proof that Barmoth was in communication with Adham somehow, and it made Kotler vacillate between disappointment in the researcher and wanting to find the man and tear him apart.

Time enough for that later. Barmoth would meet justice. For now, it was imperative that Kotler stick to the plan. Bringing down Adham was the priority of the moment.

Sifting through Barmoth's data, Kotler realized that the man was somehow flagging and tracking keywords in the reports from the other researchers. Kotler consulted with one of the IT personnel, and they found traces of a program running on all of the camp's computers, cataloging key terms and sending them back to Barmoth via an encrypted file, buried deep in the file structure of the camp's intranet. Barmoth would routinely open this file, transferring some of its contents into his own notes, tracking what others were producing. Core pieces of the information within the encrypted file were missing from Barmoth's research, however. It was this information that Barmoth was sending out of the camp.

That encrypted file was Kotler's way in.

Nothing in Barmoth's files indicated how he was communicating with Adham directly. There was still time to find that. For now, Kotler and the IT team were all set to start planting a few seeds, to see if they could get Barmoth to take them back to Adham.

Kotler contacted some friends in New York—among them a graphic designer he often worked with. He asked for some very specific designs, and within the day he had them.

From these he started building records. He created reports that were meant to be from various researchers on the project. Kotler varied details in these just enough to make it look like they were written by several different people. In each he planted the keywords that Barmoth was scanning for, which would guarantee they were scraped by his program and dumped into the encrypted file. Once these false records were finished, Kotler began seeding them among the various folders of the other researchers, making them blend in with existing reports, to give the impression that several people were sniffing out something new among the artifacts and symbols in the caves.

The trail Kotler was constructing came down to indications of another entrance to the river, north of the research site in Pueblo. Kotler's fake reports included phony speculations from the researchers about possible locations of a secondary entrance, including map coordinates. Among these was a predetermined spot where the DEA was already setting up shop, at Kotler and Sarge's request.

If Barmoth took the bait, and bought in to the story Kotler was weaving, he would leak the information to

Adham—assuming it was Barmoth who was acting as the mole. They still had no solid proof, and nothing was guaranteed yet.

If Barmoth did attempt to leak the information, however, they would be able to track how he was doing it. If Adham took the bait, then knowing how he was getting his information might eventually lead to his capture. It was a gamble all around, but worth it, by Kotler's estimate.

The information was in place. Now all they could do was watch and wait.

Kotler began spending more time with Sarge, who eventually softened a bit from the gruff jar-head persona to someone a little more relatable. It was clear he saw Kotler as a bug in a jar—something weird and unusual that he might study but wouldn't necessarily understand.

Kotler, in turn, stopped thinking of Sarge as a cliché, and started seeing him as a pretty bright man who happened to have a pretty rough and tough exterior. He knew tactics, and he understood the value of laying low and waiting. Kotler liked him.

Despite their mutual and growing good will, however, they were both feeling the strain of waiting for something—anything—to happen.

It had been nearly three days later and Barmoth had yet to make his move.

In that time, Kotler had been periodically seeding more reports to various researcher's personal folders, adding more detail to the narrative he was weaving. "Speculation" on where the second entrance to the river might be eventually grew into details and ideas that soon started to overlap, as if several of the researchers were inadvertently confirming the data. Kotler was hoping that this was all becoming too tempting to ignore, but he had started to worry that Barmoth wasn't buying it.

Just as Barmoth's encrypted file was filling with details about the river's alternate entrance, however, it was also building a second set of records on anything to do with the city of gold. This surprised Kotler. It showed a clearly divided agenda. The two ideas were not connected—at least, not for Adham. Barmoth was gathering data on both lines of research but segmenting it for some reason.

Was Barmoth double-dealing? Did he have another contact, besides Adham?

Kotler was puzzling over what all of this meant when one of Sarge's men reported that Barmoth was on the move and acting strangely.

Video cameras had been laced all over the camp by now, and the feeds were monitored not only by Sarge but by the DEA and FBI. It was definitely a surveillance state, within the borders of the dig. According to Sarge, there wasn't a space anywhere onsite that someone could wander without being monitored.

Or in Sarge's words, "There ain't a shallow spot to take a crap in this camp unless I can smell it."

The man was a poet.

True to that sentiment, as Barmoth moved around the camp they were able to switch between cameras and monitor his movements. Barmoth left the secured research area, checking out with security, and first made his way to his trailer. This, too, was a secured area, and guards on duty checked all bags and searched every person going in and out. Barmoth passed with no trouble.

He went into his trailer for a few minutes, and when he came back out he was wearing shorts, a T-shirt, and running shoes. Passing through security again, Barmoth started jogging around the makeshift avenues of the camp.

Again, they tracked his movements, and again everything seemed benign—until Barmoth stopped to tie his shoes, near one of the solar-powered lighting stations.

The lights were portable units with individual generators and batteries. They were mounted on small trailers and rolled into place to provide lighting to the entire camp. Six of the units were placed in various locations all around the site, which helped Sarge's men to monitor the area by video as well as patrolling on foot, even at night.

As Barmoth stooped beside one of the lights, he quickly looked around, checking is surroundings. When he seemed satisfied no one was watching he reached under the chassis of the small trailer, swept at the dirt with his hand, and then pulled a square panel away from the ground. He reached into a gap under the trailer and pulled out a smart tablet, then replaced the panel and covered it with the loose dirt again.

He sprinted now to one of the portable toilets nearby. He entered, closed the door behind him, and spent the next half hour inside.

"Well damn," Sarge said. "That's a boy that needs more fiber in his diet'."

"Looks like we've figured out how he's doing it," Kotler said. "He must have something very small—a micro-SD card, maybe. Something he could easily hide in the hem of a shirt or in a watch or something."

"I'll have to tell my men to start being more thorough," Sarge said grimly.

"Don't be too hard on them. A micro-SD card is smaller than the fingernail of your pinky." Kotler glanced as Sarge's meaty hands and shook his head. "Ok, smaller than the fingernail on most people's pinky fingers. Finding one hidden on someone would take a level of scrutiny the NSA would envy. You'd spend hours checking everyone going in and out of the secure sights here, and you might still miss it."

Sarge groused about this a bit, then said, "So what now?"

"Now we need to figure out the who and why," Kotler replied.

"The who is that terrorist *sombitch* Adham," Sarge growled. "The why don't matter one bit to me."

"It should," Kotler said. "We don't yet have the full story. We need to know what Adham has on him, if anything. Or what his other motives are. We need to know exactly what he's sharing."

Kotler turned to the IT guys. "Can we plant something on that tablet? A way to track what he's sending? Maybe relay it all back here?"

"No problem," one of the men said.

Kotler nodded. "Ok, then we wait a bit longer. I'll keep planting information and see what we get. In the meantime, we need to inform the DEA that Adham may be on his way."

"Should we call the FBI too?" Sarge asked.

Kotler shook his head. "I wouldn't. They ... well, let's just say the FBI and I seem to be at odds about some of this. Let the DEA call them."

"You sure don't mess around when it comes to getting yourself a mess'a enemies, do ya?" Sarge asked, laughing. "It's like you ain't even tryin'."

"I'm not," Kotler said. "Believe me. This all came looking for me, not the other way around. All I care about is getting Evelyn back safely. And I admit, I wouldn't mind seeing Adham and anyone he's working with put in a deep, dark cell somewhere."

Sarge nodded, and then grumbled some orders to his men. They jumped to, and within thirty minutes of Barmoth replacing the tablet under the trailer it was removed again, tracking software was added, and it was replaced as if it had never been touched.

Kotler and the IT team looked through the data stored on the tablet, verifying that Barmoth was in fact sharing the location of the river.

Oddly, he was also sending information about the city of gold—but not to the same IP address.

Kotler said nothing to the team. He would keep his observations to himself for the moment. Judging from what Kotler was observing, one fact became crystal clear.

Barmoth was serving two masters, and they each had separate agendas.

Chapter 17

"I shouldn't even be sharing this with you," Agent Carl Rickson said.

Denzel smiled. "I've lost count of how many times I've heard or said that phrase in the past month."

Rickson laughed. "Yeah, I know you've seen some heavy stuff lately. The only reason I'm comfortable sharing this is because you brought this case to me in the first place. Your friend, the researcher ..."

"Kotler," Denzel said.

"He's gotten us a big lead on Anwar Adham. This is a bit out of the DEA's purview, so we're bringing in you boys at the FBI. A joint operation."

"First I've heard of it," Denzel said. "No surprise."

"You still on Crispen's shit list?"

"Not sure," Denzel said. "I don't think it's quite like that. I think he wanted me out of this because I was starting to sympathize with Kotler. There's something going on there, and I haven't got the faintest clue what it is. But it's effectively put me out of the game."

"Well," Rickson said, "Do you want back in?"

Denzel laughed. "Sure. Who do I have to kill?"

"Maybe Anwar Adham," Rickson said. "I put in a special request to have you included on this operation, since you're already familiar with both our CI and our target."

"Nice of you," Denzel said. "What was the response?"

"Negative at first," Rickson said. "But my bosses are pushing. They know you brought this in, and they know what's at stake. You're not the only one who smells something rotten in the state of Colorado."

"Great," Denzel said. "So now what?"

"Thanks to your boy Kotler we have a lead on where Adham is going to be. We don't know a timeframe, but we have operatives strewn all over the area, watching closely. It's an isolated spot, so we don't anticipate there being any civilians to worry about. I'd like for you to be on this op, Roland. Do you feel up to it?"

"I'm good," Denzel said, flexing his arm a bit, and rolling his neck. "I still get a slight twinge from my shoulder, but physical therapy has helped. I was just cleared for full active duty again, so that isn't an obstacle. Getting permission from Crispen could be an issue."

"Not if the order comes from above his pay grade," Rickson said. "And my bosses tell me it will."

"Well then, that makes things easier," Denzel grinned. "Let's do this."

They chatted a bit more about the operation, about the information Kotler was sharing, and about a few personal matters. Denzel and Rickson had both served together in Special Forces and had seen some pretty serious shit during their tours. On the whole, Denzel was happy enough to be out of combat. As it turned out, life in the Bureau could be just as dangerous—and it had the added challenges of political manipulation. Something Denzel had no stomach for.

In fact, though he wouldn't tell Rickson or anyone else, he'd been thinking about moving on from the FBI. It wasn't something he necessarily wanted to do—he loved his work, and loved serving his country, and he felt the FBI really was the best fit for his skills as well as his temperament. He'd seen a bit of corruption take root in the Bureau lately, though. At least, he'd seen it in his own little corner of the agency. Where once he felt a camaraderie with the people he served alongside, he now felt a divide growing. A lot of that had to do with Director Crispen.

After getting back to New York, Denzel had laid low while finishing his PT and taking on light duty at the Bureau. He'd received a commendation for his actions in Pueblo, though he'd been lit into by Crispen for involving the DEA and for charging in on Adham without authorization. Still, he'd been shot in the line of duty, before the 'caverns of bullshit' incident, as Crispen called it. Taking a bullet while serving was something the FBI didn't like to gloss over.

For the most part, Denzel felt he was walking a thin line, balancing between doing his job with honor and keeping in Crispen's good graces. The fact that the two didn't necessarily overlap was part of what made Denzel consider leaving the agency.

Though at that thought, the question became where would he go? The DEA might be happy to take him in, but he wasn't entirely sure he wanted to spend his career busting drug runners. He'd done that for a time, and there was something to be said for taking those monsters off of the streets. It was too similar to being back in combat, though. He would be a soldier to the DEA. He was tired of being a soldier.

Denzel checked his watch and saw that he was nearing his usual PT time. Now that he was on full active duty again, the required PT had been reduced to just a couple of days per week. Denzel had kept it up daily. He remained on duty and on call during his hour-long sessions, but getting away from the office and into a gym was helping him with more than his physical recovery. These sessions were allowing him to blow off the growing stress of his job—something he'd never really felt before.

As he changed into gym togs and hit the weight machine, he thought about Kotler and the information that Rickson had shared.

Kotler was playing a pretty involved game of misdirection. If what Rickson said was true, Kotler might actually be responsible for taking out a very active terrorist cell on US soil. Considering Kotler's background as an independent researcher, that was pretty impressive. He would have made a good FBI agent, if he'd been inclined.

Denzel had to laugh about that. Kotler in the FBI was a worse fit than Denzel trying to wear Kotler's pants. It wasn't that Kotler was unqualified or couldn't do the job—Denzel had done Kotler's background check himself, and he knew what the man had gone through, the training he'd had, and what he was capable of. His skills weren't the issue.

Kotler wasn't just an independent researcher, he was just flat-out independent. He lived by a set of principles and personal rules, and those didn't always mesh well with structure or bureaucracy. Denzel couldn't imagine Kotler pulling on a dark suit and tie and taking orders without question. He wasn't the type and, if Denzel were being honest, it would make him less effective.

Kotler's strength came from that independence, in Denzel's estimate. It was part of what made Kotler so good at this. He was smart, and a tactical thinker. He was also constantly thinking outside of the restrictions placed on him. He knew how to put together pieces and solve a puzzle, and he wasn't afraid to step away from the safe and secure world of research and put himself in real danger—as long as the cause was worthwhile.

Denzel had read Kotler's file—which was actually quite long. The man had multiple PhDs, and he'd seen real action. He'd never served in the military, but had nonetheless found himself entrenched in armed conflict, and even tortured at the hands of the enemy.

What kind of man could do all that, and still bounce back to being someone who was completely fascinated with dead languages and dusty artifacts one minute, and particle accelerators and quantum computers the next? Denzel would never tell Kotler this, but the guy was probably one of the most impressive men Denzel had ever known.

Denzel shook himself. He would definitely never tell Kotler that.

The fact that Kotler was embroiled in this mess with Anwar Adham, primarily because of the actions of Director Crispen, was just infuriating. As far as Denzel was concerned, Crispen had put Kotler in danger, and then left him to be tortured by a known terrorist. It was unconscionable, if not criminal.

Since being back in New York, Denzel had more or less kept his head down. He wasn't tracking any of the information about the Adham case, nor about Horelica's abduction. And for the most part, no one was consulting him on either subject. Denzel felt a slight pang of regret about that,

however, since he had promised Kotler that he would
continue to help out.

It was time to keep that promise.

After his workout, Denzel showered and suited up, then
got back to the office. He slipped into the cubicle that served
as his desk, and opened his laptop, logging in to the Bureau
database. He was fairly certain he was being monitored, but
that was unavoidable. He was associated with these files, so
he could just make the case that he was tying up loose ends,
following up to make sure he hadn't left anything out.
Crispen might come down on him, but he could hardly
reprimand him for being thorough in his job.

He found himself locked out of some of the files. Not
altogether unexpected, but a bit annoying. It lent more
weight to Denzel's suspicion that he was being blocked, and
unduly. He didn't push, however. There was no point trying
to get at that information, if his superiors wanted him
locked out. It would just lead to trouble.

Instead, he started digging into related files—reports
that were tied to the events in Pueblo but did not mention
Adham or even Kotler directly.

He started with the file on the theft of the Coelho
Medallion.

The investigation had hit something of a stall, and
Denzel could see why: There was literally no evidence. In
fact, based on testimony from museum staff, a few patrons,
even some outside contractors, the medallion could just as
well have vanished by magic. Denzel wasn't quite ready to
believe that wizards had nabbed the medallion. Still, there
was precious little to go by.

The museum had shown no signs of forced entry, and
the internal security system had operated uninterrupted
throughout the evening of the theft. Denzel reviewed the

footage from the cameras. They showed no one entering or exiting the exhibit during the timeframe of the robbery. It wasn't until a security guard wandered through and noticed that the medallion was missing that the alarm was even raised. Less than half an hour later, Dr. Albert Shane, the museum's Curator of Human Origins, came bursting into the room and looking ready to vomit.

Denzel paused a frame of the video, showing the empty display case and Dr. Shane's reaction. He thumbed through one of the files and re-read the statements from everyone that had been interviewed during the case. There was nothing noteworthy. By all accounts, the medallion had been present at the close of the day's exhibit and had disappeared somehow before the first guard came through for the evening. Somehow the medallion had been removed from its display and carted away while the display itself was in full view of the security camera.

Like magic, Denzel said, shaking his head.

He turned back to the security footage, examining it closely. He skipped around, scrubbing the timeline from the museum's opening until Dr. Shane made his appearance. He couldn't see the medallion itself from this limited angle, but he could definitely see that large, highly-polished glass cube that enclosed the display. That glass was coated with a substance that made it nearly bulletproof—the same substance that was used on the windows of airports and government buildings—a polymer that could help spread the impact of a bullet and prevent the glass from shattering.

Despite being bulletproof, if there was an impact significant enough, it would leave a mark, such as a webbing of cracks or chips in the glass.

There wasn't a blemish on the glass, and it gleamed in the lights of the museum.

Lights, Denzel thought.

He jumped back in the footage, to earlier in the day. Museum patrons stood and gawked at the artifact, chattering to each other and then moving on to the next time of interest. Denzel had studied all of these patrons, searching to find some hint that one of them had somehow snuck the medallion into his or her pocket. But no one had even come close to the display, thanks to the velvet ropes stretching from brass stands, providing the impenetrable wall of social pressure, preventing anyone from so much as leaning into the space surrounding the exhibit.

He had studied all of these people over and over, finding nothing. Now, though, he ignored them, and instead studied the exhibit itself.

The room housing the glass display for the medallion was kept rather dark. The display itself was lit by an overhead light that shone brightly through the glass—a spotlight for the medallion, accentuated by the highly polished glass itself. As Denzel examined it, looking for new details, he noticed there was another light source reflecting from the glass. It made a yellow-tinted glint that was only just visible to this angle of the camera, and from its position it looked to be at a slight angle compared to the overhead spotlight.

Where was that second light coming from?

Denzel ran the footage forward, and the second light disappeared just after the exhibit closed.

He jogged even further along the timeline, looking for a reappearance of that light the next day, when the museum was opened again. After the alarm had been raised the previous night, the exhibit was secured, and only the NYPD was allowed inside until they brought Dr. Shane into the space, to get his statement.

The light never reappeared.

He sped things up again, watching as people flicked in and out of existence in the footage. He was starting to run out of video—the detectives on the scene had only requested footage for a 72-hour window, with the discovery of the medallion's theft in the middle.

As that window started to close, however, Denzel spotted something that seemed unusual, and so he stopped and ran the footage at regular speed.

The exhibit itself was closed now, and no one had entered the entire day, except for a maintenance crew. Denzel watched as a man set up a ladder next to the display and climbed it to work on something out of frame. From Denzel's perspective, the man was standing at the at the top of the screen, with his upper body off camera. As he stepped back down, fully into frame, he was holding some sort of small, metal cylinder, with a cable protruding from it. There was a bracket mounted to it, and the man was holding this like a handle.

Denzel froze the video and looked closer at the object in the man's hand. It looked like a small theater light, though it appeared to have multiple lenses. Denzel brought up the earlier from of the video, looking at the yellow glint of light. He was able to overlap this with the form of the man on the ladder, to determine the angle he was working at, where this light had been mounted. He flipped back and forth a few times and was finally certain.

The second light source.

The man wore a jumpsuit that had a name tag and logo on it. Denzel couldn't make out the name tag, but he recognized the logo. Jimenez Lighting. They were a local event lighting company that handled a lot of large venues. Denzel had cleared some of their personnel for big events in the past, including times when they were setting up lighting for high-profile visitors to the city. Denzel had been one of a handful of agents running background checks on vendors and crew for a large chess match that had attracted the attention of the President of the United States, several months back.

The President had a real love for chess, and the event had brought out a large crowd that had to be searched and scanned before they were allowed to enter. Jimenez Lighting had been one of the vendors on the list that Denzel had vetted, prior to the event. He knew some of their people.

He picked up the phone and started making a few phone calls. First, he called Jimenez Lighting and talked to Amanda Jessup, the Jimenez office manager, to find out who they'd had on duty at the museum on that date. That turned out to be a dead end. "We don't have any record of service at the museum," he was told. "We don't have a contract with them."

That was curious.

Denzel's next call was to the museum itself, and they showed no record of any lighting company—Jimenez or otherwise—being onsite that day.

Denzel turned back to the video. There wasn't enough. He would need access to the weeks prior to the theft.

The museum kept digital archives of everything, and Denzel requested full access. Fortunately, they kept secure digital backups offsite, accessible by remote. The museum's head of security granted the FBI full access, and within an hour Denzel was able to pull up footage from as far back as the archives would allow.

Early in the investigation, NYPD Detectives had looked at footage for a few weeks prior to the theft, to determine if anyone had been lingering, gathering intel on the exhibit.

No one had bothered going more than those few weeks back, however, because there hadn't been need. They ultimately found nothing to hint that someone might have cased the exhibit in the weeks prior to the theft.

No one else had noticed that second light until now.

Denzel scrubbed through the video as quickly as he could. He was lucky to have the second light as his marker. Even at high speed, with hundreds of people moving around the exhibit throughout the day, the glint of the lights remained stationary. Denzel was able to follow them all the way back until, suddenly, the second light disappeared again.

Or rather, as he stopped the footage and sped forward again, it appeared for the first time. In fact, it not only popped into frame, it *moved*.

Denzel slowed the footage, letting it run at normal speed. As he watched, another Jimenez Lighting crew came in, set up a ladder, and started messing around out of frame. Unlike what Denzel had seen following the theft, this time the second light made its appearance for the first time.

It glinted on the edge of the case, jiggling as the man did something off camera, and then slowly slid into its new position, where Denzel had first noticed it.

Over the following minutes there were several small adjustments, but eventually the light was steady. The man climbed down from the ladder, and this time Denzel got a very good still frame of his face. He would run this through the FBI's facial identification database later. For now, Denzel kept his eye on the display.

Nothing happened for about an hour. The museum shut down, and the lights dimmed even further. The spotlight and the second golden light were both still in place, however.

Denzel sped up the footage to about four times normal speed and kept his eyes on the display.

Several hours after the museum had closed, a security guard entered the room. Denzel stopped, jumped back a bit, and played the footage at normal speed.

The guard did something at the security panel, which was several feet from the display, and only just in frame. It was impossible to see exactly what the guard was doing, but as he finished he turned and walked to the display itself. He used a key to unlock the base of the display, then lifted the glass cube up and away. He reached in and simply grabbed and pocketed the medallion.

Denzel couldn't believe what he was seeing.

The guard replaced and locked the case, and went back to the panel, reactivating the security system, apparently continuing his rounds as if nothing had changed.

Denzel sped the footage to the point just as the museum reopened.

No one seemed to even notice that the medallion was no longer in the case.

Denzel rolled back to the moment when the guard had pocketed the medallion, watching it again frame by frame. He studied every move the guard made, which was well lit and in full view of the CCTV.

He rolled it back and watched again. And again. He repeated this several times before deciding that what he'd seen was what had actually happened.

The guard hadn't replaced the medallion, after taking it. There was no swap. No dummy version. He'd left the case completely empty.

Denzel made notes about the guard, grabbing a still from the video to both run through facial recognition and to use for identification among the museum staff. He looked now at the face of the guard, studying him.

He had no idea how, but this man had managed to steal the medallion weeks before it was reported missing. Denzel would find how. More importantly, however, he intended to find out why.

PART III

Chapter 18

VICTOR WAS NOT GENERALLY GIVEN to impatience.

He would often deny himself something he truly wanted for long stretches of time, just to heighten the experience when he finally got what he wanted. He would do this for days, sometimes for a week, maybe two. But this ...

It had been almost two months now. Even Victor's patience was starting to wear thin.

If only Evelyn did anything other than work.

She kept herself busy. To Victor, it appeared she was trying to forget her situation by burying herself in the work. Only the work. She didn't even try to make contact with the outside world. She never attempted escape. The most she ever diverged from the research was when she was eating, sleeping, or exercising.

In a way, this was fascinating. Victor watched her closely in the beginning—studying her, measuring her, fantasizing about her. He did as he always did and restrained himself to the point that his nerves were on fire, and there was a tingle in his very blood.

But his patience was fading.

His employer wouldn't allow him to simply take action, of course. The job had to be finished. Regardless of his impatience, the work, the mission, came first. Victor was a professional.

He had to be. If he got a reputation for jumping the gun, for satisfying his own urges at the expense of the work, it would be the end of his career. He'd have to go back to stalking and hunting all on his own. He'd have to go back to the days of tracking his prey in public, where the dangers were greater, and the risks of being discovered, caught, imprisoned, were much higher.

He could wait. The fire within him would fuel him, not consume him. He would use it to improve, to grow. He would use the fire the purify himself, so that he would be an even better hunter.

As he watched Evelyn work, watched her from every possible angle, he couldn't help but feel the pulse of her. He felt it throbbing within him, syncing with his own heartbeat.

It was distracting.

But soon.

The task would be done. Victor could claim his bonus.

All of the waiting would make it taste all that much sweeter.

Evelyn was going stir crazy.

She was comfortable with long stretches of isolation—she was a researcher and a linguist. You spend a lot of time alone. However …

It was one thing to be in the flow of the work, no longer noticing the world around you because you're so interested, so focused, so absorbed in the work. This forced isolation was different. She was working completely in a vacuum. She had no one else to share her ideas with, no one to turn to when she was feeling lost or stuck or simply lonely. Even prisoners in solitary confinement were given some reprieve, even if it was the voice of a guard. Evelyn hadn't heard another human voice for ...

It had been several weeks now. Well over a month. Maybe two? It was hard to tell because the clocks and calendars on the computer and the smart tablet were constantly being reset. Whoever was on the other side of the walls of her prison intended to keep her disoriented.

To keep her head clear, she kept certain facts in focus. The research, of course. Also her circumstances. She'd been forced into labor, with no real hope of escape, and she still had no idea who was doing it or why, but keeping the fact of her abduction to of mind helped her to remember to stay alert, to look for clues and resources and opportunities her captor might not recognize.

And actually, she did know the why. Or at least, she thought she did.

She was now certain that her captor wanted the city of gold. She was also certain that they were feeding her information directly from the Pueblo site. Which meant there was someone at that site who was working with her abductor. A mole. Or, for all she knew, Dr. Coelho himself could be working with her abductor. She rejected this idea, though. Eloi was such a kind man, and though they knew each other primarily through their work, she was sure she knew him well enough to eliminate him as having a role in this. The odds, then, favored someone working secretly within the dig site, stealing information to share with whoever was behind all of this.

The information coming to her was nearly always

related to the city of gold, in some way. The city was the goal.

The problem, however, was that the city of gold was not what her captor—what anyone—thought it was.

Evelyn had worked out what the city was, though, and she knew that if she revealed the truth her abductor would have no further use for her.

In any other circumstance, Evelyn was pretty sure she'd have a good laugh over what the city actually was. It was like a big historic pun or the punchline of an anthropology joke. She was pretty sure that Dan would have found hysterical. Eloi Coelho himself would have had a good laugh.

That was what made this all the more dangerous. Whoever had her abducted was after something that didn't really exist, that would ultimately make them look foolish. There was no way to know how that person would react, but Evelyn couldn't imagine that it would be good.

Keeping the location of the city to herself, and especially keeping the real nature of the city a secret, might be the only thing keeping her alive.

For now, she had to keep doing the work, and keep up the translations and the searching, as if she were right on the verge of unlocking everything. All this, while keeping the truth buried. It was a difficult balancing act, to uncover more and more but reveal less and less. She wasn't sure how much longer she could hold out.

She was getting to a point where details were starting to get thin. She could hold out for a bit longer. She could keep playing this information game for a while more. She could keep fooling her abductor for a time. But time was starting to run short, and she knew it.

Evelyn was thinking of ways she could keep up the

charade, to keep making "discoveries" about the city of gold, when something very strange started happening.

The information she was getting about the city of gold changed.

The reports were filled with new evidence—translations of artifacts that led to the inescapable conclusion that there really was a city of gold out there, and that it was exactly what her abductor was hoping for. Details were arriving that supported what Evelyn knew to be an impossible conclusion—that *El Dorado* was real, and that the Pueblo site was just one path to reach it.

It was confusing, and even a little alarming. Had she been wrong? She checked and rechecked her initial translations, and no, she'd gotten everything right. The runes, the Native American symbols, none of the symbology from the dig site supported the discovery of *El Dorado*. It was impossible.

The data just kept coming.

Day after day now, a deluge of new information flooded in. She was suddenly finding herself verifying translations made by someone else more than translating new finds herself. It was a strangely familiar experience, and a little exhilarating, if she was to be honest about it. This new flood of data and information was a welcome shift, and she felt almost as if her isolation were over. Even better, she was starting to see an interesting pattern to the information.

Someone out there was lying.

She'd seen and studied every scrap of information about the medallion and the figurehead to date. She'd studied scans of the totem and had determined that the runes and symbols carved into it were copies, likely interpretations from native cultures, replicating what they'd seen among the Vikings. She knew from what she'd read from the files of the site's researchers, and uncovered from her own work, that every artifact or carving or random piece of stonework from the Pueblo site told essentially the same story. She knew what the city of gold really was. This new information contradicted nearly all of that.

Eventually, gradually, Evelyn realized that this new information was being planted by someone. Someone, it was clear, who knew what he was talking about.

These markings and symbols, as well as the interpretations of them, were perfect. They were exactly the sort of runes one would expect to find in a Viking camp, and they pointed the way to a vast city with fortress walls shrouded in gold. They talked of vaults of the stuff, as if someone had transported Fort Knox back in time and let the raiders have at it.

The runes and markings were perfect, but they were also lies. Because they indicated a literal city of gold, when Evelyn knew for a fact that wasn't the case. There was no doubt whatsoever that the city of gold was in no way what this current influx of data and findings would indicate. So, someone with full access to the Pueblo site as well as any related research, and with an intimate knowledge of Viking culture, symbology, and anthropology ... someone was feeding the bad guys a load of bullshit.

She only knew of one person connected to this research who could fabricate a story like this and get it so perfect, and the realization that it was him made Evelyn smile.

Dan Kotler was out there.

She didn't know why he was doing it, or how, but she knew he was involved. She could tell by the syntax of the research, the timbre of the notes and observations, even though they were masked and altered to sound as if they came from multiple sources. The story itself was carefully constructed in the same way Dan would have built a narrative around an archeological find. She'd seen him do this a thousand times. She knew his work as intimately as she knew her own.

She nearly started crying when she realized it.

This was like getting a letter from home, telling her that everyone was ok. It was like seeing a distant ship on the horizon headed toward the deserted island where she'd found herself washed up and struggling to survive. This was Dan sending her a message!

Or ...

Well, no, that didn't make sense. He wasn't sending this to her. Why would he? He would likely have no idea where she was. It didn't seem feasible that he'd worked out how to get a message to her. The information coming in bore nothing personal, nothing that indicated he knew it would be here reading it. If Dan was trying to reach her, she was sure he'd use some code, some contextual reference that she'd recognize. It was unlikely that he'd done this as a message to her.

So Dan was doing this for some other reason. He had some other purpose in mind, and it required him to lay out an elaborate but false story about the one thing her abductor was after. As Evelyn thought about it, the only logical explanation was that he was laying a trap.

It was an intriguing thought, but the next one had her pulse smoking. Dan had no way of knowing, but his trap would depend entirely on her now. She could help make his ruse all the more convincing, by playing along with it. She could help shape the story, so that her abductor would make a misstep. The power to save herself was now in her hands.

Suddenly all Evelyn wanted in the world was to talk to Dan Kotler, to ask what he was planning, and to see how she could help. She wanted to pick up a phone or, at the very least, send him an email. She'd never be allowed to do either, of course.

If only she could respond!

And then, she realized that maybe she could.

She turned to the computer she was using to log her work and opened the word processor. She was pretty sure that her every keystroke was being recorded, so she had never bothered to try to hide any sort of message before. Who would see it anyway? Everything she wrote would go no further than the yes on the other side of the screen, the person or the people who had her locked away in here, toiling to solve a riddle on their behalf.

Except now, as she saw Dan's trap being laid out, she realized she might be able to communicate after all. It wouldn't be direct. She'd have to be incredibly subtle. But if she did this just right, she might be able to at least send a signal to Dan, to tell him that she was ok. That was a start.

She started typing.

This was delicate work, and she had to pause several times to think out what she should write. It took hours, but after a time she was finally getting somewhere.

She started by correcting a few things, just minor details in the translations. She worked in alternative interpretations, explaining the errors of the initial reports in language she and Kotler had used together numerous times, elaborating on a point the way she always did when she meant to annoy Dan. She corrected him, though subtly. Then, to ensure the message would be sent, she asked numerous open-ended clarifying questions. She needed more information, she claimed. She needed access to more reports, and she needed certain points clarified. She needed to consult with the people writing these observations, if her captor was ever going to get to the prize.

It was a gamble. She was taking a risk, by pushing back and asking for more information. She might inadvertently ruin whatever trap Kotler was laying. As she saw it, though, her time here was running out. If she couldn't produce results soon, she might outlive her usefulness. This, at least, was a fresh new avenue to explore. Leveraging this new information, she might be able to buy more time. Even better, she might be able to signal Dan and bring some help.

She realized, after saving the document and sitting back from the computer, that it didn't really matter what the outcome was. She was done with this place. She was tired and starting to run short on caring about self-preservation. She needed out, one way or another. She needed to take back some ownership over her life.

This was the first opportunity that had presented itself, and she was taking it.

Chapter 19

KOTLER WASN'T ALLOWED to be directly involved with the operation, but he was able to tag along at least as far as one of the observation vans. He had to admit, this was actually an interesting experience all on its own. He and two DEA agents sat in a large van surrounded by surveillance equipment, and it was every bit as dramatic as what he'd seen in the movies or on TV.

The agents seemed to get bored after a couple of hours, but Kotler was still excited and riveted. He would freely admit that he was often impatient, preferring to jump into action and put his hands in the dirt, so to speak, rather than sit back and watch.

Sitting here, however, with dozens of screens giving him different viewpoints on an actual DEA sting operation, was something new and interesting. It was a bit like sitting among the members of some strange culture or tribe as they practiced some ancient, undiscovered ritual. As an anthropologist, Kotler was practiced and studied in being able to stay still and observe, to take in every detail even if he might rather be participating in the action. It was a bonus that this scenario was intriguing to him. It made him pay closer attention.

Which was why it was Kotler, and not the agents, who was the first to spot the men crawling commando style through the underbrush.

"There," Kotler said, pointing to a screen. "There's movement there, and it isn't a small animal."

One of the agents increased the gain on the night vision and slowly zoomed in on the spot Kotler had pointed to. As they watched, at least three men crawled past a tiny gap in the brush and stone, worming their way toward the cave that the DEA was using as bait.

Kotler was now watching some of the other monitors, with feeds coming in from several miles away. It took several moments, but he was able to spot four vehicles parked and covered with brush. Poor camouflage, if this had been during the day. But at night they blended almost seamlessly into the rugged landscape. Kotler again pointed to the screen, and the agents began chattering into radios and phones.

A voice came back over the line. "Do we have eyes on Adham?"

"Negative, cannot confirm," the agent said.

This entire operation would be a bust if Adham wasn't one of the men they took down tonight. It might do some damage to his organization, if the DEA removed a few players from his team. But like the mythical Hydra, Kotler was certain that for every head they removed two more would grow back. They would have to go for the trunk of the beast—their leader—and take him out of play.

Theirs was not the only DEA surveillance vehicle operating that night. On the far side of the valley was another team, and they were sharing some of their information now.

Another small cluster of vehicles had been spotted, though these were on the move. They were positioning themselves a mile or so from the caves. The agents sitting with Kotler pulled up a feed that was streaming live from the other team's cameras.

The footage was a bit shaky because it was coming from a helmet cam, worn by one of the agents who was wriggling his way along the ground toward Adham's men. There were three such teams at the ready, moving around under the cover of the desert and mountains. The agents in Kotler's van were starting to get reports from these teams, and the numerous displays lining the van's interior began to light up and rotate between stationary cameras and helmet cams.

Kotler watched in fascination, and in hope. They needed Adham to make just one mistake. He needed to show himself, here and now. Kotler hoped that the bait he'd planted was enticing enough to get the man himself on site.

Several minutes went by. It was obvious that Adham had suspected this could be a trap, based on the way his men were making their approach. Two different teams were in motion—one closing in on the caves and the other hanging back, ready to either roll forward or make a retreat. They could be commanded remotely, if Adham was being cautious.

Kotler studied the screens, flicking from one to another in a near constant movement that was starting to make him feel nauseated. He breathed shallowly, feeling beads of sweat breaking on his forehead, and concentrated on the details.

"There," he whispered.

It was brief, almost instantaneous—not much more than two or three frames of video. But Kotler would know that face anywhere. He'd studied it, during his captivity.

Adham was here.

He pointed to the screen, and the DEA agents started the wheels turning. They would strike both groups simultaneously, in a coordinated attack. The primary objective was to capture Anwar Adham, alive if possible.

Kotler tensed as the action started. Part of him wanted to be out there, dodging bullets and returning fire. He could handle it—he'd done it before. It wasn't his favorite hobby, of course. He wasn't fond of being shot at. But this ...

This was too personal, ultimately. Given Kotler's history with Adham, there was too much risk that he'd make a mistake.

Of course, there was the fact that the DEA had no intention of issuing him a weapon and putting him in the field. He was a civilian. No clearance. He was also an asset, as the only one who had actually had direct experience with Adham, and who could identify him on sight.

Kotler resigned himself to the inevitable and embraced his role as a set of eyes at the DEA's disposal.

The night vision cameras were suddenly being washed out by flashes of gunfire and spotlights flaring to life, throwing the landscape into near daylight brightness. The agents in Kotler's van were franticly calling out instructions, offering intelligence and giving direction, switching cameras and talking to both the infield agents and their remote offices. Kotler was focusing only on those cameras that showed Adham's position.

In moments, the whole operation was over. The constant noise, which Kotler hadn't even noticed at the time, became a dense silence that called attention to itself. The images on screen reverted back to calmer actions. A mix of night vision and unfiltered cameras showed the smoky landscape and the deft movements of the DEA teams.

The enemy combatants near the cave entrance had all been apprehended. No deaths from that group.

Those men who had been flanking Adham had suffered heavy casualties, however. Kotler found himself secretly praying that Adham had survived. After everything he'd been through at Adham's hands, Kotler just wanted the man to be alive, so that he could suffer in a cell buried in some deep hole somewhere in an American prison. He wanted to face the man while Adham himself was in chains. It might be a bit petty. He couldn't think of a better way to greet his *old friend*, however, than to see him haggard and bound and facing life in prison.

The DEA agents closed up shop and drove the van to where the field teams had gathered. They had moved all of Adham's men—those who had survived—to a secure location. Agents would remain behind at the scene to arrange for bodies to be recovered.

A great number of Adham's men were severely wounded, and they were getting medical care. A triage had been set up in the impromptu camp, and medics were rushing from patient to patient, patching and sewing wounds, administering IVs, and speaking in that uniquely succinct patter that the medical profession relies on.

Kotler wasn't interested in any of this.

He had an escort—one of the DEA agents who had been with him in the surveillance van. Kotler wasn't sure if the agent was with him for his protection or for Adham's. It could go either way.

They came to a large panel van that was being used for interrogation, and when Kotler stepped up and into it he froze.

There, his head sagging and his clothes stained in dirt and blood, was ...

Not Adham.

He looked like Adham. In fact, under the right conditions—say, if one were looking at him through the lens of a helmet camera, broadcasting a night vision view of the man over several miles—he was the spitting image of Adham. It was instantly clear to Kotler, though, that this man was a decoy.

"It's not him," Kotler said quietly. "That's not Anwar Adham."

"Sir!" one of the DEA agents yelled into the van.

Kotler and his escort both turned.

"We just got a report from the Pueblo site! It's been hit!"

The lead agent cursed under his breath and turned back to Kotler. "They figured us out," he growled. "This was a trap, alright. But it just sprung on us."

Chapter 20

AGENT DENZEL WATCHED the museum guard fidget. The guard was in a small room that was typically used by the museum as a sort of informal conference room—a place for some of the staff to meet with cups of coffee in hand to discuss policies on being late to work, on keeping the museum floors clean, on what to do if a kid vomits on an exhibit. There were posters on the walls that talked about employee rights and demonstrated how to give the Heimlich maneuver if someone was choking.

Denzel had set up a camera in the room, and was broadcasting the feed to Dr. Shane's office, where the two of them sat and watched.

"I don't understand," Shane said. "Why aren't you questioning him?"

"Right now, he's confident," Denzel said. "He doesn't think we have anything on him. But there's probably a bit of worry in there somewhere. I'm waiting for that to start gnawing at him a little."

"It's been nearly two hours," Shane said. "I have a museum to run."

"Go about business as usual, Dr. Shane," Denzel said. "You were the one who insisted on being here to watch the interrogation."

"I wanted to ensure one of my people was treated fairly," Shane replied.

Denzel nodded. "You have my word. You've also seen the footage."

"I still don't understand what it means," Dr. Shane said.

"It's clear he took the medallion, so at the very least I'll be arresting him for that," Denzel said. "What I need now is to know how he did it, where he took it, and who he's working for. This case is tied to an abduction, as well as to some events transpiring in Pueblo. As such, it has to be handled delicately. That takes time."

Denzel didn't mention the other reasons this case needed a delicate touch. He wasn't even sure what he thought of it. As he'd looked closer into the details of this case, however, it had become obvious that this security guard could not have organized any of this on his own. It had become clear as well that there was someone at the top of this, someone with the authority and the power to ensure that certain bits of information got from place to place and hand to hand. Denzel was almost sure he knew who that was, he was just having a hard time believing it.

Denzel had managed to get clearance to bring two more agents with him to the museum. One was standing just outside the door where the guard was waiting to be interrogated. The other was in the exhibit room where the medallion had been stolen, seeing if there was any way to determine what it was the fake Jimenez Lighting crew had taken down from above the display.

Another forty-five minutes went by, and the museum guard was getting antsy. He got up and started moving around in the room, reading from some of the posters, pouring himself another cup of coffee—his third, Denzel noted. That was good. More coffee meant more jitters, and jitters were an interrogator's best friend.

Denzel waited just a bit more, until he saw the guard's fingers tapping absently on the Formica tabletop, and then went into the room himself.

The guard's name was Ernest Crantz. He was a little less than average height, but Denzel knew from his records that he suffered from a bit of 'short man syndrome.' He had a hot temper, had a few fist fights in high school, and had washed out of the police academy because he couldn't tolerate the instructors yelling at him. Crantz had mouthed off one too many times and found himself applying to be a museum security guard a few days after washing out of the academy.

Denzel had a pretty complete file on Crantz. What he couldn't determine from that, though, was who Crantz might have been in contact with—who might have paid him to steal the Coelho Medallion.

And he had been paid, that much Denzel knew for certain. In the space of a month, Crantz suddenly had a retirement fund bulging with over a million dollars. It wasn't enough for him to leave his job and still stay in Manhattan —cost of living alone prevented that. But it would be a nice life on the beach somewhere, in just a few years of compounding interest.

That money had been in high need, too. Judging by his financials, the man had never put a dime into savings in his life. He had a mountain of credit card debt, with a handful of maxed-out cards, some of which were in default. All Crantz had to do, however, was hold out for just a short time, suck up the job for just a while longer, and he could walk away for good.

That was speculation on Denzel's part. For all he really
knew, Crantz might be smart enough to know that quitting
his job after the theft of such a prominent exhibit might tip
people off. Or, if he wasn't smart enough to come to that on
his own, he might have been counseled by his benefactor.

The only thing Denzel knew for sure was that Crantz
wasn't staying here because he loved his work. There were
dozens of complaints about him being a little overzealous
with museum patrons and staff. His personnel reviews
contained a number of dings that might not have been
enough to fire him, but it had been justification enough to
deny him several raises and promotions.

More recently, within the past year, there were several
notes in his file about time off for medical care. There was
no list of a cause, but there were numerous notes from
doctors, as well as requests for reimbursement for reim-
bursements on prescription costs. Crantz was sick, and it
was serious enough that it was occasionally taking him away
from work.

The combination of his dicey financials, his poor work
performance, and his medical condition had all the
earmarks of Crantz being the perfect inside man. He might
be willing to risk everything for the right price. Someone
had sought him out and approached him with just the right
opportunity.

Denzel entered the room and smiled at Crantz. "I apologize for the wait," he said.

"I've been in here for almost three hours!" Crantz said. "I
have work to do!"

"Yes," Denzel nodded. He shuffled through the file
folder in his hand, then looked up at Crantz with a friendly
expression. "You've been with the museum for several years,
haven't you?" Denzel took a seat across the table from

Crantz and took out his notepad. He would take notes, of course, but he mostly wanted to show Crantz that this was Denzel's show. The notebook, Denzel knew, looked very official. Official things tended to add pressure to an interrogation. It was also human nature to accept that the one asking the questions as the one in charge.

"Yeah," Crantz said, suddenly cautious. "Almost ten years now."

"That's a long time," Denzel nodded. "Do you ever regret leaving the police academy?"

"No," Crantz replied, though Denzel could hear in his voice that he certainly resented it.

"You were on duty the night the medallion was stolen, correct?"

"Yeah," Crantz said. "My route was the East wing. There were still a few patrons hanging around and I had to move 'em along. I told this to the police already."

Denzel nodded. "There are a lot of witnesses who put you in that part of the museum, actually. Definitely a solid alibi."

There was a brief flicker of confusion on Crantz's face, followed by a subtle smile. "Right," he said. "So, what can I do for you, Agent Denzel?"

"Your whereabouts on the night the theft was reported are established, but I'm interested in where you were about two weeks prior."

"Two weeks?" Crantz thought about this and shrugged. "No idea."

Denzel nodded and made a note in his notebook, which made Crantz strain for a peek. Denzel kept the notebook obscured, then said, "I think I can help."

There was a television mounted on the wall of the conference room, used for showing training videos and presentations. Denzel had set up his own presentation in advance. He picked up the remote from the table and turned on the television, revealing a still frame of Crantz, with his hand on the medallion, just prior to shoving it in his pocket.

"Can you identify the man on screen, Mr. Crantz?"

Crantz stared, slack jawed, at the image in front of him, then slowly shook his head. "That ..." he started, but never finished. He looked back at Denzel, then shook his head.

"You don't recognize yourself on that screen, Mr. Crantz?"

"I want a lawyer," Crantz said.

"You'll have one," Denzel said. "Will you be paying him with the money you recently put in your retirement account?"

Again, Crantz said nothing.

Denzel knew he was on shaky ground. Now that Crantz had asked for a lawyer, technically Denzel was required to withdraw. He more than enough evidence to arrest Crantz and take him in for further questioning, with his lawyer present, but he wanted to delay that for as long as possible. He wanted Crantz here, in this place he hated, looking at himself on a monitor he'd probably stared at blankly a thousand times in ten years, watching ridiculous safety training videos or sitting through mandated sensitivity training. Denzel wanted Crantz to remember exactly where he was, and how much he hated the place, and why he'd taken that deal.

"There's a way out for you, if you cooperate," Denzel said.

This was where things could get tricky. He wasn't techni-cally authorized to make any deals, but he could offer to put in a good word, at least, and that did actually carry some weight. Denzel was gambling it would be enough.

He had Crantz's attention. The man wasn't looking at him directly, but he had stiffened, had turned his head just slightly, his ear oriented toward Denzel and whatever hope the agent might offer.

Denzel might not be quite as proficient at ready body language as Kotler, but he knew a thing or two. Crantz was listening.

"I need to know who paid you, and who you gave that medallion to, after you stole it."

Crantz was now staring at his hands, which were worrying their way around a Styrofoam coffee cup.

"In a minute, Mr. Crantz, I'm going to call in the other two agents I brought with me. We're going to put you in handcuffs and walk you through that museum, in front of the museum patrons and your co-workers, right out to a car we have parked on the street. That's going to happen, either way. What happens after that is up to you. I need to know who put you up to this."

"I don't know," Crantz said, suddenly but quietly. "He ..." there was a pause as Crantz took a shuddering breath. For once in his life he was keeping his temper in check, knowing full well that lashing out at the FBI was only going to end in more trouble. "He contacted me through someone else. A kid. He came up to me one day as I was making my rounds and handed me an envelope. It had instructions, and a phone number for me to call."

"Do you still have the number?"

Crantz nodded. "It's in my phone."

Denzel motioned with his hand, and Crantz reached into his pocket and removed a mobile phone—one of those prepaid smartphones with no contract. He handed this to Denzel. "It's the one named 'The Guy.'"

Denzel marveled at this. Crantz had not only left incriminating evidence right on his phone, he'd named the contact something that anyone in law enforcement would immediately assume was a drug dealer or worse.

Denzel took a small, plastic evidence bag out of his suit pocket and used his pen to slide the phone inside. He would tag it and run the number later, though he wasn't sure it would lead anywhere useful. Whoever had organized this was smart enough to arrange a throwaway number.

"When you spoke to ... *the guy* ... what did he tell you?"

Crantz shook his head, perhaps trying to deny any of this was happening. "He didn't say much. The instructions were in the envelope. He read off a bank account number. It was my retirement account. He said that he could arrange for half-a-million dollars to be in that account in 24 hours if I agreed to do the job, and another half-a-million once the medallion was in his hands. All I had to do was let in a lighting crew, and then grab the medallion a little later."

"Tell me about the lighting crew," Denzel said.

Crantz shrugged. "They were sharp guys. Definitely pros. They came in with just what they needed, and they did the work fast. I was really surprised when I took the medallion, because that projector made it look like it was still there, once the glass was back in place."

Denzel was surprised. "A projector?"

Crantz nodded.

Denzel thought for a moment, "So the equipment they installed was a projecting an image of the medallion on the glass case? A hologram?"

"Yeah," Crantz said, and he broke into a smile. "Look, I know I'm busted here, ok? And I'm sorry. But that was just cool. For two weeks everyone was paying to see a light show, and nobody knew it!"

"No one except you," Denzel said.

"Right," Crantz said, his expression turning sour again.

Denzel noted all of this, then asked, "What can you tell me about the lighting crew itself? How many men were there? Can you identify them?"

Crantz shook his head. "Three guys, but I didn't know them. I only saw one of their faces. They came here twice."

"Could you describe the face to a sketch artist?"

"Maybe," Crantz said. He was once again looking deflated.

Denzel made a note to have him sit down with an artist, and with the suspect identification system. He already had a screenshot of the man's face, but it couldn't hurt to get more detail.

So far, the database hadn't turned up anyone who matched the suspect's facial features. If this guy was a pro, he hadn't yet come onto the FBI's radar. At this point, Denzel was hoping for a lucky break.

He wrapped up the interrogation with Crantz and had the other two agents take him away. He also retrieved the camera, which had a full recording of the interview. He would log this into evidence as well.

This whole operation was very well done, well organized. It had an almost *Ocean's Eleven* vibe, but it didn't feel like the typical heist. The men who had installed the equipment were of the "for hire" variety. Which meant they were working for whoever Crantz's mysterious benefactor was. If Crantz was paid a million, the pros who had installed that holographic projector had to have been paid considerably more.

From this, Denzel was able to imagine a Venn diagram

of sorts. In one circle was everyone who had the financial resources to pull off this type of job, with millions being paid out to everyone involved. The other circle contained people who would be interested to the point of obsession with obtaining an ancient artifact. In the middle was ...

Well, Denzel couldn't think of many people who had both the money and the inclination to do this. But one name did occur to him. It was a difficult one to believe, but it fit.

Mark Cantor.

Denzel knew it was a stretch, considering Cantor was the one funding the Pueblo dig in the first place. What would be his motive? Why hadn't he simply kept the medallion, when it was first discovered?

There was no clear line on motive, and Denzel would have to work on that. He did have some theories about why Cantor wouldn't have held on to the medallion.

As Denzel had looked closer at evidence in this case, he'd come across a fact that, at first, he hadn't given much attention to. Cantor was providing the funding behind the Pueblo dig, but it hadn't started that way. He'd become involved later, after the first few artifacts and been uncovered in the region. He had approached Dr. Coelho with an offer to fund the research, and of course Coelho had accepted. A well-funded dig, with the backing of an internet billionaire, not only helped things financially, but also added a layer good publicity for the research. It was Cantor's involvement that had, in part, been the catalyst for the explosion of public interest.

And then there was the medallion.

The discovery had been so grand and so intriguing, it had sparked an instant love affair with the idea of Vikings in North America. The public was paying close attention now, eager to consume any shred of information they could get from the site. It would have been impossible for Cantor to keep the medallion tucked away for himself, with so many people watching with bated breath, studying the site from their living rooms and mobile phones.

It meant that if Cantor wanted exclusive access to the medallion, he would be in the awkward position of having to steal his own artifact.

Which brought Denzel back to motive.

What did Cantor gain by having the Coelho Medallion in his personal collection, rather than having it on display in the museum. He was a billionaire, so money shouldn't be a factor. Was it simply avarice? Pride of ownership? Selfish greed?

Or ...

Denzel remembered something Kotler had said, about zebras and horses. At the moment, Denzel was hearing the sounds of hooves, and jumping to conclusions. He needed to step back, to consider every possibility.

With Crantz in custody, Denzel finished up at the museum, thanked Dr. Shane for his cooperation, and returned to the Bureau offices. He took great pains to move through the office as discretely as possible, swinging by his disk to snag his laptop, before slipping into one of the windowless rooms they often used for questioning suspects or for privacy when working with sensitive information. Once the door was closed and locked behind him, he immediately logged into the FBI database and ran a background check on Mark Cantor. There was a lot of information to sift through, so Denzel opted to go for the highlights.

Mark Cantor had made his billions from software development. Zelot, his social media network for academics, was something of a loss leader for Cantor's business. It didn't really make any profits. Cantor kept funding the site because of, as he stated publicly numerous times, his "passion for academic research and scientific inquiry."

While that sentiment might simply be good PR, by Denzel's estimate, it was clear that the site was also a proving ground for some of the technologies that Cantor did make money on.

Here, Zelot was a goldmine. Cantor could release beta versions of his software to a group of intelligent, detail-oriented users who were entrenched in a Pavlovian social media culture of over-sharing their opinions with no compensation. It was like having a free quality assurance department and a focus group all in one. He could also mine that community for developers and subject matter experts who willing to donate their time for free, such as Cantor's assistant at the Pueblo site, David Reese.

Cantor was also data mining the site to direct new research and development, borrowing the freely given ideas, speculation, and insights of the community to determine what the next steps should be in an array of technologies and industries, and then commissioning his own team to build that tech.

From a software and technological development perspective, having a privatized social media network was good for business, even if it never brought a dime in directly. The loss leader strategy was used by companies such as Google, Apple, Amazon, and many others, and Cantor was clearly tapping into that zeitgeist.

Except, as it turned out, Zelot wasn't working out so well as a loss leader. Or rather, it was all loss, no leader, according to Denzel's findings.

The amount of money being siphoned into the well of Zelot was increasing exponentially every year. The users— once primarily reputable academics, academics, and scientists who could use the site for quickly vetting theories and safely exploring new avenues of research—had of late been abandoned ship. The increasing growth of the site had attracted a fringe element and had made the online community toxic to those serious-minded souls in pursuit of knowledge and advancement.

Kotler had said as much of the site himself, while they were back at Pueblo.

The current users were still intelligent, and still skilled, but they were mostly concerned with bickering and debating minutia, on topics that were both irrelevant and dead ends for research and development. Speculation on the existence or non-existence of God, or on whether there was a "gay gene," or whether time was real and measurable or merely a social construct—these became hot and epic debates in the community, but they led to few if any technological insights that Cantor's people could mine. They were useless in keeping Cantor's company on the cutting edge, and the cost of maintaining the social network they had infected was becoming untenable and unsustainable.

Ironically, the Petrie dish Cantor had created for nurturing new thought and new insights into technology had been tainted by the very culture Cantor was trying to nurture. Zelot was soaking up money from Cantor's portfolio and offering little to nothing in return.

It wasn't Cantor's only bad investment. Over the past few years, numerous startups and ventures had failed under Cantor's watch. His software company had started backing a lot of these failed ventures, and his Board of Directors had not been pleased. Essentially, every business Cantor touched went below the red line. Cantor was bleeding money.

He still had wealth. He could still move funds as he

needed. As Denzel dug in and took a closer look, however, it emerged that Cantor was operating above his means. It wouldn't be long before the billionaire's pockets came up empty, and he'd be just another failed former titan of technology, trying to get backing for his next big idea.

Unless, of course, he found some great windfall.

Denzel suspected he knew exactly what that windfall would be. In fact, if he was right, it might explain a lot of what was happening, not just this case but with the other connected cases as well.

He saved the research he'd found, sending a few things to the printer so he could have a hard copy for his growing case file. He folded up his laptop, exited the room, and stepped out into the bustle and activity of the offices. He looked around at his co-workers, fellow agents all engaged in various cases.

His gaze landed on Director Crispen's door.

He thought about Kotler, and how Crispen had clearly singled him out. It was odd behavior, and worse it was unjust. Denzel had looked into Kotler, had studied him, had spent time with him, and he knew that the man would never have abducted Evelyn Horelica, and he was certainly no terrorist. Crispen's attention to Kotler seemed bizarre, even suspicious.

Furthering that suspicious was the fact that Crispen had removed Denzel from both the Adham manhunt and. the investigation into Evelyn Horelica's abduction. It was as if Crispen wanted to keep anyone from coming to Kotler's aid, as if he wanted Kotler to remain off the board.

Denzel had been removed from the case, which meant he shouldn't even be following his current line of investigation. But this was a lead, and Denzel knew he would have to be the one to follow it.

He had only his suspicions, and no actual evidence—but that was part of what Agents were trained to pursue, wasn't it? It was his responsibility to follow up, to eliminate any potential wrong paths so he could keep digging to find the right ones—to find the truth. This was just one more path to explore, and hopefully close up tight.

He stopped by his desk, opened his laptop, and logged back into the FBI database. He entered a few search terms, looking for connections to confirm his suspicions. He knew that what he was thinking was dangerous. He knew what it could mean for his career, as well as the career of other agents in the FBI, and even the bureau itself.

He hurried through the results and dumped them to a thumb drive, so he could look at them later, then gathered his things and left, on his way to the airport. He would fly to see Cantor, and he needed to do that as quickly as possible, in case his searches were being monitored and his suspicions were correct.

There were bound to be red flags, and his window of opportunity to act with autonomy would slam shut any minute, if he turned out to be right.

Chapter 21

KOTLER and the DEA agents made the long drive back to Pueblo at high speed, and as they approached the research site they skidded in beside several other official vehicles. There was a strong FBI presence now, and the DEA was coordinating to offer backup.

The mission to find and arrest Adham had been a disaster, and Kotler knew that somewhere along the way he'd catch blame for it. This had been his plan, his trap, and it had backfired. He had inadvertently created a distraction that had allowed Adham to gain his objective. The entrance to the river now belonged to the terrorists.

How had Adham known about Kotler's trap?

Maybe he didn't. Maybe he had legitimately sent his men, and his decoy, with the objective of taking that second entrance to the river. Then, as a backup plan, he had decided to risk trying to take the main entrance at Pueblo, in a daring full charge.

As Kotler thought about it, the plan made sense. Adham was clearly very intelligent, and a solid strategist. He could have weighed the odds and decided that a plan to attack on two fronts would offer him a better chance at obtaining his objective.

Kotler got out of the surveillance van and walked to the perimeter. He was stopped by several FBI agents who demanded he step back. The DEA was vouching for him, but the FBI wouldn't hear it.

"Let him through," a gruff voice shouted, and everyone more or less flinched. Sarge Canfield approached, looking a bit haggard and dirty, and holding a semi-automatic rifle against his shoulder. He had one of his cigars in the corner of his mouth, making him look like a comic book super soldier, ready to take down Nazis or Viet Cong or anyone else who threatened life, liberty, and the American way. "He's with me."

"This is a Federal matter now," one of the FBI agents said. "You're a private security force. You're lucky you're still allowed here."

"I got papers that say I'm allowed here," Sarge said, pulling a small sheath of folded papers from his back pocket. "And I can hire anyone I want for my team. I'm paying this guy ten bucks to be here."

Kotler smiled. "Not my usual rate, but I assume there's a dental plan?"

"You get to keep all the terrorist teeth you can kick in," Sarge grunted.

Kotler smirked and nodded. "I accept your terms."

The FBI agent tossed the papers back to Sarge, who shoved them back into his pocket and motioned for Kotler to follow. "Stay close," he said. "I think the Feds don't like you much."

"You either," I said. "Thanks for getting me in. What's the situation?"

"Adham took the main building, and he has the entrance

to the river. We've seen his men carting in crates we think contain C-4. He's planning to blow the opening. If he doesn't bring the whole mountain down on his head, he'll be swimming in that underground river in no time. But that ain't what worries me." He looked around at the line of federal employees, all armed and armored, ready to advance on the camp. "I heard a rumor."

"What kind of rumor?" Kotler asked.

"Satellites are picking up traces of radiation, and the signature looks like uranium. The feds think Adham may have a nuke."

"A nuke!" Kotler exclaimed.

"I managed to chat up one of the feds. He said there was a robbery a couple of months ago, in New Mexico. Someone broke in and stole a warehouse full of smoke detectors. It's been on the terror watch list ever since."

Kotler huffed. "Unbelievable. They used the uranium from the smoke detectors to build a bomb? I've read about people trying to build dirty bombs that way. Scary."

"Yeah, scary as shit," Sarge said. "The only thing no one can figure is why they want a bomb like that down in an underground river. Maybe contaminate the water supply?"

Kotler shook his head. "That far down and with all the sediment and rock that will be there, even a nuke wouldn't cause much ecological damage. Nothing that couldn't be handled." He thought for a moment, staring off toward the dig site, thinking. This area had no real strategic importance. There were no military bases in Pueblo. Nothing that would cause the sort of abject terror that someone like Adham wanted to create. It was possible he just wanted publicity—the sort of press he could get by destroying a city in the interior US. But that didn't seem to match with Adham's ego, based on what Kotler knew of the man. He wasn't a showman. He was a strategist. He had the foresight to take advantage of a vulnerability, to steal what he needed, and to use it to build a nuclear device. He wasn't doing this to show strength, he was doing it because he *had* strength. That meant he had an objective.

So what else was nearby?

Nothing, that Kotler could think of. Nothing of strategic importance, at any rate. Pueblo had its share of government buildings, and was something of a tourist spot, but it was nowhere near the caliber of a national landmark or a military base ...

Kotler's eyes went wide, and he stared at Sarge.

"Whatcha got?" Sarge asked.

Kotler turned and looked around the site until his eyes landed on a small table beside a tactical van, several feet away. He rushed to this, with Sarge in tow.

"Gentlemen, is that a satellite map of the area?" Kotler asked the three agents who were standing nearby.

"Yes," one of the agents replied, warily.

Kotler bent to look at it. "It's a long shot, but it could be," Kotler mumbled.

"What's up?" Sarge asked.

Kotler looked up at him, "If you wanted to hit the US somewhere that would really hurt, what would you aim for?"

Sarge shrugged. "I don't know. Big cities, maybe? Military bases?"

"Big cities would have lots of civilian causalities and would do a lot of psychological damage to the US public. But if you wanted a tactical advantage as well—if you wanted to stir up fear but also give yourself a strategic advantage over your enemy, you'd want to take out something bigger, with more implications. Something that would not only create panic among Americans but would give you a more tactical advantage for future attacks."

"So what are you getting at?" Sarge asked.

"We've been operating under the assumption that this underground river was completely unknown. But what if someone does know about it? What if it's been mapped, and it leads somewhere that could be a perfect target?"

Kotler looked back at the map and ran a finger over it until he hit the spot he was looking for.

One of the FBI agents leaned forward. "Cheyenne Mountain?"

The other agent replied, "They're going after NORAD? Underground?"

Kotler straightened. "In 2015, Admiral William Gortney commissioned an upgrade to the Cheyenne Mountain complex," he said. "It's been shielded against an EMP blast. For all intents and purposes, that complex is the most heavily guarded and most well-protected spot on the planet. It's designed to serve as a command center for the President, in the event of a nuclear war. Think of what a coup it would be if Adham managed to detonate a nuclear device below it. He'd create a vulnerability we couldn't recover from before our enemies could initiate a second attack."

Sarge cursed. "You think Adham is going to sail a nuclear bomb all the way to Cheyenne Mountain from here?"

"If the Vikings could sail here from the North, there's every chance the river makes at least that kind of range," Kotler said. "It would likely go even further, emerging somewhere beyond the Rockies. It's essentially an unguarded passage through the mountains, with a significant military base in the middle."

Everyone was staring at Kotler for a moment, and then

the activity started. The FBI agents buzzed, started making calls and reports, and started alerting others to this new possibility. The presence of a nuke was bad enough, but the prospect of using it to take down one of the most powerful military assets in the US was too much to risk.

Kotler and Sarge were more or less forgotten in the ensuing chaos, and so they pulled back, retreating to a large Humvee that Sarge and some of his men had used to make their escape. It was riddled with bullet holes along one side. Dried blood was caked in a splatter on one of the rear windows. Kotler didn't make a point of asking who had been hit, or whether they'd survived. Sarge and his men were all business at the moment, and that was exactly what was needed.

"There isn't much I'm going to be able to do here," Kotler said. "I want to see them take down Adham."

Sarge nodded. "I think that's coming soon. There's no way they're letting him get into that tunnel with the nuke, now that they know what he's up to."

"I'm only guessing at that," Kotler said.

"I ain't known you long," Sarge shook heads head. "But I know enough that I'd trust one of your guesses over a lot of other folk's facts."

Kotler smiled a little at that and was about to respond when an explosion blasted outward from the tent surrounding the tunnel entrance. A cloud of dust rose into the air, obscuring much of the camp from view.

"What the fresh shit is this!" Sarge shouted.

"The nuke?" one of his men asked.

"Are your balls glowing in the dark?" Sarge sneered. "No, it ain't the nuke."

"They just sealed themselves in the tunnel," Kotler said,

feeling the anger rise in him. "They had all that C-4. They just closed the tunnel so we can't get to them."

There was another sound then, muffled but still quite loud.

"That would be them opening the tunnel on the other side," Kotler said. "They're insane! If the mountain hasn't dropped on them, they're just plain lucky!"

"They probably see it as acceptable risk," Sarge said. "They know that they ain't coming back out without either being shot down or carted off to a prison somewhere."

Kotler thought about this. "They have the nuke, so this is an opportunity to carry out their plan. They have nothing to lose by trying."

"So now they have a nuke and a river that you think takes them straight to NORAD. What the hell is the play here?"

Kotler shook his head. He wasn't sure what to make of any of this right now. What had started as an amazing historic and archeological discovery had turned into something so sinister. Adham and his men could do some serious damage if they managed to get to NORAD with that device. Even with advanced warning, there might not be a way to stop them.

Kotler walked away from Sarge and his men, in search of someone from the FBI or DEA. He wasn't sure what was going to happen in the next 24 hours, but despite his unfinished business with Adham he had more important things to worry about.

This had distracted him from finding Evelyn. Whatever else might come, he was determined to find her and bring her home safely.

Hopefully before the nation was thrown into war and chaos.

Chapter 22

"WE HAVE something we want you to look at," one of the
agents told Kotler, before handing him a laptop and
motioning to the screen. "That's from the computer used by
Richard Barmoth. Before Adham took the camp, a new set
of messages came through. We don't know quite how to
interpret them, but we thought you might."

Kotler was in no mood for any of this, but he had to
admit he didn't have much else to do. The trap they'd set for
Adham had failed, the FBI and DEA were scrambling to
find a way to reach the terrorists in the underground river,
and Sarge and his men were busy with re-securing the camp
and reporting in to Cantor.

This had all gone to hell.

Kotler opened the laptop and rested it on the hood of
one of the tactical vans. He opened the folder that Barmoth
had been using to transfer information to his mysterious
benefactor. All of the documents that he had created as a
smokescreen were there, but there were also new files.
These were named for existing files within the folder, but

each had a capital "Q" followed by a dash, and then the file name.

Kotler felt his pulse quicken.

He and Evelyn used that same system for tracking questions in documents without altering the originals. It had been Evelyn's practice—make a copy of the file, rename it, and then embed her questions using the inline comment feature in the word processor. Evelyn, like Kotler, was in the business of preserving documents—so she preferred to do new, fresh work—or to ask questions—in a duplicate, while preserving the original.

Kotler opened the first file and quickly read through the comments. He sat back, amazed.

This had to be Evelyn.

It had all the signs of having come from her, from the file naming convention to the language used to pose the questions. There were some ticks in there as well—little quirks in her style that had prompted Kotler to poke fun at her more than once, as well as gentle, passive-aggressive jibes she often used to rile him up. There were little bits of jargon that they had more or less invented, occasional odd and awkward phrasing of a question, and in several places it was clear that Evelyn was rephrasing and rewording something Kotler wrote just as she used to do, mostly to annoy him.

This was Evelyn. It had to be.

Kotler looked up at the two agents who were standing near him. "These new files are coming from outside?"

There were nods. "We're attempting to track them," one said.

Kotler laughed, and upon seeing the quizzical expressions on their faces he said, "She's alive."

"Who?" one agent asked, confused.

Kotler smiled. "Evelyn. Doctor Horelica. She's alive!"

"You're sure?" the agent asked, clearly surprised. He exchanged a glance with his partner, and their body language said that this was very unexpected news.

That told Kotler everything he needed to know.

The FBI was only paying lip service to the search for Evelyn. They had already written her off as dead, which meant they'd dedicated no resources to finding her. It infuriated him. since this started, Crispen and his people seemed to be more of a barrier than a help in finding Evelyn. While the terrorist actions of Adham might be of greater importance, it riled Kotler to realize that they considered her so unimportant.

It wouldn't do to tear into them, Kotler know. He needed them, particularly now. If they couldn't be trusted, so be it. He'd use them as tools.

"Yes, I'm absolutely sure," Kotler said, letting the tightness go, keeping himself calm and his words even. "Do we have any way to trace where these messages came from?"

"We've had our IT department looking at this. The tracking programs we installed have recorded the IP addresses for both outgoing and incoming messages, but these were bounced through several relay websites. Our guys think they can track it, but it will take time."

"Time she may not have," Kotler said. He turned back to the laptop and began sifting through Evelyn's messages.

She had framed all of this as if she were asking for clarification, as if she needed him to verify a few facts and provide more information. As Kotler dug into it all, however, it became clear that she had recognized his own digital fingerprints. She must have worked out that Kotler was here, and that he was laying some sort of trap, planting false information. She had taken advantage of that, playing off of the false reports he was filing. This was her way of sending him a message, the only way she could.

Maybe she'd been able to send something that would give them a clue as to where she was.

He read further, and when he came to one of her notes he stopped, read it again, and smiled.

"You found something?" one of the agents asked.

"The city of gold," Kotler said.

"*El Dorado,*" the agent nodded. "We've read the briefing. But you said it wasn't what anyone thought it was. Care to elaborate on that?"

Kotler nodded. "When I was being tortured by Adham's men, they had me researching everything that Barmoth was relaying to them. They were only interested in the river, and now we know why. But Barmoth was compiling and sending information about the city of gold as well. All of the research and translation work he was siphoning from the researchers had a split focus. Before I was abducted, we had assumed the city of gold was a possible motive, but when Adham dismissed this we all thought it was off the table."

"And?" The agent asked.

Kotler shook his head. "I discovered that everything the indigenous tribes and the Vikings wrote about the city of gold was a little misleading—though not intentionally. It really came down to an error in translation, right from the start. The Vikings were translating something the Aztecs were saying, and vice versa. And then we come along and start translating and interpreting through our own modern lens. The problem, then as now, is that irony doesn't always translate well in writing."

"Great," one of the agents said. The two of them were men Kotler had never met, and they had never bothered to introduce themselves. Kotler figured they were likely working directly with Crispen, which could explain their mostly belligerent attitude toward him. He didn't quite trust them, and he wasn't yet ready to reveal what he suspected about the city of gold.

With what he was seeing from these questions and comments from Evelyn, it was clear she had come to the same conclusions he had, which made things easier. It was a way to verify that it was her and not someone else. It also provided a key—a way to encode messages to each other that no one else was likely to detect.

"Dr. Horelica has had access to Reese's stolen files," Kotler said. "She's essentially been forced to do the same research I was doing for Adham, only her abductor has a different motive."

"So you're still asserting that Adham was not her abductor?" asked the agent.

"I am," Kotler said. "Adham had nothing to do with Evelyn's abduction. Our man Richard Barmoth is a double agent. He's providing information to two different parties."

The first agent, whom Kotler was beginning to think of as "the Jock," due to his footballer build, took out a notepad and started flipping through it. "We took Barmoth into custody, and we've been grilling him. He didn't mention that he was working with two different parties. He only sent information to one IP address."

Kotler considered this. "Director Crispen mentioned that he thought Adham might have a benefactor. A patron. Maybe Barmoth was sending his information to the patron, and they in turned shared information with Adham."

"So we're no further along than we were," the Jock said. "We still have to track down this patron."

Kotler saw an opportunity and decided to take it. The FBI had more or less lost interest in finding Evelyn, as

Adham and his plans became a priority. This was a chance to bundle everything together. "If you can locate Evelyn, there's a very good chance her captor is colluding with Adham. It's clear that Barmoth was just a patsy in this. He was working for someone else, who is in turn sharing information with terrorists. Find Evelyn, and we may be able to end this."

"There's still a nuke winding its way through an underground river," the Jock said.

"Yeah," Kotler nodded. "That does put something of a time limit on this, doesn't it?"

The agents exchanged looks, then the Jock said, "What's your plan?"

"We've finally established some sort of communication with Evelyn. The events here today may spook Barmoth's contact, so we probably can't count on being able to use this channel for long. Keep your IT guys on tracing that IP address to its source. Meanwhile, I'll dig in on all of these notes and questions from Evelyn. It's clear she realized it was me feeding the false info to the patron. She may have hidden something in her responses that can give us a clue as to where she is, or who is holding her."

The agents nodded, and after a brief exchange they left Kotler to work.

Now Kotler had to shift from the adrenaline and drama of what was happening around him and slip into the flow of using his mind to sift through the data he had. He needed to find any trace, no matter how small, of anything Evelyn was able to share. Her life, and maybe the lives of millions of US citizens, could depend on some tiny detail buried in these reports.

Kotler took the laptop with him, found a cup of coffee and shaded table, and got to work.

Chapter 23

MARK CANTOR'S home was a large estate that sprawled over a tract of land in one of the wealthiest areas of Colorado Springs. Mountains butted against the back of the property, and the main house clung to a private hillside that over-looked the city from one angle, and miles of mountains and unspoiled wilderness from another.

Denzel drove through the security gate, after a brief intercom exchange with a security guard, and cruised slowly down the long and winding driveway. The drive was walled on either side by cultivated landscape, privacy hedges and trees mean to keep prying eyes from having too much of a view into the property. It was actually a pleasant drive, as Denzel drove over a bridge mounting a rock-strewn stream below, which turned to meander alongside the drive for a distance. It was peaceful here. A retreat, tailored to the need of a technologist billionaire. Peace and privacy. Denzel was about to disrupt both.

This was Cantor's third property. His first was near Silicon Valley, close to where his companies were busy churning out ones and zeros for profit. The second home was an apartment in Manhattan, which put Cantor closer to the academics and museums and the culture he prized.

In the background check, Denzel had uncovered interviews with Cantor in which he referred to this third home as a nod to his roots. His family was from Colorado Springs, and he had been born here. His father had served in the Air Force and had been stationed at Cheyenne Mountain. It was while serving at Cheyenne that Cantor's father was killed under ... well, the file literally said "questionable circumstances." It hadn't elaborated any further, and Denzel had been unable to uncover any details in his quick and under-the-radar background check. That was curious, and a little frustrating. And no less so for Cantor himself, according to his file.

It was after his father's death that Cantor's life took an interesting turn.

His mother quickly remarried. A little too quickly, by Denzel's estimate. It seemed pretty certain that she'd been having an affair, and that her husband's death had given her the opportunity she'd needed. She and her new husband moved away from Colorado Springs. Mark Cantor, seventeen years old and already considered something of a prodigy, stayed behind to fend for himself.

Cantor filed a petition to become an emancipated youth, which was granted without contest. His mother signed the paperwork the day it was filed, indicating she'd either known this was coming or saw it as another opportunity to start fresh. Possibly both.

In a letter Cantor's mother wrote to the presiding judge, she referred to him as "difficult" and "disobedient" and even "arrogant." Not exactly matronly. It seemed clear to Denzel that Cantor's mother thought of him as a lost cause and was glad to be rid of him. She seemed to have no faith in him and was willing enough to let him fly or fall by his own choices.

And then Mark Cantor surprised everyone by becoming a billionaire, and sharing absolutely nothing with his mother, who apparently did come calling on his 20th birthday.

Denzel had watched an interview on YouTube, with a very young Cantor, in which he had stated that he didn't hate his mother, he just didn't like her very much. "She's not useful to me. She's never been useful to me." Cold words, but they matched the zeitgeist of the times, as titans like Steve Jobs, Jeff Bezos, and Elon Musk were gaining reputations as highly successful sociopaths. Being a dick to get ahead was the hotness of the era.

The deeper Denzel dug into Mark Cantor, the more nuanced his profile became. Denzel could see the threads of the man's life twining together to create someone who could be equally as capable of orchestrating an elaborate museum heist as they were of building a successful tech business. He hadn't done it alone, however.

Denzel parked the car and stepped out, pulling on his suit coat and making sure his badge was at the ready. Cantor knew he was coming, but it was always good to have the badge to flash at anyone who wanted to make things too complicated. Cantor was surrounded by employees who were trained to prevent access to him, and it might take Federal authority to get them to step aside without a hassle.

Denzel was let into the house and shown to a drawing room—something he hadn't realized that people even thought about in homes like these anymore. Cantor had a fascination with history, Denzel knew, so maybe this was an homage.

The man who had shown Denzel in and ushered him

into the drawing room had urged him to take a seat, but Denzel remained standing until Cantor came into the room.

"Agent Denzel," Cantor said. "Good to see you."

Denzel nodded.

"Can I offer you something?"

"Water would be good," Denzel said. The altitude here was playing havoc on his sinuses, and everything felt dry.

Cantor went to a set of sliding panels, which revealed a small wet bar. He reached into a beverage fridge and handed Denzel a cold bottle of water.

Denzel accepted it gratefully, and the two of them took a seat on a set of plush chairs that faced each other while angled just enough to offer an impressive view through the window. They were treated to a vista of mountains and trees that rose just beyond a well-manicured lawn.

"What can I do for the FBI?" Cantor asked.

Denzel sipped his water, then placed the bottle on the small table next to him. He took out his notepad and his phone. The phone contained all of the research he'd gathered so far—information about Cantor, and about Evelyn Horelica's abduction. But also, something else. This was going to be a dangerous play, but Denzel saw no way to avoid it. There was also no reason to delay.

"I wanted to ask you a few questions regarding your relationship with Director Matthew Crispen."

To his credit, Cantor didn't show any outward sign of recognizing the name. Denzel envied Dan Kotler's advanced ability to read body language—there might have been some sort of micro expression that would have given Cantor away immediately. But even Denzel could see that Cantor was a bit uncomfortable at the mention of Crispen's name.

"Isn't Director Crispen your superior at the FBI?" Cantor asked. "That's about as much as I know of the man."

Subtle reminder, Denzel thought.

"Hm," Denzel referenced his notepad. "Didn't you meet with Director Crispen during your last stay in New York? I have a note here that that the two of you met at your Manhattan apartment."

Cantor smiled tightly. "Well, you have me, Agent Denzel. I was told not to speak of that meeting."

"By the Director?" Denzel asked.

"Exactly," Cantor replied.

"Would you care to tell me what that meeting was about?" Denzel asked.

"No, I wouldn't actually," Cantor said. "It was a private meeting. With your superior."

Denzel nodded. This was thin ice to tread, he knew. It was also the only road through, and he'd decided to take it, no matter the outcome. "Mr. Cantor, I believe your meeting with Director Crispen was in regard to the research camp in Pueblo, and the museum exhibit surrounding the Coelho Medallion. Would you care to verify that?"

Cantor shook his head. "Maybe you should speak to Crispen," he said, a bit slyly.

"That's next," Denzel said, looking up from his notepad with a sober expression, his tone turning to ice.

The mood of the room changed from uncomfortable to guarded. Cantor stared at him for a moment, "I'm sorry, I have business to attend to. Whatever it is you're implying here, it has nothing to do with me."

Cantor stood and was walking toward the room's exit. Denzel also stood, put his notebook and phone back in his pocket, and calmly said, "Mr. Cantor, I have evidence that you and Director Crispen arranged for the abduction of Dr. Evelyn Horelica."

Cantor stopped and turned swiftly. He laughed. "Evidence? What evidence?"

Interesting, Denzel thought.

It sounded like Cantor was more doubtful that there might actually be evidence than he was worried about being implicated.

"Your meeting with Director Crispen wasn't entirely off the record," Denzel said. "There are recordings."

Cantor scoffed. "No, there aren't," he said, completely sure of himself.

And with good reason. Denzel had been bluffing, hoping to rattle Cantor's cage. He'd played his hand—he suspected Cantor and Crispen of having planned Horelica's abduction, but he actually had no real evidence of it. He was hoping he might convince Cantor to confess. It would have made going after Crispen a lot easier.

But the bluff had failed.

"Agent Denzel, I think you'd better leave. And you can expect a pretty serious conversation with Director Crispen," he said. "He will be very interested to hear that you came here and implicated him—and me—in a kidnapping."

Denzel nodded. "I know. And I'll likely take some lumps, if it comes to that. But it won't do any good to call him."

"Why is that?" Cantor said.

"He's already here," Denzel replied. "I traced him to your property. And for that, I do have evidence. I also have a confession from one of our agents—one of the men who took Horelica from Houston that day. Once I knew about your meeting with Crispen, it wasn't hard to track his movements over the following weeks. He ordered two agents to fly to Houston shortly after your meeting. And when they left Houston, they escorted an unmarked van on a cargo flight to Colorado Springs. That van was then driven to your property."

"You ... you're telling me you have proof of this?"

"I do," Denzel said. "I have satellite imagery showing the van parked outside of one of your outbuildings. None of this is enough to convict anyone, just yet. But it was enough for me to get a federal warrant to search these premises, and to hold both you and Director Crispen in custody during the search."

Cantor stared at Denzel for a moment, then shook his head.

"None of this is going to stick. Even if you do have photos of the van, there's nothing to indicate anything sinister about it. I have vehicles like that coming and going from this property all the time. And any connection I may have to Director Crispen—well, there's no crime there, either."

Denzel nodded. "That's true. But all of this was enough to convince the judge, and right now I have a number of agents searching every square inch of this property. They came in behind me I came here first, to you, as a courtesy."

Cantor cursed under his breath and went to one of the windows of the drawing room, peeking out of the sheer curtains that hung there. "You mean a distraction," Cantor said.

"That too," Denzel nodded. "You would make things a lot easier on both of us if you would agree to testify, Mr. Cantor. Care to issue a statement?"

Cantor looked at him, and it was clear that he was angry. But he hadn't gotten this far by letting his temper get the best of him. As Denzel watched, Cantor visibly calmed himself, took a breath, and said, "Am I under arrest right this moment?"

"I don't have any evidence to make that arrest yet," Denzel said. "But don't plan on leaving."

"Oh, no, I'd never leave," Cantor said. "But I am going to make several phone calls."

Denzel nodded. "I expected that. I should warn you that our warrant includes monitoring any communications coming or going from this property."

Cantor clenched his jaw. "Thank you for the heads up."

"I'll also need to know where I can find Director Crispen," Denzel said.

"Right here," Crispen's voice said from behind him.

Denzel turned to see the Director standing in the entryway to the drawing room. "Sir, I have to ask you to relinquish your weapon and your badge. I'll also need your mobile phone."

"You've just made a career-ending mistake, Agent Denzel," Crispen said. "And maybe more. You can be sure that when I've cleared this up I'll be leveling an investigation into your actions, as well as your connection to Anwar Adham."

Denzel nodded. "Might I suggest the Director find a new dead horse to beat, sir? You've been falling back on the terrorist umbrella quite a bit lately."

"Watch your tone, Agent. I'm still a Director for the FBI."

"For now," Denzel said. "But I'm guessing that by the end of the day you'll be cutting a deal to be a witness. I know you have enough pull to keep yourself out of prison, sir. But you'll spend some time in a cell. That much I can guarantee."

"Don't get too comfortable with this little coup, Agent," Crispen said.

"Nothing about this makes me feel the least bit comfortable, sir," Denzel said.

Crispen handed over his weapon, badge, and phone, and Denzel held out an evidence bag for these to be dropped into.

Denzel asked both men to remain in the drawing room. Cantor got his phone calls—all of which were recorded by Denzel's team at the front gate. They were mostly to attorneys, but one was to someone Cantor referred to as 'Victor.' That call had clearly been a coded message, and the surveillance team was scrambling now to trace where it had gone.

This whole maneuver had been tricky for Denzel to pull off, especially without alerting Crispen. He was more than a little nervous that they wouldn't find anything to implicate either Cantor or Crispen in Dr. Horelica's abduction. But his research had uncovered some pretty strong hints—enough that not only had he been able to get the warrant and the team, he had managed to convince the judge to help him keep this whole operation under wraps and off of Crispen's radar.

One of the agents helping him with this operation came into the drawing room, guided by Cantor's assistant. Denzel handed things off to him, with orders to keep Crispen and Cantor in the room and went to report in with the mobile HQ they'd set up at the front gate. He made greater speed on the drive back than he'd made coming in, the scenic path blurring by as he approached the front gate in minutes.

"Sir," one of the men running surveillance greeted him as he stepped into the van. "You're going to want to see this."

He pointed to one of the screens in front of him, part of the larger array that covered the entire inside panel of the van. Denzel leaned in to read what was coming through.

"What is this?" he asked.

"It came in from the research camp," the agent said. "It

was bounced through several relay sites globally, but we intercepted it from the trunk line coming into this property."

Denzel read it closely, and though he didn't entirely understand the contents, he did recognize it as one of the reports coming out of the research camp. He smiled. "I had heard there was a mole at the camp," he said.

"Yes sir," the agent said. "Richard Barmoth. He's already in custody."

"So who is sending this?" Denzel asked.

"According to the field agents, this is coming from them. It's being written by Dr. Kotler."

"Kotler!" Denzel exclaimed, then shook his head. "Of course it is. But that's really good news for us," he said.

"Why's that?"

Denzel smiled. "It means that the mole was sending information here. Which can implicate Cantor in colluding with Adham. But it gets better than that. I'm finally going to be able to use Crispen's own favorite card against him."

"The agents on the other end of this claim that Kotler is trying to reach Dr. Horelica with these messages. He's determined that she's sent coded messages, buried in communications that were coming to Barmoth."

Denzel blinked. "Well, now, that makes everything easier, doesn't it?" He turned to another agent, manning and monitoring communications. "Let these messages through. And keep the search going, but tell our guys to go ahead and make the arrest. We have more than enough to put Cantor and Crispen in a cell now. And I can't wait to hear Crispen try to make a deal after this."

Chapter 24

Victor hung up the phone, feeling a little disappointed. Cantor had promised him that eventually he would have his prize and now, with the FBI closing in, that could be denied to him. That would not do.

Cantor had been kind enough to give warning, to tell Victor that he was soon to be discovered, that he should run. Through key phrases and codes, Cantor had ordered that all on-site records be destroyed, which was simple enough. Everything was backed up on Cantor's overseas servers, in non-judicial treaty countries, so even with the local records destroyed the data was safe.

Victor only needed to enter one key passcode to start the server meltdown. There were no paper records—that would be foolish. There was nothing to shred, nothing to burn. The micro-EMP devices built into each server rack would wipe everything clean in an instant, and the drives would be physically melted down by high-heat plasma from jets installed like sprinkler heads at the bottom of each rack. With a few quick keystrokes and the press of the enter key,

Victor started a volcanic eruption within the stacks of pristine computers. Total annihilation.

The terminal in Evelyn Horelica's cell was a dummy, slaved to one of the servers. It had no buffer, no storage, no memory for the FBI's IT experts to hack. From Evelyn's perspective, the screens would simply blank out and become unresponsive.

Of course, her data wasn't the only thing that presented a danger to Cantor and to Victor. Her very presence was damaging.

Cantor had given him strict instructions not to harm Evelyn. He was to watch her, to provide for her physical needs, and to provide her with the research and materials she needed to do her work. If she tried to escape, he was to stop her with as little physical harm as possible. If she tried to send a message for help, he was to block it.

But what now?

If the FBI found her here, it would be bad for Cantor and for Victor alike.

As Victor saw it, there was no choice. He had to remove Evelyn Horelica from the equation. And he might as well claim his bonus.

In all the time Evelyn had been captive here, Victor had never had to intervene with her directly. The automated systems had been more than enough to keep her in check. In the event she had ever managed to get out of her cell, however, or if he'd had to physically intervene with her, he'd been prepared.

He stepped into the small closet at the back of the room. Hanging there, among the boxes of supplies and computer equipment, was a black, leather motorcycle race suit. Victor took this down and quickly pulled it on. He took a pair of black Kevlar gloves from the whisper-glide drawer of the inset dresser. He pulled these on, then slipped his feet into a pair of boots, quickly cinching the ratcheting straps along their outer surface.

Finally, he pulled on the motorcycle helmet, which had a blackened faceplate that let him see out with no trouble, but which blocked his features entirely from the outside.

In this outfit, Victor's features and identity were entirely hidden, but it provided more than just anonymity. The suit itself was lined with Kevlar and ablative plating—a few steel plates sewn into the material at vital spots. Victor enjoyed riding, but this suit had been made to give him protection from more than just road rash. It was armor, and he was dressed for battle.

Perhaps his favorite touch was the holster.

It was small, made for the slim 9mm that he kept there at all times. He checked this now. It was loaded, and a round was chambered. Around his waist, in a series of pouches on his belt, were four more fully loaded magazines. Each was slim enough that they caused very little bulge in the suit, and each was strategically placed so that he could reach them without having them interfere with his movements.

He slid the 9mm back into its holster, and its black frame all but disappeared against the suit, camouflaged further by a loose flap of leather that obscured it from view. He could walk around in public in this and no one would even notice the gun. For certain he'd be a spectacle—he looked absolutely striking in the suit. But no one would consider him armed, just to look at him.

Victor knew he was playing against the clock here, but this was a precaution that had to be taken. Now, fully uniformed, he left the guest suite and its array of monitors behind. The screens were already dropping out one by one as the servers in the basement destroyed themselves.

Victor took the personal elevator down to Evelyn's floor. He stepped out and peeked into her cell through the small window in the door. It was a one-way mirror, so Evelyn would have no idea he was there.

He punched the entry code into the pad next to the door, and for the first time since Evelyn had been brought there the door's latch made an audible click.

That got Evelyn's attention.

She wasn't working at the moment. Her days and nights were a little ill-defined—something Victor had chosen to do on purpose, to keep her off balance. He reset the clocks on her terminal and on the digital tablet daily, and delivered food, research, and artifacts at random times, all in an effort to keep her from guessing the time of day.

At the moment, she was sleeping. But when the door opened she sat up bolt straight.

"Who are you?" she asked.

"Dr. Horelica, you will come with me," Victor said.

"Where are we going?"

"Come with me, Evelyn," he said, his tone still hard.

She reluctantly got out of bed and slowly moved across the room.

Victor indicated the door, and in what could have been considered a gentlemanly fashion at any other time, he allowed her to step through first. In reality he intended to keep her in sight through all of this.

"Where are we going?" Evelyn asked, her voice small and filled with fear.

"Do not talk. Do not scream. If you scream, I will kill you. Do you understand?"

She nodded.

"Good. Get into the elevator."

She did as she was told, and Victor stepped in beside her.

The elevator was small. Added after the construction of the estate, it was one of those personal elevators that could hold two people, but really wasn't meant to. There was no way to avoid being in each other's personal space, and the ride was a bit of a squeeze. Victor pressed against the back of the elevator and kept a hand gripping Evelyn's left arm as she stood nearly nose-to-door at the front.

When the elevator opened this time, it let them out into the garage.

This was where things might get tricky.

The garage was hidden on the estate, another structure carved into the side of the mountain with a camouflaged entrance. Mr. Cantor had intended it to be a quick escape, in an emergency. Victor figured this qualified, though he knew Cantor would have preferred to be here himself.

The problem was, there was only one vehicle in the garage at the moment—Victor's motorcycle, a Ducati 1200 Enduro.

The van was still parked out by the guest house, where they had first brought Evelyn in. In all these weeks, Victor had never gotten around to moving it into the hidden garage. He'd been too busy with his monitoring duties.

He cursed the FBI—the agents who had brought Evelyn here as much as the agents who were now closing in on them. Their laziness was going to cause more problems for him.

"Stand here," he said to Evelyn, and she stood in place.

He went to the cabinets lining one wall of the garage and rummaged through them until he came away with two medium-length zip ties. He took these to Evelyn, had her hold her hands out in front of her, and tied them together with the plastic bonds. He made them tight, and then checked to make sure she couldn't wriggle out of them.

Evelyn whimpered a bit from the pain of the bonds cutting into her wrists, but to her credit she said nothing.

Behind the faceplate of the helmet, Victor smiled. Evelyn Horelica was a strong woman, and Victor appreciated that. He was going to enjoy his prize, for certain.

"We will be riding the motorcycle," he said. "You will be behind me. If you try anything, you must know that it will only end in your injury or death. Yes?"

She nodded.

"Say that you understand. Out loud."

"I understand," Evelyn said.

"Good. Come."

He half dragged her to the motorcycle, climbed on and started it with the key, then motioned for her to climb on behind him.

"You must lean in close to me, since your hands are bound," he said. "And you will shift your body in any direction mine shifts, understand?"

"Yes, I understand," Evelyn said.

Victor got the motorcycle moving toward the exit and hit the remote to open the door.

On the outside, the garage was masked to look like the mountainside. Victor had no way of knowing whether the FBI might be close to the exit, but he was counting on the fact that he had Evelyn on the bike. They wouldn't dare take a shot at him, and risk losing the hostage.

With a quick and fluid motion, Victor reed the Ducati, and they shot out of the garage and onto a manicured field —one that had been scoured clean of bumps and large stones during the construction of the garage and guest house. The sod covering this area was real, but it was growing over a thick layer of sand and soil, which lay over a hard-pack of dirt covering a concrete slab. There was no driveway or road here to make anyone suspect the existence of the garage, but Cantor had made this as smooth an area as possible, to aid in escape.

Victor throttled the Ducati and brought it to full speed. As he did, several FBI agents scrambled, raising their weapons and shouting at him. As predicted, none of them fired.

Victor raced across the field and to the service road that cut through the property. The FBI was sure to have spotted this, and likely had people at the gate in back, but Victor had no intention of using that gate. There was another way.

He went off-road on a walking path that cut through the property.

Evelyn made a noise behind him, something like a muffled scream. With her hands tied, she must have had some difficulty holding on. Victor was conscious of this, and stayed on the smoothest parts of the path, but maintained his high speed.

At the end of the path was a rounded *cul-de-sac* with a seating area of stone benches and a large, central fountain. Just beyond was what looked like an iron fence. Victor hit another button on the remote, however, and the fence slid aside, into the brick wall to Victor's right. The hidden gate gave him passage out into the woods that obscured this part of the estate, and he wound through the path until he came to a road.

Now he really poured it on. He'd been moving at top speed coming out of the garage, but he had to slow down to navigate to the hidden exit. Here on this open stretch of road, however, he could fly.

He throttled to top speed, and the engine whined as he

and Evelyn Horelica flew like a missile, away from Cantor's estate and the FBI.

They were clear. Even if the FBI could track them to this road, they would have to guess which way he went, and by the time they got cars here Victor would take another road and get to a safe place to stow the Ducati until he could come back for it.

Victor had already arranged for just the place.

As the mountain road wound and turned in hairpin curves, mounting the steep grade of the terrain, Victor finally let up on the throttle. He slowed enough to take a turn when it appeared, and then gunned his way down this gravel road at a speed that was probably not safe.

The trees arcing over him and zipping by on either side of him made him feel safer, hidden. He was confident that he'd gotten away, and when the cabin came into sight he slowed to what felt like a crawl, gliding into the little shed that served as a garage.

"Get off of the bike," he said. Evelyn practically fell from the Ducati.

Victor shut the bike down and stepped off himself. He took Evelyn by the arm and dragged her out of the garage. He paused to close and lock the door, and then dragged her again, into the cabin.

This place was in the middle of nowhere by almost any standards. It had a generator, in a small shed out back, which provided electricity for both the cabin and for the pump on the well. It had no internet or telephone access. There were no neighbors within miles, and there were no hiking trails or roads that might allow anyone to have easy access. The dense woods surrounding the cabin were a good natural barrier, but even better was the sheer drop from the rock side, only a few feet from the back of the property. Victor knew that Evelyn could not call for help here.

The cabin had few amenities. The kitchen and bathroom were both very simple, and the only feature of any note in the living space was an old, iron wood burning stove, its piped chimney ascending into a hole in the ceiling. It didn't even have bedrooms. But what it did have was his white room.

Below the house, in what was once the basement, was a converted room with pure white walls. It was soundproof, though there was hardly any need for that here, where there wasn't another human soul for miles.

In the middle of the room was his table, which he had tricked out with straps and little trays for holding his tools. There were surgical lights dangling from an intimidating array in the ceiling, and along the walls were steel tables and cabinets, adorned with various instruments of surgical steel. The overall effect was to make the place look a lot like some sort of alien environment, where one might end up being probed and dissected.

Which, Victor admitted, was quite close to reality. He shucked the leather riding jacket and the helmet as they entered, hanging both neatly on a set of hooks just inside the door. He was still wearing the Kevlar under armor, which was comfortable enough for the moment, like a slight, padded vest.

When Evelyn saw the room, she froze for a moment, then tried race back through the door while Victor was occupied with the jacket. He managed to grab her before she could make it, gripping her arms hard. She fought him to get free, and at one point she did manage it, kicking him in the knee and racing away as he stumbled. She darted for the door, and Victor tackled her, dragging her back into the room.

"This is my bonus," he told her, whispering it into her ear as he held his check against hers. "You cannot deny me my prize."

Evelyn kicked at him, and he instantly regretted not tying her feet. The leather pants and boots were protecting him from the blows, but it was a struggle to get his hands on her.

He made a fist, reared back, and punched Evelyn between the eyes with his gloved hand. It was enough to daze her, and she stumbled back before laying still. He dragged her into the room and shut the door.

He was panting from all the exertion of having wrestled Evelyn to the ground, but it was exhilarating. She had more fight in her than he had given her credit, and that was a sweet surprise. It added to the flavor of the moment. A bit of the hunt, which he'd been denied in all of this.

She was coming to, and groaning. He would have to act fast to get her on the table. But first he had a bit of prep to do.

He went to the table and turned on the surgical lights, then made sure each of the straps was loose and ready to be secured in place. He made sure his trays of instruments were within reach of him, but not close enough that Evelyn might be able to reach one herself. He made everything ready.

Now ...

"Don't move," Evelyn's shaky voice said behind him.

He turned slightly, despite the warning, and saw that she was holding his slim little 9mm, aiming it at him with a tremor.

He froze.

"What are you doing with that?" he asked calmly, genially, as if she were a child who had gotten into something she wasn't allowed to touch.

"Let me out of here," she said, her voice sharp and cold.

"Put the gun away," he told her, firmly.

She didn't budge. He knew she wouldn't. He also knew that he was wearing a Kevlar body suit—and she was aiming for his chest.

Victor rushed her, and as he did she fired. The bullet struck with a heavy thud, and it hurt. Victor could push through that pain. The Kevlar had done its job, stopping the small-caliber bullet with no trouble. He'd have a bruise, but nothing more.

He slammed into Evelyn and the two of them fell back. She struggled and kicked, and Victor once again balled his hand into a fist, preparing to strike.

She let out a guttural yell then, the sound of someone facing their own death, and in a desperate motion she started pulling the trigger on the 9mm, again and again. And as she did, she raised it, just slightly.

One bullet grazed Victor's left cheek, making him flinch involuntarily.

The next bullet caught him just under the jaw, passing through to the back of his skull.

For a very brief instant Victor had the strangest memories and sensations. The smell of freshly mown grass. The sensation of warmth on his toes, like standing in the waters of the Pacific. The sound of bees buzzing gently.

He was about to say something about these sensations, to smile and remark on them, when the entire world went black.

Chapter 25

KOTLER WAS out of the helicopter almost before it landed.

Cantor's estate had a landing pad, and there were three agents waiting at its edge, wearing protective vests with "FBI" emblazoned on them front and back in large, yellow letters. One of the agents spoke into a radio as Kotler approached.

"This way, sir," the agent said, showing him to the main house.

Kotler nodded, and began sprinting down the walkway, bursting through the door into a large hall. Ahead, Denzel was standing in the entryway of a drawing room. Kotler went to him and they shook hands. "Have you found her yet?"

"Not yet," Denzel said. "We lost him on one of the roads cutting through the pass. But we have people searching, and we've closed every way out of the area. But Kotler ..." Denzel paused, looking at him with concerns. He looked Kotler in the eye and said, "It might be too late."

Kotler considered this, took a breath, "It's not," he said. "I have to believe it's not."

Denzel accepted that.

"How can I help?" Kotler asked.

"I'm not sure there's much you can do in the search for Dr. Horelica, but I thought you might be helpful in interrogating Cantor."

Again Kotler nodded, and Denzel led him into the drawing room where Cantor was sitting on a small, ornate sofa. His hands were bound, and he looked haggard despite having only been under arrest for a few hours.

Denzel and Kotler stood in front of him.

"Hello, Dr. Kotler," Cantor said. "It seems my attorney has been delayed, so I won't be speaking with either of you."

Kotler exchanged a quick glance with Denzel, who nodded, as if giving a cue.

"I understand," Kotler said. "But it doesn't have to be this way, you know. If you help us find Evelyn, things will go a lot easier on you."

"As Agent Denzel has insisted," Cantor said. "I have asked for an attorney, as is my right. I am also exercising my Fifth Amendment right to remain silent."

Kotler sighed. "Ok," he said. "But forgive me, I have some questions anyway. Maybe I can just ask, and you can answer if you feel it won't incriminate you? For starters, do you even know where this Victor guy took Evelyn?"

Cantor said nothing, but Kotler saw the corner of his mouth tighten and rise slightly on the right-hand side—an indication of contempt. He might or might not have he any knowledge of where Evelyn was, but he was sure she was in danger, and he reveled in that. He saw it as a small victory over Kotler and Denzel.

"Would Victor harm her?" Kotler asked. Again, Cantor said nothing, but his body language indicated that he knew Victor would.

"Does Victor have any property close by?"

This time, Cantor's eyebrows raised just a tiny amount— an indication of happiness. Why would he be happy? Kotler thought about it for a moment. Victor was on a motorcycle, with Evelyn riding on the back. According to reports he had seemed very proficient with the bike. There was no reason he couldn't have had Evelyn out of the state in short order, though the FBI had acted quickly to close roads in all directions.

It was extremely likely that Victor had a place nearby, but it was good to have some confirmation. Wherever it was, Cantor thought the FBI would never be able to find it, and that Evelyn had no chance. Kotler realized that this was the sort of thing that would bring a man like Cantor a small bit of joy. Victory, even if it was a Pyrrhic victory.

This information wasn't useful, though. It wasn't going to narrow down where Victor would have taken Evelyn. Unless Cantor decided to be forthright, he wasn't going to be much good as a resource.

It was time to change tactics.

"Did you know that Anwar Adham plans to sail a nuclear device under Cheyenne Mountain, using the underground river?"

Cantor said nothing, but his eyes shifted sideways. He was hiding something, of course. He was also feeling a slight twinge of … well, it wasn't guilt, or regret. More like satisfaction. Cantor felt relief about something. He wanted Adham to succeed.

"The base is already being evacuated, and the authorities are looking for another way into that river," Kotler said. "They'll have the opening at the dig site blasted clear within a couple of hours, so at worst they'll have to play catch-up with Adham."

Now it was time for Denzel to speak up. "We know about your father, Cantor."

Cantor nodded and spoke for the first time. "I'm sure you do," he said quietly. He looked away, as if looking into the distant past, toward Cheyenne Mountain and the site of his father's death. Kotler could read the grim satisfaction in Cantor's body language. He had resolved himself to his fate, if it came to that. As long as he took away his prize.

What was that prize, after all?

Vengeance, maybe. A bit of retribution against those who took his father from him. But Kotler wasn't sure that was it. At least, not entirely. Cantor had worked with Adham in much the same way he worked with the users of Zelot. They came to the site with their own agendas, and he mined their intelligence, insight, and resources for his purposes. Kotler was starting to put it together—Cantor had become a patron for Adham, because Adham could get him what he truly wanted.

Vengeance as a bonus, but it wasn't the driving goal. Cantor had proven himself better than everyone who had wronged him using one metric in particular. He used his billionaire success as a way to say to his mother and to everyone else that he didn't need them.

So, what happens to someone like that, someone who is fixated on wealth derived from his own genius as the score-card of his success—what happens when that wealth starts to dry up? What would drive him then?

Kotler thought for a moment, then said, "We also know about the city of gold."

Cantor looked up at him sharply. "Where is it?" he asked.

Kotler studied the man before him, inhaled and exhaled, taking his time. He watched the tension build.

Cantor sat almost rigid, the muscles in his jaw and neck working and straining. He shook his head and said, "You'll never know, Cantor. We're never going to tell you where it is, and you are certainly never going to see it. You'll never lay your hands on it, Cantor. But I do have some good news. It isn't what you think it is anyway. It was never going to be the salvation you hoped it would be."

Cantor gritted his teeth, the muscles of his jaw flexing. "It's mine by right," he said. "I sacrificed everything for it."

"What did you think that would get you, exactly?" Denzel asked. "This plan of yours never had any chance of anything but to get you put away for the rest of your life."

"We know you've been secretly funding Adham," Kotler said. "You may have destroyed some of the evidence, but we have enough to connect you to him. I'm sure there are forensic accountants already at work to follow the money trails."

Kotler glanced at Denzel, who nodded.

"You were hoping the city of gold would give you the funding you needed to escape after all the damage was done, right?"

Cantor had recovered and was once again exercising his right to remain silent. His body language, however, told Kotler everything.

"Cantor, I hate to be the one to break this to you," Kotler said. "But the city of gold—it was never what you thought it was. It was never going to be anything more than a sensational historic find. You spent your life and your fortune trying to find something that isn't what you think it is."

Cantor's expression was now shifting, and there were light traces of fear and pain. The haughtiness was fading. "What is it?" he whispered. It was clear he was obsessed, even now.

Kotler shook his head. "No. There isn't much I can do to you, Cantor, for all the damage you've done. The FBI will do plenty. But the one thing I can do is deny you any knowledge about that city. It's real, that much I'll tell you. It just isn't what you think it is."

"What is it!" Cantor demanded.

Kotler was through here. He nodded to Denzel, and the two of them walked out of the drawing room even as two agents stepped in to restrain Cantor, who was struggling to stand.

"What is it!" Cantor shouted again, pushing one of the against aside as the other subdued him, throwing him face down on the floor and twisting Cantor's arm behind him.

Kotler and Denzel ignored his plaintiff screams, and Denzel led the two of them through the house and to the kitchen.

This was a modern room—stone tile, natural wood cabinetry, and stainless steel everywhere. It was a chef's kitchen, with industrial appliances that would have been right at home in a fine restaurant. There were agents set up at tables, using them as field desks as they wrote reports and communicated with agents elsewhere.

Denzel led Kotler to a door that took them out into the grounds. There was a patio here, and a pool and hot tub formed a half circle around its edge.

When they were alone and staring out at the mountains, Denzel said, "We'll find her, Kotler."

Kotler nodded. "Thanks," he said. "I know you will. I'm just worried. And once again, pretty useless."

"Are you kidding?" Denzel asked. "You just got more out of Cantor in a one-minute conversation than we got out of him the whole time he's been held here."

Kotler smiled. "That's a good start, at least."

"You going to tell me what the story is with the city of gold?" Denzel asked.

Kotler laughed. "Tell you what, when this is over I'll show you."

Denzel blinked. "You mean you know where it is?"

Kotler smiled again. "Yes. But I'd prefer Adham be out of play before I take you there."

Denzel thought about this. "So it's underground," he said. "On the river."

Kotler was surprised. "I never said that."

Now Denzel laughed. "You didn't have to. It makes sense. I'm waiting to hear from the agents back at the research camp. They should have blown open that entrance by now. The plan is to put several boats in and charge Adham. The nuke is a problem, but there's not much else we can do."

"I'm sure they'll be delicate about it," Kotler said.

"We have a terrorist cell running loose under Colorado with an armed nuclear device made from stolen smoke detectors. There is nothing delicate about this situation. Those men ..." Denzel drifted, then took a breath. "Those men may not live through this day. But they'll stop Adham, somehow."

Kotler thought about this. "I met most of those agents, and they seemed like good men."

There was a sound from Denzel's belt, and he took a small radio out and responded.

"Sir," a voice came over the air. "We've found Dr. Horelica."

Kotler and Denzel exchanged glances, and Kotler felt dread grip his stomach.

"She's alive, sir," the agent said. "She took out her captor and she was found wandering on one of the main roads. We've taken her to a hospital, but she's alive."

Kotler let out a breath, and then turned and immediately started walking back to the house. Denzel raced to catch up with him, and the two of them made their way through the home and out to the front drive, where a car was already waiting for them. Denzel took the wheel, and they sped off to the hospital where Evelyn Horelica was being treated.

Chapter 26

KOTLER WAS LOSING his mind trying to hurry things along, but there were protocols to observe. Denzel had to meet with the agents who had brought Evelyn in, and get a quick debriefing. Kotler tried a couple of times to get through and go to her room but was stopped by the agents on duty.

Finally, Denzel caught up to him. "Come on," he said.

Kotler followed Denzel through the hospital corridors, and when they came to Evelyn's room, Denzel showed his badge and they were let inside without hesitation.

Evelyn was in a hospital gown and had an IV in the back of her hand. She was sitting up, leaning against the incline of the mattress. When she glanced down to see Denzel and Kotler walk in, her eyes went wide.

"Dan," she whispered.

Kotler rushed forward and hugged her. She clung to him, and they both cried, wetting each other's shoulders with hot tears.

"I never thought I'd see you again," she said.

He kissed her forehead. "I know. I'm sorry, I wish I could have found you sooner."

Her face crinkled, and she shook her head, tears running in streams down her cheeks. "They told me everything, Dan. I know you were doing everything you could."

They chatted some more, for several minutes, and finally Agent Denzel politely asked if he could talk to her about her experience.

It seemed that despite the turmoil of the past several weeks, Evelyn was more than ready to talk about the entire thing. She told Denzel everything she knew about her captors, which wasn't much. But her details about why she'd been abducted were almost more than the agent could jot down in his notebook.

She told them both about the artifacts and papers, which they had known about. And then she said, "He was after the river, and the city of gold."

"I know," Kotler said, smiling.

"But it isn't what he thinks it is. I kept hiding the truth from him."

Kotler laughed. "I know that, too."

Evelyn rolled her eyes. "For someone who knows so much, you sure took your time getting to me."

Kotler grimaced. "Sorry," he said. "There were a few hiccups along the way."

"Dr. Horelica," Denzel said. "In your research, did you see anything that might connect Mark Cantor to Anwar Adham? Anything that might have hinted at a terrorist action?"

She shook her head. "No. I know now that the river was part of that, but other than a few ideas connected to the city of gold, I never quite knew what he wanted with the river. He was trying to track it, I know that. He wanted to know its exact course, as closely as possible. But there wasn't really much information about that, except on the medallion."

Kotler arched his eyebrows. "Coelho's medallion? The one that was stolen?"

Evelyn shrugged. "I had no idea it was stolen, but yes. It took a while to crack it, but the medallion has a pretty detailed set of directions for finding the city of gold. It gives the distance, in a sense. There are markers that the Vikings installed as waypoints. The local indigenous population rarely visited the city, but they knew the way."

"How could I have missed that!" Kotler exclaimed.

"It was subtle," Evelyn said. "We kept translating the various Native American symbols as if they were literal phrases, but they were actually references to the waypoints. Each was named for something the locals would recognize. The medallion was a roadmap of sorts."

Kotler shook his head. "Well, we ended up figuring it all out despite ourselves, I guess."

Denzel jotted some things down, then closed his notebook. "Well, we found the medallion in Cantor's home. He had it locked in a safe in his bedroom. He spent quite a bit of money he didn't actually have for it to be stolen and delivered to him. I'm still not sure why. He had detailed scans of it. He didn't need the medallion itself to find the city."

"No," Kotler said. "But Cantor likes to control these things. He demonstrated that at the dig site, with the figurehead. I think it's an ego thing with him."

"Well whatever it is," Denzel replied, "it's over now." He turned to Evelyn. "I don't want to bother you anymore. I know you two have some catching up to do. I'm going to circle up with the field agents at the dig site and see what the progress has been on Adham's capture."

He nodded to them and left the room.

Kotler turned to Evelyn, kissed her hand, and said, "One second."

He followed Denzel out of the room. "Roland," he said.

Denzel stopped and faced him.

"I want to be there, when they bring down Adham," Kotler said.

Denzel shook his head. "Not a chance. First of all, it looks like this action is happening underground. There's no easy way to get you there in the first place. And second, you're a civilian. A smart one, for sure. And you've definitely held your own in this. But I'd never live through the hearing if I put you in jeopardy deliberately, after all of this."

"Crispen is the one who got me involved in this," Kotler said, though he knew deep down that he would have gotten involved anyway, once he discovered that Evelyn was abducted. "Let the hammer fall on him. Adham tortured me for information about that river."

"I know that," Denzel said quietly. "I understand. I do. I just can't put you in danger. Just stay here, Kotler. Rest. Take care of Evelyn. She needs you."

Kotler wanted to reply to that, to say that Evelyn was another reason he wanted to go, to be there when Adham was taken down. After everything, after all that had happened to the two of them, seeing Adham in handcuffs was the most Kotler could hope for, in terms of closure. He wanted to see this through.

He had a sudden inspiration. "At the very least, you should have me there to identify him. I'm the only person you have who has actually met Anwar Adham face to face."

Denzel considered this for a long moment, then shook his head and cursed. "That's clever," he grumbled.

Kotler grinned. "Of course," he replied. "Clever is what I do."

Chapter 27

KOTLER MADE sure Evelyn was on the mend, and that she had everything she needed. She was being transferred back to Houston in the morning, and Kotler made plans to connect with her there, after Adham was dealt with. Evelyn seemed better, but Kotler had observed that she was a bit on guard with him. Maybe she blamed him for all of this—it was his little quip about the *city of gold* that had set this off, wasn't it? Cantor had been monitoring their emails somehow, and he had taken Kotler's joke as confirmation.

The damage Cantor had done might be irreparable. Evelyn might have a difficult time forgiving Kotler, even if she knew it wasn't really his fault she was abducted. For now, Kotler was just happy she was safe. He could worry about repairing their relationship later.

After ensuring that Evelyn would be alright, and that she would have guarded posted at all times, Kotler left the hospital and went to a private airport nearby. He boarded a small plane, alongside Agent Denzel, and the two of them flew to the research camp, just a short hop away. It would have taken much longer to drive, and both Kotler and

Denzel were grateful for the short respite. They said nothing, but both relaxed and dozed for the duration of the flight.

They arrived within an hour, and Kotler and Denzel were escorted to the tunnel entrance, which looked very different than the last time Kotler had seen it.

Explosives had re-opened the cave, and engineers had stabilized it while laying in a metal staircase that led down into pure darkness.

Kotler felt a great sadness, looking at the ruins of the cave. This had been a significant archeological find—they hadn't even finished cataloging all they'd found here. The archway of the cave—now destroyed completely—had been the first evidence ever found of a relationship between the Vikings and the Native Americans. They had barely scratched the surface of what this site could teach them about these two ancient cultures, and how they had interacted. There were nuances to the findings here that could have changed the known path of history.

Now it was all gone—all but the photos and video records, the scans and the data, all of which had been funded by the man who had ultimately brought the site to destruction.

Kotler stifled the sadness, and instead allowed himself to feel angry. There were a lot of crimes, great and small, that Cantor would pay for. This was just more to add to the list.

"There are already two teams down there," Denzel said as he and Kotler stood at the mouth of the downward-sloping tunnel. "There's no real justification for us to go down there until they've already stopped Adham."

"But we're going anyway, right?" Kotler asked.

Denzel glanced around at the site, looking at the hundreds of FBI and DEA agents going about their work.

"I'm not in charge, you know," he said. "They've been relaying to me because I busted Crispen. But officially, I'm just another agent. I don't really have the authority to make a call about this."

"So we do it and ask for forgiveness later," Kotler said

"I'm pretty sure that's not the way the FBI works, and it's not the best idea you've had," Denzel said.

"Hardly the worst," Kotler grinned. "I've rushed into unstable caves before, trust me. Remind me to tell you about finding the Brass Hall some time."

"If we get out of this without being nuked or shot, I'll do that," Denzel replied. "For now, let's get down these steps and see what we have to work with."

They descended into the tunnel, and at first their way was barely lit by the sunlight leaking in from above. Then the lighting system kicked in and they could see the staircase sloping down to a small platform, obscured by the curve of the cavern.

When they reached this, Kotler realized that it was a floating dock. And attached to it was a rubber raft with an outboard motor.

"Well I would have to call that a sign," Kotler said.

"You want to take the boat?" Denzel replied.

Kotler looked at him. "Look, I don't want you to jeopardize your career or anything. I just ... I have to be a part of taking this man down. If you can't live with that, I understand. I'm taking the risk by choice, though. I can go alone."

"That wouldn't be any better for my career than going with you, actually," Denzel grinned. "So I might as well have a little adventure to remember all this by."

Kotler nodded. "Are you sure?"

In answer, Denzel led Kotler back up the stairs to the trailer that held the FBI's weapons and equipment. He gave

Kotler a bulletproof vest, but tore the FBI insignia off of it. As the sound of the Velcro still rang in Kotler's ears, he asked, "Does this mean I don't get a weapon either?"

"Not on your life," Denzel said.

"You know I'm trained, right?"

"Trained but not cleared. I have enough trouble coming my way."

Kotler nodded. In a pinch, he would have to make due with whatever was at hand. It wouldn't be the first time he'd had to work this way. It was just so much easier when he started with a weapon.

They exited the trailer, walked past the guards, and as stealthily as possible made their way back down the tunnel. When they came to the dock they climbed into the rubber raft, and Denzel untied them as Kotler used an oar to get them moving.

The waters were fairly still, and in the darkness they seemed deep and intimidating. They got away from the dock and Denzel started the motor. Kotler turned on the electric lamps and a small spotlight at the nose of the raft. He looked at Denzel, and saw the man was sweating and pale.

"Oh," Kotler said. "I forgot …you're claustrophobic, aren't you?"

"I'm fine," Denzel said, clenching his jaw.

"Definitely not fine. Are you sure you want to do this?"

"Please stop asking me that," Denzel said.

They puttered along the river, pushing through the darkness at a moderate speed. The river was wide and tall enough that a fairly large vessel could come through with no trouble. So there was no moment where they had to hunker down to avoid a low ceiling, or paddle their way through a narrow spot.

Kotler marveled at this. The fact that this river existed at all was miraculous, but the added fact that the Vikings had sailed these waters, hundreds of years ago, made this surreal.

Kotler played with the lights a bit, shining one directly up to the ceiling. This was in part to get a view of the concave walls of the cavern, but also in part to give Denzel some relief. Kotler knew that if Denzel could see this place as expansive, it would ease his claustrophobia.

They ran in silence for quite some time. The team pursuing Adham had a fair lead on them, but they would be moving with much more caution. Denzel had figured they were bound to catch up if they kept their speed constant.

Several hours later they started to hear a popping sound. Minutes after that the sound became almost continuous, and as it echoed from the cavern walls and ceilings it sounded like hail hitting a tin roof.

The radio Denzel had clipped to his belt had been silent during their entire run, but now the chatter started. They heard the FBI and DEA teams ahead, coordinating an attack.

"I don't get it," Denzel said. "Are they still in the water? It sounds like they're moving on land. They're coordinating with each other to surround Adham."

"That makes sense," Kotler said. "They're probably in the city."

"The city?" Denzel asked.

"The city of gold," Kotler said. "Adham has probably found it by now and is fortifying it."

"I thought you said it wasn't real?"

"I said it wasn't what Cantor thought it was," Kotler said.

Denzel shook his head, then picked up the radio and called to the men down the way, letting them know he and

Kotler were in play. He got an earful from whoever was leading the team, but then he was given an assignment.

Denzel and Kotler were to stay in the river and see if they could make their way around the edge of the city without being spotted.

Kotler shut off all of the lights on the boat, and for several minutes they were in complete darkness. He could hear Denzel breathing heavy, but he was at a loss as to how he might help his friend.

Then, blissfully, a gradient of light appeared. And as they moved, this grew brighter. As they rounded a bend in the river, the whole cavern was lit like dusk.

"Son of a bitch," Denzel said in awe.

Ahead of them was an island.

There were dozens of stone structures that looked like huts surrounding a large, central building. Even from this distance, Kotler could see dozens of agents taking position, firing their weapons in bright bursts, and in turn ducking from weapons fire coming from the buildings themselves.

Adham and his men had taken the city of gold, and they were using it as a well-defended position.

Kotler watched the gunplay with some fascination, but he was far more excited by the city. Here, miles under the surface, was the remnant of an entire culture that was older than the United States itself. The implications of this were mind boggling. Kotler wanted nothing more but to explore every inch of this place, to find any records or hints of the civilization that built it. For the moment, he had to concentrate on not being shot.

"We'll skirt along the wall of the cavern," Denzel said. "We'll have to turn off the motor and use paddles."

"Got it," Kotler said, gripping the oar he'd used earlier.

Denzel moved them as far to their right as they could

get. Stalactites and protrusions from the walls prevented them from moving in a smooth and straight line, but those same protrusions helped provide some cover for them as they paddled. Denzel took up his own oar, and he and Kotler worked meticulously to keep the boat moving.

The firefight on the island showed no signs of slowing any time soon. The agents were well armed but so, apparently, were Adham's men. Plus, they held the ultimate trump card, with that nuke in tow.

Kotler whispered, "What's to keep them from setting off that nuke?"

"Not strategic enough," Denzel said. "They might do it if it looks like they're trapped here with no hope of escape, but for the moment they still think they can win this."

Kotler kept his opinions on that matter to himself. Because from his perspective, they very well *could* win this. They had a very well defended position, with plenty of old stone structures to protect them. Meanwhile, their backs were to the prize—all they really had to do was put the nuke on a boat with a couple of men and send it upriver to finish the mission. The rest of Adham's men could stay behind to make sure the agents never got through.

As Kotler and Denzel continued to push along the wall of the cavern, Kotler realized that this idea might have occurred to Adham, too. In fact, why wouldn't it occur to him? Adham had proven himself to be a very strong tactician. He knew how to plan against inevitable dangers, but he was also good at adapting to whatever came his way. He was smart enough to know that no matter how well protected he was in the city of gold, eventually the FBI and DEA would overrun him.

So he wouldn't risk it. Kotler realized that Adham would certainly go with a plan to send the nuke ahead.

"Denzel," Kotler whispered. "Adham isn't here."

"What? How do you know?"

"He would have taken one of the boats and carried that nuke on. He's headed for Cheyenne Mountain. This fight is just a distraction."

Denzel considered this. "You're sure?" he asked.

"Call it 99 percent," Kotler said.

Denzel looked up at the island. "We can't just dash out of here. We have to help them. They're expecting us to get around the island and provide a distraction."

"Fine," Kotler said. "But let's just make it a dine and dash, ok? Let's create a distraction and then get back in the water."

Denzel nodded. "You have a plan, I take it?"

"It's going to involve doing something dramatically stupid," Kotler said.

Denzel rolled his eyes but said, "Why not? It's worked for us so far."

Chapter 28
CITY OF GOLD

DENZEL AND KOTLER dragged their raft up onto the rocky slope on the far side of the underground island. The fighting was all concentrated downriver, and here—other than the echoing cacophony of sounds from the firefight—it was almost peaceful. There would be patrols, Kotler was sure. Most of the attention was concentrated on the out buildings of the city, on the other side of the island from where they now crouched.

They moved quickly, taking cover behind large stones and stalagmites. Ahead of them they saw men moving in bass relief against the electric lights and bright flares of gunfire.

As they got closer, they spotted two men moving in crouches, guns raised, patrolling the shore of the island for invaders such as Kotler and Denzel. They were too late in spotting trouble, however, and Denzel shot both of them quickly. He and Kotler raced forward then, stripped the men and dressed in their clothes. They pulled their coats on over their bulletproof vests. Denzel removed the FBI insignia from his own vest, in case any stray glint of light might catch it.

They also took weapons and a few other items off of these men. Kotler felt much better with a weapon in his hands. But it was something he found in one of the terrorist's pockets that really made him grin.

"Grenade," Kotler.

"Give me that!" Denzel snapped.

"Have you had live fire training with grenades?" Kotler asked.

"I'm going to pretend you didn't ask that."

They left the two bodies there and continued on as if they were resuming patrol. They moved closer to the back ranks of the terrorists who were engaged in the firefight. Most were obscured by tumbled stone walls, but a few were wide open from this angle.

"Ready?" Denzel asked.

"Ready," Kotler said, raising his weapon.

Denzel held up the grenade. "I think we'll start with this," he said. He pulled the pin and then lobbed the grenade in a low arc, right into the area immediately behind a cluster of Adham's men.

In seconds, the grenade detonated, killing several of the men close by while wounding numerous others.

Kotler's heart broke to see some of the buildings had taken damage as well, but there was little to be done about it at this point. Instead, he raised his weapon, just as Denzel did the same. They laid down fire from this side of the island.

Adham's men were taken completely by surprise, and it took several seconds for them to scramble and adjust to this new threat. They'd lost a significant number of men to that grenade, but their numbers were still high enough that they could hold their line for quite a while.

Kotler and Denzel backed away, keeping low to avoid the shots, and scrambled to get back to their raft. Denzel keyed his radio. "We've done all we can," he said. "Adham is upriver with the nuke. We're going after him."

The voice on the other side of the radio came back, "Take him. We have this under control. Thanks for the assist!"

"I may need you to return the favor when you're done here," Denzel said.

"I'll have men running your way."

Denzel started the motor for the raft and the two of them sped away, angling back to the wall of the cavern where they at least got small bit of cover. Miraculously they avoided being shot, or even taking a hit to the raft itself. The raft was sheathed in Kevlar, but there was always a chance of a puncture. Kotler shivered at the thought of ending up in these dark, unexplored waters, and decided it was best to keep his mind on the task ahead.

There was no way to know for sure where they were in relation to the surface. It was possible they were closing in on the Cheyenne Mountain facility by this point. They might be close enough that if Adham set off that nuke it would accomplish his goal.

Adham had not seemed like the suicidal type to Kotler, but then you could never underestimate terrorist zeal. Adham was clearly an educated man, and incredibly intelligent. Whatever his reasons for wanting this war with the United States, he seemed willing to sacrifice himself in the cause of it. Or was it possible that Adham had an escape route in mind?

Actually, now that Kotler thought about it, why wouldn't

he?

There was no need for Adham to be present when the nuke detonated. In fact, he could theoretically leave it floating just under Cheyenne Mountain while he made his escape up river. The Vikings had gotten into this underground river somehow. Adham must have been counting on finding that entrance and using it as his exit. He had never intended to die for this cause.

Which also explained why he, personally, had left with the nuke in tow. He might have some of his men with him, but it was a sure bet that Adham had hopped into his boat with the intention of leaving the nuke somewhere and making his escape.

What a coward, Kotler thought. The man was brilliant, and dedicated to his sick cause, but not so dedicated that he'd die for it if it could be helped. He'd rather create a holocaust that impacted millions of people while keeping himself safe, as far away as possible.

They continued running upriver for the next few hours, and Kotler was starting to wonder about their plan. This was already an unsafe place, by its very nature. Add in a group of armed terrorists with a nuclear device and things were even more harrowing. But other minor concerns— food, fuel, a means of escape—were starting to worm their way into Kotler's mind as the tension and excitement of this little adventure began to fade.

Denzel must have felt that as well. "Do we have any way of knowing how much further it is to Cheyenne Mountain?"

Kotler shook his head, despite knowing that Denzel likely couldn't see him. "I suspect we're already under the mountain itself," he replied. "The base is further in, but judging by the way this cavern runs I'd guess that we're not far from it. Just a guess, though."

"And no sign of Adham," Denzel said.

"No," Kotler replied, and the word was bitter. He had half hoped they would come across Adham and his men after the first bend, and with each subsequent twist and turn the river took that hope was halved. Now it was anticipation mixed with dread. Kotler was feeling impatient.

Luckily, the wait was abruptly over.

They rounded yet another stony bend in the river and were greeted immediately by a wash of bright lights. Kotler quickly snapped off their own spotlight and dimmed the lanterns, while Denzel cut the motor to the boat. They used the oars to once again paddle their way to the outcroppings of rock on the side of the sloping cavern wall, keeping themselves as hidden as possible behind a small outcropping thrown into shadow.

Ahead, Adham and his men—four of them, by Kotler's count—were shifting from one boat to another. They had tied off their second boat, and one of Adham's men was leaning over to tinker with something inside.

"That's going to be the platform for the nuke," Denzel whispered.

Kotler nodded and whispered back. "What should we do? We're too far from the island for anyone to get here in time."

"We'll have to take them down," Denzel said. "We'll paddle closer."

"There's another option," Kotler said, though he was inwardly screaming at himself. "We can let them go."

"What?" Denzel asked. "Why in the hell would we do that?"

"We can disarm the nuke, and then go after them again. They're looking for the entrance the Vikings used to get down here, and who knows where that might be? Miles from here, for sure. It's going to take them days to get out, if my estimates are right. We have time."

Denzel considered this. "It's a good plan, but we really have no idea how they're arming that nuke. There may not be a way to disarm it, once they're gone. Or Adham may have some kind of remote."

"So we can't risk it," Kotler said, letting out a breath. "That's a relief."

Denzel laughed lightly. "I knew you didn't want to let him go."

"No," Kotler said, raising his weapon. "Shall we go save the day?"

In answer Denzel started the motor and they were suddenly racing toward Adham and his men.

"Don't shoot the nuke," Denzel said.

"The chances of that device going nuclear from a stray bullet hit are almost incalculable," Kotler said.

"But the chances of hitting one of the explosive charges and setting it off, releasing radioactive material into the air and water while possibly collapsing this cavern in on us are a little more likely," Denzel said.

"Good point," Kotler admitted.

He aimed at the four-man boat, high enough to avoid hitting the nuke.

Adham and his men were taken by surprise but recovered quickly. Someone in the boat gunned their motor and they shot forward, taking evasive action. They headed straight for one of the bends in the river, with a jagged array of stones that could provide cover.

"They're going to try to fortify that spot," Denzel shouted over the motor.

In answer Kotler let off a bleat of gun fire, tracking splashes in the water until he had a bead on the boat's outboard motor. In the next instant this was chewed into so many twisted bits of metal as Kotler dismantled it from afar with the automatic rifle.

Adham's men dove into the water, trying to get away from the hail of bullets. Two of them had the presence of mind to gain purchase on the stone walls of the cavern and start returning fire, but their angles and position were so awkward they were having a hard time aiming.

From the boat, however, Adham stood with a rifle of his own.

Kotler shouted, and Denzel took evasive action, angling toward the wall and putting a jut of rock between them. Kotler heard the report of the rifle echoing through the cavern, and the ping-whiz of bullets on stone near where they were taking cover.

"We have to take him down!" Denzel shouted.

Kotler thought for a moment. "I have a plan, but you're not going to like it."

"Sounds perfect," Denzel grated.

Kotler crawled out of the boat and clung to the jagged rocks. He reached in and turned on the spotlight at the nose of the boat, aiming it dead forward. He motioned for Denzel to get out as well. Kotler began tinkering with the outboard motor, tilting it up and out of the water. Using a strap from his rifle, Kotler wrapped the throttle and tied it in the open position. The propellers of the motor spun at high speed, and the whine from it filled the cavern, cutting off any other sound.

Kotler had Denzel help him position the boat, and then he quickly tilted it down again, so the props were back in the water.

The now empty raft shot out and away, angling in the general direction of Adham.

Kotler and Denzel swung around the jutting stone that was giving them cover, and as Adham began firing at their raft they each took aim and fired their own weapons.

Kotler could see Adham in the light from their raft's spotlight, and he was able to get a better bead on him. It was difficult, dealing with the water and the rifle, trying to keep steady with his head above water as he aimed. It paid off as he watched plumes of blood erupted from Adham's back, glistening in red streams lit by the spotlight of their abandoned raft.

Adham staggered, letting his rifle fall to his side, and then fell, tilting backwards over the side of the raft and into the dark waters of the river. Kotler watched intently, but never saw Adham surface.

From their vantage point they were able to spot Adham's men. Two had died in the firefight, but two more survived. They were exposed, in their positions, and were firing at Kotler and Denzel while screaming something Kotler couldn't decipher, among the noise and echoes within the cavern. Denzel and Kotler focused their fire, and because they were in a much better position they took the remaining terrorists out with just a few shots.

The gunfire and motor noise slowly died out. Their raft continued on down river, and Kotler watched its light fade in the distance. Denzel turned on a flashlight, which he was able to clip to his vest.

"Great," Denzel said. "The bad guys are dead, and we're stuck. Now what?"

In answer Kotler dropped his rifle, letting it sink into the darkened waters, and quickly swam back toward the boat that contained the nuke.

Denzel cursed before doing the same.

Chapter 29

KOTLER AND DENZEL had dried off, changed clothes, and debriefed.

Denzel took some flak from the field agent in charge, especially when it was realized that Denzel had brought along a civilian to a firefight. There was some dressing down, and some threats. In the end, that seemed to be as far as the agent was willing to take the reprimand. Given that Denzel and Kotler had just risked both their lives and saved one of the world's premier military bases, not to mention the city of Colorado Springs and its populace, there was an unprecedented level of leeway given. Terrorist threats with nuclear devices turn out to be great tension breakers, Kotler surmised.

They spent the rest of the day repeating the details, as they knew them. The nuke had been brought back in their boat, having never been fully armed when the two of them had attacked Adham's men. The bomb itself was dismantled and contained, and Denzel and Kotler were relieved to hear they had suffered only minor radiation exposure.

Once the debriefings were complete, Kotler called Evelyn

to fill her in on as much as he could share. He'd been warned that he was not to mention the nuke, or how close Adham had gotten to his objective. That was now classified information, and Kotler was more than happy to leave it that way.

Evelyn was thrilled to hear he was alright, and that he had helped save the day. "I'm leaving for Houston in an hour," she said. "And once I'm cleared there I'm going to gather my things."

"Are you coming back to Manhattan?" he asked. In all this, he'd come to realize just how much he missed Evelyn, and how much he'd risked by not being who she needed him to be. He wasn't sure, even now, if he could truly be that for her. He knew himself, perhaps better than he knew anything. He knew his faults, which were many. But for Evelyn, he would try. He would put in the work. He would ...

"No," she said, and there was a note of something in her voice that Kotler couldn't quite place. He felt it, like cracking glass within his chest. "I'm going to take a bit of a break," she said. "I'm going home. For a while, at least. I just ... I need to feel safe. "

"I understand," Kotler said quietly. "Can I visit you?"

There was a pause. "Dan, I'm sorry—I don't want to sound ungrateful after everything you went through, to help rescue me. I just ..."

Kotler cut her off. "It's ok," he said, and forced himself to smile, so she could hear a note of it in his voice. "I understand completely."

"You do?" Evelyn asked, laughing nervously. "Because I'm not sure I understand it entirely myself."

"This has been traumatic," Kotler said. "You've been through something ... terrifying." He had started to say *extraordinary*, but he was glad he had stopped himself. It wouldn't do for him to sound in any way fascinated by her ordeal. It wasn't what he meant, but he knew that in her current state she might take it that way. He didn't want to start one of their familiar patterns, the argument over nothing more than his insensitivity. She needed him to be better than that. "Go home," he said. "Be with your family. If you ever want to talk, I'll be here."

"Good," she said quietly. They hung up, and Kotler rubbed his eyes with one hand.

"How'd it go?" Denzel asked him.

"She's going home," Kotler said, pausing a moment before looking up. "I have a feeling I won't see or hear from her for a while."

"I'm sorry," Denzel said.

Kotler smiled, marveling at Denzel's intuitive insight. Of course, it wouldn't take someone of Kotler's expertise to read his body language at the moment. Still, he appreciated Denzel's empathy. After all they'd been through, Kotler had started to think of the agent as a friend.

He realized Denzel had been studying him during his slight pause. "I'd rather she be safe," Kotler said. "It's fine."

Denzel nodded, clearly not convinced but not pushing it any further. Kotler was grateful for that.

"So what's next for you?" Denzel asked. "Now that all of this is over, where do you go?"

"Well," Kotler said, grinning and chuckling. "I'm hoping to go back to the City of Gold, once it's cleared. It's an amazing historic find!"

"About that," Denzel said. "I have clearance to return to the site. I figured you'd want to come with me. I convinced them that your expertise might help us close any loops that could still be open in this case."

Kotler laughed. "Well, how could I turn that offer down? I appreciate the vote of confidence."

Denzel nodded, and the two of them went for a meal and a night's rest before embarking on their trip to the City of Gold.

EPILOGUE
CITY OF GOLD

THE FBI HAD CLEARED some of the research team to assist in setting up a new camp in the cavern. The island that was home to the City of Gold was large enough to support a few dozen people, as well as the equipment and resources they brought with them.

Kotler was temporarily in charge of the site, guiding the researchers in where they should concentrate their search for historic artifacts, but also guiding the FBI in where to place lighting and surveillance equipment. The FBI was very keen to keep any unauthorized personnel from going upriver. That path would be restricted until they could be sure no one was attempting to replicate Adham's plan.

Denzel stood beside Kotler as he pointed out details and features of the stone structures of the island. The agent was patient with Kotler's geeky enthusiasm for the history of this place, but after a time Kotler could see he was growing bored.

Denzel sighed. "I still don't get the joke. Why was this place referred to as the City of Gold when there's no actual gold here?"

Kotler laughed. "Sorry, I forgot—I haven't officially told you. I put it in the report, but you may not have had a chance to read that yet."

"So what's the story?"

Kotler shook his head. "Context is everything, isn't it? Mark Cantor wanted to find this island because he believed it was literally a city of gold. *El Dorado*, perhaps. Or maybe just the basis of the legend for it. His fortune was pretty much exhausted by his bad investments and the gambles he took with new technologies and new industries. What little he had left was quickly depleted after he started funding Adham's work. He really did want revenge for his father's death. The fact that he was enabling a terrorist to kill millions of American Citizens probably didn't bother him in the least. From all accounts, Cantor would have been happy enough to go bankrupt as long as Adham managed to blow up NORAD on his way out."

"He was pretty close anyway," Denzel said. "But then, why go after the city of gold? If all he wanted was revenge, why bother?"

"Cantor has a fixed mindset," Kotler said. "He defines himself by his wealth and success. When he emancipated himself from his mother and stepfather, he pored himself into studying and excelling, building his empire on his genius. His identity was tied up with that success. If he failed, who would he be? Without the fortune he'd made, who was he? So, when he came across the information about the river, about its proximity to NORAD, and found that it tied in with the legend of a city of gold, he saw an opportunity to have everything he wanted."

Denzel shook his head. "I guess the gold from this place was a way for him to have his cake and eat it too."

"Except, as you can see ... no gold."

"Right," Denzel said. "So what gives?"

Kotler laughed. "Ok, this is where it gets really funny. See, the Vikings managed to make their way through this river. Miles and miles underground. They must have found this island and set it up as a sort of base of operations. This was home, after spending weeks and months on this river. They knew how to get back, and they measured the distance with markers they placed along the way. It wouldn't have been that difficult. But this was a treasure too good to ignore. A fully fortified city in the underworld! At least, from the Viking's point of view, that's what all of this would seem like."

Kotler waved a hand at the stone structures. "They were a proud people, and the idea of conquering the underworld and taking a piece of it for themselves would have been incredibly appealing. And then, once they had this place established, they continued on down river until they came to the cave where they eventually met the Native Americans."

"And struck up some kind of friendship with them," Denzel said.

"In a way," Kotler replied. "Remember the totem? Some of those natives revered the Vikings, seeing them as great spirits who rose up from the depths of the Earth. There was a bit of worship happening. And chances are, after the alliance was formed, some of the natives went back with the Vikings, to this city." Kotler waved a hand to indicate the stone walls of some of the ruins.

"So what about the gold?" Denzel asked, impatient.

Kotler smiled. "Well, if you were from a race of people who had never seen blonde hair before, how would you describe it?"

Denzel blinked, then made a guttural noise, shaking his head. "You're kidding," he said.

Kotler laughed. "The City of Gold was named for the blonde hair of the Vikings! The Native Americans had never seen it before, and that was one of the traits they assumed made the Vikings into great spirits. Coming here, seeing an entire Viking culture, and with underground stone structures no less—that must have made quite an impression! One they documented in the best way they could."

Denzel shook his head. "So no gold. Ever."

"Not even a nugget," Kotler agreed.

"So what happened here?" Denzel asked. "Why aren't we standing her chatting with an entire culture of underground Vikings or something?"

Kotler shook his head, and his expression softened. "The river, actually," he said.

"What about it?"

"Remember the crushed bits of wood from the research camp? The remnants of the Viking ship? I was curious about that. How did it get so far up into the caves, when the river itself was so far down? There were not slopes or rises that the Vikings could have used as a slip. But look at these stones," Kotler pointed to the stone structures. "See that? Dried algae. These have been underwater, probably numerous times. In fact, I'd say that these were under water fairly recently, maybe within the past two or three years."

"So the river rises?" Denzel asked, looking around him and obviously a bit more worried.

"It's probably something that happens once or twice in a century," Kotler said. "It's probably tied to the same seismic activity that buried the tunnel entrance in the first place. There's every indication that the Vikings were here when the waters rose, and it must have happened so suddenly that they couldn't escape. They boarded one of their vessels, but before they could make it to the caves it was crushed against the cavern, and all hands drowned. The remnants likely floated up into the cave opening itself, and when the waters receded they were left behind."

Denzel shook his head, then shivered. "That's ... that's just horrible. I can't imagine going out like that."

"Chances are they couldn't imagine going out in a nuclear explosion," Kotler said. "This story is full of horrible ways to die."

"So that's it then?" Denzel asked. "The City of Gold was named for the Viking's hair color, and they were killed by the same river that brought them here? That's the whole story?"

"Not by a long shot," Kotler laughed. "We still have to figure out how they got here in the first place, and what sort of arrangement they had with the indigenous tribes of North America. What impact did they have on the culture here? What permanent marks might they have left? We have the whole of ancient American history to redefine." Kotler smiled at this.

Denzel rolled his eyes. "Ok. Well, I've had enough of ancient American history and Vikings and terrorists. I'm on the next boat out of here, and I'll be back in Manhattan tomorrow. When will you be going back?"

"A few days," Kotler said. "And then I'll be working on documenting all of this. Dr. Coelho will be thrilled to be updated."

Denzel nodded.

As Kotler walked him to the makeshift dock, at the island's edge, he shook Denzel's hand and said his goodbyes. They would remain in touch. Denzel was a good man, and a good man to know. If nothing else positive had come from all of this, Kotler was pleased to at least have made a new friend.

He returned then to the stone structure and had a chat with several researchers. Everything here was thrilling and new, and the implications for American history were astounding.

But even as he continued to talk and speculate and muse about possibilities, Kotler could feel himself detaching from all of this. The new head of research would take over soon, and Kotler would return to Manhattan, to writing, to speaking and touring. He would talk about this find as much as he was allowed, and he would be thrilled that he had been such a large part of the discovery.

And then he'd be on to the next thing. Whatever else he could discover about the world was already beckoning him.

He could hardly wait.

STUFF AT THE END OF
THE BOOK

This book was written on a dare.

Well, not really. It was more like the kind of thing that happens when two guys are drinking together and one of them says, "You should totally ask that girl out." And then, emboldened by the booze, the other guy does it. And by some miracle she says yes.

My friend and writing partner, Nick Thacker, was the first guy.

Nick is a thriller writer. And he's good at it. He writes books that smack of the kind of storytelling mastered by James Rollins and Dan Brown and Robert Ludlum. He writes about some of the mysterious things that happen right in front of us, in a contemporary world filled with more magic than we're usually willing to admit.

Nick and I have worked together (and really well) for the past two years or so. He's read some of my work, and he claims to like it. And so, he thought I should write a thriller of my own—mostly to see what that would look like.

Lately, over maybe the past year, I've been shifting the type of storytelling that I do. I always wrote genre fiction—

primarily science fiction and a bit of fantasy. And some of that is of the "space ships and high science" variety. But in 2015 I wrote a book called *Evergreen*, which—while still a bit of science fiction—had a much more thriller feel.

And I fell in love.

The thing is, that book was set in a more contemporary universe, even with its fantastic and far out premise. And that's something that I love. That's the type of book I enjoy reading, it's the type of movie I enjoy watching, and it was inevitable that it would be the type of book I'd enjoy writing.

I wanted to play around with that theme a bit more, so I wrote a three-book serial called *Think Tank*. That was meant to be my bid at a story similar to the televisions series *House*, only without the medical drama. *Think Tank* features a cast of characters who have no super powers, no magic weapons, no spaceships. Instead, they have their brains and their attitudes and a super wealthy benefactor.

That little series did well. It was loved by the readers. It ended a bit short, I'll admit, and I'll eventually get back to it and write more 'episodes.' But for the most part it served its purpose with me.

It let me explore the idea of writing fiction in a contemporary universe, without any tropes or gimmicks to fall back on.

In a way, that series was a bike with training wheels. And between that and *Evergreen*, I was feeling pretty confident about what it was I wanted to do with my writing career.

When Nick essentially dared me to write a thriller, then, I could hardly say no.

The funny thing about thrillers is that they're almost always thinly veiled science fiction stories.

Seriously—read any given thriller and there will be

some element of science fiction to it. A laser on the moon. An Amazonian tribe that has a mind control drug. A relic that unlocks an ancient, buried city that contains forgotten technology. It's all there.

But the thing about a thriller that makes it different than science fiction is that it's a very grounded story.

The science has an explanation. There's a reason why it works.

In most actual sci-fi, the super science is just there. It doesn't need an explanation other than, "This is what came to pass."

Knowing that about thrillers, it was a little easier for me to agree to write *The Coelho Medallion*. It made it simply a matter of toning down one type of storytelling and amping up the other.

The other key component of a thriller? A mystery. Or, more accurate, a puzzle. We read and love thrillers because we get to tag along with the hero and help him or her figure out what's happening, based on some pretty interesting clues. That makes us feel smart, and it makes us feel excited about all the twists and turns the story can take.

Now all that is well and good, but in order for me to start a story like this I needed a few foundational pieces. I needed a solid idea with some quirky little puzzles to solve.

In the prologue of this book there are four little vignettes [AUTHOR'S NOTE: There are now only three vignettes. I removed one that really had no place in the book, and that served to weaken the story. If you'd like to read it, I've included it in the back of this edition of the book]. The very first, about the theft of warehouse full of smoke detectors, was actually the last vignette to be written. In fact, of the four, it's only one written specifically for this book.

The other three were imports.

Back before I'd actually published my first book, I started a story around a character named Xander Travel. And if you've read my fantasy series, *Sawyer Jackson*, you'll recognize that name. Xander is an Exemplar—the model upon which all humanity was based. He's quirky and funny and quick witted. Think *Doctor Who*, but instead of a TARDIS he moves around the Omniverse using buttons and bits of string.

But back when I wrote those three opening scenes, Xander Travel was going to be a Dan Kotler.

I had this whole story in mind that involved an Indiana Jones-type explorer who becomes embroiled in an ancient mystery with modern-day repercussions. Xander Travel would be that character, originally.

But like so many starter books back then, this one petered out and was never finished.

Until now.

True, the names were changed to protect the exemplary. And the premise would have had nothing to do with Vikings or cities of gold or a psychotic billionaire. But the gist of the opening was almost exactly as you read it. I'm pretty sure it would have been a fun read.

But those little bits of story sat on a hard drive (actually, they sat in a Google Doc) for years. Nearly a decade, if I'm counting right. And it wasn't until Nick pushed me to write a thriller, and I started thinking about ideas, that I dusted those bits off and put them to work.

Time and experience can really change your perspective.

Since writing those scenes originally, I've published more than twenty novels, novellas, and non-fiction books. I've started hosting three different podcasts. I've left the full-time job I had at the time (advertising copywriter with a

Houston-based agency), and a couple more jobs besides. And I've actually gotten pretty good at this book thing.

So the book I wrote this time around, starting with those three scenes, was nothing like the book I would have written back when those scenes were originally penned. It's better, I believe. It has more nuance.

So, I guess I'm saying that I'm glad Nick talked me into it.

Now will I write more books like this? Well, the short answer is "absolutely." Because I enjoyed writing this book. Immensely. I enjoyed the characters. I enjoyed the pacing. I enjoyed the nuances themselves.

I learned a lot on this book, too. Because it took a bit more time than my other books. It took more planning, and more attention to detail. It wasn't more difficult, but it was more involved.

I'll write more like these. But I'll also continue to write science fiction the way I've always done it. Because those stories are important to me too.

Actually, if you promise not to tell anyone, I'll let you in on a teensy little secret ...

I still consider these books to be science fiction. So it's kind of like cheating.

A NOTE ON THE NEW EDITION

When I published *The Coelho Medallion*, back in 2016, I had no idea what I was in for. If you just read the previous section, you know this was all started on a dare. What I didn't realize then, and have come to realize now, is that dare was fate, putting me on a path I never even knew I wanted to take.

Also, from the previous section, you read that I would continue to write the same science fiction and fantasy books I had written prior to *The Coelho Medallion*, and that was true. For a time.

It isn't that I decided to abandon those other genres. I actually did write a handful of new books, between then and now, that fit into both sci-fi and fantasy. As I wrote each, though, I had this nagging feeling that I needed to *get back to work*.

Thrillers, it seemed, had become my genre.

As of this writing, I've just published the fourth Dan Kotler Archaeological Thriller, *The Girl in the Mayan Tomb*. After hitting publish on that book, I decided it was time for me to loop back and fix some things that have bothered me about *The Coelho Medallion*, since its release.

If you happened to have read earlier editions of this book, you may have picked up on a few errors. There were typos, of course. There are always typos. I can't escape them, no matter how many editors, and how many dollars, are dedicated to that purpose. But there were also greater errors —plot holes that a few smart readers spotted and asked about, and for which I had no excuse.

These nagged at me. Always. To the point that I would sometimes balk at recommending the book to people, because I was ashamed of the errors. The book had won awards and had been a bestseller, but I still felt shame over my goofs. That's no way to live.

I am a proponent of something that drives some authors and editors to drink. It's something I've talked about at author conferences, and on podcasts and at speaking engagements. It's a process I truly believe is part of the evolution of literature, but there are people who break out the torches and pitchforks when I mention it.

It's called *iterative publishing.*

The idea, put simply, is that an author should get his or her book to the best possible condition, given their personal means and resources, and then release it, even if it isn't perfect. Put it out in the wild, for consumers to purchase, even if there are a few typos or other gaffs.

You can see why this isn't a popular idea, but bear with me.

This idea is borrowed from a product development philosophy known as *MVP,* or *minimum viable product.* In short, you make your product "ready enough," and you release it with the intention of improving it over time.

It's a popular model with the software industry, but people in publishing want to stab you for it. Trust me.

Don't get me wrong, I'm not advocating that a book should be released without editing. Typos are annoying. It's just that they're also inevitable. I find typos even in works of classic literature—books that have been read and re-read by millions of discerning and intelligent people, for decades. No one ever seems to blast Dickens or Hemingway or Faulkner over typos.

The thing is, unlike those guys, I have a huge advantage, and it's one I press constantly. Because of the nature of publishing today, and the tools I have at my disposal, I can actually go back to a book, make some changes, and have that book available for sale again, all within a 24-hour period. At most, 48 hours.

Since that's the case, I decided long enough that good enough was good enough, as long as I was committed to making it better.

The Coelho Medallion was always a serious effort. I produced the best book I could, at the time. Perfect? No. There were plenty of errors and problems. And yet, somehow, the book became a bestseller and won some awards, and it has consistently been a favorite for my readers. It gets solid five-star reviews on Amazon, and it has brought me praise and kudos from some discerning fellow authors. Some of the people who read it are quick to point out the problems, but most get so engrossed in the story, they are able to easily overlook my goofs.

So that was Version 1.0.

Because I believe in iterative publishing, though, I decided a month back that I would spend some time reading and editing and rewriting, to make *The Coelho*

Medallion a better book. And as of right now, I believe that's exactly what I've done.

This book means a lot to me. It started something wonderful in my life. I'm grateful for it, and grateful for those readers who loved it. I'm also very, very grateful to finally have the chance to come back and fix all those little annoyances, those things that really bugged me, so that I can present to you a better version of this book I love.

Will I ever revisit it again? Do another rewrite in the future? Probably not. Other than a willingness to fix any typos that readers might point out to me, I think I'm finally done with this book. I have more Dan Kotler stories to tell. I'm going to look and move forward. And you're invited to go with me.

Kevin Tumlinson
    February 13, 2018
    Pearland, Texas

THE LOST VIGNETTE

AUTHOR'S NOTE: *The following scene originally appeared as the second vignette, in the opening prologue. Funny thing, this was actually the very first scene I wrote, for this book. Although it wasn't actually for this book. It was a scene I had started and never finished, and when Nick Thacker dared me to write a thriller I cast about for something I could use as a starting point.*

The story of Hal and Heidi really had nothing to do with the main plot. It did set up the underground river, which was the principle reason I left it in. But honestly, it does nothing to move the story forward, and therefore has no place in the book. Hal and Heidi's problems really should have stayed private, I guess.

However, I wouldn't want you to miss out. So I've included the scene here, at the end. You don't have to read it to understand anything about the story, and it has little to nothing to do with the things Dan Kotler and Roland Denzel faced. But it is kind of a cute vignette, with a happy ending. So enjoy.

Northwest of Pueblo, Colorado

Just when Hal thought that every inch of mountains, trees, and rivers in the world had been catalogued and named and pixeilized by Google Maps, he crested another Colorado ridge. There, stretching out in front of him, was a world that couldn't possibly be known.

How could it? Not a road for miles. No houses or barns or derelict old gas stations. Even airplane flight paths skirted this spot. For once, all Hal had to show for civilization, as far as his eye could see, was himself. His collection of Gander Mountain hiking gear was the closest thing to human intrusion for miles.

And then his mobile phone rang.

He fumbled in the pocket of his cargo shorts and pulled out that one vice he'd never been able to kick. Cigarettes and booze were nothing compared to his iPhone, which now caught a glint of sunlight and blinded him for an instant before he blinked and answered the call.

"Hello?"

"Hal? Where are you?"

Heidi's voice had that amazingly subtle but unmistakable tone that said she was annoyed with Hal to the point of stabbing him. He'd know it anywhere. He heard it often.

She was back at the cabin, probably sipping a glass of Pinot Grigio while complaining about him to her folks.

He sighed. "I took a hike. I had to get away from you for a while."

"Oh God," she said. Hal recognized that tone, too. Now she was annoyed and disgusted with him. That was her tone that said he was too pathetic to believe. It was the tone that said she thought he was a loser.

Or ... that's how it always felt to Hal, anyway.

"Get away from me? That's a really nice thing to say to your wife, Hal. I can't believe you went without me. Where are you?"

"I just needed a break," Hal said. "I'm a few miles away. I found a trail. I'll be back before dark."

"We're supposed to go on a hay ride this evening!"

"I'll be there," he said, and then abruptly hung up.

Just like that.

Which as something he wouldn't usually do—he would typically argue with her until they were both so furious they were saying unbelievably hateful things, which he would later apologize for, even though he thought he'd done nothing wrong. That was the dynamic of their relationship —each of them went for the throat, but he was the only one who ended up apologizing for it.

Not this time.

The fight had already happened, and he was still pissed at her for making him the bad guy—one more time— just for wanting to do more with his limited vacation days than sit and stare at the mountains and remain totally silent while she said anything that came into her head and ...

He took a deep breath, looked at all the nature around him, and willed himself to just let it go. It wasn't really her fault. She was stressed, and he knew that. They both were. It had been a rough year. It was just—he couldn't always be the bad guy, could he? He couldn't always be wrong.

When she called back he ignored it, sent it to voicemail, and just kept walking.

Actually, it wasn't really that he was still all that pissed. In fact, he'd gotten over the fight hours ago. The whole thing had been really stupid—one of those fights where you eventually figure out you're both saying the same thing, but you're spewing acid and molten lava anyway, so you might as well burn each other to ashes.

Stupid. Pointless.

It had started when he woke up that morning with an

urge to finally go on a hike, but Heidi had vetoed. She didn't feel like hiking, she said. She just wanted to "relax for once."

Which, by Hal's estimate, was all they'd done since getting to Colorado. He'd made it clear when they left that he was perfectly willing to go along for the ride on anything her parents wanted to do. His only stipulation was that he wanted at least one day of hiking and exploring—soaking in the kind of countryside he didn't get to see much these days, since moving to the city. Heidi had agreed, had even smiled lovingly and talked about how wonderful it would be for the two of them to find some secluded spot, away from all the chaos of life, and maybe have a picnic. She had legitimately seemed enthusiastic about it.

But once they arrived, and her parents had shown up, the hike seemed to continuously get pushed further back on the agenda. And by now Hal knew, it wasn't likely to happen at all.

That was pretty much how these things went. If it was something Hal wanted, it steadily drifted down the priority list, falling below sitting and staring, apparently.

Of course, Heidi accused him of being "a big baby" when he complained that he hadn't gotten to do the one thing he'd wanted to do here. She reminded him that this trip was supposed to be about her parents and their anniversary, and about spending time with family. Hal reminded her that they'd just spent nine days with her family—which just ended in Heidi rolling her eyes and saying something condescending under her breath.

That had been his limit.

"No problem," Hal had told her coldly. "I wanted to go by myself anyway."

And that was the start of all the yelling.

They'd had this fight before. Hal was a fairly independent guy, and always had been. At times, he had his fill of quality time, and so he would make plans to take a road trip or just hit a movie, or maybe just go for a walk by himself.

Somehow, Heidi always managed to invite herself. And what could he do? Nice guys—stand up guys who respected and loved their wives—didn't say things like "I don't want you to go." That made things tense and stressful. It made resentment flare up. It made life suck.

So despite his objections Hal usually just closed his mouth and let her come along. It sucked, but it helped keep the peace at home.

This time, though, he had been adamant. He was going by himself. She, equally as adamant, assured him that he was not—maybe not in so many words, but she did make it plain that he would have to wait until she was ready before he could even step foot out of the cabin.

Hal stepped down onto a natural staircase of rocks and brush, looking outward as he did, into the forever expanse of wilderness and nature. He was alone here. Not a soul to be seen. Not Heidi nor her parents nor anyone else in the world.

He liked it.

As he came to the bottom of the inclined terrain he found a path. It looked like an animal trail, and for a minute Hal paused and reconsidered.

There are big cats here, he thought. Or some kind of predatory animals, anyway. Not to mention snakes. Were there snakes in this part of the country? He was sure there had to be. TV and movies always showed huge rattlesnakes in places like this.

He had a walking stick that had a pretty decent heft, and he was reasonably sure he could fend off most small to medium animals if the need arose. He didn't think there was anything bigger around, now that he reconsidered. Nothing he'd have to worry about right now, anyway. He hoped.

But the trail was here, and it was too good to just pass up. It wound its way through brush and large rocks and disappeared just past a rise in the landscape.

Hal set out, the hefty walking stick in hand, and followed the trail until he came to a river.

He stopped abruptly.

He checked his iPhone.

The map didn't show a river here. He turned on the satellite view and was greeted by nothing but rocks and trees. No roads. No towns. No river.

Was he lost?

With a slight panic he checked the GPS and saw that it was on and working.

Was there something else wrong?

He turned to look back up the path. On the map, he located the rise he had come down, and traced his finger along the route he had just taken. He came to where the dot indicated he was standing, and ...

There was no river there. Not on the map anyway.

Now he worried.

He had heard stories about heavy rains causing a flood somewhere out of visual range, and walls of water suddenly gushing through gullies and dry creek beds—low patches not unlike the one he was currently standing in.

Hikers would sometimes get caught unaware by these flash floods, dashed into the rocks and trees and anything else that happened to be in the path of the rushing water, their bodies disappearing into the wild.

He checked his iPhone for weather reports and saw no rain anywhere within hundreds of miles. There was also no indication that it had rained earlier in the day anywhere that would be upstream of this place. Nothing that should cause a flow of water here.

As far as he could tell, this river was just somehow overlooked by the satellites and mapping technology.

Hal held up his iPhone and took pictures of the river as it stretched in both directions. He made sure the GPS coordinates were attached, so that he could find his way back here again sometime—assuming, of course, he would ever get a chance to make a trip like this again.

He thought about posting about this place on Facebook and Instagram right away—but stopped.

It was a beauty of a river, he had to admit. A really nice spot, and totally worth sharing. It would make an interesting story—I was just hiking along and there it was, completely out of nowhere. The map showed nothing at all. But look at these shots!

Maybe later that would be exactly what he did. He'd take a few selfies, write a few funny comments, and share it with everyone he knew. Probably most of his friends wouldn't care even a little about some river that appeared out of nowhere. Heidi wouldn't care, for sure. The fact that he cared would probably make her roll her eyes.

He'd deal with all the potential scorn later. For now, this was his river. This was his moment. He was the only one who would 'Like' this for now.

It wasn't a very wide river, and it seemed shallow. In fact, if he was so inclined he could probably wade across.

The waters ran a bit still at this spot. Further down river he could hear the sounds of rushing water and rapids, so it might be much more turbulent there. But here it was calm, and the water was crystal clear. If not for glints of sunlight on its surface, Hal might start wondering if there was really even any water there at all.

He stepped forward and knelt on a stone by the river's edge, then dipped a hand into it. The water was cool—almost cold—and it felt refreshing. He looked around, though he wasn't sure why, and then scooped water up to his mouth to take a drink.

He knew he shouldn't. There could be all kinds of bacteria or parasites or other nasties in the water. He might end up getting sick, and then he'd have to miss the hayride after all. Or spend the rest of the trip in bed. Or maybe even fly home early.

But it was worth it, just to taste something truly fresh. Silly, he knew. Dangerous even. But worth it.

The water had that earthy quality that stream water always has. To Hal it tasted pure and clean, with just a slight metallic tingle on his tongue.

For the first time, he realized he was actually pretty thirsty. That cold sip of water was a pleasure, after his hike, and he smiled and laughed a little.

It occurred to him how nice it would feel to take a dip in the river, and before long he was peering around again, making sure no one was in sight while he stripped off of his clothes and laid them with his walking stick and his iPhone on the stones by the river's edge.

He waded out into the water, letting the coolness wash over him. There was something ridiculously thrilling about being naked, here in the wilderness. And the cold water made the experience feel even more exotic and taboo.

His heart was thumping. Maybe it was a slight shocked reaction to the sudden change in temperature as his hike-warmed flesh met with cool water, or maybe it was just a bit of excitement and a feeling of getting away with something as he slipped, naked, into this forgotten river, off the map and off the beaten path.

Either way, it felt good. He felt good. This was the first moment he'd actually felt relaxed since he and Heidi had stepped off of the plane here. And as he stretched and floated on the river's surface, every thought of Heidi or her parents or hayrides drifted away from him, along with all the stress and anxiety and anger. It was wonderful. It was freeing.

And then the river was gone.

It wasn't until his butt bumped a stone on the river's bottom that he opened his eyes to see that he was now laying in a shallow pool, with no river in sight. He got to his knees, and then to a crouch, and he watched as even the pool around him began to drain away into the stones and soil of the riverbed. The water seeped into the stony ground below him until every drop of it was gone, and only the moistened and slightly muddy soil of the riverbed remained.

Hal hurried to his clothes and pulled on his underwear. He grabbed his iPhone and quickly shot video of the fading river, the upriver current dwindling to a trickle and then to nothing. Even the distant sounds of rapids faded and disappeared.

The remaining pools of water were all vanishing as he watched, but he managed to get a few seconds of footage of them as their levels fell and the stones began to dry.

What was this? What did this mean? It was strange enough that he'd stumbled upon this uncharted river in the first place, but to see it just vanish in front of him was like suddenly discovering that ghosts were real. It was creepy and unnerving.

Was there an underground river running through here?

That had to be it. The water table must have risen slightly for some reason, filling this old river bed just in time for Hal to see it and swim in it. There were probably aquifers all through this area, filling up and pushing water to the surface for just a little while, then ebbing and drawing it all back down, back into the Earth.

Which was amazing! He'd gotten to see it. Not only that, he'd actually recorded it! This was going to be huge on YouTube, for sure! Probably. Maybe. Hal really didn't have a good sense of what was actually sensational to other people, honestly. But it was huge for him.

Hal finished dressing, then climbed back to the top of the rise, finding the trail he had taken to get here. He looked back as he went, but never saw a trace of the river again. After an hour or so he was so far away, and the view was so obscured, he wasn't even sure he could make his way back there, even with a map and coordinates.

As he approached the spot where, earlier, he had stood and talked to his wife, he used his iPhone to send the photos and the video clip to Facebook, along with a brief description of what had happened—minus the part where he was swimming in the buff. No sense giving Heidi any more ammunition than she already had.

The GPS coordinates were embedded in the meta data of both the photos and the video, so any of his friends who cared could come find the river again someday. Or, at least, they could find where the river had been.

None of them ever did.

The images just didn't sell the story for them. It didn't make any of this exciting or interesting enough. With attention spans crammed full of funny kitten videos and pointless political arguments, how could a river possibly compete?

So the whole weird event faded into the background for

Hal, just like the fight between him and Heidi eventually became irrelevant history.

In fact, a lot of things faded into the background for Hal and Heidi, who went on to become parents as a result of 'making up' after he got back to the cabin. Soon Hal's Facebook wall was crammed full of newborn photos, and laments about late-night feedings and ironic jabs about how he'd only thought he'd had no 'alone time' before. And with every new baby photo and 'baby's first everything' video, the forgotten river became more and more forgotten—by almost everyone.

HERE'S HOW TO HELP ME REACH MORE READERS

If you loved this book, you can help me reach more readers with just a few easy acts of kindness.

(1) REVIEW THIS BOOK

Leaving a review for this book is a great way to help other readers find it. Just go to the site where you bought the book, search for the title, and leave a review. It really helps, and I really appreciate it!

(2) SUBSCRIBE TO MY EMAIL LIST

I regularly write a special email to the people on my list, just keeping everyone up to date on what I'm working on. When I announce new book releases, giveaways, or anything else, the people on my list hear about it first. Sometimes, there are special deals I'll *only* give to my list, so it's worth being a part of the crowd.

Join the conversation and get a free ebook, just for signing up! Visit https://www.kevintumlinson.com/joinme.

(3) TELL YOUR FRIENDS

Word of mouth is still the best marketing there is, so I would greatly appreciate it if you'd tell your friends and family about this book, and the others I've written.

You can find a comprehensive list of all of my books at http://kevintumlinson.com/books.

Thanks so much for your help. And thanks for reading!

ABOUT THE AUTHOR

Kevin Tumlinson is an award-winning and bestselling novelist, living in Texas and working in random coffee shops, cafés, and hotel lobbies worldwide. His debut thriller, *The Coelho Medallion*, was a 2016 Shelf Notable Indie award winner.

Kevin grew up in Wild Peach, Texas, where he was raised by his grandparents and given a healthy respect for story telling. He often found himself in trouble in school for writing stories instead of doing his actual assignments.

Kevin's love for history, archaeology, and science has been a tremendous source of material for his writing, feeding his fiction and giving him just the excuse he needs to read the next article, biography, or research paper.

Connect with Kevin:
kevintumlinson.com
kevin@tumlinson.net

ALSO BY KEVIN TUMLINSON

Dan Kotler

The Brass Hall - A Dan Kotler Story

The Coelho Medallion

The Atlantis Riddle

The Devil's Interval

The Girl in the Mayan Tomb

Citadel

Citadel: First Colony

Citadel: Paths in Darkness

Citadel: Children of Light

Citadel: The Value of War

Colony Girl: A Citadel Universe Story

Sawyer Jackson

Sawyer Jackson and the Long Land

Sawyer Jackson and the Shadow Strait

Sawyer Jackson and the White Room

Think Tank

Karner Blue

Zero Tolerance

Nomad

The Lucid — Co-authored with Nick Thacker

Episode 1

Episode 2

Episode 3

Standalone

Evergreen

Shorts & Novellas

Getting Gone

Teresa's Monster

The Three Reasons to Avoid Being Punched in the Face

Tin Man

Two Blocks East

Edge

Zero

Collections

Citadel: Omnibus

Uncanny Divide — With Nick Thacker & Will Flora

Light Years — The Complete Science Fiction Library

YA & Middle Grade

Secret of the Diamond Sword — An Alex Kotler Mystery

Wordslinger (Non-Fiction)

30-Day Author: Develop a Daily Writing Habit and Write Your Book In 30 Days (Or Less)

Watch for more at kevintumlinson.com/books

THE CHANGE LOG

This is a list of the amazing readers who helped shape and improve this book. And you could be one of them!
If you spot any typos or errors in this book, you can send them to me using my Typo Report tool:

https://www.kevintumlinson.com/typos

If I use your suggestion, and you give me permission, I'll include your name in a future edition of the book, where the whole world can be as grateful to you as I am.

Again, thank you for your help!